BROTH
IN BLOOD

DUSTY RICHARDS

BROTHERS IN BLOOD

PINNACLE BOOKS
Kensington Publishing Corp.
www.kensingtonbooks.com

PINNACLE BOOKS are published by

Kensington Publishing Corp.
119 West 40th Street
New York, NY 10018

All Kensington titles, imprints, and distributed lines are available at special quantity discounts for bulk purchases for sales promotions, premiums, fund-raising, educational, or institutional use. Special book excerpts or customized printings can also be created to fit specific needs. For details, write or phone the office of the Kensington special sales manager: Kensington Publishing Corp., 119 West 40th Street, New York, NY 10018, attn: Special Sales Department; phone 1-800-221-2647.

PINNACLE BOOKS and the Pinnacle logo are Reg. U.S. Pat. & TM Off.

ISBN-13: 978-0-7860-3195-5
ISBN-10: 0-7860-3195-6

First printing: November 2013

10 9 8 7 6 5 4 3 2 1

Printed in the United States of America

First electronic edition: November 2013

ISBN-13: 978-0-7860-3196-2
ISBN-10: 0-7860-3196-4

CHAPTER 1

Christmas Eve was in full swing at the sprawling Byrnes house in Prescott Valley—or Preskitt as most folks called it. Chet's family members had gathered to celebrate the holiday, and the piano music coming from May's fingers on the grand piano in the crowded living room added to the holiday spirit.

May, his brother's widow, was now married to one of his ranch foremen, Hampt Tate. Beside her on the bench, Chet's two nephews, Ray and Ty, fingered keys and added notes to her music at her nods to them. That trick by his all-cowboy nephews amazed him the most. Their stepmother had been in the family for years before anyone knew she could sing like an angel and play the piano so well.

Hampt, a big-shouldered great cowboy, married her six months ago, and a short while after that she showed up singing. May, like his own wife Marge, was going to hatch in the spring.

He met Marge coming from the kitchen, shaking

her head as she brought out more treats on a tray. "She's so talented, isn't she?"

"Amazing what she can do. May, who sat around all those years and never sang a note."

"You said one time that your brother married her to babysit his three kids."

He nodded and smiled. "I better go check on my partners, be sure they're ready to take the stage in the morning."

She frowned. "Why didn't Cole and Jesus come up here and celebrate with us?"

He wrinkled his nose. "I asked them. They said they'd be too self-conscious."

Leaning forward, she kissed him. "We can talk later."

Nice thing about having a woman as tall as Marge, she was easy to reach over and kiss. She'd had several miscarriages in her two past marriages, but the twice-widowed woman fit him well and, so far, the baby situation was going along fine. The baby had begun to kick and she said that had never happened before.

Chet tended to believe it was more a matter that she hadn't ridden her jumping horses since she learned about her condition. But he shrugged that off, 'cause he knew so damn little about such things. All he really knew was they would have an offspring. Boy or girl, he didn't care, as long as it had five fingers on its hands and five toes on each foot.

Inside the back porch, he slipped on his

sheepskin-lined coat, then walked out into the frosty night. The bunkhouse lights were on and, when he stepped inside, the warmth from the pot-belly stove struck him in the face. The men sitting around were eating fudge, cake, and cookies. Three were *vaqueros* that worked for Raphael, the foreman for this ranch. Some of the other men who worked the ranch had families and lived in nearby *jacal*s.

"How are you doing, boys?"

"Fine," Jesus, a Mexican youth in his late teens, said.

"We'll be ready to go in the morning," Cole Emerson, a bright faced young man in his mid-twenties, replied. "You heard any more?"

"No. Nothing. I guess we're lucky JD even got that one letter smuggled out of the jail."

These two were his appointed companions. Marge insisted, and his ranch foremen agreed, he needed them to back him wherever he went. He didn't know how he got by for thirty-four years, handling his own problems.

"I guess we won't find out anything about JD's troubles till we get to Socorro, New Mexico. I'm supposed to have the best law firm in the territory coming to clear it all up."

One of the other *vaquero*s spoke up. "Good luck, *señor*. We all like JD and are sorry he is in jail."

"Thanks, Raoul. We'll get it settled."

In Spanish, both men told him Merry Christmas.

He thanked them. Then, satisfied his two side-kicks were set to go, he went back into the cold night air. Outside, he looked at the million stars overhead and recalled a story from his cattle drover days in Abilene, Kansas. They said when the Texas cowboys got to Kansas, they shot so many holes in the sky it was daylight at midnight there. He chuckled to himself. Those days had been wild all right.

He slipped back in the kitchen and hung his coat on a peg. Their housekeeper-cook, Monica, was busy getting two large beef roasts out of the oven.

"They all right out there?" she asked.

"Doing fine. They've got more sweets than a candy store."

She wiped her damp forehead with a towel and smiled. "You round everyone up and say grace. Then we can eat."

"I can do that."

He went out into the great room. "The food is ready. Let's all stand and bow our heads to pray.

"Our dear heavenly father, we are here to cele- brate the birth of your son. If we sound irreverent, that is because we feel it should be a joyous occasion. We thank you for our good health, and ask you be with Susie's husband and his crew who are driving our cattle to the Navajos, and with Reg and his wife Lucy up on the top ranch who had to stay home and work. Lord, we ask you to be with JD, who is in jail in New Mexico tonight. Give us the strength and wisdom to get him free and exonerated. Lord, bless this food and all gathered here and on our other ranches. And, dear Lord, when you are ready for us, have a staircase to heaven for all of us. Amen."

"Amen," everyone repeated.

His sister, Susie, joined them. In a low voice, she spoke to him. "I told Sarge before he left about the baby, and he agreed it was no problem for him. I'm going to have Leif's child, but it will have Sarge's name."

He hugged her tight. While chasing rustlers with Chet, her husband had been killed in a horse wreck. Shortly after that, Sarge Polanski, the foreman at the Windmill Ranch up on the high country east, married her. Sarge had always been fascinated by Susie, but never so much as danced with her before he learned she'd married Leif—but he wasted no time in coming to her aid after her husband was killed. They made a good couple and they'd work out well.

"When things open up, you two will have a great life."

"I warned him this might happen, but he said not to worry that he wanted me anyway."

"If I can get JD cleared of the horse thief charges, maybe things will settle down for all of us." He shook his head and started to join his wife at the table.

Susie caught his arm. "They won't ever settle down for you. You draw trouble."

He couldn't help chuckling. She might be right.

Seated beside Marge, he soon had his plate full from the food dishes being passed. My, how he'd miss Monica's cooking on this trip. His wife was a hand, but her cook was the world's best. For a while it looked like a gray-headed rancher might steal her, but evidently the rancher's grown married daughter didn't think he needed a Mexican wife. Monica might be better off working right here than to get entangled with a prejudiced family.

"Susie talk to you?" Marge asked quietly.

"Yes. Back when she was considering the marriage, she thought she might be expecting. But it isn't any scar. Sarge knew then and knows now. He's accepted it. I think they'll have a great life, and this family will be blessed with another baby."

"I'm trying to be cheerful, with you leaving me in the morning and your son kicking me inside."

They both laughed.

Later, in bed, they kissed and tried to breach his absence coming up. He was so glad he married this woman. He wasn't sure at first about the rich girl that paid all his small bills behind him when he first came to Arizona looking for a ranch. When he found out what she spent, he paid the money back to her. Before he left to get his family and bring them from Texas, he told her not to wait. He had other obligations to take care of, but if things worked out they might, or might not, find some common ground.

In the semi-darkness, he gazed at the tin ceiling squares and recalled Marge coming to his aid after stage robbers killed his nephew, Heck. She took him through the funeral and all, but he never let his guard down, still shying from marriage.

When he returned to Arizona Territory, he had

no obligations to anyone in Texas. She joined his camping trips to explore new range up on the Rim, and lived in a tent. His conscience made him marry her, to save her reputation. But, for his part, he never regretted a day of it.

He turned over on his side, kissed her, and they were back on their honeymoon.

CHAPTER 2

Cole and Jesus were already at the kitchen table eating breakfast when he joined them. When he spoke, they replied, "We're ready."

"Get a plate. Food is on the range." Monica pointed his breakfast out to him.

He took a dish, added scrambled eggs with chilies and cheese, fried potatoes, and ham, plus biscuits and gravy.

When he sat down, she brought him steaming coffee and patted his shoulder. "I love the housecoat and dress you gave me for Christmas."

"Marge did that. But I approved."

"How long will you be gone?"

"Long enough to get JD's name cleared."

"Oh, men." She shook her head as if disgusted. "Months? Years?"

"Monica, if I knew that, I'd know so many things I'd be rich."

"Well, you are that. I just wonder how long I will

have to put up with her being upset that you're gone."

"No telling. Mexican people, unlike you, are slow to do things."

"You can kick them in the seat of the pants and hurry them."

His men laughed at the banter between him and Monica.

"Maybe we should take her along to help us," Cole said.

Busy eating, Chet only nodded in agreement, knowing full well this was probably his last good meal for a while.

They rode out the ranch gate in the cold predawn. In the frigid air, both men and beasts breathed steam. One of the stable hands went along to bring back their horses. A packhorse carried their bedrolls and war bags to where they'd meet the Black Canyon Stage line to go on to Hayden's Ferry. The stage usually left the night before, but with Christmas, they changed the schedule to leave that morning.

Once they reached the station, they loaded their gear in the back, climbed inside, and wrapped up with blankets. The canvas curtains over the stagecoach windows kept out little cold, so they got in their cocoons and the stage rocketed out of Preskitt.

As the day progressed, the temperature rose and they shed the blankets. At stations where they changed horses, they got out and stretched and walked around. Chet promised them a good meal that night at Hayden's Ferry, so they skipped the food offers. Monica had sent along cookies and snacks aplenty. By the time they crossed the Salt River, it was eighty degrees in the valley and the sun was down.

When they arrived at Hayden's Ferry, Chet led them to a café. Business was slow and the southbound stage didn't leave for Tucson for an hour, so they ate a leisurely meal. Cole teased the pretty Mexican waitress while he and Jesus watched. They left her a nice tip, and she kissed Cole on the cheek before he left.

They reached Tucson about noon the next day, where they'd shift to another stage line to Lordsburg. They sat outside the depot in the hot sun.

With a frown, Cole asked, "They ever had a street cleanup crew in this town?"

"You talking about the dead animals in the street and the buzzards feeding on them?"

"Boy, it is bad here, isn't it?"

"This is Arizona's other capital," Chet said, amused. "They switch down here, back and forth with Preskitt."

"Well, at least there ain't any dead pigs in the streets at Preskitt."

"You're right, and it's cooler in the summertime than it is down here."

"Are we getting closer?" Jesus asked.

"I hope we're about a third of the way there."

"Well, no doubt we're going faster than we could on horseback, but that stage isn't a feather bed."

They nodded in agreement and laughed.

"You met your wife on this stage line?" Cole asked.

"Yes, we met on the one going north from here, and we rode on to Preskitt together."

"What did you think? She is a pretty lady."

"I guess I was impressed. But I had a woman in Texas then. In the end, she couldn't come out here and leave her parents. So, when I came back, I guess I thought as fancy as Marge was I'd lose her by offering to take her on a camping trip. No way. She went right along. That's when I discovered the real Marge. My sister, Susie, kept saying Marge had gone to a finishing school. That really impressed a Texas ranch girl, but now she agrees I couldn't have done better."

"Thing I saw, you two are like a team together. When I first come here, I thought you'd been married to her for years."

"Easy for her to look like she always belonged here," Jesus said. "He's such a slick talker."

Laughing, they scrambled to load their saddles and gear to the other stage line. A woman in black clothing also waited for the stage. Obviously, from her dress, she was a widow.

Chet helped her in and told her the back facing seat was the best place to ride in the stagecoach. She thanked him and the four were soon off in the rocking coach, with whips cracking and the driver scolding the horses as they clattered through the narrow streets of Tucson.

"Ma'am, these two are my men, Cole and Jesus. I'm Chet Byrnes and we work the Quarter Circle Z Ranch at Preskitt and Camp Verde."

"Elizabeth Karnes. My husband was Captain Loren Karnes. He's recently departed."

"I am sorry to hear that. If we can help you in any way, let us know."

"Thank you. The three of you are much better company than the three drunk drummers I rode with from El Paso when I came out here two years ago."

Chet smiled. "Where will you return to?"

"Texas, of course. My parents have a farm near Austin."

"We hope you have a safe trip."

She thanked them, then Chet and her talked idly about his wife and his business. They swept across the chaparral country and made the stops to change horses—eat if they dared and back in the coach and the churning dust. Lordsburg was a sleepy Mexican village past the large area of playa lakes.

Deming, the next town, was the terminal for the railroad tracks coming west, and was on fire with business. But there was no track building going on. Either they were out of money, out of iron rails, or out of help. Progress had halted. A train car with a locomotive going backward headed for Mesilla. On this part of the ride, Mrs. Karnes was more talkative.

"You know, it isn't easy for me to go back home. Who wants a soldier's hand-me-down? I married Karnes expecting to be a colonel's wife someday. He died of a heart attack in, of all places, a brothel. Now I can go home and hope some desperate poor man comes along who wants a wife to raise his eight snotty-nosed kids."

Amused, Chet about laughed. He gazed out the open window at the passing sagebrush and mesquite with fuzzy brown mountains in the distance. "I can see your situation."

"You said you married a woman twice widowed?"

"Yes, and I wouldn't trade her for anyone else."

"Tell me why."

"I knew other women. Some were damn nice. As I told you, I had to leave a great lady in Texas. Then, here I was with this woman who I thought was too fancy for me. But whatever had happened in the past, I didn't care. We came together and we have a life. Of course, she didn't have eight snotty-nosed ones, either."

"You're telling me I may have to give up a lot to get a real man."

"No, I just told you my story."

"Thank you. You have been most kind. I hope you get your nephew released from prison."

"Oh, I'll do that."

She nodded as if in deep thought. "I know you will succeed. You are a forceful man. It has been nice to share my misfortunes with you."

"Yes, ma'am."

They made it to Mesilla and took the stage north the next day. The country they passed through looked dry and desolate.

"A cow could starve to death out there," Cole said.

"Or die of thirst."

"Yeah, Chet. That would be easy, save for the water in the Rio Grande over there in those cottonwood trees."

"I have no idea what we'll run into up here. We'll play it by ear. The first thing is, don't go for your gun unless it's life or death. In a new land, we need to learn all we can and be unseen."

"What do you figure they're like?" Cole asked.

"New Mexico Territory is mostly Spanish. They've been here for centuries, and they do things their way."

Jesus agreed. "I'd say you are right. I will listen. Here, you will need the Spanish side of things."

"They must fear something. Not letting him mail letters, so that he had to smuggle them out."

"That is strange." Cole shook his head. "I hope it isn't long. I like northern Arizona, pines and grass for cows. What else did you learn from the widow who left us back there?"

"Hardest thing in her story was that her husband died in a whorehouse. She's a real nice-looking woman. I ain't seen many women in that business that good looking."

"All you saw in her was the package. Contents are another thing," Cole said.

Chet shook his head. "Aw, I saw more. I wonder if she was cold toward him? I don't know, but when you open up a package, sometimes the contents can shock you. We all thought JD's wife Kay was so ignored by him. I even danced and talked to her. I believed her story, but whatever she did to him spun him around so I can't figure it out for the life of me."

"Women can do that to you."

Cole didn't say any more, but Chet knew his man had been burned, too.

They found Socorro in a full-fledged dust storm. Heads bent down, they went inside the stage office to escape nature's force. The stage agent agreed to keep their gear.

"The Pearl Hotel is two blocks south. Best place in town to stay."

After thanking him, the three set out for the hotel. They made it into the lobby, grateful to escape the face-stinging diamond bits. Once inside, Chet stopped to brush off some dust.

"This happen often?" he asked the clerk.

"Not every day."

"Good. That might make us glad when we see an open day. I need two rooms for a week."

"Pay by the day or all?"

"How much is all of it?"

"Fourteen dollars."

He paid the man and he gave them rooms beside each other on the second floor.

"Where's a good place to eat?"

"The cantina next door. They're the cleanest and best place in town."

"Thanks," Chet said.

"Are you here on business?"

"Exactly. Where's the courthouse?"

"Two blocks west."

"Thanks."

The clerk at the hotel was right about the cantina—the food was good. The waitress told them they also did breakfast and supper.

After supper, Chet and Cole walked to the court-house. They entered the sheriff's office and asked the man at the desk for him.

"Oh, *señor*, he won't be in for a week. What can we do for you?"

"I am here to speak to a prisoner he has."

"Who is that, *señor*?"

"JD Byrnes."

"I don't know who you speak about."

"Let's get things clear. I am a US Deputy Marshal and I want to speak to this man." He showed him his badge.

"Oh, I am sorry, but he is not here."

"Then find him. I'll be back in an hour and I want him here. If he isn't, there'll be a federal grand jury here to see how this jail is operated."

"How can I find someone who isn't here, *señor*?"

"He's here. Get to cutting."

The man turned his palms up. "I can do nothing."

Chet and Cole turned and left the courthouse. Fired up and angry, Chet went to find the lawyer who had represented JD. His office was in a small room in the alley behind a mercantile store.

Chet pushed in the door. A young man seated behind the desk jumped at the sight of him, and almost knocked over a green desk lamp.

"Josh Raines?"

"Yes."

"Chet Byrnes. Where is JD Byrnes?"

"Why? Why? In the county jail."

"They say he isn't there. How can I find him?" He was fast growing weary of all this double talk.

"Did you speak to the sheriff?"

"No. He won't be here for a week."

"Where did he go?" Raines asked.

"Who knows? They're dumb down at that courthouse. I want to speak to my nephew. What can you do?"

"I guess go and demand they let us see him."

Chet pointed his finger like a pistol. "Get your ass up and I'll accompany you down there."

Raines blew out the lamp and put his coat on going out the door. "You have to realize this isn't Texas. They don't do things here like they do there."

"We are in the United States, aren't we?"

"A territory. Yes."

"Was his trial in Spanish?"

"It was—but that is usual here."

"Will that hold up in the territory appeals court?"

"Probably."

Chet double-stepped the lawyer toward the courthouse in the dust-biting wind.

"Your client was not Mexican. Was he provided a translator?"

"No."

"Good, because I've hired the most powerful law agency in Santa Fe and I expect you to support them.

Where are those horses? What did they do with them? I want them returned and examined. We'll find their owners."

"I don't know if we can do that."

"Why in the hell not?"

"I think they were sold."

"By bid?"

Raines shrugged. "No, just sold."

"Then the sheriff benefited from this frame-up, didn't he?"

"You're saying he did this to sell those horses?"

"He sold the horses. Right?"

By this time, they were inside the courthouse lobby and Chet cut off his questioning.

Ahead of him, Raines walked into the sheriff's outer office first, and the deputy frowned at him. "What are you here for?"

"I came to speak to my client, JD Byrnes."

"He ain't got no business to talk to you about."

"Diego, go get him."

"I don't work for you or that *gringo* behind you."

"I am his attorney, and you can't deny me talking to my client."

"Get out of here or I'll arrest both of you."

"Where is the sheriff?"

"He is not available."

"Tell Hernandez to come see me. The State Attorney General is coming from Santa Fe to talk to him, and he can be prosecuted if he is found failing to uphold the laws of the territory and nation."

"What can that *bastardo* do?" the deputy asked, motioning toward Chet.

"They can charge Hernandez and try him in court."

"He is the sheriff. They can't do that."

"Diego, there are higher men than a county sheriff. Tell him we need to talk before the State Attorney General gets involved."

"He won't care. They can't tell him what to do."

"Give him the word. Also tell the judge and prosecutor that we need to have a meeting."

"All for this *gringo* with you?"

"Tell them this is serious. He won't want the governor down here, too."

"I will tell him, but it will do no good. He is the law here and what he says is the law. No one sees his prisoners unless he says so."

Raines held up his hand to silence him. "Do what I said. Tell him we mean business."

Then he turned to Chet. "He will listen to good sense. Come on."

Not satisfied with the way things stood, Chet followed the young lawyer outside. Once back in the wind, he pulled down his hat. "What do I need to do?"

"If you have a room, go back and rest. We will work this out."

"Does this sheriff think he's above the law?"

"Pretty much so, since no one has ever challenged him. A Texas rancher paid him two thousand dollars to get his son released, when all the kid did was shoot someone who was beating him up. I think the sheriff thought JD's father would do the same."

"I'm his uncle, and a Deputy US Marshal. I intend to clear his name of this hoax."

"Maybe we can reach some compromise at a meeting with the county officials."

"I am not paying a sheriff to release an innocent man."

"I understand. I also understand the court business in this county. He will call for a meeting."

"I'll be at the Pearl Hotel." He ducked his head away from the wind. "Where is the telegraph office?"

"Across the street." Raines pointed.

"Thanks. Does he run that, too?"

The lawyer shrugged. "I will let you know what we need to do next."

"Thanks." They parted and Chet went to the telegraph office where a clerk was sending a message out on the key.

"Be right with you," he said.

Chet nodded and took a yellow paper and wrote on it in pencil.

To: Mrs. Marge Byrnes. Prescott, Arizona Territory.
We are in Socorro. Looks like a long affair. What is the Santa Fe lawyer's name? When will he be here?

Love you, Chet.

"I can send that right away. It'll get there in twenty-four hours. Anything else?"

"No. How much?"

"Seventy-five cents."

Chet paid him.

"Thanks. Where can I reach you for the reply?"

"Pearl Hotel."

"I know where that is." The short man with the celluloid visor nodded. "Any time you need me, pound on the door. I'm here twenty-four hours a day."

Still filled with fury, Chet went back and found his men in their room.

"Do any good?" Cole asked.

"Not really. Raines is setting up a meeting with the sheriff."

"A meeting about what?" Jesus asked.

Chet sat down and told them the entire story about the Texan who bought his son's freedom.

When Chet finished. Cole said, "This smells worse than the sheriff's office at home."

"Yes, it does. I wired Marge for the name of the lawyer coming here from Santa Fe. I guess all we can do now is wait." He knew one thing for sure—he must sit on his temper. Things in this dusty town weren't going to move fast enough to suit him. He got up and paced the floor. "I just hate that I can't talk to JD."

"We don't have an answer, either," Jesus said.

That was the problem—there was no answer.

CHAPTER 3

Firecrackers popped like gunshots. Rockets exploded overhead in the night air and threw out blue and red fans. It was New Year's Eve and the Chinese population filled the sky over Socorro with colorful explosions.

Louise, the waitress from the café, hung on to Cole's arm. Chet and Jesus went along with them to the dance hall down the street for what she called a New Year's Eve *fandango*.

The fireworks were interesting, but Chet's mind was on JD's problem. Herman Thomas, the lawyer from the Santa Fe firm of Sullivan, Branch and Alter, was on his way. Chet had sent them a telegram introducing himself and telling them where he was staying. The sheriff's meeting was set for January second in the courtroom. Raines made the arrangements, but acted like that was too sudden for them to do anything.

Chet wrote a long letter to Marge about his impatience at how things were creeping along despite his moves to hurry it up. Luckily, he found a local man who said JD was in the jail and all right, which eased his mind somewhat.

When they were inside the dance hall, Louise asked, "Will you dance with my aunt? She can dance very well."

"Of course, if I can step on her toes."

"I don't believe that. I bet you can dance real well."

"She will see."

Wooden benches lined the walls around the large room. Louise took him to an empty space, then she and Cole went to find her aunt.

"Her aunt, she is a widow," Jesus said. "I think she is tall. Louise said she was. So she will be pleased to dance with a tall *hombre*."

Antoinette Carmichael was tall. Almost as tall as his wife, and a beautiful woman with a light tan complexion and a smooth-skinned face graced with dancing brown eyes and sleepy eyelids. Her hair was pinned up and she wore an expensive blue dress that flattered her full figure.

"Ah," she said after her niece introduced them. "She says you will step on my toes. Let's see if you do." And she held out her arms.

The music was playing, so he swept her away. Head high, she could damn sure dance and he could lead. They swung around the floor almost by themselves, but he knew he had a partner that could really dance.

"Louise says you are married."

"I have a lovely wife back in Arizona."

"You have not been married very long?" She dropped an eyelid to look at him for an answer.

"No, only near a year. She was a widow and now she's expecting in May."

"You never had a wife before her?"

"No. I was serious about some nice ladies, but never married before."

"She must be a lovely woman to snare a bachelor like you were."

"Yes, she is. Do you have any children?"

"No. Two died soon after birth and I never had any more. My husband was killed in a mine cave-in. He was a big tall Texan like you."

They whirled around as if they had danced together for years. She was so quick to take his lead it was automatic. He couldn't understand why someone hadn't chosen to court her.

"You have no man at your door?"

"No. My husband has been dead over a year. I no longer wear black, but I am too fussy. I don't like drunks. Louise says you don't drink."

"I have a beer or two. I've only been drunk a few times and didn't like it."

"I won't marry a drunk, so you see that narrows a tall woman's chances of being courted."

"I'm certain you'll find a man. You dance like a ballerina."

"Oh, have you seen one of them dance?"

"Yes, I did. In Abilene, Kansas, at the end of a cattle drive. It was a traveling company of dancers."

"I've heard of them and seen pictures. I am flattered by your words. Tell me about your nephew who is in jail."

"It's a long story. We finally have a meeting on the second with the sheriff. They've denied me talking to him. JD had to smuggle a letter out of the jail to tell me about his phony trial. Did you ever meet him when he was cowboying around here?"

"No. I heard some gossip is all."

When the dance ended, he showed her to a place on a bench where Jesus sat. They sat and he began telling her about JD's case.

In the end, she agreed the sheriff had too much power. She'd also heard about the other Texas boy whose father had to buy his way out of jail.

"You didn't offer them money?" She smiled knowingly at him.

"No. I want him cleared of those charges. Might have been a damn sight easier to pay them than go this route, but I can't stand for injustices to go on."

"There are many that agree, but Hernandez counts the votes. Excuse me." She rose and took Jesus' hand.

"Come with me. You can dance, can't you?"

"Yes, ma'am."

"Some of my family girls are seated on a bench over there and dying to dance with you."

She turned back to Chet. "I will be right back. This nice cowboy needs to dance. It is New Year's Eve."

Chet agreed, amused at this strong woman who led his man across the room to meet her girls. She reminded him in many ways of Marge. He'd like to be home to take her to the schoolhouse dance, but this JD jail business had to be settled.

Antoinette returned, swept her skirts underneath her, and took a seat beside him. "Young men that age can be so shy. You have two polite nice young men that work for you. Do they go everywhere with you?"

"Yes, they do. My wife and my main ranch manager say I need them with me because of the things I get into."

She laughed. "They know you well then."

They danced again and then, sitting, he told her about Texas and why they had to leave.

"Oh my, you have an empire going for you now."

"Yes, I'm told that. Did your husband leave you set up?"

She nodded. "I have three men that work for me on the ranch. We have two hundred mother cows, and growing. The Rafter A is my brand. Like your wife, I rode with him and we had lots of fun. I can run the ranch by myself—another reason I am so choosy. I don't want to be set back as a wife in the house and have him run the ranch."

Chet nodded. "Let's dance. Dancing with you helps me forget how mad I am."

"I bet your wife does that to you."

"Yes, she does, and I treasure her for that very thing, as well as for other things. After I bought the big ranch, I headed home with JD's younger brother, Heck. He was about sixteen and had really straightened up. In a stage holdup, not fifteen miles south of Preskitt, some outlaws robbed us. I knew one of them, but in the dark he didn't recognize me. He and the other men took the boy as a hostage. I chased them down on a stage company horse, but they'd already killed the boy for no reason."

"Oh, no."

His hand in the center of her back, he straightened and they danced on. "Toughest day of my life, bar any others I ever had. Marge heard about it and she drove there in a buckboard to help me take his body back. His father was killed in the feud up in Kansas while taking our cattle to market. When Heck was killed, I was struck all over again by the entire situation."

"Did that convince you to marry her?"

He shook his head. "I was grateful, but I still had ties in Texas. In the end, that lady couldn't leave Texas because her parents needed her. So I came back to Arizona, but I wasn't ready for a wife. I wanted to make a long camping trip to see more of the territory, and I was going to ask Marge to go along. My sister said that since Marge had been to finishing school, she wouldn't go with me. She was wrong, though. Marge agreed, without any hesitation, to go. My conscience bothered me about her being single and going, so we made that trip our honeymoon."

"That was thoughtful. You are a wheeler-dealer, aren't you?"

"I guess you could call me that. Was your husband one?"

"Yes. When he died, he still had many irons in the

fire that I had to settle. Some were good, some worth
nothing. That was fine, only he could have made
them all work."

They danced until midnight when someone blew
a trumpet and confetti fell from a high net onto the
crowd. At that, he kissed her and wished her a Happy
New Year.

She thanked him and they walked slowly back to
the bench.

"Are you going home tonight?" he asked.

"Yes. I'd love to talk you into going home with me.
I know you don't want to be invited by a Mexican
woman to go home with her tonight. But I appreciated your stories. I was well entertained by a gracious
man. If you are here for a few days, I want you to
come to my ranch house and have a meal. Bring your
men and Louise and I will feed you well, with no
strings attached. I am so glad you kissed me. I think
it will bring me good fortune in the coming year.
Good night, Chet Byrnes." Then she kissed him
softly and they parted.

He told the boys he was going back to the hotel.
Jesus said he'd go along. Chet didn't argue with him.
They were his aides and they took things serious. He
told Cole to stay if he wanted, but be careful.

When he and Jesus left the dance hall, they
started down the hill in the cool night air. When he
glanced over his shoulder, he saw two horseback
riders across some open lots riding parallel to them.

"You see them?" he asked in a stage whisper.

"You think they could be trouble?"

"I think so. If they try anything, get down and shoot back." He slid his gun from its holster, and Jesus did the same.

"I can do that. They are acting suspicious."

Chet caught his sleeve and motioned toward a nearby wagon. "Get around behind that empty wagon and we can watch them."

A dog barked somewhere close to where the two silhouettes sat on horseback. Hard to make out what they were doing, but no doubt they were watching him and Jesus.

Then one shouted to the other, "*Vamoose.*" In a pounding of hooves, the riders were gone.

After they charged away into the night, Chet and Jesus holstered their guns. Chet knew they couldn't identify either man or their horses. More things to think about. He had little faith the coming meeting would prove much, but he wanted his high-priced lawyer from Santa Fe to arrive. Because of the holidays, he doubted the man could be there before the third.

Back at the hotel, Jesus asked if he should go back and see about Cole.

"Yes, but be careful. Cole may have plans. I think those men intended to shoot or scare us. Either way, I think we better have eyes in the back of our heads from now on."

"Yes. I'll go warn him anyhow."

"I'll see you in the morning."

"Sure. If I can get Cole up."

"You can both sleep in."

Jesus shook his head. "No, not after tonight."

"See you then, and be careful."

Jesus waved that he would and left.

Chet still had hints of Mrs. Carmichael's perfume in his nose. What a lovely woman. Not for him, but she was nice and some man was missing a lot. She steered on the dance floor like Marge—amazing on her feet. Oh, well, time for some shut-eye. Morning wasn't far away.

He awoke about dawn. The hotel rooms weren't well heated and frost made a pattern on the windowpane. He didn't take long to get dressed. Out in the hall, he knocked on the boys' door.

Jesus opened it. "Cole slept in. I'll be right there."

"Fine."

When Jesus came out putting on his hat, he was grinning. In a low voice, he said, "He came in late and needs to sleep."

Going down to breakfast, they both chuckled at Cole being so tired.

"Did you see anything else last night?"

Jesus shook his head.

Raines joined them for breakfast in the café. He had his head down, and Chet thought he acted nervous as a long-tailed cat in a room full of rockers—busy glancing around. Finally, he spoke. "I have an offer you might not like—for a thousand dollars they will hand him over to you and nothing will be said."

"Will his criminal record be wiped clean?" Chet asked.

"No. That costs another thousand."

"I think we can get a new trial and his sentence set aside."

"But that will cost you more money than their offer."

"But it may straighten out this county court system and the sheriff."

Raines shook his head. "Not in New Mexico."

"We'll see. They've denied me access to JD. They've ignored my Marshal badge. They did the trial in Spanish and had no interpreter for him. The whole thing was a frame-up and the sheriff and deputies sold the horses for their own gain. I'm not biting on this buy-out offer. My lawyer is coming from Santa Fe."

"Who is that?"

"Herman Thomas."

Raines' eyes flew open. "He's real expensive."

"I told you I was getting this straightened out. I'm not a lawyer, but I know a few things. And when I get done, the sheriff may have a new look at things. Perhaps from behind bars."

Raines gave up. Chet could tell the man had collapsed after the cash offer was turned down. His mention that a high-powered lawyer was coming might shake some fear into all of them. The threat of expensive lawyers had its way of impressing people.

"The meeting is at noon tomorrow in Judge Penso's office. You don't need your men there." He motioned toward Jesus.

"They go where I go."

Raines shrugged. He left his half-eaten breakfast on the plate and hurried out the café's front door.

Their waitress shook her head. "He didn't pay for his meal. Is he coming back?"

"I'll pay for it. He's upset."

"He must be." She took his plate of food and went back in the kitchen.

"Will we have trouble in the morning at the courthouse?" Jesus asked.

"With him for a lawyer, we may. If our man arrives, I think they will take notice and he may solve it."

"He's that powerful?"

Chet nodded. There was something afoot and he wasn't certain with Raines running around—maybe looking for a counter offer before the meeting. He had already cut it to half of what that Texan paid. But they still made no offer to clear JD's name. That might come later.

Back in his room, he wrote Marge a long letter about everything happening in New Mexico—but left Antoinette Carmichael out of it. Marge might think she was competition. He had no intention of telling her. It had been a nice interlude, but, in fact, he'd rather have been at home with her. The letter was about finished when there was a knock on the door.

When he opened it, an out-of-breath Raines stood there.

"We are meeting in the sheriff's office in ten minutes."

"Oh? What for?"

"He wants to talk."

Jesus walked up behind Raines. "Need me?"

"Yes. Get your coat on. We're going to the court-house." He turned to Raines. "I don't intend to pay him a damn thing. You have that right?"

"I understand. Oh, the courthouse is closed today, so go in the back door."

"We can do that."

"See you there." Raines rushed off.

"What now?" Jesus asked.

Chet smiled. "I think we may have a deal cut."

"Should I wake Cole and get him up?"

"Sure. I'll tag along."

Jesus threw the hotel door open. "Cole. Wake up. We've just got more news. The boss thinks they want to settle with him."

"You serious? I'm getting dressed. Be ready in a minute." Cole threw his covers back and reached for his pants.

When they started toward the courthouse, the sun was warming things up. Chet figured it was close to ten. Not that time bothered him, but there was a lot to do and think about. Up in the north, Sarge was de-livering six hundred head of cattle to the various Navajo agency divisions. He hoped things went with-out a hitch. Sarge's wife, Susie, would be glad when he returned to the Verde River Ranch.

Another concern was the house Chet had to get built for them on the Windmill. And maybe the US Government would pay their past bills for the cattle delivered so far. The amount due staggered him, but his banker said the government would pay it.

The three men walked the next two blocks discussing the night before when the two strange riders shadowed them.

"You really think Raines has got them to settle?" Cole asked.

"This morning, he came with an offer that we could have him for a thousand bucks. But they wouldn't clear his record for that amount. So I told them hell no, that we'd fight them."

"Isn't it unusual to meet on a holiday?"

"I told Raines our lawyer from Santa Fe was on his way."

"You think that changed their minds?"

"Yeah," Jesus said. "When Chet told him that, he went white as a sheet."

"He didn't finish his breakfast, or even pay for it." Chet chuckled at the thought of how the little lawyer had scuttled from the café.

"So what do you think will happen now?" Cole asked.

"We'll see here shortly."

When they entered the courthouse, a deputy told them to follow him, then he relocked the back door. The building was semi-dark, no lights on anywhere as they made their way upstairs.

Their guide knocked and the deputy from the day before, Diego, opened the door. Four men sat at the long table, one of them a white-mustached man seated at the head. Chet suspected he was the sheriff. The man to his right looked judicial, and the other man in a suit looked like an official, probably the prosecutor. Raines made the fourth one in the party.

"Please be seated," Raines said.

The sheriff cleared his throat and stood. "There may have been some misunderstandings. First, I found out you're a Deputy US Marshal, sir?"

"I am."

"I learned from a wire I got from US Marshal Sam Sloan in Santa Fe that we were incorrect in not allowing you access to our jail and helping you. For this, I apologize. It will not happen again. Are you satisfied?"

"If you intend to allow me access, then I will not complain anymore."

"Will you sign a form that your demands have been met?"

"As we proceed, I will take it under consideration."

"Judge Penso. Your turn to speak." Sheriff Hernandez sat down.

"After a review of this case, I have decided to set aside the conviction of JD Byrnes for horse stealing. He will be released today and his record cleared of all charges."

"Good. Thank you. Now, I want compensation for the lost horses, his saddle, and personal things."

They all looked shock-faced at each other.

"I think five hundred dollars might cover his losses."

The sheriff made a face. "We are turning him

loose today and he has no record. You still want five hundred dollars?"

"He wasn't guilty in the first place."

The third man cut off any more talk. "The county will pay you in the morning. Deputy Diego, go get the prisoner and his things."

Raines handed Chet a court order that released and exonerated JD. Along with it was the paper Hernandez wanted signed. The third man gave him a note for five hundred dollars on the Socorro County account.

"The money will be paid in the morning at my office," the man said.

When JD walked in the room, Chet rose and hugged him. Boy, the lad felt lean in his arms.

"Thank God. Is it ever good to see you, Chet. You, too, Jesus and Cole."

"Good to see you."

He turned to the four men. "Get me a pen and ink. I'll sign this letter for you."

Now that it was settled, he was eager to get moving. He had plenty to do. Wire Marge it was over. Try to stop the lawyer from making the trip from Santa Fe. And then get their asses back to Arizona.

They left the courthouse in a hurry. With the wires sent, they all headed back to the hotel. Before they got there, Mrs. Carmichael reined up beside them in her fancy two-row surrey.

"How did the meeting go?"

Chet smiled. She knew all about it. She may even have been in on encouraging them. The "word" travels fast. "It went very well. JD, meet a great lady, Mrs. Antoinette Carmichael."

JD removed his hat. "Nice to meet you, ma'am."

"Better yet, you are out of jail, huh? That uncle of yours is a tough *hombre.*"

She looked at Chet. "Get in my buggy. I want to feed your men today at my ranch. Where is that boy who went with Louise?"

Cole had disappeared. "I think he must have went back to his room to rest."

"What a shame. Should you stop and leave him a message where you'll be?"

"We can do that. You are very generous. How did you know JD was released?"

"News travels fast in a small place. The word was out that those people in charge might be in for a big legal mess over this matter. Even that, if it went on, Governor Betting might take over the county government. He could do that, you know."

"They did act upset."

"For them to settle it the day before the scheduled meeting meant they were afraid."

"Maybe someone will investigate them."

She nodded, stopped the horses at the hotel, and turned to JD. "I bet you're glad to be free."

"Oh, ma'am, I really can't believe it. I'm just sitting back here saying over and over again, 'I'm free at last.'"

"That is good. You're the lucky one. That big man come to your rescue."

"He ain't new at the likes of that, either," JD said, which made them both laugh.

Jesus hurried out of the hotel and joined them. "I left Cole a note. He was tired, so when they let JD go he decided to go to the room to sleep."

"He will miss all the fun."

"I don't think he's missed much of that," Chet said.

The drive to her ranch was short. The large house sat under the tall leafless cottonwoods along the Rio Grande. Mrs. Carmichael had her arm around JD, who acted self-conscious as she herded him through the ornately carved front door into her palatial home.

Chet excused himself and made a swing around the ranch's headquarters on foot. He spoke in Spanish to some of her men, and they showed him their remuda. They were a good set of horses, not some bangtail mustangs. When he bragged on their horses, the men's faces showed pride in their stock.

When he went into the house, a young lady greeted him at the door and took his hat.

"Thank you. You must be a niece of Antoinette's."

"Oh, *sí*. My aunt is our favorite. She will have many good things to eat and drink today. She has a reputation as the best hostess in the area."

"It must be nice to be a part of it?"

"Oh, *sí*."

He moved on through the house toward the voices and music. In the two-story room, a band played and several guests stood around drinking wine. He found JD and Jesus and asked them what they thought.

"Fancy," JD said. "Much better than that damn jail. How's my brother and Lucie?"

"They were fine, last we heard. Lucie is going to have a baby, like the rest."

"No kidding."

"Then May and Hampt, Sarge and Susie, and Marge and me as well."

"I knew Lief had been killed in a horse wreck. Susie married Sarge?"

"Whirlwind courtship. They decided they needed to be man and wife."

"Good for her. I sure love her. She's been so great to Reg and me. But I'm glad she married Sarge. He damn sure will appreciate her. I liked Leif, and it was a damn shame he was killed, but, to me, Sarge is a real man. What else happened?"

"Not much. I saw the land north of the Grand Canyon and I don't want it."

"What was that about?"

"They were holding a man for ransom up in Utah. We rounded up some more killers on the way up there and back."

"It was damn cold, too," Jesus added.

"I guess I missed a real run?"

Jesus wearily shook his head. "It is a tough country."

JD started to laugh. "Boy, four babies in the family. Man, we are going to be a tribe soon."

"We are now," Chet said. His hostess asked him to dance, so he took her hand and they danced away.

"What's he laughing about?" she asked.

"Oh, my wife, my sister, my sister-in-law, and my niece are all with child."

"That is a lot. It will be your first, right?"

"Yes, but my wife has never carried one full-term before. So far, though, things are going well."

"Oh, I bet she bites her nails. I was like that and I tried so hard. The biggest disappointment in my life was that I never gave my husband a child. I will light a candle for your wife."

"Thanks. Did I tell you that you could dance with anyone?"

"I am jealous of your wife. She has a great dancer and a serious *hombre* in you. I thought when you took this bunch on that you would lose. They underestimated the cowboy who rode in here." She gave a throaty laugh.

"A cavalier will find you, Antoinette, and he will have a prize."

"That would be nice. Be careful, *hombre*. Those bastards are real poor losers."

"When Jesus and I went back to the hotel last night, I think they sent some hired killers after us."

She shook her head in an upset way. "When will you go home?"

"Tomorrow, after I cash the note they gave me for JD's horses they sold. There's a stage to Mesilla around midday."

She frowned. "Be careful. If I could see your wife I'd tell her how lucky she is to have you."

"I think she knows that. We appreciate each other."

"Let's eat. We are celebrating that young man's release." She clapped her hands over her head and whirled around. "Time for food, everyone."

JD sat with her at the head of the table as her guest. He laughed and teased her, acting like he used to. Chet felt better about the thin, quiet, young man they'd freed earlier. Maybe he'd make it out of the shell Kay put him in. There was a lot more to it than that—maybe he'd never know it all. But they were taking him home. And, to Chet, he appeared normal again.

Later, he thanked Antoinette for such a good time. A young man drove them back to the hotel in her buggy.

"She was a fun lady," JD said. "Most of those Mexican men are a foot shorter than she is. I think that's why she likes you so much."

They were laughing and in high spirits when they met the sleepy-eyed Cole upstairs.

"You boys go to another party?" he asked.

"Yes, and we had fun, too," Jesus said.

"No trouble?"

"No. But Mrs. Carmichael is concerned they may want revenge."

"Does she know anything for sure?"

Chet shook his head. "But she damn sure knows these people we've dealt with."

"You got a gun for JD?" Cole asked.

"He'll have one in the morning. I plan to buy him a new one. We'll catch the stage at one o'clock tomorrow."

"Whew. I'm sure ready to go home."

"So are all of us." Chet included himself as well. He simply dreaded the trip back and the days of weary travel ahead.

By nine o'clock in the morning, they stood in the county courthouse lobby. The clerk accepted the note and went to get the cash. An air of tension filled the near empty building and made the hair on Chet's neck rise.

While they waited, he thought about how the Santa Fe lawyer congratulated him by telegram on JD's release. He hadn't left Santa Fe before he got the telegram, but the lawyer would still cost him.

The clerk returned with the money and counted the cash out to Chet at the window. "Anything else, *señor*?"

"No, thanks." He put the money, mostly fives and tens, quite a wad of bills, in a cloth bag.

He handed it to JD "Here's your new start in life."

JD unbuttoned his shirt and dropped the bag inside. "I owe you for a gun and ammo."

"No. That's a gift from me."

"Thanks."

During their walk to the stage office, the skin crawled on the back of Chet's neck. This might be the last chance for the sheriff's men to jump them—if they had the nerve. They might think before tackling four experienced men with handguns on an open sunny street.

A cold wind made small puffs of dust sweep across the hard-packed surface. Nothing but a slinking black dog crossed the street, eyeing them with his fang teeth showing. The mangy thing needed shot, but that wasn't Chet's job. Maybe that's what needed to be done. One shot to start a barrage of them.

There was heat in the stage office's stove, and Chet warmed his cold hands at the hot iron's radiant heat.

"You four going to Mesilla?" asked the clerk under the visor.

"We have tickets. Anything wrong?"

"No, *señor*. I was not here when you bought them. I only asked to see if you had them."

"We do. Thanks."

Cole turned from the window. "There's three men on horseback leaving town, headed south. Do they look like the two you saw the other night?"

The window Chet looked out of was dirty and he only saw their backs. "Can't tell if they were."

Jesus didn't get to see them at all. "Our stage leaves at one?" he asked.

Chet nodded and sat down. "You and Cole go buy us some fresh burritos for lunch. We have time to eat before the stage pulls out."

"Good, then we can eat in Mesilla," JD said. "They have lots of good food down there."

The two left and returned in a short while with

burritos from a street vendor. During their absence, Chet hadn't seen anything suspicious—maybe they would finally get away from this place without an incident and head for home.

They ate their lunch in the stage office. When they finished, Jesus filled a canteen at the city well across the street and they washed their meal down with it. He refilled it later to drink on the way since some stopovers only had gypsum-water.

They loaded their gear into the back of the coach and covered it with a tarp. Since the coach carried a large load of freight, it was a tight fit. At last, they climbed on the stage and it rolled out of Socorro. Chet knew he wouldn't miss the sleepy town. His guts still crawled when he thought of the arm of the crooked law that operated there. He'd slapped that local ring in the face. They might not be through with him yet.

CHAPTER 4

The rocking of the stage almost had Chet lulled to sleep, when he heard the pop of gunshots.

"*Banditos! Banditos!*" the driver shouted and urged his horses to run faster.

Everyone in the coach did some searching of each other's face. Cole stuck his head out, then drew it back in. Gun in hand, he said, "Looks like there are three of them. They're masked. Hold your fire until they get close enough to shoot them," he told the others.

After a little distance, the driver reined in the horses, locked the brake, and shouted, "We give up."

"Throw your guns out, *gringos.*"

"Who in hell knows there's *gringos* in here?" Cole asked.

"They do," Chet said.

A bullet crashed into the side of the coach, splintering slivers of wood on them. By some miracle, no one was hit. From the side windows, the robbers couldn't be seen. They stayed behind the coach, not taking any chances until the passengers unloaded.

"Get out here or die!"

At once, more of their bullets struck the freight in the back. A couple of shots ricocheted off the coach with a sharp whine. A few more holes in the coach showered them with dust and splinters. Damn, the three masked men held a position behind the stage where they couldn't shoot at them without sticking their heads out the windows.

At last, the robbers' guns clicked on empty.

"Now." Chet opened his door to lean out and began shooting at the one on that side. JD and Cole were slinging lead out the other way.

In no time, JD was out of the coach with his reloaded pistol and took three more shots.

Quarters inside the stagecoach were too tight for both Chet and Jesus to fire at the same time. Jesus resolved that by taking Chet's empty pistol and giving him his. "I'll reload yours," he said.

Three masked men lay on the ground. One raised his pistol to take aim and both Chet and JD shot him in the face. Then, when they reached the outlaws, they had to shoot two of their injured horses.

"The driver's been shot," Cole said from where he stood on the front wheel. "Help me get him down."

Jesus traded Chet his pistol for his own and ran over to assist in getting the man eased to the ground.

Chet knelt by the first man they'd finished off and pulled the flour sack mask off. His bloody face wasn't familiar. When he rolled the next limp body over, he thought he knew the big man. When he jerked off the mask, he right away recognized the main deputy, Diego. Barely alive, Diego cussed at him from behind clamped teeth.

"You better be praying, brother. There won't be any last rites said for you out here today."

JD scowled at the first one. "That other guy we shot is a deputy, too. His name is Balleras."

Chet bent over and pulled the mask off number three.

"They call him Ajo."

"Jesus, put the masks back on them. I want them found in their costumes. And find their badges and pin them on, so they will be easily identified."

"How bad is the driver shot?" Chet asked, looking back at the stage. The driver had set the brakes and tied off the reins, so the coach and horses stood waiting for them to go on.

"He's bleeding bad," said JD, knelt beside him.

Chet rose and went to see what he could do for the driver.

JD said, "He's shot in the shoulder. He may make it to Mesilla."

"You and Cole can handle driving the stage on to Mesilla. Jesus and I will try to make him comfortable and stop the bleeding."

"We can damn sure do that," Cole agreed.

"Load him up."

"One more thing. When we get to Mesilla," Chet said, "I'm buying three more .44s and cartridges to go with them. JD had his reloaded before a lamb could shake his tail."

They all nodded, acting impressed with his nephew's new firearm.

"What about the outlaws?" Jesus asked.

"We can wire their boss where to find them. We've got to get this driver to a doctor."

"Damn right," JD said. "I evened the damn score here tonight, men. That damned Diego took away my owner papers on the horses the night they arrested me. I've been kicked around and beat up by them three bastards. They sure deserved what they got."

With the wounded driver inside the coach, JD and Cole climbed on top. They headed south with a shout and the crack of a whip. Jesus bandaged the wounded man's shoulder with what they had to work with. The driver was Mexican and damned sure made of tough stuff.

They'd be asked lots of questions at each of the stage stops. No matter, as long as they got out of New Mexico Territory before someone tried to arrest them for the killing of those three. He could get into the damnedest situations, when all he wanted to do was get home.

Marge, I am coming home quick as I can. You and that baby keep doing fine.

CHAPTER 5

Throughout the night they changed fresh horses at the various stage stops. Everyone on the route knew the driver and was concerned for him to make it. Chet bought a bottle of whiskey for the driver who was in great pain, but not complaining.

The stage operators were all shocked about him being shot, because he was well liked by them. They quickly changed the horses, and at most of the stopovers they served fresh hot coffee to the four tired men before they went on. Noontime the next day they reached Mesilla and, when word of the robbery spread, the town turned out.

Jesus and JD named the three robbers as lawmen turned outlaws. Chet knew that information would set the tone when the newspapers printed it. As soon as the exhausted men could get away from the curious crowd, they ate a big meal furnished by a grateful local restaurant owner. Then they checked into a hotel and slept twelve hours.

Right after breakfast, they went west by train to

Deming. A stage took them to Lordsburg, then into Arizona, and on to Tucson. Papago Wells, the next stop, set on a crossroads that forked to Yuma and San Diego, or on north to Hayden's Ferry and then Preskitt. But it all took time, seated on the leather-covered horsehair-stuffed seats in the dust-filled, rocking stagecoach. Jesus, Cole, and JD took turns sitting on top the coach with the driver.

Chet was sure of one thing. He needed to take a great long bath when he got home. There were parts of New Mexico and Arizona dirt blocking every pore of his body. His hair was so dirty it would stand straight up. The weather was still warm, but everything was dry, and dust swept over them with every breath of strong wind. When they crossed the Salt River on the ferry past Hayden's Mill during the night, he knew in twelve to fourteen hours they'd be in Preskitt.

He was ready. He'd wired Marge their arrival time, so she would meet them or send buckboards. He intended to soak in a hot tub of water until the cows came home, then hug his wife for hours, just to savor her closeness. Bone tired, he was ready to stay home as long as he could.

When they started north, he wrapped in a blanket, because he knew as the elevation increased, so would the temperature drop. But it would be great to be back there.

They arrived close to sunup to find bonfires across the street from the stage office and scads of folks there to welcome him and his boys back.

Marge tackled him from one side, and Susie the other.

"You made it, and you got him freed."

He kissed his wife hard. Susie was hugging JD. Tom and Millie were there, and even Hampt and May got involved in the hugging. Jenn and her girls were on hand to congratulate him, and his banker, Mr. Tanner, was there to shake his hand. Everyone showing up for the homecoming impressed Chet. He accepted a steaming cup of coffee with gratitude. It felt so damn good to have his boot soles on solid ground and out of that swaying coach.

The banker grinned from ear to ear. "I have good news for you, Chet. The government will pay for the first two or three deliveries in a few weeks."

"Damn, Tanner, that will be great."

"I told you they always pay—sooner, or later."

They both laughed.

Tanner turned serious. "This was a serious matter you've been through, getting that boy out of jail."

"We were lucky. But he's a free man with no record."

At a touch on his shoulder, Chet turned to see Leroy Sipes, the man he'd rescued in Utah, and his wife Betty Lou, there to greet him. With them was Kathrin Arnold, the woman he'd brought back from Utah on that same trip.

She smiled up at him. "I knew when I heard about this that you'd succeed. JD's like me, very lucky you came along."

"How is your life these days?"

"I'll be fine. A divorced woman's path is not a great place to walk, but it will work out. And I'm grateful to you for getting me out of there. I saw no way to escape."

"You'll do fine, and I wish you all the happiness."

Marge returned to take his hand and lead him away to meet other folks. Quietly, she asked, "Is JD all right?"

"He acts like himself again. I am, too, now that I'm back here. Damned long, tense, trip. I need a shave, a bath, and a night or two with you. How are you feeling?"

"Great, but I think the baby will be here sooner than I counted."

"Fine, I'm ready."

CHAPTER 6

Chet rose before daybreak and left his wife sleeping. Dressing quietly, he slipped downstairs. The light was on in the kitchen and the big fireplace in the living room was blazing. It was even warmer in the kitchen.

Monica, in a fresh apron, smiled at his appearance. "Well, you never set out on a mission and not come home the hero."

"Oh, I don't win them all."

"You sure do all the ones I see you go after." She handed him a cup. "Have some coffee. How was the trip?"

"Well, JD is back. His reputation is restored and he's free again. Socorro is very Spanish, of course. The Chinese had fireworks on New Year's Eve. We went to a large *fandango*. Argued with the law, and I worried them enough they let him go."

"Your wife has behaved herself well. And, of course, worried about your welfare way off over there."

He took a sip of the hot coffee. Sure tasted good. "Has Susie been by?"

"She's fine. Excited about her condition, of course. You are going to have lots of diapers around you. She's been concerned about you, too. I have to console all these women when you are gone."

"Good about the babies. We need replacements."

"Deputy Roamer came by. Marge was gone to town. I think he had something on his mind, but he left no message—said he just stopped to talk to you."

"I'll check with him," Chet said. "The rest of the ranches all right as far as you know?"

"Seems to be." She put a plate of scrambled eggs, fried bacon, biscuits, and gravy before him. "Is that enough?"

"Just fine."

After breakfast, when daylight arrived, he joined Raphael, the foreman for the ranch on top, and his men. He'd dressed warm for the cold.

"I am so glad you made it back all right, *señor*, and that the boy is free."

"Thanks. We all are happy about it."

All Raphael's men were *vaqueros*. They were top of the line cattle handlers, but this morning they were unloading two wagons piled high with split firewood at the bunkhouse and main house.

They'd never run out of firewood up there. They had plenty, but it was better to be ready than without. Later, they'd have to feed the cattle hay. They were up and bawling already, but there was plenty of hay stacked up there to get them through the winter, too.

Cole and Jesus joined him and asked what the plans were for the day.

"After Marge gets up, I'll go into town. That may be a couple of hours."

"Fine. After we help unload this wood, we'll be at the bunkhouse," Cole said, and Jesus nodded in agreement.

Those two were good to find work while waiting on him; nothing lazy about them. Back in the house, his wife was up and in the kitchen with Monica.

"How's things?" he asked, joining her at the table.

"Oh, fine as I can be and the baby is, too. Here's a letter from Lucie." She read:

"Dear Folks, Things are fine up here on the mountain. My husband is running off elk every day. They fight the cattle for hay now that they've discovered we have it on hand. They also eat very good, of course. Not much is happening. The workers plan to have all buildings here completed, inside and out, in a month. Then they'll move to the Windmill. I know Susie is anxious, too. More maverick cattle are also coming in to the feed. We have added over a hundred and fifty head more since we started haying. I am shocked how many cattle strayed from passing herds. We sure didn't ever have that many head on the loose over west of Hackberry. At this rate, the place will be stocked by spring.

"Is Chet back from New Mexico yet? We are anxious to hear all about his trip and JD. Love, Lucie and Reg"

"You going to answer her?" he asked his wife.

"Yes, but you can put in a page about New Mexico. I am just so pleased to have you home."

"I'm going to town. You want to go along?"

"Nice to be asked, but I went yesterday and my back still aches."

"I'm sorry. You all right, otherwise?"

"Oh, yes. And other than that, I feel wonderful. But I do have some aches and pains in this cold weather. I guess I'm a baby at times about my aches."

"No, no. You have every right to be that way."

"JD went to the Verde with your sister last night."

"I thought he would."

"Does he have any plans?"

"Darling, he's pretty withdrawn right now, because of what he's been through. You have to pry words out of him. I hope he finds himself. He may join his brother. They used to be real close."

"I hope he's learned a lesson. That was some trouble of his for you to have to resolve."

"That's what I'm here for." He kissed her. "Then I'll go to town and take care of business. Anything going on in there I need to know?"

"Nothing I can think of. Susie and I paid all the bills while you were gone. Tom and the two of us did payroll, too."

"You all are sure handy. Thanks. I'll get the boys off firewood duty and we'll go see the bright lights."

She frowned. "Is Raphael using them?"

"No, they're just helping him."

"That's fine, then."

He kissed her, then sent word for the two to saddle

some horses—and not to pick the broncy one for him. On a cold morning like this, some of their horses used that as an excuse to buck.

In a short while they were saddled and on their way to town. Chet's horse, Chug, a big bay, walked on eggs until he passed under the crossbar at the open gate, then he calmed down. They trotted their mounts to town and stopped at Jenn's café to warm up.

"Where is the man of the hour?" she asked, looking for JD.

"He went home with Susie to the Verde last night. They had lots to tell each other."

"I see."

"How are things going here?"

"Oh, fine," Jenn said. "I can meet the payroll and pay for my groceries and the rent. That's all I need to do."

"I'm going to see my banker and Bo and talk to the machinery man—the new man that runs the mercantile. He has mowers, rakes, and stackers coming for us—I hope."

"You know his wife left him? The woman you brought back from Utah is doing his housekeeping."

"Yes, Kathrin Arnold. She came to welcome me home last night. I bet she's handling that job just fine."

Jenn nodded, but made no further comment.

He wanted to laugh. It was obvious Jenn didn't think Kathrin was a respectable enough lady, but she needed someone, too.

He and his two shadows visited the bank next.

"Good to see you," the banker said. The two went into Tanner's office and he showed Chet a chair. "Well, I got the telegram today. They are going to pay for two cattle deliveries. You know that's over a hundred thousand dollars?"

"Yes, I've known that all along. Kinda worried me at the start, but they had to pay someone for their cattle. Glad it was my outfit."

"Oh, you've helped a lot of local folks, buying their cattle, as well."

"I aim to do more of that. And when that family settles the Rankin estate, I plan to add that place to the rest of our holdings."

Tanner nodded. "Their lawyers here are very interested in you stepping in to manage it until it is settled. Would you do that?"

"I think that would be like shooting myself in the foot. The way it's run now is going to make that place less desirable, say to someone like me, who wants to buy it. What would I gain by fixing it and then buying it at some inflated price?"

"I don't blame you. But how have you managed to make your holdings work, as large as it has grown?"

"Damn good people I managed to hire."

"You willing to manage some more? I have some folks that could use you."

He shook his head. "I don't need any more. Thanks."

"I'm keeping informed about any changes regarding the Rankin place, so you will get a chance to buy it."

"Good."

"Your land man is on the lookout, too. My, he is busy. I know you sobered him up. He was so deep in the bottle, I told my wife he'd never make it. But it worked." He rose to shake Chet's hand. "Good doing business with you, as always."

Chet left Tanner's office feeling good. He was back on his feet, financially, and that situation would only get better. He buttoned his coat before setting out for the Palace Saloon to have lunch with his two men.

They usually went to Jenn's, but today their destination was the watering hole across from the courthouse. When he joined Cole and Jesus, they were already seated at a side table. All three ordered beer and a lunch of chicken-fried steak, German potatoes, and sourdough bread.

"What's new in town?"

"Frye at the livery wants to see you about some draft horses," Cole said.

"Good. We'll need lots of them."

"Did Tom tell you that John's really making barbed wire at the Verde ranch?" Jesus asked.

"Yes. That should make Hampt and Tom happy."

"How many years 'till you have all your places fenced?" Cole asked, setting down his beer mug and wiping foam off his upper lip with his kerchief.

"A hundred, maybe? I don't know, but it will become more and more a problem. Folks keep turning cattle loose 'cause they have no place or hay to winter them."

"Tom mentioned that lots of years the cattle didn't need hay up here. But after a dry fall like we had, hay's important."

"Lots of things to think about, ain't they?" Cole looked at him with a grim nod.

"Lots to learn. This country is much drier than Texas. And I thought Texas was bad enough."

"Not tomorrow," Cole said, "but some day, I'd like to know enough to be in a job like Tom or Hampt has. So I need to ask you lots of questions, when you have time to answer them."

"I'd love to do that. Ask me anytime, Cole. I sure don't have all the answers, but we can work on them."

"Mrs. Carmichael asked us about the Barbarossa stallion. I guess she never had a chance to ask you about him?"

"No, she didn't."

"She knew all about those horses and the place they came from. We were so busy with JD and every-thing happening, I guess she never had time to talk to you about breeding some mares to him."

"It's a long ways to bring mares, and he's busy now."

"Did those men ever come from Mexico and get the Barb last fall?"

"Yes, kinda like the wind. They swept in here, got their reward, and left. I wasn't there, but they im-pressed Susie. I'd almost forgot all about that."

"How many colts will we have next year?" Cole asked.

"I hope twenty of our own."

Jesus nodded and smiled at the bar girl who served

their lunch. "We may be on the way to having many great horses."

"At one time in Texas, we produced about that many every year. That damn Reynolds killed several of my best mares for no damn good reason but hatred nd jealousy."

"That must have been hard on you."

"Jesus, I hate to even think about it. Those were such bad days in my life."

With that, they fell silent and paid attention to their lunch. After eating, they went by to see Bo at his land office.

"Still got those guys that keep you sober, I see," Bo said, indicating Chet's sidekicks.

"Still have them."

"News all over town is you got your nephew back."

"We did. Any information I need to know?"

"The Atlantic Pacific Railroad has sections of land for sale that go back and forth across the tracks. You know the pattern, like your land east of Hackberry."

"How much?"

"Couple million, I guess. They need money now."

"Could we buy what we want?"

Bo shook his head. "No, it's all one big package."

"We could never use that much land, or pay for it. Some of it over east isn't much, and I haven't been to the border over there on the west."

"Okay. Oh, I bought a homestead in the canyon north of you. It straddles the Oak Creek stream. Has several fruit trees and a log house."

"My young nephews will love you. They fish."

"The papers are about through. You want to go look at it?"

"I trust you. After we go check it out, I'll find a man to run it."

"It'll be yours in thirty days, but you can go look whenever you want."

"Make me a map. Jesus can wait for it. I need to see Ben Ivor at the mercantile."

He and Cole cut across the courthouse yard and soon were inside the large store. The place, heavy with smells of spices and leather, bustled with business. He shook hands with a few familiar ranchers while making his way back to Ben's office in the rear.

The door was open and Ben welcomed him.

"I heard you'd settled with them in New Mexico and was back. You are a wide traveler—Grand Canyon one time, the next New Mexico."

"Throw in Utah, too."

"Yes, there, too. Close that door. I need to talk to you." He pointed at a chair in front of his desk. "Have a seat."

After Chet was settled, the storekeeper spoke in a confidential way. "You know my fancy wife up and left me a while back. Did Kathrin tell you she's taking care of my house?"

"She mentioned it."

"Will you tell me what you think of her? She speaks very highly of you."

"Kathrin was in a fix-up in Utah. But she was very ladylike. When I heard her story about her husband marrying two sisters, and how she made such a big effort to care for Leroy Sipes when he was their prisoner, I knew she was a good woman."

Ben looked at his crowded desk and nodded. "Don't say a word, but I plan to marry her when my divorce is final."

"I'd say you did well, Ben." Chet was pleased she'd have a good place with the storekeeper.

"Thanks. Now, I have six mowers and rakes, plus the hardware for several beaverboards. They should be here by March. You want them all?"

"If you can't sell them, I do. But I have those two you delivered from Kay's place. They're going to Hampt's. Two are going to the Windmill Ranch, and two are going to Reg and Lucie up on top. So, you have two to sell. My blacksmith has the used ones on the Verde place all fixed to mow next year."

"Good. I have buyers for them, and some more if I can get them here. But you were first on my list."

"Thanks."

"No, I have to thank you. Your cattle buying around here is sure helping folks pay me off. I think that's great for them."

Ben sounded real pleased over the debt settling folks were doing with him.

"If they don't hijack the freighters, we should be in good shape on mowers then."

"Without rails up here, it's a big operation to get them up here. They have to come to Deming, New Mexico, then the freighters haul them on to here."

"I just came back from there, so I know all about that."

"Need anything else, you holler." Ben shook his hand. "Thanks for Kathrin, too. You thought enough of her to bring her here, so I'm in your debt."

Chet headed for Frye's livery where Jesus joined him and handed him the Oak Creek place map. They'd have to make time to go see it. Marge might like to go, too.

When they walked into the livery office, Frye's wife Gloria smiled and stood up—and she was pregnant, too.

"You made it back, stranger. He's been wondering when you'd show up. I heard all went well over there?"

"Yes, ma'am, we got it settled."

"Well, he's coming right back. You men have seats. I keep this office hot, so you may cook in here."

Gloria was a nice-looking woman in her late twenties. Marge knew her well and had told him her story. Her first husband only did day work for ranchers, so when he died, he left her with three small children and no way to make a living. Out of need, she was forced to turn to working in a brothel. When Frye learned of it, he got her out of the business and married her. Gloria could do books, so they hired a housekeeper to keep the kids. It worked out all right for them, and for her children, too.

Frye came in unbuttoning his wool coat. "Hey, you made it back and never got your nose skinned." When they laughed with him, he went on. "Oh, yeah.

I have a man coming from California by the name of Rose. You met him. He's bringing a hundred head of good horses over here and said you could pick choice. Thanked you, too, for getting him to a dentist to fix his tooth."

"Crazy guy. He needed to see one bad. He was headed for Utah and there wouldn't be no dentist for days. I'm sure in the market for some draft horses. Just send me word."

"Was that a big deal in New Mexico?" Frye asked, walking him and his men out into the sunshine.

"Naw, we got it settled."

"He can say that now," Cole said. "But it was a big deal and he handled it."

Frye laughed. "He does that all the time."

They went for their horses, then stopped by Jenn's and had a cup of coffee with her. Everything was all right and she had no news to share.

By the time they made it back to the ranch, the winter sun was setting.

"How was your day?" Marge asked when she met him on the enclosed back porch.

He hung up his great coat and hugged her tight. "Over a hundred thousand dollars better."

She squeezed him in return. "Your cattle plan has worked."

"It worked fine. What else?"

"I think you better go see Hoot tomorrow. He's failing, Susie said. But we've all been so busy."

"I'll do that. That grand old man really helped me at the start and he got all these boys, along with Jenn.

Or she found him for me. Anyway, he helped, and found Tom, Hampt, and Sarge, just to name a few."

"You've got part of your cattle money then?"

"Yes. The first two shipments are paid. And Bo has bought us a place in Oak Creek Canyon that straddles the creek. Has apple trees and fruit orchards."

"What happened to the old owner, Mr. Kemp?"

"I don't know. But I'll need a man to look after it and I plan to build some cabins up there."

"That would be wonderful."

"May's boys will love it."

"Oh, yes, the fishermen. I'm so amazed to think about how you come up with so many good ideas."

"Or they come floating downstream to me."

He hugged and kissed her. Damn, he was lucky to have her. He'd had affairs, knew some good women in his past, but a wife like Marge exceeded his sweetest dreams.

CHAPTER 7

Chet and his two men had their horses saddled and ready at dawn. A cold north wind blew, and their breath looked like steam locomotives as they moved about in their heavy clothes ready to ride for the Verde.

When he put his boot in the stirrup he felt the hump in Sagebrush's back. His leg thrown over the cantle and boot barely in the other stirrup, the big bay horse broke in two. His legs were on springs and he shot sky high grunting like a mad hog. Then he leaped out in a space wide enough to cover the Grand Canyon.

Came down in a head-shaking stomp that about jarred Chet out of the saddle, but instead he stuck spurs to hide. That caused another explosion, but Chet could tell they were getting weaker by the hop. But the pony was still a quarter of a mile from being over it.

On the road, Jesus and Cole caught up with him on some high-headed horses of their own.

"Nice romp," Cole said, and drew a laugh from his companions.

"You ever been thrown off?" Jesus asked.

"A few times, but that ground out here is too damn hard to land on."

He wasn't satisfied the boys hadn't picked that horse on purpose as a joke, but he didn't really care—in his book, they were great guys. The three made the lower place by mid-morning and Susie bundled in a coat waved in greeting from the porch.

"We here for long?" Cole asked.

"I imagine so."

"Give us your horse then and we'll go out where they're feeding hay."

"I'll just hitch him. I may want to see them, too."

"Fine." The pair rode on.

By then Susie had him by the waist and they were headed for her kitchen.

"How is Marge?"

"Wonderful. No, she's a little stiff, she says. Hey, I have some news. We bought a farm with an orchard in Oak Creek Canyon right astraddle on Oak Creek."

"We did? That's such a sweet place. I went by that orchard. Will that be our place?"

"I figure to build some cabins up there for all of us to use. I need to hire a man to farm it soon."

Susie beamed with the news. "Wait until those boys hear it's ours. They'll want to live up there."

"Keep it under your hat until we sign the final papers."

"I will. You know my husband will be back here in a week."

"If he rides a good horse to death. We've received payment for our first two deliveries. So we're in line to get more. This one makes three they owe us for."

"This reminds me of when you used to return from Kansas bringing money home to Texas."

"Same effect as those sales. It's a big financial help to the ranch operation. We won't make as much money sending our neighbors' cattle over there, but it'll make money for everyone. It's going to help the area's economy too. Our mowers and rakes are coming for all three places as well. Delivery should be April."

"You never cease to amaze me. We are flying high, aren't we?"

"The move here is going better than I thought, and making places for all of us. The Rankin lawyers want me to step in and manage that place, but that would only cost me money."

"Oh, yes, Lucie sent me a letter. Do you want to read it?"

"Sure."

The message was close to Marge's, except some notes for Susie. His sister spoke up, "Lucie is a great lady for being such a cowgirl and ranch hand."

"A grand gal for him."

"Yes, I never expected—well, for Reg to pick her out after his last wife was so pretty."

"Lucie is more than pretty. I think she is so real and so damn good at it."

"She is. Next summer, we can all have a baby convention, huh?"

"Sure enough. There'll be a lot of us then."

Susie frowned before she said, "JD hasn't figured out what he wants to do yet. I hope he does soon. But he's still acting like he's not certain of his future. I think he wanted to strike out and do something himself."

"Perhaps. He's never talked much to me about anything since I offered to help him down at Kay's. And she turned it down. But since then he's sure not been the person we raised."

"I think he's having a hard time inside."

"I wish he was better grounded, but I don't know what to tell you. Anything here I need to look at?"

"No. Marge and I did the whole thing. I'll miss doing the books up at the Windmill."

"I'll miss your attention to details."

"I guess this baby and moving up there will change it all, won't it?"

"Not how much I appreciate you."

She chuckled. "I can still recall riding down and telling you they'd stolen all our horses. That kicked it off—. Oh, I hear a horse coming in hard." She looked out the window, then turned back to him. "It's Deputy Roamer."

Chet stepped to the front door and opened it. "What's wrong?"

Roamer swept off his wide brimmed hat and

shook his head. "You got time to talk? I tried to catch you before you left this morning, but got around too slow. You guessed it. I have a problem."

"Come in. Susie will fix us some lunch and we can talk." He closed the door behind the deputy. "How are you?"

"Aw, fine.

"Hello, Susie. I guess Sarge is over at Gallup?" Roamer asked.

"No, he should be back shortly."

"Tell him hello for me."

"I will, and I can fix lunch while you two talk."

"Thanks."

Chet motioned. "Have a chair."

Roamer settled into an overstuffed chair near the fireplace. Elbows on knees, he whirled his hat on his hand. "I understand you had a successful trip."

"We did. Monica said you came by, but left no word. I thought you were all right or I'd of checked with you yesterday."

He kept whirling the hat on his hand. "I guess I'm going to need a job."

"What does Simms have in mind?"

"He says he has too many deputies. Budget cuts, he calls it."

"When do you want to start working?"

"I guess in two weeks. What do you have for me to do?"

"To start, you can help up here. You need to learn all you can from Tom and then we'll find you a place."

"I want to be a hand."

"What else are you doing?"

"Oh, some breed stole a horse and beat up a squaw off the reservation, so I have a warrant for his arrest."

"Where do you think he's at?"

"Somewhere hiding out on the Verde, they say. Cold as it is, he may be holed up anywhere."

"What's his name?"

"Jack Kay."

"Maybe the four of us could find him. Jesus is a great tracker and Cole and I can scatter out and search for him. Tell me something. You really like your deputy job. Maybe if I went and talked to Simms about it that would help you."

"I wouldn't mind, but you and him don't agree on much."

"He might listen. Where's this Kay liable to be?"

"I heard there's a camp of breeds somewhere east of here."

"I've not heard about it. The crew will be in soon for lunch and you can ask Tom about it."

"Lunch is ready," Susie announced.

They rose and went into the kitchen filled with good smells. She'd fixed fried ham and German potatoes, plus her fresh-made sourdough bread.

After pouring coffee, she took a place with them. "Is this Jack Kay dangerous?"

"Who knows? These people are not really Indians or whites and they don't fit well anywhere. Most were raised as Indians, so they tend to live among them. But they don't get government food allotments, so they have to steal. But he beat up a woman, typical of the Indians, but it ain't allowed on the reservation, either. Then he took her horse to get away. That's breaking the law, too."

"Chet helped the Indians." She looked at him. "Didn't you?"

"They were starving back then and had a bad agent. We fed them cull bulls and lame horses to get them by and the agent even threatened us for doing that. General Crook had him removed and they must be doing fine now."

"These breeds will be a problem until they find a place like a reservation."

Chet nodded in agreement.

"How's your wife?" Susie asked.

"She's fine," said Roamer. "Have you met her?"

"Once at Marge's. Tell her hello for me."

"I'll do that."

"When we finish here, we can go down and talk to my men at the kitchen," said Chet.

"They told you about Hoot?" Susie asked.

"Yes, I'll see him."

"Good."

After thanking her, they headed to the cowboys' kitchen. Hoot sat in his rocker by the stove under a fancy trader blanket. He looked very weak and his eyes were drawn.

The old man looked up. "I ain't worth much to you, boss man. I'm not able to do much these days."

"We're just glad you can visit with us. You've done

your part for this outfit. Stop worrying. We just want you to be comfortable."

"It's grown to be a big outfit. I'm proud I was here from the start."

"So are we. You need anything, ask Tom."

"Hell, he's a good one, ain't he?"

"The best. Marge told me to tell you to keep kicking."

"You tell her this rocker she sent me is the best one I ever set in."

Chet went out to where Roamer and Tom were talking about the breed problem.

"I haven't heard much about that camp. But I bet if they are in that country over there, Hampt knows about them," Tom said.

Roamer agreed. "That's probably right. We'll check with him tomorrow."

"How are the Herefords doing?" Chet asked.

"Great. I have three boys up there full time. And one line rider out on the western side turning any cattle back or running any strays off our range."

"How many of the cattle are you feeding here?"

"About two hundred fifty mother cows. That means about a hundred of the cows are still out. We have lots of weaned stock and yearlings here, too. Cows outside are some of the wilder cows, but we try to bring them in as we can find them."

"You've made this program work well, Tom."

"Ryan never used to feed and we'd lose lots of stock in tough years like this one. But he was pocketing the money instead of spending it for hay."

"We're doing well. I have draft horses coming, and I plan to complete the other outfit's hay operations as well. Let me know how Hampt's fencing operation is going. I'll go over and look at it."

"We're making the wire," Tom said.

"John is really turning the wire out?" Chet asked.

"He has two helpers and they're sending a wagon load a week over there."

Chet nodded in satisfaction.

They got home late after making a search circle with Roamer. They decided to talk to Hampt the next morning to see if he knew anything about a breed camp in that area, then Roamer headed home.

Since the crew in the bunkhouse was already in bed, Monica fixed supper for Chet and the boys. While she put together a hot meal, Cole and Jesus took care of the horses.

Marge had coffee with them while they ate. After a good meal and some small talk, Chet's two men promised to be ready at daylight to meet Roamer and try to locate the breed camp. Then they headed for the bunkhouse.

After he thanked Monica for feeding them, Chet and his wife went upstairs to their bedroom.

"Everything alright down there at the ranch?" she asked.

"Yes, Tom has things running better than smooth."

"Who is this breed that Roamer is after?"

"Jack Kay. I don't know him, but he's broken the law."

"You be careful. Those men on the run get desperate."

"On top of that, Simms has threatened to fire Roamer again."

"Oh, that man has lost his mind, hasn't he?"

"I guess. I may talk to him about it."

She kissed him. "Don't lose your temper with him."

"I'll try to act nice."

The next morning, Roamer met them and they rode over to talk to Hampt. He and his men were feeding hay, and his two stepsons were riding their horses around the herd. The boys loped over to meet them.

"You two okay today?" Chet asked them.

"Really riding our horses hard. Lots of herding for us to do."

"Well, I see you're doing a good job gathering them up."

He told them to keep up the good work and rode over where the others talked with Hampt.

Roamer reined his horse around. "He says that camp is across the river and north of your property. Let's go see if we can find him." He moved his horse off and Jesus and Cole followed.

Chet lingered for a few words with Hampt. "Cattle look good," he said.

"If I didn't have to run off Rankin's cattle, it would be easier."

"I imagine it would be. How's the fencing coming along?"

"Good. We're really moving on that."

"Any problems?"

"Just doing it." Hampt laughed. "We're fine. Good to see you. JD doing all right?"

"I think so. He ain't himself yet."

"That can come. I promised May I'd do something for her today, or I'd go along with you."

"Take care of her." Chet set out at a lope after the others, but taking time to look around at the land. This country had lots of junipers and some sagebrush about it. Everything tilted east from the ranch house to the hayfields below on the Verde. The previous owners had badly overgrazed this ranch. It would be several years recovering.

The others were way off the mountain before he caught up with them. Before long, he spotted a trail of smoke to the north. He pointed it out and they agreed it came from a campfire across the river.

Headed toward the smoke, they passed the fencing crew rolling out wire from a reel slipped on a smooth post. They had two wires up and were working on the third one of five. New posts set in a straight line and stays, to be placed between the posts to keep the wire in place, were on the ground. Looked good to him. It would look better when completed. He spoke briefly to the fence crew and rode on.

They crossed the Verde at a ford where a cut in the far bank allowed them to ride up on top on the other side. The camp was spread out and little children ran for wickiups at the sight of them. Someone opened fire at them and they dismounted and returned a shot or two.

"There's three of them shooting at us," Chet said. "Be careful not to shoot a woman or child."

When there was a break in the gunfire, they divided up, crouched low, and ran for the camp. But the shooters had taken cover in some tall junipers.

Chet heard a baby cry, then a small teenage girl ducked coming out of her shelter. Bare-breasted despite the cold air, she carried a crying baby.

"Is he all right?" Chet asked.

"Yes."

"Good."

"Gun shots scared him."

He nodded and turned to see the others approaching. "They've headed for some horses," he shouted.

Roamer joined him first, then the other two. They watched as other squaws and a few men dressed in rags, all unarmed, began to appear. All he saw told Chet these breeds were a ragged, hungry-looking bunch.

"Who is your leader?" he asked.

"Rump," one woman said, and pointed out a skinny man with lots of gray hair.

Wrapped in a thin blanket, he came forward. "I'm Rump."

"Do you have anything to eat here?" Chet asked, frowning at the Indian and his situation.

"Pinion nuts."

"Tomorrow, one of my men will bring you a cow or old bull to eat. I will find you some frijoles and have them delivered to the river."

"Wait," the man said with a pained expression on his old face. "Why do that for us?"

"'Cause hungry babies cry in your camp. I won't be able to sleep hearing them."

The man used the flat of his hand to touch his forehead sideways and send it toward him. "I thank you and your people. We can do nothing about the men that shot at you."

"We can, and we'll be back tomorrow to track them down. If they're in camp when we come, put up a white flag so we know they're here."

Rump nodded his assent.

Jesus and Cole rounded up all the crackers and jerky in their saddlebags to give to the women.

"We can go home tonight, get some pack horses and go after those three," said Chet.

Roamer shook his head. "You never cease to amaze me, Chet Byrnes. You are one generous guy. It wasn't the shooting made that baby cry. He was hungry, wasn't he?"

"Yes. It'll be dark when we get home tonight, and looking for these varmints is going to take a few days. We have nothing with us and these folks need the things I promised them. We'll set out tomorrow to find them."

"Like we always do." Jesus smiled with confidence. "They can't run far enough on their poor horses."

Cole rubbed the sleeves of his coat. "I only wish it was warmer."

Roamer laughed. "Then wear two suits of underwear, Texas."

They smiled, mounted up, and headed for Hampt's.

When May heard the story about the handful of breeds starving, she was ready to take them food right away. Hampt hugged her. "Darling, we'll get them an old bull to eat, and frijoles, and whatever else you want them to eat. And do that first thing in the morning."

"Can I give them a case of canned milk?"

Chet said, "Fine. There's probably a dozen or so babies down there. I'm going to take them a few blankets from my place."

She looked at Hampt. "We have a few blankets I saved."

Hampt nodded at her, then looked at Chet. "I guess I'll be in charge of them, too?"

"Yeah, feeding them and looking out for them until we find a charity to do it."

It was late when they reached home, but Marge was up holding supper.

"May wanted to feed us, but we told her you'd be up."

She filled coffee cups around. "I'm glad you did. I sent Monica to bed. And those poor Indians up there are starving?"

"Bad shape."

"Those men shot at you?"

"They had some old rifles they shot at us with," Jesus said. "We were out of range."

"We'll go find them and Roamer can arrest them," Chet said.

"I have several blankets we can send. How will these people fend for themselves?"

"Come spring, they can plant a few acres of garden at the edge of Hampt's irrigated ground and grow what they want. But that's a long way off. Till then, we'll help them get through it."

"Why did they camp there? Isn't that on your land?"

"Probably. I think they fished a lot and ate them."

Marge looked shaken by the Indians' problem. "My, how many people like that could starve and no one know it."

They made plans to get up in a few hours and go back with packhorses to track the breeds down. Roamer thanked Marge for her offer to put him up at the house, but said he'd stay at the bunkhouse.

Chet and his wife got ready for bed, but both still thought about the Indians' situation.

"I think the Methodist Church will help them. I'll ask this Sunday," Marge said.

"They won't take much. But they're so pitiful, I was shaken. No one cared, but then, no one had any way to know their plight, either."

"I'll get some folks working on it."

"Good. I figured you would." He hugged her to him and kissed her. It was great to have her by his side.

* * *

Blue cold at peach dawn, they set out on dancing fresh horses with pack animals following. The steamy breath of men and horses almost made a cloud. They left in a long trot for Hampt's place. When they arrived, he joined them with two of his men who said they knew where there was a crippled bull the breeds could eat.

They rode off to drive the bull down there, and the posse crossed the river to meet with Rump. Soon, blankets were handed out, along with a hundred pound sack of frijoles, canned milk, and some ground corn meal. Chet told Rump that his men had brought the bull for them to slaughter.

The chief stood wrapped in a newer blanket and tears ran down his wrinkled cheeks. "How we pay you?"

"Be well. We must go."

When they joined Jesus, he'd found the breeds' tracks, so they rode south. The day warmed under the sun and they trailed them close to the river. Jesus was confident the breeds' horses weren't very strong and they'd catch them by dark. Everyone stayed on alert. Even old worn-out guns could kill. These men probably had no food, either, and that would make them desperate.

As they rode south, Chet smelled a fire. He made a sign for the others to spread out and they scattered.

Cole took out up the mountainside with a rifle in his hands. His horse cat-hopped up the steep side of the slope, from where he could oversee the valley. Jesus went right, six-gun in his fist. Roamer and Chet rode straight into the opening.

The three breeds stood and raised their arms. Pitiful looking in their ragged dirty clothes, they appeared haggard and hungry. Long stringy hair hung shoulder length and on their faces—not whiskers, like their white fathers—but lanky hair.

Jesus gathered their guns, while Cole found their hobbled horses. Roamer handcuffed them and sat them down. Chet put an iron grill over their small fire and the others gathered axes to find better fuel. They soon had flames blazing, and Jesus cooked some food and made coffee.

"We're kinda overdone for capturing these three." Roamer chuckled and shook his head.

"Naw, we'll feed the breeds. That may solve their stealing to survive. Those people's living conditions still bother me."

"Oh, no. You've been generous to them. I agree those poor people back there need it. But it's pretty well a waste of time taking these three back. The county will have to clothe them, feed them, defend them, and then imprison them."

"That's the way it works. It's called the American way."

Roamer looked him hard in the eyes. "I still wasn't opposed to the answer you gave those killers over on Rye Wash."

"These breeds ain't worth the cost of a rope. Besides, they didn't rape an innocent woman and murder two good men in cold blood, plus steal a bunch of horses."

"I agree those men were real worthless. And rotting in prison wouldn't have helped them or their ambitions in the future."

"Under all circumstances other than those I've been more mindful of the law. I try to obey it."

"It damn sure took lots of guts to do it by yourself. I've always regretted I wasn't there to back you." Roamer shook his head as if in disgust.

"The Preskitt Valley foreman, Raphael, does, too. He tells me about it all the time."

"That desk deputy wouldn't let him go and help you. It wasn't his fault," Roamer said.

"I know. He knows. Just how it turned out."

"There isn't a man I know in this county does more for law and order than you. That's why you're a US Deputy Marshal. They want you on their side."

After the meal, they gave the prisoners a blanket apiece so they didn't freeze to death. The next morning, Jesus served everyone an oatmeal breakfast, then they mounted up and headed north for the crossing. Their horses were slow, so when they got about half way, Chet sent Jesus to Hampt's to get three fresh ones. He planned to leave those three weary animals at the breed camp, and maybe they'd find some forage and get rested.

They made the exchange at the ford and Rump thanked him for the horses' return. They pushed on to Hampt's where May fed the posse and offered them a place to spend the night. Chet and Roamer decided they should push on to Preskitt Valley.

They made it there about midnight and put the prisoners to sleep on the bunkhouse floor. With the horses put up, Chet breathed steam and headed for the dark house. It had been a long day.

When he went inside, Marge had come downstairs and lit a lamp.

"How did it go?"

"We caught them. Been all night getting here."

"Didn't they put up a fight?"

"No, they were starving, too. Horses worn out. They'll be in jail tomorrow."

"I'm glad you weren't hurt and are back with me." She hugged him.

"I smell like a horse and campfire."

"You smell good to me anywhere, anytime, anyplace, Chet Byrnes."

They went off to bed.

CHAPTER 8

In the morning, Jesus went with Roamer to deliver the prisoners and bring Hampt's horses back to them. Cole helped the *vaqueros*. Chet took a bath, shaved, and sat in the living room reading the *Miner* newspaper editions that he'd missed.

"Well, world traveler, what are your plans?" Marge asked.

"I need to check with Sarge to be certain everything is fine in Gallup. That's a very important part of this operation. Our sales over there will keep us expanding."

"Are you concerned about it?"

"Not concerned, but the potential is there. They're pleased we delivered on time and good well-fleshed cattle. But I worry people might try to underbid us. They say their experience with us has been what they expected, but it could be fragile."

"Do you need to go over there?"

"Maybe later on."

"Maybe it will be less pressing on you in the future."

"All I care about is you and the baby first. Family, ranches, and my people next."

"Oh, I can't complain. I miss my horses. I miss being more active, but I have you and the baby warms my heart."

After supper, they went to bed and he slept hard.

Come dawn, he was up, ate breakfast and told his men they were riding for the Verde. Sarge should be there with his wife, plus he might have any news on the state of their contract with the Indian Bureau. It would make him more settled to know everything was all right.

The day was sharp, but warming, like so many winter days did. They dropped off the mountain into the Verde Valley and it heated more. Midday at the ranch, Sarge and his wife, Susie, came out on the porch to greet them.

Chet gave Jesus his horse's reins, hugged his sister, and shook Sarge's hand. "How did it go?"

"No problems." Sarge led the way into the house. "I spoke to all the agents we delivered to. They liked the cattle's condition for this time of the year. I think we're secure."

"Good. Tom has the next herd scheduled to take up to you at the Windmill."

"Yes, he told me."

"Good. Any ideas how we can do it better?"

"We're getting along well, I think. I listen to everyone's comments up there, but I think we're solid."

"I'm glad you two get to have a little time together."

"So am I," said Susie, who'd lingered to listen. "I'll fix some lunch."

Over lunch, Chet told them about the breeds and their pitiful condition, along with the arrests they helped Roamer with. Susie said they'd be on the lookout for things the Indians could use or needed.

"Mostly food. They're too damned starved and poor to even think."

"Reg sounds busy," Sarge said.

"He must be. He's building a ranch out of the mavericks that come in for feed."

"Did you see that many when you were up there looking at it?"

"No, but there were signs of cattle being there. We really had a lot to look at. But even Lucie said in her letter to Marge that they ranched way west of here and never realized that many mavericks were loose up in that part of the country."

"Well, it hasn't hurt us."

"No, it's made a big difference in developing that ranch. Reg and Lucie may have a money-making operation up there. Is JD still here?"

"No, he went up there to see them. The weather was holding so we told him to go," Susie said.

Sarge nodded. "He wanted to see things up there, and see his brother, plus Lucie."

"I don't blame him. Lucie is a treasure."

"May is, too, and it took Hampt to bring it out of her. I was around her for years and she never showed a sign. Then she marries Hampt and overnight she's an opera star."

Susie laughed. "Good men help." She clapped Sarge on the shoulder.

"I better get back to home. Good to see you two. Sarge, the construction crew is coming your way. Barring weather setbacks they should be done up there at Reg's."

"We have a lot of lumber already there. Robert sent us several of the loads you ordered."

"Glad it arrived."

"I'm ready to move now," Susie said.

"I know you must be."

He reached for his hat. "I'm ready to go home. Sarge, keep your mind on those folks up there at Gallup. We sure need to hold on to that beef contract."

"Do the best I can."

"I know you've really tried, but it's important."

"See you," Susie said.

"You two have a nice visit."

"Get out of here," she said, blushing.

He found his two men at the blacksmith shop watching them twist three-strand barb wire.

"Either of you want this job?" he asked.

Cole spoke up first. "Hell, no, but it makes impressive fencing."

"After we saw it strung up at Hampt's, I wondered how they made it," Jesus said. "They'll have those fields cowproof, won't they?"

"It's supposed to work that way. We need to get back to the Preskitt Valley ranch."

"We're ready," Cole said.

Chet congratulated John on making the wire operation work and told him how much it meant to the ranch. John beamed and bragged on his two helpers.

They made it home after supper, but Monica fed them. About eight o'clock, someone knocked on the back door and Chet went to see who was there.

"Mr. Byrnes?"

"Yes."

"My father said to get you to come help us. They shot him and took four of our horses."

"What's your name, young man?"

"Raft Boone. My paw's Henry Boone."

"How bad is your dad shot?"

"He said not for me to worry. He said get Chet Byrnes and he'll get them boogers stole our horses."

"You tell the sheriff?"

"Naw. Paw said come here and if'n you weren't home to send the word for you to come at once."

"Where do you live?"

"Below the Rankin place. My paw knows you."

Cole and Jesus materialized out of the darkness, probably after hearing the ruckus.

"You heard of a Boone down there?" Chet asked Cole.

"Yeah, but I don't know him."

"Okay, Raft. We'll saddle up and ride back with you. Should we get a doctor for your paw?"

"He just said get you."

"Come in and eat something. Is your horse done in?"

"Yes, sir."

"We'll saddle another for you." He turned to Marge.

"Are the panniers packed and ready?"

"Yes," she said. "I make sure they're ready anytime you need them. We usually don't get too much warning." She smiled at him.

"Jesus, bring a packhorse. We may have to go after them from down there."

"I'll get our bedrolls, too," Jesus said, and left at a run.

"I better help him," Cole said, and hurried after his partner.

"Shall we notify the sheriff?" Marge asked.

Chet nodded. "Someone can do that."

"Or should we send the news to Roamer, instead?"

"That would be better," Chet said.

"I'll send the news to him in the morning. You know it's cold out there," she reminded him.

"I know it's January and the coldest month of the year."

He looked up to see Monica come in from the kitchen where she'd fixed the boy a plate. "What's happened now?" she asked.

"Some rustlers shot a rancher and stole his horses. We're going to see what we can do for them."

"Does this sheriff do anything?" Monica made a pained face.

"So far, we're waiting," Marge said to her.

In a short while, Chet and his crew headed out behind the boy. Chet was proud of how his men worked as a team. Jesus handled the packhorse unless they needed to track someone. He had tracker duties and cooked. Cole led the pack string. No one was a glory hog, and they were all sensible enough when in a tight spot, like the stagecoach robbery in New Mexico. After that shootout, they all wore the new .44 center fire cartridge Colt pistols. Chet felt they were much more dependable and powerful than the older cap and ball.

The stars were out in the sky's ceiling when they rode past the Rankin place road. With no time to spare, they rode on and it was well past midnight when Chet saw lights of a ranch house flickering in the distance. He'd never been there before, but the boy confirmed they'd arrived.

"That's our place," he said. He'd been quiet most of the way, no doubt concerned about his wounded father. When he reached the yard fence, he bailed off his borrowed horse and headed for the tall woman in the doorway.

"How's paw?"

"Not good, son. You bring Mr. Byrnes?"

"That's him, maw."

"How's your man?" Chet asked, taking in the raw-boned woman dressed in a wash-worn dress covered with a shawl for warmth. Red faced, her nose looked redder, perhaps from crying, and her graying hair hung to her stooped shoulders. Her lips were chapped and cracked.

"He's not good." She dabbed at her nose with a frayed handkerchief. "I'm Irma Boone."

"My name is Chet; Jesus and Cole are with me."

"I sure hate to impose on you, sir. I don't consider my man's doing very good."

"Should we get a doctor?" Chet asked, concerned.

"He don't believe in 'em. They cut off his brother's leg in the war, and he says he would of lived if they'd left him alone."

"Where is his wound?"

"His shoulder. Me and the boy got him in the bed by the stove. Come look at him."

A tall thin-bearded man lay sleeping in the light of a candle, his face drawn and white. The torn sheet bandages showed fresh blood, so he was still bleeding.

"How deep is the bullet?" asked Chet.

She shook her head. "I don't know."

"If we can get it out, that bullet needs to come out. That's the only way I know to stop the bleeding. I fear if we don't, he'll run out of blood."

Cole, standing beside him, nodded. "We don't have a forceps to get it, either. We can take a thin-bladed knife and try to locate it." He shed his jacket and hung it over a chair.

With a grim face, Cole agreed. "We still have some black powder that we used in our old pistols. Is there some hot water, Irma?"

"Yes, on the stove and I can make some more. I've run out of coffee, sorry."

When Chet looked up, Jesus came in the doorway unbuttoning his coat. "Jesus, get us some coffee for this lady. We'll need that bottle of whiskey, too."

"I'll help you carry it," the boy offered.

"Cole, how long is your jackknife blade?"

"It's longer than yours." He fished it out of his vest.

After Chet opened it, he shaved the hair off the back of his hand. "Sharp enough. You can sharpen mine next time. I'm not as good at sharpening as you."

"Better get Jesus to do it. I can't, either, but he can."

"I learn more about you two every trip." Chet shook his head in amazement.

The woman put more wood in the iron stove and clanged the door shut.

"I need to wash my hands and anyone else touches that area needs to wash theirs as well." Chet looked at the woman hovering nearby. "I guess I should have asked you, Irma. Do you want us to do this?"

"Of course. I didn't know what to do. He's so contrary about doctors, he wouldn't hear to me getting one."

She brought a wash pan and a bar of home-made lye soap to the table. Then she filled the chipped enameled pan with hot water from the kettle on the stove.

"Should we take him off the bed to do this?"

She shook her head. "No, the mattress is already

ruined. If you can do it with him on the bed, that's fine."

"Tell us more about the men that shot him."

"Those three rustlers rode in late afternoon. Their horses were worn out. They called Henry out to talk. I knew they was outlaws when they come in the yard out there. I told him—I'll get you a clean towel." She rushed over to the crate box cabinets to get one for him to dry his hands on before she continued.

"The one they called Curly wore a big black hat. The old man had white whiskers, and he was short. The young guy looked only half here in the head to me."

"Tell me more about this Curly." Sleeves rolled up, Chet removed the bandages. Jesus and Cole, shirt sleeves rolled up, too, had washed their hands and stood by to help.

The heat from the large stove was intense, but Chet decided the room wasn't that warm at his back. At last, he got down to the site of weeping blood. About four inches below the collarbone, a black hole disfigured the man's stark white skin. Chet thought it might be a .45 slug, but only time would tell. Minutes earlier, he'd sterilized the blade in the stove's fire. Drawing in his breath, he probed gently in the wound. Henry, still asleep, moaned.

With a nod of his head, Chet drew the knife out. "If I knew more, I'd cut the bullet out, but I figure I'd cut more blood vessels and muscles that don't need to be cut. Unless you three complain at me, he can wear that slug."

Grim faced, they all agreed. Cole brought the gunpowder in a hollow cow horn over and took off the cap. He poured some in the wound on the man's shoulder. Using a matchstick, Chet poked the powder into the wound against the blood flow. No easy job.

"Put a towel over his face," he told Irma. "And when I strike a match, close your eyes. There'll be a blinding flash and he'll jerk in pain, but, Jesus, you and Cole hold his shoulders down." He pointed to her and the boy. "You two hold his feet down hard now."

The match struck, he touched the powder, and the blinding explosion showed through his eyelids. A bitter smell of burnt flesh and spent gunpowder filled his nose. The blinding smoke was bitter to breathe in and Irma rushed over to open the door for air. They were all coughing, but Chet saw one thing about their handy work that relieved him. The black hole the size of his thumb pad no longer flowed blood.

Irma, fists squeezed in front of her, looked relieved, too. "Oh, thanks, dear Lord. Make my husband live. Please, dear God, we need him so much."

"Amen," Chet said. Still no blood flow, so he stepped back. "You can't let him roll around a lot for three days, or he'll bust it open."

"If I have to, I'll tie him down. Thank you. There's coffee made. We all need a cup."

Cole hugged her shoulders because she was shaking

so hard. "Irma, he'll be okay. I've helped do this three times in my life. Every man lived."

"If I can keep him from opening that, he should make it."

Jesus poured the coffee in every kind of chipped cup he could find.

They seated her at the table and the boy stood behind arms wrapped around her thin shoulders.

Chet sat across from her. "Now tell me more about these outlaws."

"He had curly black hair, bigger chested than you. Bossy as all get out. On his right cheek—no—on his left one he had an ugly scar from the corner of his eye to his mouth. He wore a gold ring and rode a Mexican saddle. If his gun hadn't misfired after his first shot he'd of shot Henry again and might have killed him."

"How old was he?"

"Thirty to forty. I ain't sure. I don't age many folks."

"The old man?"

"He was fifty, sixty years old, maybe fifty-five. He only had three fingers on his right hand. I noticed that when they got a drink from our well. The last two fingers were gone. He had one eye that I don't think he could see out of."

"Raft said the boy was crazy?"

"He'd break out and say wild things. Cussed a lot. I tried my best to avoid him."

Raft spoke softly. "He went riding off laughing and

screaming, 'You got that old son-of-a-bitch. You got him.' Over and over until I couldn't hear him."

Irma still looked in shock.

"Which horses did they take?" Jesus asked.

"A big black horse. He was Dad's roping horse for chasing mavericks. He's black except for a white scar on his neck. He wears our brand on his right shoulder, a BO brand. And a blaze-faced three-year-old sorrel I was breaking. I sure hated to lose him. A bay horse with a Keystone brand on his right shoulder. Three more broke bay horses with our brand. They also had three more worn out ones they'd rode to death to get here. Lucky I had Shorty in a pen by hisself. He's the one I rode to your place. We've got a few more, but they're turned out."

Irma nodded and clasped her long hands on the table. "When they rode up, we didn't think anything. People pass by here often enough though we're off the road. I think most of them get lost. Some that come by, we've known good and well they were on the run. But all of them were polite and offered to pay me for my food. If they looked down in the heel, then I turned their money down. Those three rode in here like they owned the world."

"They say much we could use?"

"One mentioned a lady of the night named Crossett," Raft said, looking as if his mother disapproved of him telling about it.

She shook her head. "Henry shot and laying on the porch. We were covered in his blood. All over us from moving him in here. Henry said to Raft, 'Go find Chet Byrnes, son. He's the only man will get them dogs.' Raft asked if he should go on and tell the sheriff. Henry said, 'He don't do no good. You find Byrnes.'"

"He can be proud of his son. He must have rode the hair off that short horse to come tell me."

"There ain't no law in this country. Every rancher and miner we know thinks you should be the sheriff. We all know you're busy, but who else would have dropped their life and rode over here this late at night?"

"Can we sleep on the floor in here for a few hours? We'll need some sleep and we can't track at night. Whoever needs to wake us at daybreak."

"How many of those horses are shod?" Jesus asked.

"Three of them," Raft said. "Mom or I'll wake you."

Chet thanked them. He unrolled his bedroll and wished he was at home in a warm bed with Marge. Sleep evaded him and when he finally did sleep, Raft woke him up.

Jesus provided the flour, shortening, and baking powder for Irma's biscuits. She also made ham gravy and fried several slices for their breakfast. They left her half their coffee.

Henry was awake enough to thank Chet. The bleeding had stopped. The man had a long recovery coming, but Chet felt better over his crude doctoring.

Busy enjoying the hot breakfast, he knew the trail ahead would be cold. It would turn warmer when the sun got cooking, but it still wasn't Texas. He hugged Irma and saluted Henry, who she'd given some laudanum for his pain. Then he shook Raft's hand.

"You're a helluva good hand, son. Don't overdo it being the main one here, and be sure she don't."

"I'll do that. Thanks."

They rode south, Chet wondering where they'd find the outlaws. They had a good head start, but probably had no notion there was any pursuit. Still, their previous crimes no doubt made them fugitives—desperate and on the run. Shooting Henry Boone was just another small hitch in their day. But, like other criminals in this kind of situation, they struck the isolated ranches for their supplies and that called for more abuse of the innocent to show their power.

That was why he and his men rode southward. He wanted the likes of them stopped.

"Them folks were poor, weren't they?" Cole asked.

"I'd say so. Proud and poor. There's several folks like that trying to ranch over by Rye, living year round under a squaw shade."

"That would be cold. No walls?" Cole hugged his jacket sleeves. "That would be worse than Nebraska."

"No walls, either. It isn't as cold as up here, but it frosts down there. I'll tell Tom to contact Henry about selling us some of his cattle. A few sales would sure help their standard of living."

"Reg is getting a real winter up there." Cole tossed his head north.

"He's got a wife to keep him warm, too," Jesus added.

"Boys, that's a good reason to have one. Reg is such a hard worker, I bet he don't hardly notice the weather. You just wait. His brother JD will be back down here looking for a place. JD works, but his brother is a damn hard worker."

Midday they moved into the saguaros on the south slopes of the mountains they crossed. Lots of century plants and yucca marked the step ups and downs in the mountains they rode over.

"Where does this trail lead?" Cole asked, looking back over the tough country they'd already covered.

"I've heard there's an outlaw trail comes out of Utah, like we took the way back across the Grand Canyon. It runs east of the Black Canyon stage road down through here to the big valley and then into Mexico."

"I heard her say that when they got company she suspected some of them were outlaws."

"I don't know, but she never did say if these men came up or down the trail."

"I'm like you, Chet. I thought they came from the south. But all she said was they rode up." Jesus nodded his head. "Maybe they are on the run from up north."

"Wherever they came from, we need to get to where they're going. We better trot these horses over this mesa."

His men smiled and picked up their pace. An

hour before sundown, Chet decided to make camp where they found some water for their horses in pot-holes in a dry stream. They unsaddled and gathered firewood. Jesus set about boiling some beans for supper, adding fried chunks of bacon to the pot.

Chet and Cole unloaded the packhorses and hobbled all of them. Jesus made Dutch oven biscuits to go with the beans, and they thanked him as they ate their meal long past sundown. They had enough wood to keep the fire going all night and to cook breakfast in the morning.

Chet slept more that night, and while it wasn't toasty getting up, it was a lot warmer than at the Boone Ranch. Jesus worked on the fire and made oatmeal and coffee. When they finished eating, they gathered horses, saddled them, and got the pack-horses ready. A peach rose light of dawn came over the mountains in the east. They had another short winter day to run those outlaws down.

In the saddle again, they headed south on the trail. He wondered what they'd find this day. Jesus had mentioned he saw signs in their horse turds that they were getting closer.

Chet hoped so, and made his mount trot. Cross-ing the flat desert floor, the midday sun's heat made them take off their coats. They couldn't be over thirty miles from the Hayden's Ferry. Chet wondered about his own ranch holdings and business. His back muscles ached from sleeping on the ground and the rough mountains they'd rode over. He sure wanted to catch them, and soon.

CHAPTER 9

Passing through chaparral greasewood brush and into some open grass flats, they smelled smoke. Chet twisted in his saddle trying to see the source of the campfire. He spotted five burros standing around hipshot and he turned his horse in that direction.

"Morning." He reined up. A whiskered man held a rifle in his arms and looked skeptically at him.

"US Marshal Byrnes."

"Adolph Gunner. What do you need?" His stoic German pronunciation told Chet he wasn't looking for any company. His packsaddles lay scattered around his camp. He must ride one of the burros, too.

"Three men ride through here? One big man on a black horse?"

"Dey bought some food from me about noon. I kept my gun on dem. Didn't trust dem, but they had money and several horses."

"They shot a man up north and stole his horses."

"I didn't know dem. I was glad whey dey were gone."

"You're lucky they didn't kill you and take your things."

"Others have tried."

Chet touched his hat, reined his horse aside and rejoined his men.

"Friendly old sumbitch," Cole said, glancing back at him.

"At least now we know they aren't far ahead of us."

"Those old hermits like him hate people," Jesus added.

Cole agreed. "And maybe for good reason."

Jesus was satisfied they were following the outlaws' horses' hoofprints. They reached the edge of the irrigated land and rode on. They found a place where the horses had turned east on a farm road.

"Reckon they wanted to avoid the ferry?" Cole wondered.

"Maybe being seen. At this time of year, the river will be lower and they can ford it upstream about anywhere."

With their jackets tied behind their cantles, they passed many recently planted citrus orchards. Large herds of sheep brought back from the mountains for the winter grazed fields of green barley and alfalfa.

They crossed a shallow river, came out the other side, and rode south. By evening, they stopped at a farm that the outlaws' tracks passed. Chet wanted to buy some good hay for their horses. The farmer, Al Holmes, came out, introduced himself, and looked them over.

"You a lawman?"

"Yes. Chet Byrnes. We're trailing some outlaws that passed by here earlier."

Holmes nodded. "They had some loose horses, too."

"They stole them. We've been tracking them for two days. Our horses could use some good feed."

His wife, a short woman, joined them. "I'm Nell. Al, you can show them where to put their horses and I'll get these men something to eat."

"Thank you, ma'am. This is Jesus and Cole, and my name is Chet."

"You all are lawmen?" she asked.

"Yes, we are."

"My, my. I'd better get inside and fix you something to eat." She disappeared inside the house.

Her husband showed them a corral to use and told them to store their gear in his harness shed. The horses were forked some of his fine hay. Soon, they had their chores completed and were talking with him about Chet's operation up north.

"You're a big rancher. How can you do all this lawman work?"

"You don't understand," Cole said. "Chet's the only one ready to enforce the law up there. They made him a US Marshal because of his efforts."

"I'd heard something about him bringing in a man who held a Prescott man in Utah for ransom?"

"That's us."

"Well, I'm honored you stopped here tonight."

"What time did those men pass by here?" Chet asked.

"Oh, about three hours ago."

"Then they aren't too far away from here."

"When will you arrest them?"

"When we catch up with them. Maybe tomorrow or the next day. We're on their track now, but they don't know that and they can get lazy."

"How can you three be so calm?"

Chet shrugged. "Just another job we have to do."

Just then, the farmer's wife told them the food was ready and to come to the kitchen. She directed them to seats. "All of you sit down. This is just a quick meal I made up so you could eat. Sorry, I'd of done more, but I knew you must be hungry. It isn't much."

"Looks good to us," Cole said, "we didn't have to fix it."

"This'll be just fine," Chet added. "It looks good. We thank you for it."

After they were all settled and enjoying the food, she asked, "Marshal, do you live in Prescott?"

"I'm just Chet, ma'am. We live on a ranch east of there. It's my wife's place."

"Oh, what's her name?"

"Her name is Marge, and we've been married about a year."

"Is this your first marriage?" she asked.

"Yes, no one else would have me."

His men shook their heads and laughed.

"I'm sorry if I ask too many questions."

"No, Nell. I don't mind. I'm proud of my wife."

"Have you been in the territory long?" Al asked.

"No, I brought my entire family out here last spring."

"My, you sound like a busy man."

Cole passed the basket of her sliced sourdough bread to Chet. "Ma'am, he is busy. Try some of this, Chet. It's wonderful."

Toward the end of the meal, Nell offered them coffee, so Chet figured they must not be Mormons. Lots of Mormons lived in the Territory, and he knew they avoided the use of coffee as if it was poison.

The meal finished, they rose from the table and thanked Nell again for the good food. He told the Holmeses they'd need to get up early, but there was no need for them to get up then.

"I'll have breakfast on before sunup. You three come eat with us," Nell announced.

"We sure will, and thanks much. If you ever come to our country, you come and stay with us at my ranch."

"I don't know when or how that could happen, but I'd love to do that." The round little woman beamed.

They slept in the hay barn that night. The weather wasn't as cold as it was at home, but wrapped in his bedroll he thought of his warm wife at home and wished he was there with her.

Nell fixed them a large breakfast the next morning. Then she sent several loaves of sourdough bread with them, along with two jars of her peach jam.

They rode off laughing and teasing her that if she got tired of her husband they'd marry her.

Out of the gate, they trotted their horses south. Midmorning, they found where the outlaws had camped and slept. Chet hoped to catch sight of them by midday.

The sun warmed things up quickly, so they shed their coats. They rode around most of the irrigated land that the outlaws had probably avoided in order to not be seen.

Late afternoon, Chet and his men spotted some loose horses at a building at a well. Then they saw a big black horse hitched with others out in front. The unpainted building had a sign: GOLDBERG STORE/SALOON.

"They don't know us, so we can be some dusty cowhands needing a drink. They'll be nervous. Unless we need to shoot, hold your fire. Walk up to the bar and act like we don't know them."

"Hey, I'm going to wash a ton of this dust down my throat," Cole said.

"Me, too. Damn, this country is dry," Chet said.

"It is a *malo* country," Jesus said.

They hitched their horses outside and Chet entered the open doorway first. Out by itself, there was no need to have batwing doors on the saloon. No women passed by on the boardwalk that might not want to see the contents and activity going on inside.

"Hello, *amigos*. You ride a long ways?" the Mexican bartender asked.

"From the border," Chet replied.

He'd seen the big man at the table and the other two, but avoided looking at them as he and his men bellied up to the bar and ordered beers. In the shadowy light, he could see the three in the mirror behind the bar. The bartender brought their beers and asked if he should wake up the *putas* out back for them.

"No, we're just passing through."

The man nodded and took their thirty cents off the counter.

Chet saw that Curly was swilling down whiskey by the shot glass and looked mad about something. No telling what that was about. And no reason to stall.

He turned from his beer. "Put your hands on the table."

"Who the hell are you?" Curly asked, then swallowed at facing the three pistols pointed at them.

"Lawmen. You're under arrest for horse stealing and trying to murder a rancher. Disarm them, men."

"How in the hell did you find us?" Curly demanded.

"We followed your horse apples here."

"Those guys *banditos*?" the bartender asked, sounding upset.

"Yes, they are. You ever seen them before?"

"No, *señor*. I never seen them before today."

"Well, they'll soon be serving time in jail in Preskitt."

"Are you the sheriff?"

"No. I'm the US Marshal." He motioned to Jesus. "Get the handcuffs."

"Do something. Do something, Curly!" the kid screamed.

"What the hell you expect me to do, kid?"

"Shoot them. Shoot them, like you did that old sumbitch up there."

"Shut up," Curly said.

"Yeah, do that, kid. If he dies, you three will hang." Jesus clamped the cuffs on him. "You better listen or we'll have you gagged."

"What's your name?" Cole asked the old man when he cuffed him.

"Barnaby Stove."

Chet never heard his name before, either. No telling where they came from, but he had a good idea there was blood on that back path. He also had an idea of a simple way to get back to his wife real quick.

"Let's take them to Hayden's Ferry. I'll go with them on the stage, and you boys can take your time driving these horses home."

Cole looked at Jesus. "Can you drive them home alone? One of us better ride with the boss."

Jesus agreed. "You're right, one of us needs to go with him. I can drive them by myself."

"Take your time doing it. And take no chances," Chet said.

Late that night, they arrived at the ferry and put the three in the local jail. Chet bought five tickets for the morning stage. They left their saddles and gear to go on the stage, then put the horses up in the livery. The ticket man told them of a cantina where they could eat before the stage left. They slept a few hours before waking to get their grumpy prisoners out of jail and herding them to the café for breakfast.

The local law dropped in and handed them a wanted poster for the pair from Wells Fargo. It offered two hundred apiece on the three men for holdups they'd done in Utah.

Chet smiled over his cup of coffee. "You boys are going to do all right for sleeping on the ground while going after these three."

Cole whistled. "Me and Jesus here may go on a spree with that much money."

"Could I get married?" Jesus asked.

"Do you have a girlfriend somewhere?" Chet asked. He'd never heard his man even mention one.

"Yes. She is in Sonora. I have sent her letters and she has answered them."

"We can get you a small house up at the Preskitt place. What's her name?"

"Carmellia. I can still ride with you and Cole if I am married?"

"I don't see why not."

"Good. I will write her when I get home."

He nodded and went back to his coffee. By the next day he'd have those three in Simms's jail. Before they left, he'd send his wife a telegram they were coming home on the stage, and for her to have Roamer there to take the prisoners to jail.

When he drove them out of the livery, he gave Jesus money to eat on and for ferry charges. No telling about the quicksand in the river crossing down there, they'd better use the ferry.

The horses were used to each other and drove easy down the hard-packed main street past the mill to the ferry.

Two trips across and Jesus was on his way home. He could stop to rest at the stage stops and use their corrals for the horses. He should make it home in three or four days. In a few hours, they'd pass him in the stagecoach.

Cole rode inside the stage with their prisoners, and Chet rode on top with the driver named Lum. They crossed the river on the ferry with his big horses impatiently stomping the barge's floor as they hand-cranked them over the Salt's low winter flow.

In a cloud of dust, Lum sent them north through the desert and back toward the small town called Phoenix. There, they went through more irrigated land before heading north through the flat desert toward the Bradshaw Mountains.

At New River Station they changed to fresh horses and pushed on to Bumble Bee. They'd make Preskitt by eight o'clock that night. Jesus would be three days making the same route. He'd have to send a few men from the ranch to meet and help him.

The rocking stage climbed higher in elevation, and despite the sun Chet put on his jacket. A tall cloudbank hung up in the northwest. At Bumble Bee, deep in the canyon, it wasn't visible, but when he and Cole took the prisoners to the outhouses behind the stop it looked like snow was headed for them.

"Be our luck, huh?" Cole smiled as they waited outside the open doors of the stinking outhouse. "Maybe we can ski home."

"Maybe we'll have to."

Weary of the prisoners, Cole shook his head. "I'd shut these grumbling bastards up. They sure get tiresome to listen to, and that kid is crazy as a loon."

"Just keep thinking that they're worth over three hundred dollars to you. That's damn near a year's wages."

"I know, and I'm going to buy me a small place."

"What then?"

"I know it's crazy, but either of those girls that works at Jenn's would have me, I'm going to marry one of them."

"Bonnie and Valerie, huh?"

"Yes. I know all about their past. You think I'm crazy?"

"No, but they may not want to be housewives."

"If they turn me down, I'll still have me a place."

"Personally, I like both of them. They're attractive and they've been abused. I can only wish you good luck."

"Thanks. Ah, hell, we'll see, huh?"

"Right. We better load up. Lum will be ready to leave."

He'd never considered either of the young women as a possible wife for anyone. But they had every right to be. While searching for Jenn's daughter

Bonnie, he'd found both her and Valerie and brought them back to find themselves a place in this world. He hoped Cole could make a good marriage with one of them. JD's efforts with Kay had left him a sour apple, and he'd probably never change.

Valerie might be the best choice. She gave it up long before Bonnie. But it wasn't his problem. He simply wanted the best for a man he considered as almost his son.

They arrived home in the dark. Roamer had a buckboard waiting to haul the prisoners on to jail. He also had another deputy with him cradling a shotgun. And when Marge ran over to hug him, it began to snow like their reunion had caused it.

Chet gave Roamer the wanted poster on the three and said, "The reward money goes to Jesus and Cole."

"They must be happy to know that."

"Hey, they slept on the ground long enough to earn it."

Roamer shook his head. "You three are relentless."

"How is Henry?"

"He's doing fine. Said you were a doctor, too." Roamer laughed, holding his hands out to ward Chet away. "I ain't sick, Doctor. We better get them locked up. We can talk tomorrow or the next day. Good to see you, Marge." He tipped his hat and drove off in the buckboard for the jail.

"What's this doctor business?"

"Oh, Henry was bleeding bad and I poured black

powder in his wound and ignited it. That stopped his bleeding."

She made a face at him. "My, that was severe."

"It worked and he's alive. Jesus is bringing the horses back. I'll send him two of Raphael's men to help him."

"Good. I'm always so glad to have you back."

"Me, too. Let's go home. Who drove you here?" Chet looked around for her driver.

"I drove myself here before dark. I'm not a cripple."

"Don't tell me I have to have those two galoots with me and then you drive to town all alone."

He motioned to Cole. "Get in back. We have no horses to ride."

"This is fine. Good to see you, Marge."

"Thanks for bringing him home," she said.

"You're welcome. I'm so glad they have to listen to that crazy kid I've heard for the last ten hours. Bad situation."

"Why was that?" Marge asked Chet.

"Too long to tell. Raft Boone said the kid was crazy. Before long, we decided he knew him well." Chet laughed.

They rode easy through the snow. In the darkness, the flakes obscured his vision of the road, but he trusted the horses to find their way back to the ranch. At last, the house lights, filtered through big snowflakes, welcomed them.

Marge offered to feed Cole, but he went to the bunkhouse. He told them he'd drive in for their saddles and gear the next day. Chet figured that would give him the chance to speak to Bonnie and Valerie. He was happy he had Marge and they were going to bed where he belonged.

In the morning, he had Raphael send two men south to meet Jesus and help him distribute the horses where they belonged. The Boones could have the extra ones. Jesus knew their horses, and he'd bring them home in the four inches of snow on the ground.

Monica fixed them breakfast and she sounded happy. "So you rounded up more bad guys, huh?"

"Three of them. They were wanted in Utah, too. Cole and Jesus will get a big reward. Jesus wants to bring a young lady up here and marry her."

"Oh, yes, he has one in Mexico. She writes him letters, or has someone write them for her."

"Carmellia is her name."

"Robles is her last name. Marge and I have seen his letters."

"I told him we'd build a small house for them."

Marge agreed. "Sure. He's a big part of our lives."

"Is Cole going to marry someone, too?" Monica asked.

"He says he wants either of Jenn's daughters, Bonnie or Valerie."

"Really? They are pretty women—" Marge stopped and frowned.

"I thought the same thing. But I'd give either one a chance at having a real life."

"We need to find him a big farm girl," Marge said. "Like Robert from the mill is going to marry soon."

They laughed.

He shook his head at his wife's solution. "She is pretty and she does look more like what Susie thought my wife should be."

He spent the day reading the newspapers. A story about the Boone shooting incident never mentioned his involvement, but said the sheriff was looking for leads to the shooter and the party that stole the horses.

He went on to read about the mining activity at Horse Thief Basin. A new mine opened down there and claimed its gold and silver excavations were producing ore worth over three hundred dollars a ton. Their stock on the Denver Exchange was selling for eighty bucks a share. Mining was not his game. There were some fast and furious deals made in that business, but he wanted no part of it.

David Ellis had listed his EKO ranch west of Preskitt for sale. He had three sections of deeded land and ran two hundred mother cows. Price negotiable.

Maybe JD would want that place. He'd send word to Bo to look it over. Money wasn't floating around and it might be what JD needed for a place of his own. No telling. They may want way too much for it. Plus, he didn't know the situation or the range conditions, either. Oh, well, he'd let Bo look into it.

"Did Roamer say anything about his job last night?" Marge asked, standing in the doorway drying a plate.

"I guess he still has one. Have you ever been to Dave Ellis's ranch?"

"No, why?"

"It's for sale."

"Just what you need. Another ranch to worry about."

"Hey, I thought it might work for JD."

"As sugar-footed as he is, in six weeks you'd have to run it."

"I'd like to give him a chance to do something he likes."

"I know, but he's not dependable enough today to turn over a ranch to him."

"We'll see how things go. They may only want to see what people will offer and have no plans to sell. People do that all the time to find out their ranch's worth."

"What would you sell this kingdom for?"

"Hell, I don't want to sell. I love all this country we own."

"No, give me a price."

"A million dollars."

She shook her head. "No one will pay you that for it, which is good. I won't have to pack and move."

"Me, either. I'm still not over the tough time we had coming here from Texas."

"No, really. Where else would you even consider going?"

"Eastern Kansas, where the bluestem grows six feet tall and cattle get fatter on it than eating corn."

"You never looked up there for a place?"

"No, there's too much resistance up there to southern drawling folks—left over from the Civil War. There's folks up there still fighting that battle. I saw and heard lots of their hatred when I took the first family herd to Abilene five years ago. They aren't through fighting it, either. But it's a swell country for cattlemen, best grassland I ever saw."

"I understand. No need to leave one fight for another."

"That's why I came west."

"You ever consider California?"

"I'm far enough from Texas here."

She laughed. "I can see I'm not budging you one inch."

"No, that baby of ours will be a native of this place. I hope our children will take care of all these places we're fixing and see this territory become a state."

"What do you plan to do next?"

"Sit around here and enjoy my married life."

"That sounds good. Then, tomorrow, what?"

"Aw, you beat all. I don't know if the snow is melting yet. I may get ready to check on things around the circuit."

"One day is enough to sit around the house, isn't it?"

"I've got some sharp men looking after our interests, but we can always do better."

"Hay operation shaping up?" She took a seat on the end of the long couch.

"I still need some stout horses for that job. Rose is bringing some from California and he seems like the best source to supply them. All these folks around here have to sell are bangtail mustangs."

"I know. But you'll have them ready to mow next spring. Is Hampt going to grow more?"

"I think him and Tom both have plans to plant more acreage."

"Who will run the new place with the orchards?"

"Leroy Sipes, I think would be a good man. They can barely eke out a living at their small place. Maybe he and Betty Lou would take it over. She could oversee the cabins and he could help harvest the orchards and berries and plant the food crops. There's plenty of water up there. We could grow a lot of food up there and can it to feed the ranches next winter."

"When are you going to talk to them about it?"

"Tomorrow. Cole will be back and we can ride up there and see them."

"Where did you learn so much about people and what they're good at?" Marge asked.

"I guess dealing with them. Leroy drove that big shire team down here, no trouble. He never complained one minute and helped my men at every stop. I watched him and he's good. I had no place for him then, but I will in a few weeks."

"Who will build the cabins you're planning?"

"The crews at Windmill won't be done in time. I want the cabins finished so we can stay in them next summer. Leroy may have ideas on that. You do a drawing of a floor plan for a cabin that each of our families could camp in."

"How many will we need?"

"Say, three, and a bunkhouse for help and single men to stay in. I may have to expand the main cabin. They have kids."

Marge looked up at the copper ceiling tiles for help, shaking her head. "Do these ideas swirl around in your head like millers at a light?"

"I guess so. We can spend more time on things like that as these ranches settle into operating."

"You going to learn to fish?" she asked.

"I may do that, too. Do you think Ray and Ty should go to college back east some day?"

"No, not really."

"I disagree. I think May could teach them, in addition to their regular schooling, and get them smart enough to do that."

Marge nodded her head. "You're right. I bet she has enough education to do it too. Wouldn't that be something, to have a Byrnes really educated?"

"There's time enough left in my lifetime to see it, too."

"Chet Byrnes, you can imagine and make up some of the wildest schemes and make them come true.

I never thought you'd do any good at selling the Navajo agencies your cattle. But you did."

He scooped her up in his arms. "Monica has things to do. Let's sneak off upstairs and have our own private talk."

She shook her hair back and smiled. "I thought you'd never ask."

CHAPTER 10

Jesus wasn't back yet, so Chet and Cole went to town. Bo was hunched over his desk in the land office, working on some land transaction, but looked up at the two men. "The Arizona Rangers are here," Bo said to his helper.

"Where's the other one?" the young man asked.

"Bringing our horses home and the ones the outlaws stole."

"I guess Simms knew you were after them. He said he was looking around for them. Maybe in the garbage cans behind the Palace. What can I do for you?"

"The Dave Ellis ranch was for sale in the *Miner*."

"Way overpriced," Bo said. "Two hundred thousand. What would you pay?"

"I'd have to look. Thirty to forty thousand, if it's real."

"I say thirty."

"Good. Look at it for that. If he really wants to

sell, we might buy a ranch. Oak Creek going through all right?"

"You bet. His heirs back east accepted the eight thousand I offered."

"I'll try to hire a man today to run it."

"So soon?"

"He may turn me down, but I'm going to ask him."

"I'll look at that ranch you mentioned and get you more details."

"That'll be fine. Good to see you two," Chet said.

When they left the land office, they rode out to see Leroy and his wife. He was busy busting firewood with an axe, and the yard was littered in split wood. He looked relieved to see them.

Betty Lou came to the door. "How nice to see you two. Come in. I heard you three got the outlaws that shot Henry Boone. You're life savers. Where's Jesus?"

"He's bringing all the horses back. We brought the outlaws back by stagecoach to get rid of them."

"When will folks stand up and elect you sheriff?"

"Not my job. I'm here to talk to you two about moving up to Oak Creek. I bought Mr. Kemp's place. I haven't been there yet, but they say it has lots of fruit trees and berries. Plus water to grow vegetables."

She nodded. "I know the place. We were up there a few years ago and bought apples from him to resell."

"Would you think about moving up there and running things?"

Leroy looked at his wife. "Well, Betty Lou, say something."

"That time we were up there, you said you'd love to have it."

"I did sure enough. We work hard, but this place of ours doesn't yield much."

Chet decided to throw in an incentive. "I would pay you so much a month and a percentage of the profit on the rest. We're going to build some cabins up there for my families to camp in. I'll hire a crew and want them done by summertime. You could move in anytime you want. Take your cow and chickens. Act like it's yours."

"We finish our term of school the first of February and we can go anytime after that," Betty Lou said.

"We can move you. We have farm wagons to do that."

"That's a relief."

"I'm going to start you at forty bucks a month."

"That's sure acceptable," Leroy said.

"I'm looking forward to you two working with me." Chet shook his hand and hugged Betty Lou. "Don't be worried. It will all work out. Would a twenty-dollar advance help you two out?"

She looked at Leroy for his answer, and he nodded. She said, "That would be wonderful."

After Chet gave him the advance, they rode back and had lunch at Jenn's where Valerie waited on them.

"You have a job here in Preskitt," she teased.

"No, but I'm thinking about getting one."

"You two want the meat loaf special today?" she asked, amused by his answer.

"Sure," they agreed.

She rushed off to fill their order.

After she left, Cole said, "I came by yesterday and talked to her for a long time after she got off work. She told me Bonnie has her cap set for JD. I can believe that. Can you?"

"I don't doubt it."

"Well, Valerie agreed to go out with me. We'll get to know each other, maybe go to a dance. She's a pretty stable person and not in any rush to get married, which I'm glad of. Could she come out to the ranch and go to the schoolhouse dance sometime?"

"I think we can arrange that anytime she wants to come."

"Thanks, Chet."

That evening, Jesus made it home. Monica baked him a cake and they had a small party for him at the bunkhouse.

He entertained them with stories of their adventure. "I headed back as fast as I could, and then it snowed. Manuel and Rudy found me and helped take those horses to Boone's. They made us stay there until most of the snow melted. They sure did appreciate getting them back, and his wound is healing."

"Doctor Byrnes," Marge said with both her hands clasped on top of his shoulders.

"Don't get sick," he warned her.

"If I did, you'd figure something out." She tossed her hair back.

It was time to leave the bunkhouse party. He wanted some private time with his wife. Monica accompanied them across the frozen yard under the starry sky to the big house.

"Thanks, Monica. You think of everything. I know Jesus appreciated that cake."

"Oh, sometimes, I do."

After saying good night to Monica, Chet threw more wood in the open fireplace, then hurried upstairs to their bedroom and his waiting wife. He savored his life and his wife. Arizona had been good to them.

If JD found a place in life, he'd feel lots better. No telling. When he slipped under the covers with his wife, he said, "I sure do love you."

CHAPTER 11

All bundled up, Hampt, May, her toddler daughter Donna, and both stepsons came by in the buckboard. Hampt carried the three-year-old girl and May came smiling and joking with her stepsons. Chet couldn't miss seeing the close relationship the five had gotten into since the marriage. Ray and Ty used to tell him they were sorry when they made her cry, but she was so hard to please. That phase had passed and they even helped her play piano. What a change in a woman and her life.

"Come in. What are you doing out in this cold? Frost bite," said Chet.

"No, we were caught up on our work and May wanted to see Marge," Hampt said. He set Donna on her feet inside the kitchen and she walked away after the boys, while May whisked past headed for the living room. "A woman gets to wanting to see company after so much time being a lone housewife."

"And how are you doing?"

"Hell, you know me. I've never been happier in

my life. Those three kids are great and we'll have one of our own come spring. Three years ago I was struggling along and you found me. I had no idea I'd ever be this lucky."

"Hey, you've earned it. What did you do to open May up?"

"Lands, I don't know. She told me one night, sitting on my lap, that she used to sing, and I said, 'Well, sing for me.'"

"That was it?"

"Yes. And after she sang for me, I told her not to hide that anymore, to sing out louder. And she did. The boys heard her and told her to sing, too. Pleased us all."

Piano music came from the other room. Then they were all singing a trail song, "Oh, Suzanna, don't you cry for me . . ."

"We all have to hand it to you. You really brought her out of a shell and we're proud about it."

"The two boys are, too. They told me, 'Hampt she never used to be any fun.'"

"By the way, how are the breeds doing?"

"We've got them meat, beans, and corn meal. Had to show them how to open a can of milk. But they're grateful. Two of their bigger boys are learning how to build fence. The crew is showing them how. I pay them a little."

"Turn the cost in. We can afford it."

The visit went fast, and in the late afternoon their company headed home. After they left, Marge was telling Chet what a great day she'd had and about how Ray played a song all by himself on the piano. Then someone knocked at the back door.

Chet went to answer it, and it was a young man who handed him a telegram.

"Come inside. You look cold."

"I'm fine, sir. The key operator said for me to wait for your reply."

"Get in here. Marge, make this boy a cup of hot chocolate. He's brought me a telegram from Chief Marshal Bailey in Tucson."

"What's your name, young man?" asked Marge.

"Toby Parsons."

"I'll get some milk and make a big cup. Take your coat off. He'll read the telegram and want to answer it, I'm certain."

Chet unfolded the yellow paper and read it.

DEPUTY MARSHAL CHET BYRNES

THE ARIZONA GRAND BANK WAS ROBBED

TODAY BY FOUR OR FIVE MEN STOP THEY ARE

HEADED NORTH STOP COULD YOU MEET ME

AT HAYDEN'S FERRY? IF THEY GO A DIFFERENT

WAY I WILL TELEGRAM THE TOWN MARSHAL

THE INFORMATION TO GIVE YOU STOP TWO

OF THEM ARE RIDING WHITE HORSES THAT

IS ALL I HAVE RIGHT NOW STOP I CONSIDER

THEM ARMED AND DANGEROUS STOP DO NOT

TRY TO APPREHEND THEM BY YOURSELF STOP

CHIEF MARSHAL DON BAILEY

"What is it about?" Marge asked.

"Five men robbed a bank in Tucson and are headed north. He wants me to meet him at Hayden's Ferry."

"Does he say what they look like?"

"I'm writing a telegram and sending it to Tucson, Casa Grande, and Hayden's Ferry that we're coming. It'll take us two days to get down there. But if we have a chase, we'll need a couple of packhorses to follow them."

"I guess you'll go talk to your men."

"Yes. After we get this boy warmed up and on his way."

He found a pencil and wrote out the telegrams with the three addresses so they would catch the marshal on the move. He gave the boy money to send them and a silver dollar for his services.

That impressed the youth and he thanked him. Then he started on his mug of hot chocolate. "Ma'am, this is sure wonderful. I'll head right back and get these sent for you."

"Don't hurry," said Chet. "You did me a big service. Take your time on that chocolate."

"I need to talk to you," Marge said.

In the living room, she whispered, "You think he's a Mormon?"

"I'm not sure, but he's sure enjoying the hell out of your cocoa." They both laughed.

When the boy finished his chocolate, Chet walked to his horse with him and saw him off. Then he went to the bunkhouse to find Cole and Jesus. They talked in low voices by the door.

"Tucson bank robbers are headed north. We're to meet Marshal Don Bailey at Hayden's Ferry in two days. Packhorses, and we leave at dawn."

"Who are they?" Cole asked.

"Two of them ride white horses is all he knew at the time he telegraphed me. They must be a tough gang to rob a bank in a town like Tucson. If they turn another direction, he'll telegraph the Hayden's Ferry town marshal with word for us where they've headed next."

"You reckon he knew Simms wouldn't do anything to help him?"

"Oh, if those robbers rode up Whiskey Row, he might see them," Chet said.

"Did he ever send you a thank-you for getting them three?"

"No."

"Well, he's as sorry an excuse for a law as there is in the territory." Cole spit out the door.

"We better get some sleep. You already refilled the panniers?" Chet asked Jesus.

"Oh, yes. When we got back. We have food and everything ready to go."

"Let's lighten the load on that one and use another horse for our bedrolls and tent."

"Good idea, if we have to move fast," Cole agreed.

"Monica will have breakfast ready early."

"She does a helluva job. Jesus and I will re-check the packs, too."

He thanked them and went back to the house. It was suppertime, and Monica and Marge were setting the table.

"All set?"

"I sure am. By the way, I volunteered Monica to make breakfast in the morning before dawn."

"No problem. I think they should make you three Rangers."

"We'll be fine as Deputy US Marshals."

"I guess there must be no one else who wants to take on the lawbreakers."

Chet nodded. "I guess that's how it works."

"You simply be careful," Marge told him. "Monica and I will wait for you. I thought if it thaws enough we could go to the dance down at the Verde."

"I sure want to go, too."

"Great day yesterday with May and Hampt, wasn't it?"

"Yes, it was. Those boys told Hampt that she never was any fun until she married him."

"Those boys are getting so big. Did you hear Ray playing the piano? He's good."

"I sure did. I thought for a long time Susie might take them boys to raise herself. But she has her own life now, and besides, May wouldn't give them up."

"It's working great with both families."

Chet paid a lot of attention to his wife that evening. She'd be upset at him leaving again so soon. Being pregnant made her jumpier, but with two husbands killed, she had a right to be upset. He wanted her to feel good when he rode out—for he'd sure rather share their bed than sleep on the cold ground.

Before the sun rose, he and his men headed south under the stars. A light frost covered the ground, but the day promised to warm up fast. Most of the snow had melted except in the shade. The horses danced some, so they let them lope. They dropped elevation by midday down into the saguaro country and shed their coats. Galloping the good horse they'd chosen for him, he knew it would be a two-day hard ride to the ferry.

If the bank robbery gang headed north, they might meet them at the Salt River. All he had to watch for were two white horses. Most experienced outlaws rode nondescript mounts without brands and dressed plain to match the rest of society. But these five held up a bank in a crowded narrow street town and rode off on two white horses, with telegraphs clacking in every direction.

The day warmed as he'd expected. They made it to Hassayampa City and stabled the horses, had them grained, and went to eat at the café.

The young waitress looked up and said, "Oh, oh. Trouble must be brewing around here. That's usually what it means when that man and his sidekicks come to town. Who are you after this time?"

"Bank robbers."

Her eyes opened wide. "Where?"

"Tucson."

She drew back as if shocked. "Oh, that's miles away."

"They may be heading up here."

"I'm not afraid. You guys will stop them." As if that was settled, she went back to business. "You want lunch? We have roast beef, mashed potatoes, and sourdough rolls."

"That, and coffee for the three of us," Chet said.

"We'll have to move tomorrow to reach the ferry, won't we?" Cole asked, glancing around at the other customers.

"Yes, and it's a long ride yet to get there," Jesus said. "And even longer driving horses. I thought I'd never get home with them."

"You made good time, even with the snow and all." Chet moved his arm to let the harried waitress set their coffees down.

Cole spoke up. "Did Simms ever thank you for us doing that?"

"Of course not."

"That sorry sumbitch."

"But he hasn't fired Roamer yet."

"You know, boss, we still have lots we don't know about these outlaws we're after."

"I know, but maybe when Bailey arrives at the ferry we'll know more, unless we meet them on the road."

"Someone has to know more than we do."

Chet agreed, but he looked for a telegram, or else Marshal Bailey, to be there when they arrived.

Before they left, the lady cook wearing a clean

apron promised she'd have their breakfast waiting at five a.m., which Chet thanked her for.

Sarge was probably headed back to New Mexico with cattle, in case a storm delayed them. His pregnant sister, Susie, was no doubt walking the floors. He hoped JD was helping Reg and Lucie. Most in his thoughts, though, was how much he missed Marge.

They slept in the hay at the stables. When they got up it was still dark, so they saddled up by a candle lamp. Both packhorses loaded, they walked in the chilly air down to the café where a light glowed inside. At least they'd have a hot breakfast.

They rode through the chaparral country that spread out along the stage road, but soon reached the flatter desert land and galloped several miles with their coats tied on behind their cantles. The sun bore down as they rode into it and temperatures rose. His front cooked, though his wool vest felt good on his back on the shady side.

It was near nine in the morning when they crossed the Salt on the ferry. He asked the operator if any men with white horses had crossed that day.

The man spat overboard, continuing to crank on the winch that drew them across. "Naw, they ain't been no one here like that."

"Thanks."

His next stop was the telegraph office where the key operator handed him two cables. Eager for information, he read them right there.

WE ARE ON OUR WAY NORTH STOP THEY SAY THEY
ARE THE GRISHAM GANG STOP WANTED IN NEW
MEXICO FOR TWO OTHER BANK HOLDUPS STOP
DEVIN GRISHAM IS FORTY, SIX FEET TALL, WEIGHS
TWO HUNDRED POUNDS STOP JESSIE COMBS AGE
ABOUT THIRTY LOST HIS RIGHT EYE FIVE EIGHT AND
ONE HUNDRED FORTY POUNDS GRAY HAIR AT
TEMPLES STOP SHOT ARKANSAS SHERIFF AND TWO
DEPUTIES IN ESCAPE WHILE AWAITING TRIAL FOR
THREE MURDERS STOP OTHERS ARE ESCABAR
HOLDRIDGE A MEXICAN, JOJO MARONEY SMALL TIME
CROOK, ELROY DUNBAR WHO'S WANTED IN TEXAS
FOR ARMED ROBBERIES AND KILLINGS, ALL ARMED
AND DANGEROUS STOP I WILL BE A DAY LATE
MEETING YOU STOP HOPE YOU AND YOUR POSSE
CAN CUT THEM OFF THERE STOP
MARSHAL BAILEY

He handed the telegram to Cole. "We have their
names and more descriptions now."

"That'll help."

"Yes, so now all we have to do is find them."

The second one he read aloud to his two men.
"Chet, I have good word they passed through Papago
Wells headed north. So far as I know, they are still
going toward you. Use caution, they are very dangerous. They shot four innocent people that got in their
way in Tucson. Marshal Bailey."

"What should we do?" Jesus asked.

"Take turns watching the ferry today and tonight.

If they try to cross on it, they'll try for it in the dark."

"We're going to sleep at the stables?" Cole asked.

"What we can. It's on the main street and they have to ride down the main street to get there, because of the small butte on the right. Town's dark enough at night, who'd worry about some riders going through, but us? They aren't here by dawn, I say we go east and see our friend Al Holmes to see if they passed that way."

"You think they may have gone by the Fort McDowell way?"

"I don't know. This gang obviously robbed some banks in New Mexico and eluded the law. They aren't dumb as ducks. They may have someone among the gang who knows the way. The law don't do much up there, we know that. Roamer rode a good horse half to death trying to get assistance from the Globe sheriff. There's lots of small ranchers in that country who might even hide them for the money."

"Let's eat," Cole said.

"Lead the way." Chet didn't blame him. It had been a long time since breakfast.

After they ate, they grained their horses, watered them, and stabled them. With no sign of the outlaws by time to turn in, Jesus took the first watch, with Cole up for the second, and Chet the last.

Before sleep caught up with him, he couldn't help

wondering what the morning would bring. Daylight, they could head east and see what they found over there. By that time, Bailey would be there. One sure thing, after a day in the saddle, no one had to rock him to sleep.

CHAPTER 12

When dawn broke, no one had shown up. The town night watchman came by several times during the night to check with them, and at daylight made his last appearance.

"Well, Marshal Byrnes, they never made it, did they?"

"No, but that doesn't mean they aren't coming. They may have cut east. I'll leave Marshal Bailey a note where we went."

"The police here will watch for them, too."

"Good, but remember those men are cold-blooded killers."

"I'll tell them."

By then, they had their outfit saddled and packed. They went to eat in the main street café, keeping alert the entire time, but no sign of the gang.

"You believing they went east?" Cole asked, sopping up gravy on his half biscuit.

"My guess."

"Jesus and I are ready to ride, anytime you are."

"We may see a lot more miles before this is over. I'll leave Bailey a note at the telegraph office as well."

By midmorning they were at the Holmes farm. Al Holmes had seen three men go by, then two more an hour or so later, all headed for the Salt River crossing.

"Yesterday, when I finished mowing some barley for hay, I saw them headed north in a hard trot," he said. "There were two white horses in that group. One was in the front three, and one in the back pair. That's what caught my eye."

"Is there a neighbor boy can take a message to the telegraph office for me?"

"I can get one to do that. Write it out." He turned to his wife Nell.

"Honey, get him some paper and a pencil."

When she brought a stub of a pencil and a half sheet of penciled tablet paper, he wrote:

Bailey.
  They went east. I imagine to Fort McDowell or places north. I will leave word at the Fort where we went.

  Marshal Byrnes

"Don't fret. I'll get this there in no time."

"I know you will." Chet shook his hand and patted Nell on the arm. "Thanks. We're off again."

They forded the shallow Salt River, only knee deep on their horses, and went up the steep bank on the other side headed for the road and Red Rock

Mountain. The sighting of the gang by Holmes was all they needed. Jesus knew their tracks well by this time and easily found the direction they took from there.

Looking at the far off Four Peak Mountain, towering to the east, Chet felt pleased. They trotted toward it on dusty wagon tracks. If nothing happened, they might catch up with the outlaws before they reached the Mogollon Rim in the north. He hoped so anyway.

Past noon, they sidetracked to the Fort McDowell reservation. Chet spoke to the lieutenant in charge. The five men hadn't stopped there, nor had anyone seen them on the road that lay over a mile south of the camp and agency.

From there, they went on to cross the Verde and ride north toward the mountains. This was the road to Rye from Hayden's Ferry and they were soon in the desert-mountains, winding their way on a narrow road over some steep climbs and descents. They watered their tired horses in a few trickles and potholes they found in some of the nearby dry creeks that bisected the road.

A man driving a pair of mules pulling a wagon headed south reined up for them, and Chet rode in close.

"Afternoon. You pass five men on horseback back there coming down today?"

"I know you. You're the law from Preskitt, ain't you?"

"That's me. US Marshal Chet Byrnes. Did you see them?"

"Yeah, I seed 'em. They was five."

"How far back?"

"Above the cutoff goes to Globe. They got a fair start on you. What did they do?"

"Robbed a bank in Tucson. Shot some people."

The man nodded his head. "Yep, they looked tough."

"Two had white horses?"

"Sure in the world they did. Two white ones. They just rode past me and I wasn't displeased one little bit. You tie into them, you'll have your hands full."

"There's a posse coming behind us with Marshal Bailey. Tell them we talked to you and you saw the bank robbers and us on their trail."

"Be proud to do that. I hope you get them scallywags. I recall you did good on them damn pig farmers before. Keep your head down."

"We will. Thanks."

"No problem, boys. Hee yah, mules." With a flip of his reins, the mules moved off.

Jesus halted them a few miles north of the Globe cutoff. The sun was getting low in the far west. "They turned off here."

"I wonder why, unless they aimed to find a ranch for food and to rest their horses. Let's ride on up north. These horses need a drink and we need to make camp. I saw a sign said Sunflower two miles. So we should be close to it and can take up the chase in the morning."

The Sunflower Store and Bar wasn't much. A mustached man in an apron came out of the store and showed them a corral for their horses with hay and water. He charged them twenty-five cents a head. His wife would cook them supper for the same price and Chet paid him for that, too.

The owner, Willie Jackson, was all business. His price for most anything was two bits. He was six feet tall and had coal-black hair that kept falling down in his face, which he'd push back. From his drawl, he was a Texan.

"She'll have your vittles ready when you get unloaded, boys. Nice to meet y'all."

The winter sun was about to vanish. Concerned about the bandits' plans, Chet knew they couldn't do anything in the dark. There were candle lamps burning in the store where its interior smelled of dry goods, leather, and beer.

The storekeeper's wife was a tall lean woman with her light hair braided and piled on her head. The dress she wore would have fit her and someone else.

In the midst of it all, she set a table and brought them a kettle of stew. She filled their bowls with a cup and told them if they needed more to holler. By Chet's standards, her coffee was weak and the cornbread cold. But they ate good and thanked her.

"Why you boys up here?" she finally asked.

"Looking for some bank robbers."

"Oh, I hope they don't stop here."

"Probably nothing to worry about, ma'am. Do you serve breakfast, too?" Chet asked.

"Why, sure. When will you be up?"

"Crack of dawn."

She made a firm face. "It'll be here on the table."

After thanking her, they retired to their bedrolls.

"We're close to them," Cole said. "Maybe we can run them down tomorrow."

"Sounds too easy, but we are close." Chet rolled over and went to sleep.

In the cool starlight of early morning, they scrambled around to saddle and load their horses. A light was on in the store, and Chet could smell smoke from the cookstove. Their hostess was no doubt up cooking.

Breakfast was oatmeal with bugs (raisins) plus fresh biscuits and prickly pear jelly. Her coffee was stronger and Chet wondered if she might be a Mormon and didn't drink it. The jelly had its own flavor, but everyone complimented her cooking.

"You simply peel the ripe prickly pears, mash them, then stir in some jell and sugar?" Chet asked.

"That's about my only fruit on this place." She laughed, and they did, too. He'd have to tell Marge about it. When they ripened in the fall, the ranch hands could pick them for her and Monica.

They headed back south and took the side road where they'd seen the tracks turn the night before. Jackson told them the KT ranch was up that way. The owner, Art Kelly, had a wife and two kids. When they rode up the wagon track road, they soon saw the squaw shade and corrals.

A woman with a rifle came out and challenged them. She looked distraught.

"Ma'am. I'm a federal marshal. Is your husband here?"

"No. They took him."

He rode in closer. "Took him? What do you mean?" He dismounted, feeling satisfied she was too upset to shoot him. "Could you explain?"

"They took him hostage to make him show them how to get over Four Peaks last night." A sob caught in her throat and her voice rose. "I fear for his safety."

He moved in and took her rifle. "Is there a trail over those peaks?"

Through her tears, she nodded. "Oh, he will try to kill them, I know, for what they did to me. I know he will try."

"They assaulted you?" He put out a comforting arm, but she drew back.

"Yes, I fought them, but it did no good."

"Don't worry. No one will blame you. Those men are animals. We want to catch them before they hurt anyone else. How tough is that trail?"

"Very steep and dangerous, but Art has used it a time or two. It goes over on to Tonto Creek."

"I see. And where would they go from there?" Chet asked.

"To Young, and over the Rim, I guess."

"How will they go?"

"Oh, take the ferry across the Salt, then go east and cross the Salt again, and there's a road goes north to Young."

"Why did they take him?"

"To guide them. They said if I told the law where they went they'd kill him." She wrung her hands. "Oh, I'm sure they've killed him already. I have two small children, what will I do?"

"Ma'am," he spoke in a low soothing tone. "My name is Chet Byrnes. This is my man, Cole. My other man, Jesus, is already scouting their trail. If we catch them, we'll try to save your husband. Did they say they were being chased?"

"No, but the leader said they needed a twist on their way out of this damn place."

"They never mentioned anyone being after them?"

"No, but I think he was scared there was, and he cussed this spiny land. He must have got into some jumping cactus. His gun hand was bandaged."

"They left when?"

"Before sundown."

He knew Jesus had probably already found their trail. "Ma'am, there'll be others coming after us. Will you tell them we went on and they might better go around?"

She said she would. "And if you can save my man—oh, dear God, I hope you can."

"We'll do all we can. You take care of yourself and your children."

Damn, her husband's situation got to him. He thought back to when those men took his nephew, Heck, after robbing the stage they were traveling back to Texas on. And how he found Heck's body discarded with his throat sliced open. Silently, he prayed for her man.

"Ma'am, we must be on our way. I'll check with you later. I wish I could do more."

"I thank you for trying to find him. God, I hope he's alive."

"Yes, ma'am. Me, too." He remounted and nodded to Cole.

"She's going to be all right?"

"Yes. In time. I bet Jesus has their trail." Cole gave him Jesus's reins and he led the two packhorses.

"Trail look tough?" he asked Jesus when they joined him.

He took his horse reins and mounted. "Not to a billy goat."

Chet laughed, but it wasn't funny when they started up the steep narrow path. In places their horses' hooves sunk into the crushed gravel. Other sections were exposed slick rocks. They wound up the face of the mountain on an angle. After a while, the climbing narrow trail looked hundreds of feet from the bottom below.

"They came over this last night?" Jesus asked. "That was a helluva trip. If there was a place to get off my horse, I'd lead him."

"I agree. These horses are surefooted, but one misstep and we won't have to worry about anything ever again," Chet said, and booted his horse skyward.

When they got to the top, there was no place to dismount, either. The trail plunged down the face as steep as the one they'd just come up. Their horses were forced to almost crouch on the turn-backs. Tonto Creek down below looked like a thin silver thread.

No sign of anyone. One of their packhorses lost his footing, went to his knees. There was nothing Chet could do except watch his own mount's heading.

"He's all right," Cole called at last from behind.

Chet nodded. *Thank you, Lord.* They continued on until they reached a flat where everyone could dismount and let their anxiety calm down. His legs about didn't support him, so he grasped the saddle horn.

"Watch your sea legs," he said over his shoulder.

"What legs?" Cole asked.

Jesus laughed. "I am so nervous, my hands are shaking. I thought I'd been over some rough country. That ride over Four Peaks, or at least around them, is damn sure gut-wrenching."

"That was a bad way all right. I hope Bailey goes around." In the thin air, his heart throbbed so hard it gave him a headache.

"I say this, they're damn tough to have gotten over that at night," Cole exclaimed, and they mounted back up.

Past noontime, from the base of the peaks, they struck out for the ferry. A man waited there with a wagon.

At their inquiring looks, he said, "There won't be any ferry. A little while ago they yelled over to me that someone cut the ferry loose and it went down the Salt River into a narrow canyon and was smashed. So there'll be no ferry service until they can get another."

"The gang did that?" Cole asked. "This damn sure cuts us off from crossing. Mister, can we go upstream? Tonto Creek isn't that big. Could we get across the stream and then go around to the Young road?"

"I don't see why not. With my wagon, I've got to go clear back up the road fork and then to Hayden's Ferry, then around to Globe."

"You have a fur way to go," Chet said. "A long way."

"Why're you men going to Young?"

"Bank robbers went that way."

"I hope you catch them."

"We do, too."

"I wonder what happened to that lady's man?" Cole asked.

"I was thinking the same thing. No sign of him so far."

Two hours later, they'd crossed Tonto Creek and circled around on the north bank to reach the Young road. There set the grounded ferry, and a man on foot was sitting on it.

"Are you Art?" Chet asked.

"I am. How did you know?"

"Your wife told us you were kidnapped and is worried that they killed you."

"Them sons a bitches might have, but when I told them I couldn't swim they laughed and cut the ferry ropes so I'd be stranded over here."

"We crossed Tonto Creek and rode around here. That isn't too far across there to swim. We can take our lariats and swim over there and get it hooked up."

"I can do it," Cole said, and began undressing.

Jesus rounded up their ropes.

"Let me tell them over there what we're going to do." Chet stood in the stirrups and called loudly, "We're tying on the rope and my man is coming across with it."

"Yeah!" went up a cheer from the opposite bank.

"How deep was your crossing on Tonto Creek?" Art asked.

"Not much over our horses' knees." Chet stepped off his mount and hung his gun belt on the saddle horn.

"You get in trouble, I'm coming after you," he said to Cole who was down to his long handles, standing in water up to his knees. "I can swim good enough for both of us."

Boots off, his shirt shed, Chet dropped his pants and watched Cole swim for the far shore. The current took him a ways downstream, but not bad. Jesus threaded out the tied together lariats. The current was pulling on them, too.

The four men on the far side waded out to meet Cole. They took the rope and tied it on a heavier one. Then they hauled it back and tied it so they could hook it up to the winch on board the ferry.

"Launch it," they shouted.

The barge was well up on the shore and they had all they could do to inch it through the mud and, at last, in the water. Then they climbed aboard and winched it across.

Chet redressed, and Jesus took a blanket and Cole's clothes to him. He told Chet that Cole looked frozen over there standing huddled by the fire on the south bank.

"You men are life savers." The older man shook their hands. "None of us swim that good."

"Dry landers," Cole said. "You've never drove cattle to Kansas like Chet and I have. You'd learn quick how to swim good or drown."

"What do I owe you three?"

"Not a thing. Glad to help. They said you lost the other ferry they cut loose?" Chet asked.

"I did for a fact, and I'll be months getting another to replace it. Oh, we can cut down some pine trees in the mountains, I guess, and make a temporary one."

"Sorry we can't stay and help, but we want those five men. Marshal Bailey should be coming along. If he does, you tell him we're headed for Young."

Chet turned to Art. "In your condition, don't you try to go over that dizzy mountain. Your wife needs you, but not that bad or dead. She's powerful upset and told me what they did to her. Take your time and hitch a ride the long way home. You have a good woman there. None of it was her fault, and these outlaws need hung for their deeds. Get us back across, men. They're getting away."

On the ferry, Art shook his hand. "I'm glad you stopped and saw her. I worried she might go crazy.

People do that over like experiences. Tell them when you run them down that Art Kelly hopes they hang."

"We damn sure will," Cole promised.

In a short while they were trotting their horses north on the wagon road. Jesus estimated the gang was four hours ahead of them. In these short winter days, by then it would be sundown.

When the sun started to set, they found a campsite for the night. They unsaddled the horses and gave them all grain in the nosebags they'd brought along. Chet and Cole drug in enough firewood, while Jesus cooked.

"It's good to be sipping your coffee again," Chet said, squatted on his heels. "That poor woman at the Sunflower store didn't know how weak hers was."

"It sure wasn't this good." Cole took another swallow of the steaming liquid.

"You should have seen that boy who brought Bailey's telegram. I bet he never had tasted hot cocoa until Marge made it for him. But he sure smacked his lips over it."

"Folks don't know what they're missing." Cole shook his head.

While they turned in, Chet wondered how much longer this chase would continue. Would shutting down the ferry system make the outlaws feel more secure? Maybe they'd let up somewhat and drop their guard. He'd bet they were wanted all over, besides Arizona and New Mexico, so they'd be running scared.

Sleep tight, Marge. I miss you.

CHAPTER 13

When they reached the little community of Young, it consisted of a small store, a blacksmith shop, a saddle and gun repair shop, and a Mormon church.

"Welcome," the burly blacksmith said. "What can I do for you three?"

"We're tracking five men who came through here today or yesterday."

"You the law?"

"That's right. US Marshal Byrnes."

He drew off his heavy work gloves and reached to shake Chet's hand. "You're about six hours behind them. I hope you catch them. They were thugs. Ordered folks around and shot at two people. Some of us would have shot them, but we were afraid of them shooting an innocent bystander. My name's John Orr."

"Nice to meet you. Quiet town you have here. I understand it must have upset folks."

"This is too nice a place to put up with the likes of them."

"They sank the ferry that crosses the Salt to go to

Globe, and they beached the one that comes up here. We got it back in the river and it works, but the other one is gone."

"What have they done besides that?"

"Held up a bank in Tucson, besides shooting three townspeople. They raped a woman west of Four Peaks. Robbed two banks in New Mexico. Lord knows what else."

"You and your men have been in some tough places getting here."

Chet shook his head wearily. "Don't even talk about it. That trail crossing over Four Peaks is real bad."

The blacksmith rubbed his forehead. "Never been over it, but I can imagine. I do appreciate you men putting your lives on the line for the rest of us."

"Any idea where they might try hanging out up there?"

"Horse Head Crossing, on the Little Colorado. There's lots of stolen horse business goes on up there and the no accounts hang out there."

"I passed through there when I moved my people to the Verde Valley from Texas. No trouble, but we avoid it when we ship cattle to Gallup every month."

"Good place to stay away from. But it's two days' hard ride from here."

"Can we cross the Rim?"

"There's a few roads go up on top. They aren't hard to find or follow."

"Thanks. The store here have any fresh meat for sale? We're tired of beans."

"He sure might."

"Jesus, go buy us some. We'll put the horses up."

John Orr gestured toward the back. "Put them in my corrals. I've got hay and grain. Anybody looking for outlaws is a real sight to see up here."

While they unsaddled and unpacked, John brought them a huge armload of cut wood for cooking. "I'll get you one more load of wood. Grain's in the shop in my bin. Feed them mine. You and them horses are my guests."

Jesus brought some nice beef back from the store. "They found out who we are and wouldn't take your money. I thanked them."

They enjoyed the beef cooked on a grill and savored canned peaches for dessert. This trip was sure dragging out, but they still had the trail of the five. Chet worried they might split up at Horse Head Crossing and go five different directions. They'd need to push harder.

Had Bailey given up finding him? Hard to tell, but without success posses get the quits in about three days. They might have run them in the ground somewhere.

Chet and his men topped the Rim two days later. Saddle weary, they rode through the tall grasslands that the Windmill Ranch shared with this country. It went clear back to where the Rio Grande sliced through New Mexico.

They saw a steady stream of smoke in the sky and stopped on a rise. Chet used his field glasses to focus in on the dots that were horses by a weathered gray

wooden building. Two white horses stood among the
five hipshot animals at the hitch rack.

He handed the glasses to Cole, who nodded and
passed them to Jesus.

"Thank God they are there." Jesus crossed himself
and handed the glasses back to Chet.

"Cole, you take your rifle and ammo and get behind
that outhouse and cover the back door. Jesus and I will
take the front. We'll hobble our horses and leave them
here. Keep down. Only shoot when shot at."

Their horses under control, they each took a Win-
chester and ammo and with care circled around to
the front of the cabin. They were close enough to
hear the men raising hell inside.

One man stuck his head out the front door and
Chet and Jesus flattened themselves on the ground.
He never saw them, but went back inside and closed
the door. A woman's high-pitched scream made him
and Jesus frown at each other. They remained on the
ground where they could cover the front door. Guns
beside them, they listened. It sounded like there was
another female in there as well.

"I'm going to put two shots in that rusty stovepipe
on the roof. You be ready. It should spook their
horses out of the way."

Jesus nodded he understood.

Chet took aim, and the first shot made every horse
tuck his tail between his legs. The number two shot
made them panic and reins were broken. The horses
jumped on each other and broke their headstalls.
The first white one led them away, bucking like a

hellcat was raking his butt. The stovepipe had disappeared, and he heard lots of loud cussing and coughing coming from inside.

"You got the stovepipe," Jesus whispered.

Chet nodded and looked through his sights at the front door.

Two quick rifle shots and someone shouted, "They're out back, too."

"They've found Cole. Or he found them." Chet smiled.

After a lot of coughing, two half-naked women ran out with their hands high and screaming, "Don't shoot."

"Watch behind them." He nudged Jesus.

A man came out next, with his hands in the air and threw away his pistol.

"Get on the ground. Face down and spread eagle. You jump up, you're dead. You hear me?" Chet demanded.

"I won't move." He sank to the ground and followed orders.

"You girls get way north of here. We'll shoot you if you do anything wrong."

They waded through the tall grass. "Is this good enough?"

Chet rose to his knees. "Far enough. Put your hands down."

At the sound of more shots from out back, he whirled around. Someone must have gone out the back door firing his handgun. There were two loud reports from Cole's rifle, then quiet save for the coughing men still in the smoke-filled building. One man tried to crawl out the front door on his hands and knees aiming his gun. Jesus shot him and he went face down.

Chet heard someone inside say, "Go ahead. We can get them."

He whispered to Jesus, "You get number one. I'll get number two."

The first one burst into sight his six-gun blazing, but slumped face down from Jesus's two quick shots. The big man came next. He fired too high and was slammed into the wall by Chet's bullets in his chest. He slid down the wall and the gun spilled out of his hand.

In the following quiet, a meadowlark sang and the wind in the grass sang a hymn. The two women huddled together. They cried more from being scared than any losses, Chet figured. He looked the downed outlaws over, then checked on the one-eyed outlaw who ran out and gave up. He still lay face down.

"Handcuff the one-eyed one," he told Jesus.

"The two out back are dead," Cole said from the side of the shack.

"These two here are, too, or will be shortly. Jessie Combs is the only one we have to take back. You boys better round up your horses that you'll have to sell. We'll need the bank money, too. They usually pay twenty percent as a reward for its return."

"How much are they worth?" Cole asked, indicating the dead men.

"Five hundred apiece," Chet said. "You guys are doing all right."

"What about us?" one of the doves asked, still seated on their butts in the grass.

"You get a chance to go find a new place to entertain your company. Get your things and get to hiking."

"But it's a long ways—"

"You got here. You can get back where you came from."

"You damn sure ain't nice to ladies." They stomped off down the wagon tracks headed north.

"It's the company you keep," he said after them.

He and the crew got what was left of the stovepipe back up and drew the smoke out. After that, they gathered up their horses. Then, with a rope, and on horseback, they dragged the four corpses around and lay them in a row for Bailey to see if he ever came. Chet wanted to spare chopping off their heads to take back as evidence they'd gotten the wanted men. He covered them with an old blanket to keep the buzzards away.

Jesus fixed supper. Chet and Cole rounded up all the money that was in the outlaws' saddlebags and a valise. It was too much money to count. If those outlaws had ever reached civilization, they'd have had a wild party. They had a pretty good start on one and were probably drunk when the gunfight broke out. Those two women must have had a supply of whiskey on hand. After a brief search, Cole discovered some full bottles in a wooden crate.

The sun was about to set when Chet heard horses coming. Led by a hatless Indian, he had no doubt these men in suits and high-crowned hats were Bailey and his posse. Plate in hand, he stood in the doorway and waved as they dismounted.

"Boys, welcome to the Horse Head Crossing Brothel. Come on in. Jesus has plenty of beans."

"Thanks. I'm Bailey, and you must be Byrnes. You're a hard man to catch. What in the hell happened here?"

"We rode up about midday, saw two white horses at the hitch rack, and surrounded the house. When we ordered them to come out hands high, one man and two whores came out. The others decided to fight their way out. If you check under that blanket, there's your gang, except Combs who's cuffed and resting. I think his head still hurts from the moonshine he drank."

All the men with Bailey looked like businessmen or large ranchers. When they looked under the blankets at the four bodies, they all reacted, shaking their heads or looking away.

"I'm glad to see you. We were fixing to chop their heads off and put them in a sack to bring to show you," Chet said.

"Chet Byrnes, you ever shoot a wanted man, your word is good enough for me. You don't have to bring in any dead heads to prove it. You think they were drunk, huh?"

"Yeah, the evidence of that is inside. I ran off the shady ladies, but they had a good supply of untaxed lightning. I think they thought they'd stopped everyone from finding them and they might have done it, but we didn't take no for an answer."

"We know that. We've been on your trail. Thanks. The money?"

"More than we can count. We have all we could find on them in their saddlebags and a valise."

"That Kelly woman told us you three went over a trail even a goat would resist."

"I've been over better ones, I can tell you that."

One of the posse members chimed in. "Byrnes, we kept asking each other where you'd go next."

Bailey smiled. "We heeded your advice and the woman's, too. We went around."

"Just be grateful you did," Cole said. "You didn't miss anything but hell."

Busy eating their supper, some of the posse members sipped on the liquor. They all agreed it wouldn't take much of it to get real drunk.

Afterward, the men took turns using Jesus's short-handled shovel to dig a common grave, then dumped the four bodies into it and covered them up.

When Bailey had a chance to talk privately with Chet, he brought up the reward money. "You know that you're entitled to the rewards for these men and a percentage of the money recovered."

"That money goes to my men, Jesus and Cole."

"It'll be a pretty large sum."

"Good, they need it. Jesus is getting married this spring to his sweetheart, and Cole is courting a young woman back home. They'll put it to good use."

Bailey shook Chet's hand. "Without you, we'd never of made it up here. And you've put an end to a dangerous gang who'd have gone on robbing and killing until someone finally stopped them."

"I'll write Mrs. Kelly and tell her about their end. People like Grisham and his men raping her bothers me the most. She would have fed them and never said a word, but she was violated by men too cruel to live in anyone's world."

"You're right." Bailey nodded. "I guess lots of us in the law business know about that article in the *Globe* newspaper about the Rye lynchings. When I heard the entire story of their crimes, I understood how you felt that day. This one ended well. When I write the news release on their capture, I'll mention you and your men's names, if you don't mind."

Chet shrugged. "We were just doing our duty."

"Hell, that ferry problem about shut us down. Who swam the Salt and brought the rope over? They really bragged on him."

"Cole did it. If you ever took cattle to Kansas on one of those drives, you had to learn to swim or die. After that first run to Kansas, Cole and I both learned to swim better. I came home and swam all summer until the creeks went dry."

"How will you go home?"

"Ride west. I have a ranch at least one day's ride west of here."

"Then how?"

"We'll ride the next day to the Verde ranch, and

then up to the Preskitt Valley place. From there, we can ride south to the Hayden's Ferry."

"We're going back with you," Bailey said. "How much land do you own?"

"We have five ranches."

"I know folks say you're busy and I can see why, so I sure appreciate you helping us get these outlaws."

Next day, Chet and the entire posse and their prisoner rode to the Windmill Ranch, spent the night, then went on to Camp Verde. Sarge and the main crew were on the move with a herd to Gallup.

Jesus and Cole brought the horses and gear they received for capturing the gang. Chet suggested when they got home they take them to Frye's Livery to sell, and they thought that was a good idea.

Chet knew they'd overheard Marshal Bailey talking about the rewards they'd get and wondered if they'd quit him when they received it.

They were close to the Verde Ranch when they stopped for a short rest and a chance to empty their bladders. The wind was cold out of the north, and the sky looked like the belly feathers of a goose. Apart from the others, Jesus and Cole approached Chet to talk to him.

"Would it be too much to ask your wife to help us invest this reward money?" Cole asked. "Jesus and I talked about not blowing it away. I don't think we'll be so rich, but if we invest in the right things it can grow, right?"

"I bet she'd be flattered to help you."

Cole smiled in relief and exchanged a look with his partner. "Thanks."

"Yes, thanks," Jesus repeated.

"I'm glad you decided that. I thought you two might quit me and go into business for yourself."

"Naw, we're grateful to get to do this with you."

Jesus nodded in agreement. "It gets to be work sometimes, but we've seen more country working for you than we'd have seen in our lifetime."

"I'm not quitting. It gets sure exciting at times," Cole said.

"Fine. I'll tell Marge about what you two want her to do."

A tall older man by the name of Kyle Riley, who ranched down on the border, spoke to Chet as they rode west. "How long have you been out here?"

"Oh, from start till now, about two and a half years. Why?"

"Just wondering how you put all your holdings together."

"Not so much me, but I bought a badly managed large ranch. I hired the men he fired and they're the ones who put in the real effort to make it work. My family had some money from cattle drives we made to Kansas at the height of the market. I was able to invest that in places here that were in trouble. One man bought several sections of land on a railroad right of way, where the sections go right and left alternate. They weren't near a river so he got them to trade for land close to the Colorado River. He traded, but didn't know the river was in the Grand Canyon. They wouldn't trade back, so it was up for cents on the dollar."

"How did you ever learn that?"

"There's a land agent in Preskitt that does it for me. He's a whiz at finding them."

Appearing amused by Chet's story, Riley said, "Sounds like you fell in a pile and came out smelling like a rose."

"I have been lucky."

"I wouldn't say that. You convinced that Navajo agency in Gallup to let you supply them beef. I have to sell mine to Old Man Clanton and he has all those federal contracts in southern Arizona sewed up."

"Well, up in Gallup the last contractor wasn't delivering on time and the tribe members traveled long distances to get their commodities. Waiting days for their beef didn't work for them. Quality was another issue. Hard pressed to get them there, meant the cattle were drawn and tough after the rush."

"That's why you have the Windmill Ranch?"

"Yes. We assemble the cattle there, where there's good grass most of the year and makes us closer to the market."

"You have hay, too?"

"We plan to improve on that. A dry fall like we had this year means no feed on the range for the stock. Or a big snow amounts to livestock losses."

"Which way are you going, Hereford or Shorthorn?"

"I have a small purebred herd of Hereford mother cows. So I'm betting on the white face cross."

"I have some of both. I thought Shorthorns might be better since they're from Scotland in the North Country."

"I never thought about that. We're late getting to crosses, since the last foreman charged the owner for them and used longhorn home-raised bulls instead."

"That was no help, was it?"

"No, and it also made the stock less valuable when I bought it."

"Your success impresses me. Compared to your work, I feel lazy."

Chet, amused, demurred. "Lucky, like I said. Things broke open for me. Kinda like lots of eggs hatching under one hen."

"No, Byrnes, you're a doer. What will you do next?"

"I'm working on another ranch tied up in an estate. That's not for public record, since it's still in the works."

"Where is it?"

"Right beside one I own."

Riley chuckled and gigged his horse on down the road.

They reached the Verde Ranch late that night. Susie quickly dressed and welcomed them. She offered to feed them and set about doing it. Jesus and Cole helped her while the tired men sat in the living room.

"This is not your home?" one of them asked, gazing around.

"No, we'll be there by midmorning. That's my wife's home and where we live. Susie, my sister here, will move up to the Windmill Ranch soon where her husband is foreman. So this house needs a family to move into it."

One of the posse said, "Don't tell my wife this nice large house is available. She'd make me move here."

They all got a chuckle out of that.

The next morning, they reached home. Monica served them pastries and coffee. Meanwhile, Jesus and Cole reshod one of their horses so they could go on.

Within an hour, Bailey, his men, and their prisoner left for Tucson. Marge made sure they had enough supplies on their packhorses for the rest of the trip.

"Bailey is an interesting man," she told Chet when they were alone.

"He thanked me for helping out."

"Where did you finally find them?"

"Horse Head Crossing, up on the Little Colorado. They thought they were safe and were celebrating in a house of ill repute, and drunk when we arrived."

"Oh, my."

"They decided to fight and all but one was shot down."

Marge came into his arms and held him close. "I'm so glad you're home."

He squeezed her to him. "How are you doing?"

"So far, so good. No problems, except worrying about you."

"No need to do that. How are Lucie and Reg?"

"Fine, but—"

"What else?"

"JD left them. They weren't sure where he went, except he said he needed to find his way. Neither Reg nor her could talk him out of it."

"Nor could I, I'd bet."

"What will he get into next?"

"I have no idea, Marge. I know I need a bath and I really missed you."

"Later on, draw me a map where all you've been. Did you see any better place than here?"

"No. Nothing to move me out of here. Oh, the boys want you to help them to manage their reward money."

"I'd be glad to. Were you glad they were along?"

"Hey, they are super help to me."

"I have the boiler heating." Then she whispered, "I don't have to have you shiny clean for you to love me. It'll be another hour till the water is hot enough for your bath."

"Let's sneak upstairs."

"Go," she said, giving him a shove.

Whew, was he ever glad he had her to come home to.

CHAPTER 14

Up to date on the rest of the operations, Chet and Marge were eating supper that night when someone knocked on the door. When he answered it, Jesus and a ranch hand from the Verde Ranch stood there.

"They found some cattle today, killed by a grizzly. Tom sent Nate to let you know he thinks the bear has rabies," Jesus said.

"Have you had supper?" Chet asked the cowboy, then wiped his mouth on a linen napkin.

"Yes, sir."

"What happened?"

"I was with them when we found the cattle. It was bloody. I figured those tough old longhorn cows that hadn't come in for hay could fight a buzz saw. But he tore 'em up."

"You sleep in the bunkhouse tonight. Tomorrow morning, you two come up here and have breakfast and I'll ride down there and see what we can do. I know Cole is in town, but the three of us can handle it. See you then." He closed the door behind them.

"Who was there?" Marge asked.

"Jesus and a Verde cowboy named Nate that Tom sent about a cow killing done by a grizzly bear."

"What are you doing to do?"

"Go hunt him down. There's lots of superstitions about grizzlies. They're simply a larger fierce bear that lead can stop."

"Oh, my dear husband is going off on another chase."

"Bear hunting. It should be fun. Cole is in town courting Valerie and selling the outlaws' horses they recovered. Jesus and I can handle a grizzly bear and be back in a few days."

"You may freeze in this cold weather. Why isn't he sleeping? The rest of the bears hibernate now."

"You have a point. Male bears down in Texas seldom sleep very long. The climate in the valley is not as warm as there, but not as cold as up on the Rim."

"Maybe someone woke him up. You be careful. Grizzlies or not, they're man killers."

"I'm always careful."

She reached over and tapped the top of his hand. "Still, be careful."

He promised.

Predawn, Jesus and Nate were already seated at Monica's breakfast table when Chet joined them. After exchanging greetings, he sat down.

Monica poured him a cup of coffee and he thanked her.

His housekeeper pointed a finger at them. "Crazy men, rushing off in the cold to shoot a dang bear."

"Somebody's got to do it," he said.

"I guess so, but you have better things to do than run down a bear."

"No, Monica, a grizzly is a tough adversary. I'm taking along a .50-caliber Sharps rifle that can kill a buffalo at almost a quarter of a mile."

"That's where I'd be. A quarter mile away from him," she said on her way back to the kitchen.

"She'd probably kill him with a kitchen knife," Jesus said quietly.

Chet shook his head at him. He didn't want her to hear their comments. They were only kidding, but he didn't want her feelings hurt. She faithfully fed them and did nice things for everyone. She was probably thinking how his being gone would make Marge unhappy. He sipped his coffee, wondering why his wife hadn't come down. He sent the men on and went upstairs to kiss her good-bye. He had no intentions to leave without doing that.

He hurried upstairs and sat on the bed, leaned over, and kissed her.

She woke up with a start and sat up. "I—I slept in. I'm sorry."

"I wasn't going to leave without kissing you."

She put her arms around him and kissed him. "Thanks. Be careful. I'll pray for your safety. Come back soon."

"I always do."

"I know you have to go. So much work to do. I know Bailey sure appreciated you. You're making this territory a place for common people to live and survive."

"Take care of the baby." He stood up. "And be careful."

He buttoned his coat on the glassed-in porch and pulled up his collar as he ran to his horse. It would be a cold morning, but they'd be there early enough to head up into the bear country. The sun came out when they were halfway off the mountain, but it offered little heat. In his wool long johns, heavy clothes, and great jacket, he was warm. He regretted some he wasn't back in Texas, but if he was he'd probably not have half the things he was building in the Territory. So he wouldn't complain about the frigid temperature and booted his horse downhill with the others.

At the ranch, he went to speak to Tom who was at the blacksmith shop and met him at the door.

"Sorry, Chet, but I'm not a bear hunter, so I need your help. I thought about calling in the man in Camp Verde with the dogs, but he told me once you need tougher dogs than he has to tree a grizzly. I don't know anyone who has Airedales, and he says they're the only ones tough enough for that."

"Why isn't the bear sleeping, my wife wants to know?"

"It was warm down here last week and he may have woke up."

"He's up in the north country."

"Yes. That's where they found the dead cows. I figured those old tough cows up there came from the Texas brush. They were some of the ones wouldn't come in and eat hay. But he killed them like they was rabbits."

"How many bears you think there were?"

"I thought one, but I'm not a good tracker."

"We're going up there and find him."

"I'll come up tomorrow when I get things lined out, and help."

"We'll be at Thorp's Spring. Nate said the slaughter was close to there."

"Be careful. He's a killer, not only of cows, I figure."

"How's John?"

"Making Hampt lots of wire. I still need to go see him. My men that haul it over there say it's stout."

"Will you fence your farmland?"

"Yes. That wire and stake fence we have is hard to repair and expensive to maintain."

"Sounds like what you need to do. See you, Tom. Tell Millie I'm sorry I missed her."

"I will. You talk to Susie?"

"Of course. See you tomorrow."

"Right."

He galloped his horse to catch up with the other two men.

"Was it all right?" Jesus asked.

"Sure. Tom handles things well. A grizzly is a big deal. I guess they were the bane of the mountain men that trapped the beavers out."

"Mountain men?"

"Yeah. Grizzlies were a lot more plentiful a hundred years ago. An old man once told me if you ever stab one, don't take your knife out of him."

"Why do that?"

"He said then the bear would fight the knife stuck in him and not you. Take it out and he'd take you on."

Jesus frowned. "I hope I never have to fight one with a knife, but I'll remember that."

Nate agreed. "I saw them cows, and when I tried to ride closer, my horse about bucked me off. I guess he could still smell him."

Chet shook his head. "No. The bear pissed on those carcasses."

"They do that?" Nate asked.

"Yes, and that scares other predators away from their kills."

"Well, it damn sure spooked that cowpony."

Jesus pointed up. "They're having a gathering up there."

What looked like a hundred turkey vultures circled in a high loop over the mountainside ahead of them. The winged foragers had found the death site and called all their buddies to join them. Where there was any shortage of the big scavengers, ravens filled in.

Several slinky coyotes ran off at their approach, and two red wolves slunk away as well. It was feast time and all were there, except the silver tip.

Jesus dismounted to examine the ground, and when he did, vultures scattered into the air.

All the horses spooked at the smell of the dead cows, whose entrails had been opened in the bear's attack. Nate held on to their horses' reins as well as the packhorses. The cows were large framed Longhorns, no doubt driven originally from Texas to stock the ranches. There were no calves or yearlings with them. The complaining of the disturbed vultures and the ravens made a lot of racket. Then they started acting brave enough that Jesus moved outside their feasting area. He looked at the mountain face and pointed north to indicate he thought the bear went that way.

Chet and Nate rode around and joined him.

"Get a lead?" Chet asked.

"Yes, he came and went this way, I'm certain."

"You think he came back to this kill?"

"I don't know, but there are tracks of a big bear going north."

"We better be ready for most anything, men." He drew the .50-caliber Sharps out of his scabbard. Jesus took out his .44/.40 and so did Nate.

"Shoot him in the head. One of your bullets in his body will only make him madder."

Jesus acted like he had a good track and went on afoot. They stayed back and let him lead. The cow track they followed was just a single path the range cattle used to come and go on. Other animals, like deer and maybe even elk, used them because the path was already marked for them.

They'd gone high enough to look down into the trough of the Verde basin, walled in on both sides by towering mountains. Chet sat his horse to wait while Jesus covered some ground looking for sign.

Chet noticed several good-sized pine trunks where the bark had been clawed by the bear sharpening his claws. From the height of the scars on the trunks, he was a giant.

"I think he has a cave around here," Jesus said.

"Secure the horses with a lariat. If anything spooks them, we don't need to be afoot."

"I'll do that," Nate offered. Jesus had gone out of sight into the timber.

Chet set out to follow. The sun had warmed enough he unbuttoned his coat. He kept looking around, not wanting to be surprised by anything showing up. From a rocky point, Jesus waved for him to come up there.

After Chet climbed up, Jesus pointed. "I think he uses that cave over there. It has an opening big enough."

Braced against a pine tree on the steep ground, Chet could see the entrance a hundred feet away. If that was his lair, it was strange the bear hadn't caused stock loss before. But no telling. He may have lost a mate or was looking for one and moved in there for the winter.

"What shall we do?" Jesus asked.

"I'm not fool enough to go in there and wake him up."

Jesus nodded vigorously in agreement.

"If there's enough fuel, we can build a fire and smoke him out. But if he went back to hibernate, he'll be hard to get out. They say they breathe very little in that state."

"I'd say he has us in a draw, huh?"

Chet nodded. "He very well does. We need to make camp closer to the spring. It'll be dark soon and we'll be fumbling around without any light."

"Good idea. Where's Nate?"

"Downhill, watching the horses."

"Jesus, was there a letter for you from Mexico?" Chet had wondered some about it since they got home, but hadn't checked. He knew Jesus had sent a letter to his girlfriend in Mexico before they left to run down the bank robbing gang.

Jesus looked disappointed. "No word so far."

"Maybe she will answer you and you'll get it when you get back."

"I hope so."

"You did a good job tracking that bear. We'll keep an eye on things and see if he comes out again."

"Cold as it is up here," Jesus said, "I'd sleep, too."

"It isn't toasty warm, is it?"

Jesus explained to Nate what they'd found. Then they mounted and went near the spring, far enough from the bear kill to not smell it or hear the animals fighting over the remains.

They snaked in firewood and let Jesus set up for cooking. Things went smooth, the wall tent up, horses hobbled and grained. Jesus had raided the ranch kitchen supplies and had elk steaks broiling while he fried sliced onions and potatoes for the side and made biscuits in a Dutch oven. Seated on a log, they let the heat from the cook fire reflect into their faces while waiting for the meal.

"Why, he don't need a wife," Nate teased while they ate. "He'd beat most females at cooking anytime."

When the laughter died down, Chet added, "And keep you warm at night, too." The mellow smoke from the dead live oak they'd found filled his nose. Stars were out and he was tired enough to sleep. But he'd miss his wife, too.

CHAPTER 15

Sometime during the night, Chet decided he needed to search inside the cave the next day. To leave that killer in there happily sleeping worked on his conscience. They'd need a few pitch torches to light the way inside the dark hole. He didn't want anyone hurt, but until they looked inside they wouldn't know if the big bruin was there.

"We'll need some torches to go see if he is or isn't in there."

Both men quit eating their oatmeal and turned toward him.

"You want to go in there?" Jesus asked in disbelief.

"What if he kills us?" Nate asked.

"Oh, Tom will be along in a little while and recover our bodies."

They laughed, but uneasy sounding.

After breakfast, they hacked three torches out of some junipers. Full of pitch, Jesus said they should make good ones. They left their horses hobbled to graze in the valley by the spring and climbed the mountain. Armed with rifles, they hiked up to the cave entrance. Chet's rifle at the ready, he checked inside and decided the cave must be deep.

He couldn't hear the bear sleeping, but that didn't mean he wasn't there. Bears had low respiratory sounds during hibernation. Not hearing him was not an indication that he wasn't inside. He handed the rifle to Jesus who stood ready for him to light their torches.

Flames and smoke spewed from the heavy torches, and he entered the cave holding his high. They went a good distance inside the natural shaft before it narrowed with no sign of the bear. They were down to a crawl space tunnel when Chet stopped them.

"He's in here. I can smell him. He's in the back. We'll have to build a large fire at the cave opening and see if we can drive him out."

Jesus looked relieved. They went back to the opening and started back to camp. Tom and another hand named Joe were waiting for them at camp.

"Any luck?" Tom asked.

"We think he's in a cave up there on the side of the mountain. We're glad you arrived. We need lots of fuel, so go to dragging things up there."

In a few hours, they had the cave entrance stacked full with dead pine logs and other debris. With it stuffed floor to ceiling with flammable fuel, Chet and Tom lit it on fire. They moved outside the cave to wait while Nate and Jesus made lunch.

About then, Chuck, a new cowboy, rode in on the scene and he couldn't believe they went in the cave to try to find the bear. The six of them wound up abandoning lunch to sit outside the cave as smoke and flames poured out. Meanwhile, the fire was getting red hot inside the cave.

Then Chet spotted a large bear roaring loudly, headed down the canyon next to them, running full steam, and with his fur smoking and on fire. The bear had found another way to escape from the cave. Chet jumped up and ran to Tom's nearby horse. His big rifle in hand, he charged off the mountain.

The horse slid on his butt off the steep side and Chet wondered if the pony would ever find its footing, but he did and scrambled some more. They were off again and hit the flats where Chet made a downhill shot at the furious bear. The bullet struck, but never stopped him. Chet sent the big horse off more mountainside, and when they reached the valley floor, the bear whirled and rose to face him. That bear must have stood eight feet tall.

Chet reloaded the Sharps and closed the trap door. Then he shouted, "whoa," at the horse; the animal obeyed and slid to a stop. He took aim at the raging mouth of the bear. The loud report echoed up and down the valley. The bear folded up, and the spooked horse had to be checked. The bear, to his relief, was dying.

His heart pounded in his chest. Tom, Jesus, and the other two were coming pell-mell off the mountainside, sliding on their butts part of the way and cheering.

Squatted beside the carcass, he decided the fire-scorched hide wasn't worth much and stunk as bad as any male bruin, but he would mount the head. Even dead, the bruin's worn eyeteeth still looked dangerous.

"Well, big game hunter. I thought for sure you and Star were going to crash and burn coming off there," Tom said, laughing.

"I didn't want him to get away. We can skin his head so it can be mounted."

"Let's eat lunch first. It's ready," Jesus said. "So he found another exit, huh?"

"Yes, he had a back door," Chet said. "Thanks, boys. He won't kill any more Quarter Circle Z stock."

He and Tom walked back to camp, discussing ranch business, but Tom ended with, "You're a damn tough man, Chet Byrnes."

"Nah. Just doing what needs to be done. I figured if I didn't, he'd kill some unsuspecting cowboy. Now he won't."

"No, he's damn sure dead."

"Damn sure."

"After lunch, we'll pack you up so you can go home."

They reached the base ranch long after sundown. After he showed the bear's head to everyone, he went to Susie's where she fixed him a hot bath and fed him supper. Then, over supper, she listened to his bear story.

"What's next, brother?"

"Home to my wife."

"Marge will be glad, I bet. I sure miss Sarge a lot.

I never thought I'd feel like I do about a husband. But he's a great guy."

"I'm the same about my finishing school wife."

She gave him a shove. "All right, my concern about her education was wrong. She's a great woman and I love her."

"You know," he said, growing serious, "I've been thinking about all we've accomplished here, and it isn't bad. I doubt we'd have found this kind of opportunity in Texas. Folks tease me about having an empire. But, I guess, we do, as a family, have one started."

"I know, and it works because of you, so don't let any bears get you."

"Yes, ma'am." He yawned. "I want to get an early start tomorrow so I'll be up before sunup."

"I'll have breakfast for you and Jesus."

"I'll go up and warn him."

"Where did you say Cole is?"

"Courting a young lady."

"Oh, do I know her?"

"Her name is Valerie. She works for Jenn."

"I guess I don't know her."

"Back when I was searching for Bonnie, I sent Valerie up here from Tombstone. She helped us and wanted no part of life in a brothel. Cole was impressed when he met her again in Preskitt, and they've had some face-to-face meetings."

"Sounds serious."

"Yes, Cole is serious. I gave him a few days off. And Jesus has sent for his woman in Mexico."

"Oh, he has one there?"

Chet shrugged. "She hasn't answered his letters so far. But letters get lost down there, too."

"Oh, I do hope that works for him. He's such a sweet man."

"Pretty loyal to her, too, I'd say. We've been lots of places where he's had the opportunity and never strayed. That takes willpower."

"How about Nate? I don't know him very well."

"He's just a cowboy. Happy to have work, but he won't ever make a foreman or boss. He'll work, but he's not a deep thinker."

"Do you fret about DJ taking off again?"

"I can't nail his foot to the floor. I don't think he's ever got over Marge's friend, Kay, and he took lots of risks she never appreciated him for."

"No, he started changing when you were out here buying this ranch. I saw it then and wondered what he was trying to do. Reg had Juanita, and JD was left to his own devices."

"Was Reg happy with her?"

"I think he was—dedicated. But she showed a fiery side I'd never seen when she worked for us. He was so happy when he found out she was with child. Then she had the crash—and I blame that on the impatient streak she'd begun to show."

"I simply wondered. Lucie was such a great fun person with us on our honeymoon, but I never saw her as a wife for Reg."

"I did. She rides everywhere he goes. Maybe not

now, but she can out rope him and he admits it. He's also the best looking man up there, huh?"

"I remember she told us there wasn't a man up there worth marrying. Then Reg showed up."

They both laughed at how things worked out for those two.

After supper, he went upstairs to bed. He could still smell that fire-singed stinking grizzly. Well, he was gone. They could go back home. Sarge would be back any day from New Mexico.

And he needed to talk to Tom about something pressing him. Oh, he'd think of it in the morning.

Marge, I'm headed home. I love you.

He and Jesus headed for Preskitt Valley in the cold air of dawn with Chet sunk in thought about the ranch business. Another six weeks and things should break wide open into spring. Tom had the cattle assembled for the next shipment, and he'd even talked to the Boones about them selling him some cattle in the spring. Tom said they were looking forward to it.

That cattle sale would set the Boones on their feet. They were frugal folks and they'd make it with a good cattle sale next spring.

"Jesus, if you don't get a letter soon, you want to go down there to see if you can find her?" he asked his helper.

"You have many things to do, *señor*. I do not wish to trouble you about my cares."

"Hey, you and Cole are like my sons. If we need to go down there, we can do that."

"*Gracias*. I will send her another letter this week."

"Don't forget. We can go down there, if you want us to."

"We will see."

They arrived home midmorning, and after he dismounted by the house, Jesus took his horse along with him. Marge was waiting on the glassed-in back porch and hugged him when he came inside.

"Get the bear?"

"He's dead and he was a big stinking one. Bigger than any bear I ever saw."

"Monica has the boiler going. It'll be heated by the time we eat lunch. Is Susie all right?"

"Waiting for Sarge."

"Oh, yes, he's coming home. I'm so glad you're back safe and sound. How are the others doing?"

"Tom has things well in hand, of course, and they're getting lots of cattle fed. I know this is a droughty year, but our plan to stack that hay was good. But as we increase our herd size, I see us having to expand our hay operation."

"You've been buying irrigated ground as it comes available along the river. How much more is there?"

"Not a lot, but if more of it comes up, I need Bo to be ready."

"You going to be in charge of farming, too?"

"No, I'll make Jesus the boss of that and he'll do good." He hugged her. "No worry, so far. Tom takes care of the valley, Hampt the land over there, and Reg does the top."

"What will you do next?"

"Keep her all rolling."

"Good, you can do lots of that around here."

"Fine with me. I'll go to town tomorrow and make the rounds. If it isn't bad, you want to go along?"

"Sure. I need to get out once in a while."

"I don't want you to get too tired."

"I won't. Besides, I've not heard another word about Roamer being laid off. Nor any good gossip, or anything. I'll go by the dress shop and get filled up on gossip again."

"Fine. The water must be warm by this time, so I'll go take a bath." He walked toward the stairway.

"Can I go along?"

"You can go anywhere I go." He held out an arm for her.

"Well, I do get anxious when you're gone. I don't know if I'll really like this baby. I'll miss the time I had taking care of you."

"Oh, you'll spoil the fire out of it."

"I don't spoil you."

"Not too much, but, yes, you do, and have since we met."

She looked at the ceiling for help.

Chet undressed and sank into the tub of hot water. How great that her father had seen an ingenious contraption in Pennsylvania and installed it in this house. The hot water came gravity fed from a boiler on the second floor and filled the large metal washtub. A windmill also fed the copper house tank upstairs.

The water was hot, but would cool fast, so he kept slipping in deeper and deeper until he was soon immersed to his neck. It sure felt good to simply soak. Nothing better than this, being back home, and not a thing wrong that he needed to straighten out.

After he finished his bath, Marge brought him clean clothes. He shaved, then dressed, looking forward to catching up on the news in the *Miner* newspaper. But when he came out of their bedroom, he heard someone talking downstairs. He paused at the top of the stairs, looked down, and saw that Marge had started up.

"Wait there. I'm coming down. Is something wrong?"

She nodded, a concerned look on her face.

Three men stood in the entry, a small room at the foot of the stairs with doors that led to the living room on one side and to the dining room on the other. Dressed for the cold, they all wore scotch-plaid wool caps.

"Chet, this is Mr. McElroy and his sons. I'll go make some coffee. Gentlemen, just hang your coats on the wall pegs by the door."

Chet came the rest of the way down the stairs and shook their calloused hands. They told him their names: Lord the father, Shawn the oldest, and Kevin.

"What can I do for you?"

The older man placed his coat and cap on the rack beside his sons' coats. "It's their sister I came to see you about. Her name's Sheila, and an outlaw has taken her and we can't find them."

"Is it a gang?"

"The Turley Gang," Shawn said.

"Never heard of them. Let's go in the dining room and you can tell me all about this business. Marge will bring coffee." He always worried about offering coffee to any of the many Mormons in the area, but he figured they could always refuse.

"A wonderful house you have here, sir," Lord said, admiring it.

"My father-in-law built it before I came here. He's a very educated man and studied house design across the country before he built this one."

After they were all seated at the table, Lord folded and unfolded his large calloused hands on top of it. "Well, to begin with, Sheila is only seventeen. John Turley, maybe thirty. He's a man who dresses well and acts like he's a prince. How he does that on a two-bit cow outfit is beyond me.

"He has three men with him who I'm sure are wanted back in Texas. Since they showed up, there's been disappearances of several men over the past two years—mostly strangers who looked like they had money. Never saw them again. Sheriff Simms said they likely drifted on."

"But we never believed that," Shawn said. "We think the Turley Gang killed them and hid the bodies of over a half-dozen men."

"Ever see the horses they rode in on again?" Chet asked.

"No, and we've damn sure looked."

"Horses are sure harder to hide."

"They could have them over to the Bill Williams mining district and sold them, no questions asked."

Chet nodded his head. "That's been done with a few of our cattle."

"Anyway, Turley took a shine to Sheila at the dances. I warned her against him, and she agreed that he was probably mixed up in something outside the law. But three days ago, she up and disappeared. We think he kidnapped her and left the country. I knew the sheriff wouldn't do anything but say it was just romance. But me and the boys don't agree. I'm here to offer you five hundred dollars to find her. If she wants to come home, fine. She don't have to, and if you're certain that it's her own heart-felt idea to stay with him, I'll accept that."

"I understand."

About that time, Monica and Marge arrived with coffee. They brought fresh-baked pastries along with it and the two boys smiled when they saw it.

"You and the boys have searched for him. Where did he go?"

"We think south. A few folks saw them with pack-horses. Shawn can show you their tracks."

"That'll help. But you three feel certain Sheila didn't go on her own with him?"

Kevin swallowed hard. "She and I are pretty close. She told me that he scared her and she wanted no part of him. I'll never believe she went willingly with him."

"I know you're a busy man, but I feel you're our

only hope to find my girl," said Lord. "You have a reputation in this country for getting things like this done. I know your wife is expecting and you have several ranches to look after, but I also know there ain't another man in this country who could do this."

"You realize I could fail, too?"

Lord nodded, face somber. "I would accept that."

"Kevin, there's a Mexican boy in the bunkhouse. His name's Jesus and he's a little older than you. Tell him I need to see him. He'll have to find my other man, Cole, and then be ready to search for her in the morning."

Kevin left the room almost at a run.

"Then you'll look for her?" Lord let out a sigh of relief.

"We'll try. We'll be in your country about two hours past sunup and Shawn can join us."

He turned to Shawn. "Bring your bedroll, rifle, and warm clothes, and be ready for a long ride."

"I will, sir."

"This ain't an army. My name's Chet, Jesus and Cole are the other two that ride with me. Jesus can track, and Cole isn't afraid of any man we've met. Both men are good at this kind of work."

"I'll be proud to ride with you—Chet."

"I don't expect you to do this for free," Lord said.

"We haven't done anything yet. Anyway, you can't put a price on your daughter."

"I know folks have bantered this around. Why aren't you the sheriff?"

Chet chuckled. "I'm too damn busy running five ranches."

Kevin came in the door, Jesus following.

"Jesus, meet Lord and Shawn McElroy. You've met Kevin. He told you the circumstances we're up against?"

"Yes, he did. I will get Cole and be back. Breakfast here before daylight?"

"Yes, as usual. And two packhorses and shod horses for the three of us."

"Cole and I will be ready."

"Shawn's going to meet us over at their place in the morning."

"Good. Does he cook? Nice to meet you all." Jesus turned to leave.

"Don't let him touch a skillet," his father said, and they all laughed.

The McElroys started for home, and Marge hung on Chet's arm as they watched them mount and ride off. "You were't home even a day and someone needs you."

"I guess you married a gadabout."

She gazed fondly into his eyes. "No, I married a man who cares about others. I'm proud people count on you when the law won't do anything for them. You better be thinking hard about finding someone to sit in that swivel chair and administer the law better. And Roamer isn't the man. He'd be bored to death. And you would, too."

They both laughed, and he folded her in his arms and kissed her. Damn, he was a lucky man.

But while he held her, breathing in her fresh scent of lavender and fresh-baked bread, he couldn't help thinking about Sheila McElroy. Where was she? And did she want to be there? He'd have to find out.

CHAPTER 16

Everything was set. He stood outside in the cold and darkness talking to his men while they saddled and packed.

"How is Valerie?" he asked Cole.

"She sent her best to you and Marge. I think things are going fine between us. Say, I hated I missed helping you get that grizzly."

"I know. Glad things are going so well."

"They really are. Hey, that Jenn is a great gal, too. She sent her best wishes, too. Jesus told me about this girl that's missing. What do you think about her?"

"I think we have to find her and ask just what she wants to do. She may be with them on her own, but it don't sound like it. You just never know."

"Right. You think they're killers, too—that bit about the missing men?"

"Not till we can prove it."

"Right. We're about done here. We'll wash up and join you up at the house in a few minutes."

"I'll be there. Good to have you back."

"Still, sure wish I'd come on the bear hunt—"

"Jesus and I knew that. But we only had one bear. We figured we could handle him."

They laughed, and he headed for the house under the cold clouds overhead.

Over breakfast, Cole asked Marge if she thought it would snow.

"It may. Right kinda clouds, aren't they?"

Jesus nodded and swallowed a sip of coffee. "If they make water, it would be good anyway."

"Dry as it was this past fall, I agree," Chet said, cutting pancakes on his plate with the side of his fork.

Breakfast over, he kissed his wife good-bye, hugged Monica, and went to dress for the outside.

Marge watched while he buttoned his coat before leaving the cool enclosed porch. "You know the routine now. Just be careful for the baby and me, Chet Byrnes."

"I'll do that." He kissed her and left as quick as possible, not wanting to prolong the leave taking that always tugged at his heart.

The roan horse acted a little upset, breathing vapors out his nostrils. He danced sideways going down the drive and was still upset when he passed under the bar. Chet watched his mount close. He expected the horse really wanted to buck, but was held in check by his past training. They turned west and headed for Preskitt. While the days had lengthened some, they still were short compared to the summer months.

Shawn joined them on the road south of Preskitt, riding a stout-looking bay. He shook hands with Cole, and after transferring his bedroll to the pack-horse, they rode on.

A few snowflakes whirled around them, but none of any consequence, before they started off the mountaintop. Far below lay the desert, and it would be warmer down there, but it was a steep and long winding road to get there. They camped that night at the bottom at a ranch with water and feed for their animals for a small fee.

The man recalled the gang and Sheila passing by there. He said he knew she looked distressed but never approached him for help. "Them buzzards with her was tough and I knew it, but she never asked anything of me. I was glad when they went on. They were like you said—sure enough hard cases."

"Any idea where they went?" asked Chet.

"I figured they were headed for Mexico, but I'm not certain."

"Any reason to think that?"

"Yeah. The three were wanting to go to the broth-els there, they said."

"Anything you can tell us about their names and looks?"

"One was called Slick; he was about five-eight. Maybe twenty, and had slicked back hair. He was a cocky sumbitch with ivory-handled guns."

"Who else?"

"Denver, he was forty, I bet, but he was tough. Those other boys didn't cross him none."

"What else?"

"He wore a low-crowned, light-colored hat with rawhide strings to keep it on."

"And the last one?"

"Claude, they called him. He wore a derby hat and cowboy gear. Another cocky bastard. All told, they were asking for trouble, but they listened to Turley when he said something."

"Thanks. You've been a big help. We know enough now to find them."

"They kidnapped that girl?"

"Yeah, we're pretty sure they did," Shawn said. "She's my sister."

"Ride easy, men. You're the posse been bringing them in, aren't you?"

Chet nodded.

"I'm damn glad to meet you and hope you catch those bastards."

"Thanks, we'll find them."

"I'll leave you all to turn in," the rancher said, and headed for his house a short distance away.

"Well, we have a good picture of them. I'm going to bed," Cole said.

"It'll sure help us down the road." Chet kicked out a place for his bedding. Once the space was clear of rocks, he spread it out. He was ready for some sleep. Plus, his wife was all right at home. It always eased him to get home between these trips to check on her. When he yawned big, a coyote answered him. He laughed as he crawled inside his bedroll and was asleep right away.

In the early morning light, they rode on to the small village called Phoenix, named for the old ruins of a past civilization that they thought was from the Aztecs. Chet had heard some called them Hohokam ruins, for a people who vanished before the white men came. In his travels, he learned the territory was full of such former civilizations.

It was a long day in the saddle. When camped for the night Cole visited a few cantinas, but learned nothing about the Turley Gang.

The next day, though, the Hayden's Ferry man remembered seeing them and said that Sheila was still with them. The gang had a two-day lead, but they wasn't moving very fast. Chet and his men had gained some time on them. It may be that Turley had no concern about the McElroys' chasing them. Knowing nothing about the man's plans, they could only keep tracking him.

In Casa Grande, a blacksmith told them he'd shod a horse for one of the gang. That shortened their lead, but Tucson lay ahead. It was a big place to cover and try to learn something about the men they followed.

When they rode into the city, Chet wished he didn't have on long handles. They damn sure didn't have to worry about any snow there. It was hot. He sent Shawn and Cole one way, and he and Jesus went the other.

Tucson had the usual crowded streets—peddlers and cart sales, burro trains with water and firewood. The firewood consisted mostly of sticks from the desert, stacked high on sleepy burros' backs. A boy guided the animals with a switch, giving them sharp voice commands. The man who owned them hawked his ware and sold bundles to women for their cooking. Goats, too, that they milked into the housewives' buckets, with the bleating herd gathered around the sale.

They found a cantina and went inside for a beer and information.

"I don't know any John Turley," the bartender who brought their beer said.

"Four tough *gringos*. One was a cowboy with a bowler hat."

"Oh, they were in here last night."

Chet slapped a half-dollar on the bar. "What else do you know about them."

The bartender hesitated, and Chet placed another half-dollar on the scarred dirty bar.

"They said they'd go to Mexico, that my *putas* were too high-priced for them."

"What did you tell them?"

"I told them yeah, but all those down there had the clap."

Jesus laughed, and the bartender joined in, pleased at his joke.

"They have much money?" asked Chet.

"They had money to pay me for the bottle of whiskey they drank. That big man, I'd seen him before. Yes, in El Paso. I don't know his name now. Them others I hadn't ever seen before."

Chet paid him another half-dollar and thanked him.

"Oh, *sí, señor. Muchas gracias.* I hope I can help you again."

Chet drank only half of his warm beer and they left the place. When they cleared the door, Jesus said, "That money was probably more than he makes in a day."

They were only a day behind. Turley's outfit probably took the King's Road south to Nogales. Determined to catch them, they rode out in a trot. Stopping at a cantina down the road, the whiskered barman said they'd been there that morning.

The three of them remounted and hurried their horses along. Jesus found tracks where they'd turned off the road. After following their trail for a distance, they smelled smoke, dismounted, and drew their rifles.

"Shawn, don't shoot too quick," he cautioned the younger man. "We don't want anyone shot that doesn't deserve it."

"Yes, sir."

The boy acted level-headed enough, but he might overreact when he saw his sister. Chet set out, making his way through the willows. The smell of wood smoke from a campfire grew stronger. Soon, he found a path that led there and he took it.

Moving with caution, he spotted a man and two horses. The rest may have gone on to Nogales.

Then he heard the man say, "Don't try to get them ropes free, little girl. You ain't escaping John Turley's camp with me here. Besides, I may wanta take a peek at you naked."

"You do, and when he hears about it you won't ever see anything again."

"Ha, ha. He only took you along to sell you to a rich hacienda owner. He's gone to get him right now."

Chet stepped out of the willows, his gun pointed at the man. "Make one move and you're dead."

The girl screamed, then saw her brother following close behind Chet. "Shawn, you found me." Then she began to cry.

Chet disarmed the man and sat him on his butt beside a log, while Shawn comforted his sister and untied her. Jesus checked around the camp and removed a rifle from the scabbard on the outlaw's horse. Then Chet and Jesus tied the man up.

Chet squatted down on his boot heels beside Sheila as she used her hands to wipe the tears from her eyes.

"Sheila, did any of these men rape you?"

She shook her head and took Shawn's kerchief to dry her eyes.

"I'm not trying to embarrass you, but we have to know. Neither Turley nor any of his men molested you?"

"No, they were saving me to sell to some rich Mexican rancher as a . . . virgin."

"I understand. Your father, mother, and brothers want you home. You know that?"

"I sure hoped they did."

"They do, they said even if you married Turley but wanted to come home, bring you home to them. That's pretty strong, isn't it?"

"I would never marry him. He's an outlaw. And I think I know where they buried one of the men they killed."

What a piece of luck. "Where's that?"

"Under a shed on the place he had up there."

"When you get home, tell Deputy Roamer where that is. No one else. He'll dig it up. When the others come back to camp, we'll capture them. After that, I'm sending you home on the stage, so you get there quicker." He patted her arm and stood up.

Chet pointed at the man on the ground. "Gag him. Then hide our horses down the road a ways, so they don't see them. We're going to have a big welcome party for them."

"Can I kiss you, sir?" she asked, getting to her feet.

"Sure." He bent down and she kissed his cheek.

"Oh, thank you. And thank God, too. I never thought anyone would ever catch them. I'd gave up all hope and decided I'd have to be a captive mistress for someone."

"Well, you're safe now, missy."

They laid plans, and Jesus fed them before darkness came. They built up the campfire, sat the gagged man near it, and concealed themselves in the nearby willows. Stars came out before two riders came into camp.

"Denver, where the hell are you?" a voice called out.

"Get your hands high, or we'll kill you." Cole

slipped in on one side and Jesus the other and disarmed them, then forced them on their bellies with
their hands behind their backs.

"Where's John Turley?"

"He went to San Marie to see a man about selling
her to him. He won't be back till tomorrow."

"You better not be lying. If you are, we'll cut your
throat and leave you here to die."

"No, no, I'm not lying."

"He went there all right," the one called Claude
said.

They put the three in handcuffs, then Chet posted
guards to watch them throughout the night.

Chet told them that if any one of them let out a
peep to warn Turley, he'd shoot them dead. Then
they waited.

Jesus and Sheila fed them a breakfast of oatmeal,
then beans for lunch. Shortly after lunch, riders approached and everyone cleared out of the camp,
taking cover in the willows.

A big dark-complected man rode in, then a well-
dressed Mexican on a fine Barb horse came in with
two *pistoleros*. Chet and his men got the drop on
them, made them get down, and disarmed them.
They cuffed the men together, but each was cuffed
so they faced front to back.

The *patron* made wild threats at Chet until he
showed his Marshal's badge. Then he slumped into
silence.

"You'll be charged with kidnapping and slavery in
the Federal court at Tucson. Miss McElroy will give

testimony there, and you'll be tried in a federal court. I'll also ask them to hold you for murder charges in the Coconino County courts."

Since they now had seven prisoners, Chet sent Jesus and Shawn to rent a wagon to haul them to Tucson. That process took two days, and lawyers hounded Chet in front of the courthouse. Someone told him the Mexican authorities wanted their citizen, Fernando Vasquez, released immediately. If not, they threatened there would be an international incident with Mexico.

Chet shook his head. "No. He broke the law in the Arizona Territory. He doesn't have any special privileges in this country."

"You don't understand," said one of the lawyers. "He is—"

"Oh, but I do. He broke the law in the United States. You can't sell people anymore. He came here to buy a white woman. That breaks our federal laws."

"You trapped him!"

"Talk to the judge. He'll rule on this business."

News reporters flocked him for a story about what happened and why he was there.

"A young woman was kidnapped at Preskitt and her father asked me to look for her. We found her and learned Turley and Vasquez were arranging a sale for her."

"They say Mexico may send troops to free him."

"Come on, men." He frowned at them. "Mexico ain't going to send any troops up here to free some farmer who tried to buy a young innocent woman for immoral purposes."

"You said it pretty frank, Marshal," one reporter said, chuckling.

"I mean it that way. We'll also file murder charges against Turley and his men up in Preskitt."

"What do you call this agency you run?"

Chet sighed. These reporters just wouldn't let a body alone. "I call it, Don't Mess With Me."

He met at the hotel with his men and Sheila. "We have one more night here. After your testimony, Sheila, you can go home."

Cole spoke up. "Jesus and I can take the horses back."

"Okay, you and Jesus take the horses home from here. Sheila, Shawn, and me can go home on the stage."

"That won't work," spoke up Jesus. "One of us has to be with you."

"Not my words, but my wife's and Tom's."

"Well, I will not be the one to explain to her why we left you."

"Shawn and I can take the horses," said Cole. "That Mexican's horses are good Barb horses, too."

"Federal law says they're ours. That means you and Jesus. So take them along."

"We can sell them?"

"Yes. And the sheriff here is searching for reward notices on Turley and his bunch that the three of you can share."

"Is that for real?" Shawn asked.

"It is, that and more. My deputies share all rewards that we collect."

"I think I want to help you more."

"It ain't always that easy to find folks, nor do they give up so easy every time."

"I still want to be on your team," Shawn repeated.

"We'll see how that goes."

He persisted. "Will you really consider me as one of your team?"

"I said I would think on it, but yes, I think we could do that."

"Great. And I can sure help drive the horses home."

"Sheila, it's suppertime. Let's lead these tough *pistoleros* of mine to supper downstairs."

She took his arm and they went down to dine.

"I don't really like to even think about living in a city," Sheila said as they descended the stairs.

"I agree. I'd miss the coyotes howling too much."

"I might not miss them, but I would miss breathing clean air and not being hobbled by traffic in the street. Do you have any other nice cowboys on your ranch?"

"Maybe you can come to the house and go to the dance at Camp Verde some Saturday night, and look them over for yourself. Marge would love to take you with us."

"That would be a big treat for me. I can dance some." Her smile was sweet and Chet felt certain her brother being at her rescue put her more at ease with his bunch. After she testified to the grand jury, they could go home until she needed to return for the trial.

Over supper, they went over their plans for the trip home. Early in the morning, Shawn and Cole would set out with the horses for the drive north. Chet, Sheila, and Jesus would catch the stagecoach to Hayden's Ferry, which would take a day and a half. Then they'd take the Black Canyon Stageline to Preskitt, and be home.

He'd already notified Marge they were fine and in Tucson. Now he could wire her from the ferry to tell her he'd be home on the stage in two or so days, and for her to send word to the McElroys he was bringing Sheila.

They left Tucson for Papago Wells, then went on the ferry, arriving in late afternoon in time to catch the northbound stage, and with time enough for him to send his last telegram. When he came back across the street, Sheila and Jesus were in the coach. The gravel-voiced driver said, "We like to left yuh here."

"Frog, I'd sue you for all you're worth if you'd done that."

"Huh, all you'd get is a half chaw of 'baccy, two swallows in a whiskey bottle I got at home, and my old worn-out pair of overalls. They have to bury me in these good'uns."

Amused, Chet shook his head. "After all that, you ain't worth suing. Get up there and earn your keep."

"By doggies, I can do that. Nice to have you, too, young lady, you brighten up this whole coach."

"Don't laugh," Chet told her. "It only encourages him some more."

The side lamps were on as the stage swayed from side to side going down to the ferry. Impatient horse hooves pounded on the hollow barge and they crossed the Salt. He slumped down in the seat beside Sheila to try to sleep. He had lots of that to catch up on. He'd need to retrieve his jacket before this night was over. Farther on, he'd freeze to death without it.

When they changed horses at New River, he opened his war bag from the back storage, got his jacket out, then pulled the drawstring tight and reloaded it. Right away he felt warmth surge through his body. He smiled and helped Sheila back in the stage. "We will get there before this night is over," he assured her.

"How will I ever repay you for all you've done for me?"

"Just live your life with your head high and savor every day. That'll make me proud."

"I will. Thank you."

He wished the canvas covers on the windows fit tighter. The cold night air leaked around them, and the higher they climbed into the mountains the colder it became.

Jesus's soft snoring told them he was asleep, but they continued to talk.

"I'm going to try to not be too nosy," she said. "But how did you meet your wife?"

"On this stagecoach, when my nephew and I came up here to look for a ranch."

"Did you fall in love right away?"

"I didn't. At the time, I didn't consider myself free, because of a lady in Texas. I told Marge that."

Sheila smiled. "She never gave up getting you, though, did she?"

He smiled at the memory. "No, and when stage robbers murdered my nephew, she helped me get through it. Mighty tough days those."

"But you went back to Texas after that?"

"I did, and never promised her a thing. Turned out the Texas lady couldn't leave her elderly parents. We parted friends, so I came back still single." He chuckled. "When I wanted to take Marge on a camping trip on the Rim, my sister told me Marge had gone to a finishing school and would never go with me. Well, she was wrong. Marge agreed to go. But then I went to worrying about folks talking about her, so we wound up going camping all right, but it was our honeymoon."

"Have you ever regretted it?"

"No, ma'am. We have a great life together. When I'm gone, she worries a lot 'cause she lost two husbands before me. But I'm very grateful to have her."

"Sounds like a fairy tale come true." A soft sigh escaped her lips.

"It was that."

"Maybe some handsome prince will find me some day."

"Oh, I'm certain he will."

"I'll keep my hopes up, but now I'll have a tainted background."

"Don't ever think that. You're still the same as you were before this happened. Don't let yourself fall into a case of self-pity."

"You give good advice. Thanks so much."

"Meantime, I know your mother and father will be excited you're coming home safe."

They arrived in Preskitt in a light snow. As soon as he helped her down from the stagecoach, her mother was there hugging her. Jesus gathered their gear and put them in the waiting buckboard. Sheila's entire family was waiting, and her father about wrung Chet's hand off thanking him—and tried to pay him.

"You can pay Cole, Jesus, and your son. Shawn and Cole are bringing the horses and will be here in a few days."

"What else can I do for you?"

"Hug that girl. She's been through some tough days. She'll be fine, but she needs lots of love."

"Count on that. We love all our kids." He paused and ran a hand over his whiskers. "You know, people spin yarns about you. Some aren't true, and the next time I hear someone telling one of them, I'll knock his block off. You had—"

"Excuse me, my wife is here."

"Tell her thanks from all of us for letting you go find our Sheila."

"I will." He turned and caught Marge in his arms and kissed her. "You all right?"

"Wonderful since you've come home to me."

"Oh, Mrs. Byrnes." It was Sheila's mother wanting to hug her.

He stepped aside and both Sheila and her mother hugged Marge. While light snowflakes fell in the starlit night, tears streamed down their faces.

"Oh, thank you so much. No one else would have ever found her. Your husband's a treasure. We know it's hard on you to be apart from him, but we do appreciate him finding her."

"He's part yours, too," Marge said. "He's very generous with foks."

"Oh, Marge, I was so afraid I'd never see her again."

"I know how you must have felt."

The younger McElroy, Kevin, was there to shake hands with both Chet and Jesus. "Did Shawn help you get her back?" he asked.

"Big help. Cole, Jesus, and Shawn did a great job helping to arrest them."

"You going to hire him?"

"I'd consider it, if I ever needed a good man." Chet wondered what they were getting at, but nothing else was said. He hustled his wife to their buckboard and nodded to Jiminez, her driver.

"Let's go home."

Jesus hopped aboard just as Jiminez popped the reins at the team.

"Is Sheila all right?" Marge asked in a low voice.

"Yes, they didn't molest her. They planned to sell her to this big hacienda owner as a virgin. So, besides thinking all the time that she'd end up some slave mistress, she's fine."

"Oh, my. What were they going to sell her for?"

"Several thousand is the amount I heard."

"Did they shoot at you?"

"No."

"You surprised them?"

"That we did."

She twisted sideways in order to reach over and kiss him. "Glad you're home in one piece."

At home, bathed, shaved, and in bed, he felt a great letdown, so he reached for his wife and drew her to him. "Good night," he whispered.

"It is. I have you safe at home."

CHAPTER 17

By dawn, Chet was up, dressed, and in the kitchen drinking coffee with Monica.

"What kinda trouble are you looking for today?" she asked.

"Are there any mice in the house?"

"No, I have a cat who stays around the house and gets them."

"El Gato gets them all?"

"He's neutered, so he don't chase females."

"I've seen him a time or two."

"What else worries you?" She got up to peer in the oven, then sat back down.

"How are my ranches being run?"

"As good as if you were there. They know what to do and they do it. So you can go on another wild goose chase."

"Getting that girl back home wasn't a goose chase."

"No, but if that family had any sense they could have trailed them to the border and jumped those *bastardos* themselves."

"In other words, you think I can be replaced."

"If I find someone can do that, I'll send him to you. I'm looking hard, so she doesn't panic every time you leave."

"Oh, she doesn't panic that much."

"You don't have to live with her when you're gone." She slid his plate in front of him.

He sure couldn't solve this impasse with her. He'd better eat his eggs, potatoes, biscuits, and gravy, and shut up. And go see if those horses had ever arrived.

Jiminez saddled him a horse and he rode off for town by himself. Jesus needed some rest, so he let him sleep. His other men were coming with the horses. He only needed to check on things in town. Then see if the horses Rose was bringing from California had arrived.

He stopped and drank coffee with Jenn. Valerie asked him about Cole.

"He's fine. Bringing our horses back. He'll be here in a few days."

"Good," she said, and nodded, smuglike. "We've been talking. He's a pretty swell guy."

"I think so."

She winked at him and disappeared toward the kitchen.

"You think she's got a winner?" Jenn asked when she was out of sight.

"He walks on his boot soles. Been a bachelor a long enough time."

"I guess she could do worse."

"Lots worse."

"I got the word, your nephew ran away again?"

"JD can do what he wants. But, yeah, he left his brother up there on top."

"What ails him?"

"That I can't imagine, nor can I nail his foot to the floor."

"Oh, I know. Young people get so restless. I learned that the hard way."

"How is Bonnie?"

"She's still here. But I'm afraid her life is too boring. Same disease as JD has, I think."

"I was so damn busy holding our ranch together, I never had a chance to be bored."

"She worries me, like he does you. But I don't know anything else I can do for her."

"There are those like Reg who lost a wife and picked up the pieces. JD's different. But any way I can help, let me know."

"Mister Byrnes! Mister Byrnes!" A boy raced into the café. "They said you were in town. I have a telegram for you from the Marshal in Tucson."

"Here, let me read it." The message covered two sheets, so Chet unfolded them and began reading.

DEPUTY BYRNES
I'M THE NEW CHIEF US MARSHAL FOR ARIZONA
TERRITORY. I UNDERSTAND YOU WERE HERE A FEW
DAYS AGO AND I MISSED YOU. MARSHAL BAILEY
RESIGNED WHEN HE RETURNED, THEN I TOOK
OVER. I FOUND WE'RE HAVING MANY RAIDS ON
RANCHES BY MEXICAN BANDITS OUT OF SONORA.
SINCE THE NEW RULES CAME DOWN FROM

CONGRESS, THE US ARMY CAN NO LONGER INVOLVE
THEMSELVES IN LAW ENFORCEMENT. SO THESE
OUTLAWS ARE RUNNING WITH A FREE REIN IN
THE SOUTH HALF OF THE TERRITORY. SHERIFFS
ARE SEPARATED BY COUNTY LINES AND THESE
CRIMINALS DON'T KNOW WHERE THAT IS. BAILEY
TOLD ME YOU HAD DONE GREAT WORK FOR HIM
IN THE PAST. CAN YOU RAISE A GROUP OF MEN
TO STOP THIS CRIMINAL ACTIVITY, ONCE AND
FOR ALL? I REALIZE YOU HAVE RANCHES TO RUN
AND OTHER OBLIGATIONS, BUT YOUR SUCCESS AT
APPREHENDING CRIMINALS IS WELL KNOWN. MOST
OF MY OTHER MEN ARE WHAT YOU'D CALL OFFICE
DEPUTIES. IF YOU CAN BRING A HALF DOZEN OF
YOUR CHOICE OF MEN TO TUCSON AND BEGIN I
HAVE FUNDS TO COVER YOUR EXPENSES, AND YOU
CAN HELP ME MAKE ARIZONA TERRITORY A SAFE
PLACE FOR ALL.
HOWARD BLEVINS, CHIEF US MARSHAL, ARIZONA
TERRITORY, TUCSON, ARIZONA.

"Man, he wrote you a book," Jenn said. "You have
an answer for him?"

"I'm going to answer him." Chet leaned over and
lowered his voice. "He wants a law enforcement
patrol to clean up the bandits in south Arizona."

"He knew who to call on," she said, nodding her
approval.

She turned to Valerie who'd returned when the
boy came in. "Get Chet some paper."

The girl brought two sheets and a pencil. "Enough?"

"Plenty."

He put pencil to paper, but didn't need all the space the Marshal had used.

Marshal Blevins
  I'm not sure if I can manage my business and do as you request. You will have my answer in three days.

Chet Byrnes

He gave the boy from the telegraph office two dimes, one to send the message, and the other a tip.

"Thank you, sir," the boy said, and raced off.

"Who will help you?" Jenn asked, a frown wrinkling her forehead.

"That's what I need to decide, as well as tell my pregnant wife what's happenng." He shook his head. "That may be even harder."

"I can't help you there. Good luck, brother. I'm rooting for you."

He went by the livery to check with Frye about the horses Rose was supposed to bring.

"I may be gone for a while. Tom, at the Verde Ranch, knows horses and what I'll need. When they get here, send word to him."

Frye frowned at him. "Where're you going?"

"Can't say. Government business. All right?"

"Sure, I won't tell a word. Be careful. Folks around here count on you."

Lots do. Some more than others. He better go home and talk to Marge.

She read the telegram through. "Where are those Rangers the legislature voted for?"

"They had no money to fund them."

"Well, that is sure stupid." She dropped her hands and the paper in her lap. "I know you can handle this, but I'll sure miss you. I promise not to cry on Monica's shoulder when you're gone. You have to be extra careful. This baby and I will need you. Who will you take with you?"

"If they will go, Jesus and Cole first. Then, I'd like to borrow Roamer, if he'll still have his job here when he gets back. Then, Shawn McElroy, he's a good capable young man."

She agreed with his choices. "Who else?"

"I'd love to be able to take Hampt. When it comes down to it, he's the toughest guy."

She shook her head. "You need him at that place and May needs him."

"I know, and Reg would be my choice, too, but he's in the same situation. I can find another. I'd even like to take JD, wherever he's at. He handled himself well in Tombstone. I'll find someone."

"Jesus was upset you left him behind to sleep. I told him you wouldn't get into much in Preskitt, or he'd of rode in there. He asked if there was a letter for him, but there wasn't. Do you think his girlfriend gave up waiting for him?"

"I don't know much about it. He said he'd write her one more time."

"I hope that works out for him." She sighed. "I know you need to go. You live on challenges and do a great job. I couldn't be prouder. I accept that you have a job to do, so you make your plans—whatever."

"I love you, Marge Byrnes. God gave me a beautiful wife and a future baby. I treasure both of you. But we do need to make this territory a safe place to live. I have many things to do before I leave, but I'll attend to that tomorrow. Let's go to bed."

"Yes, and do something cheerful for a change."

Arms entwined, they went off to their bedroom laughing and teasing each other about lighter matters.

CHAPTER 18

The next morning, while Monica fixed them pancakes and fried ham, he and Jesus talked over coffee in the kitchen. After she put their plates in front of them, she told them the coffeepot was on the stove and left the room.

"No letter from your girl, huh?" Chet asked.

"No letter. I don't know why. But it has been two years since I told her I would make us a place up here."

"Did you write her other letters?"

"I did, but maybe my letters discouraged her. I was only a stable hand then. I will wait a while longer. Thank you for your concern. Did you want to talk to me?"

"Yes. There are lots of bandits on the border that come up and raid in Arizona and then go back. The Army can't stop them. The new head Marshal in Tucson wants us to stop them."

"The three of us?" Jesus frowned.

"No, six men. I wanted to ask you and Cole first."

"Oh, we will help you. I know how he thinks."

"Still, I'll ask him."

"Yes, you should do that. Who else?"

"I think Shawn McElroy will make a good team member."

Jesus was quick to respond. "Yes, he is very calm, and quick thinking, too."

"Roamer. If I can get Simms to hold his job for him until we finish."

"A good man."

"Yes, but I need two more."

Jesus held the coffee cup in both hands. "They have to get along with the rest of us, yes?"

"Otherwise, we'll damn sure get tired of each other."

His words made Jesus laugh. With a shake of his head, he said, "That rules out some I know who might be tough enough."

"You think of any one special, tell me. I trust your judgment to find men we can work with."

"I will do that, Chet."

"You and I are going down and talk to Tom today. The other two should be back when we return late tonight. We need to choose the best horses and have them shod. You tell Marge what you need to feed us and fill the panniers."

"For that many, we will need four packhorses."

"Right. When you finish your coffee, get us some horses saddled and we'll head for the Verde."

Jesus drained his cup and set it on the table. "Will you ride one of the roans?"

"Yes."

"I will be sure he is shod today, and I will ride the big bay they call Tally."

"He's a stout horse."

"*Sí*. We will meet out front in a short while?"

"After I tell my wife good-bye, I'll be out."

Hurrying upstairs to their bedroom, he decided it wasn't nearly as cold as yesterday. He found Marge sitting on their bed in a robe, brushing her hair.

"I'm off to speak to Tom." He bent over and kissed her.

"Are all expectant mothers this sleepy?"

"Darling, I have no idea. You're the first one I've ever had."

"You haven't even been around a woman expecting, have you?"

"Only May, before she had Donna. And she wasn't mine. My brother pretty much ignored her."

"Well." She popped up. "I'm glad you don't ignore me."

"Send word to Hampt today to come over tonight, if he can, so I can explain this business to him. May can bring the kids, too, and spend the night."

"Boy, this house will rock with Ray and Ty and their little sister."

"I'll try to be back by supper, but probably later."

"More than likely," she teased.

He kissed her and left.

He and Jesus pushed their horses hard and reached the Verde Ranch by midmorning. They stopped at the big house, and Sarge came out putting on a coat. Chet sent Jesus to find Tom.

"Well, how is the cattle-driving business going?" Chet asked.

"It's so simple, I'm afraid I've left something out. No renegade Indians. No stampedes and no weather holdups. I'm going back up to Windmill with the new cattle tomorrow. In case of bad weather, we'll set out for New Mexico the next day."

"Have you seen my building crew yet?"

"Susie got a letter from Lucie. She says they're coming down when some of the snow melts."

By this time, Susie had joined them, and he hugged her.

"Get your cold self inside. Coffee's on," Susie said, and herded them into the warm house.

When they were settled, he asked her, "What else do you know?"

"JD is back up there and is coming down here any day."

Chet wondered if he would make a team member or not. He'd have to see. At this point, he didn't want to weigh the good versus bad of picking him. So he put off thinking about it—almost.

"You act in a hurry. Is something wrong?" Sarge asked.

"There's a new US Marshal in Tucson. He's asked me to put together a group of men and stop the raiding by Mexican bandits in southern Arizona."

"Doesn't he know you have several ranches to run?" Susie asked.

"He knows. And he asked for my reply."

"What will you tell him?"

"I'll decide that later."

"Tom's here," Sarge said, and let him inside.

"I'll get coffee." Susie excused herself and went to the kitchen.

After the three shook hands, they sat down at her big oak dining table. Chet handed Tom the telegram to read.

He frowned at the two pages. "Why, he sent you a whole letter." After he read it, he looked up. "That sounds like a Texas Ranger job to me. Didn't they vote for Rangers?"

Chet nodded. "Yes, but the Legislature never allocated any money for them."

"Sheriffs like their tax collector job too well. And no wonder. They get ten percent of it."

"Nothing to rock their job, huh?" Sarge asked.

"Exactly. Tom, can you and your men manage all this for as long as three months, with me gone?"

"Sure, no problem. I'm getting ready to hire a farm crew for here. You said we could plant twenty acres of field corn this year. Are the draft horses coming?"

"Frye says that California bunch are bringing them. I want you and whoever to choose enough teams for all four places."

"I have some I'm hauling hay with, but I'll need two more pair," Sarge said.

"The mowers, rakes, and beaver board hardware are coming for you, Hampt, and Reg. Tom has his old equipment and John has them repaired. Raphael has two farmers make his hay, and that works for now. One of those machinery setups is at my top place—Ivor repossessed it from Kay. We can send it, I guess, to Reg so he can put it together. Two mowers, two rakes, and a hay sweep. He has some wagons, but, Tom, you check on what he needs. I'll meet with Hampt tonight."

Tom nodded. "We can handle it smooth. I guess you're going ahead and do this?"

Chet nodded. "Sounds like something needs to be done. If we're ever going to become a state, we need these outlaws handled."

"I don't envy you at all." Tom shook his head as if he thought it would be a real tough job.

"I still need two more men. If JD shows, I'll ask him, if he really wants to go. I have no idea about his answer. So far, I'm going to ask Roamer, Cole, and Jesus, plus Shawn McElroy who rode with us to get his sister back. If he doesn't want to go, I'll need one or two more."

"Shame Hampt Tate can't go," Sarge said. "He's the best fighting man I know, besides you. He's tough and a good shot, too."

"May would kill me, and who would run that place?"

"And we may get the Rankin place thrown in on him, too," said Tom.

"Yes, there's that, too," agreed Chet.

"Hey, I want to check on those cattle we have bunched to go up to Windmill. I don't want any crippled ones." Sarge grabbed his hat and headed outside.

"Be careful," Chet called after him. "No life is worth risking herding them. We're doing great, even as slow as the government is paying us."

Sarge turned at the door. "I will. You be careful, too. The four of us sure need you to keep this place together."

"Oh, I will."

Then he and Tom discussed everything from payroll and labor needs to the cost of farming and buying more British breed bulls. Their Hereford yearling bulls they'd have coming in the spring were not, in Tom's words, going to be strong enough to turn out on the open range. They'd be better, Tom suggested, holding them off till the next year and buying some older bulls.

"Then you better start looking for them now. They will be high-priced and hard to find."

"I'll start doing that."

"That rounds this up then. I think we've covered everything."

"Looks like it." Tom stood, ready to leave.

"Hey, I have lunch about ready. Where's Jesus?" Susie asked from the kitchen door. "I know my husband went to check cattle, but I can feed him later."

"I'll send Jesus back here, and thanks, but I'll eat with Millie," Tom said, and excused himself.

"Tell her hello. With Sarge here, I don't get much chance to talk to her."

Tom winked at her. "I understand." Then he left with her scowling after him.

Chet laughed, but quickly smothered it when Susie turned to glare at him.

After lunch, he and Jesus rode back to the upper ranch. They were home before sundown and Hampt's unhitched two-seated buckboard was already parked by the house.

The big man came outside and joined Chet at the hitch rail, shook Jesus's hand, and exchanged greetings. Jesus took their two horses toward the barn.

"Any sign of Cole?" Chet asked Jiminez who had also come to claim the horses.

"Not yet, *señor.*"

"They're coming, I'm sure." He turned back to Hampt. "They'll be here by dark, I bet."

"They probably will," the big man said. "Marge told me about the Marshal asking you to take on those border bandits. Damn, I wish I was free to go along, but I've got so many irons in the fire. Fencing is slow, but it's bull tight. I have thirty some acres ready to seed to alfalfa and barley for a nurse crop. Hay feeding. And all the rest, but I just hate you going off and me not riding with you."

"Add three kids and a pregnant wife, looking for number four."

"I never thought I'd get to be a dad to anyone. See, my mother raised me. He got killed in a drunken gunfight when I was little. Oh, I had some dads, but they weren't like a real one—uncles and cousins tried to fit in—but not someone to talk to me like I talk to them two boys. And they tell me some tall stories about their uncle Chet."

"In Texas, them boys trailed me around asking questions."

"Yeah, they do the same to me, but, damn, I'm proud they accepted me."

"I'd sure like to have you, but I knew you couldn't go. I have some good boys. I want Roamer to go, but I need Simms to hold his job till he returns."

"No telling how that will come out, but if he thinks you will be out of here, he might promise anything."

"That's true. I got word that JD is back at Reg's and may be coming down."

"He's been a worry, hasn't he?"

"He may want to go along. I'm unsure about it, but, in the end I'll have to decide."

Hampt nodded. "Just remember, if you ever need me, send word and I'll be there for whatever you need done."

"I appreciate your saying that, though I always know that. But Tom and I count on you. You're doing a great job as ranch foreman. And your marriage to May has been a song in our hearts."

"I ever tell you I come home one day, tired as dirt, and she was singing and never heard me come in." Hampt smiled, remembering. "She about swallowed her tongue. I said, 'Girl, sing like that to me,' and kissed her. And she did."

"A miracle. Susie and I never heard her sing one note in all those years she was married to my brother."

"You told me once you thought he only married her to take care of his three kids. But she's never complained once about him. We have a good fun life together, and she's an angel to me. I'm so glad God sent her to me."

"I am, too, pard. If I'm ever going to be gone off to the Mexico border, we better go inside and talk about ranching."

"Chet, we've all been put on this earth to do a job. When you came here, I was so glad to be back cowboying. I thought my life couldn't get any better. Next, I got up my nerve with May and, holy cow, that worked. Then this job running the ranch. Those kids, and now one of my own coming. Great life, every day."

"I have one, too. We're both lucky."

About then, the boys ran over to hug Chet, with sister right behind. He swung Donna up and kissed her. "You all right?"

"Yes, the boys take care of me," she said.

"They're doing a great job." He set her down and hugged May. "How are you, sister?"

She smiled up at him. "You've never called me that before."

"Well, I always thought of you as my sister."

She hugged him tight and buried her face in his shirtfront. "I love it. I love it. Oh, I will worry about you being down there. He'll be worse for not getting to go along. But I can't run that ranch, not carrying him." She stepped back and pointed at her round belly.

"I understand. I count on you two. I told Marge that when all hell breaks loose I'd rather have Hampt with me than anyone I know."

"How long will it take you to do the job?" she asked.

"If I knew that I'd be the smartest man in the world."

"I think you are." Then she blushed.

After supper, an exhausted Cole and Shawn rode in with the horses. Marge fixed them supper and told Shawn he could sleep in the house or the bunkhouse. He chose the latter and thanked her.

When they finished eating, the room was cleared and the men left by themselves to talk. Chet explained the border problem and the Marshal's request. The two of them agreed they'd like to join him.

"How many days do I have before we leave?" Cole asked.

"Maybe two or three. Why?"

"I want to marry Valerie and have a couple of days with her before we go."

"When are you going to marry her?"

"Tonight or tomorrow. Can I have two days and catch you?"

Chet shook his head at the young man's situation. "You can marry her, but you may be gone for a while."

"No problem. I made up my mind coming home

that if I don't marry her now, I may never get another chance."

"The boiler is on, Cole," Marge interjected from the open doorway. "You can go upstairs when you're ready and take a bath. I have some of Chet's clothes ironed that will fit you. Leave yours and we'll wash them. Are you sure she'll marry you?"

"Yes, ma'am. We've talked enough about it."

"Don't break your neck, but you can take our buckboard. Get a room at the Brown Hotel, and eat at Jenn's. Chet will pay for it. Now, Chet, show him the bath."

"I—I don't know what to say," Cole sputtered, looking flabbergasted.

"Say, 'will you marry me' to her," Marge said.

Cole fell back in his chair. "I know that."

They all laughed and sent Cole off to bathe and shave.

"Who will marry them this time of night?" Marge asked.

"Marrying Sam," Chet said. "He don't care what time it is, as long as you have two dollars."

"Oh, my, we could have saved some money doing that," Marge said.

In thirty minutes, Cole was on his way to town. They waved him on his way, and hoped he didn't fall asleep and out of the buckboard.

The kids were in bed and Hampt and Chet sat in

leather chairs before the fireplace. Logs crackled in the fire and spewed sparks that blazed in arches.

"We've all come a long way," Hampt said. "In my darkest hour, you came with a job for us ex-hands. Poor old Hoot, he broke the ice back then when he called us all up here so we could take this big place away from Ryan and his outlaws."

"Man, oh, man. I wondered if I'd ever get this ranch straightened out, even after they sent him to prison." Chet wagged his head, thinking about all the problems they'd overcome.

"You and that boy, Heck, went clear to Hackberry and got him."

"I guess I'll wonder the rest of my life what Heck would have grown into."

Hampt agreed. "We was proud of him making a real hand. He sure cowboyed up fast working cattle with us."

"One of my big mistakes."

"Hell, no, it wasn't. Lady Luck shifted cards on you."

"Thanks, Hampt, but I'll always labor over Heck's death."

"Listen, boss man, we can't do everything right in our life. But being sincere is important. In that case, you did all you could."

Chet hated even thinking about the loss of his nephew. "Tell me about your alfalfa planting."

"I've talked to three different ranchers that have successfully planted it. You need a grain nurse crop.

Sow it less than a crop for grain, but still it's needed to protect the alfalfa coming in. You need some kinda dust to treat the alfalfa seed. They sell it, too. I have it all ordered from Ivor, along with my seed. If I can get as good a stand as those three have, I'll whoop my head off."

"You're going to have quite a bit of that acreage wise."

"Yes, but the cattle really shine when we feed it to them."

"Barbed wire and alfalfa. Folks will soon begin to think you're a farmer."

"Call me what they want. I'm going to make that place as good as the Verde Ranch."

"You will, Hampt." Chet smiled at the pride the man showed.

"May says we will."

"Tom's going looking for more bulls with some age on them. He's worried the home crop isn't developed enough to take the range conditions."

"We'll need them. And ten years from now, we won't have any Longhorns left."

Chet shook his head. "I never believed that, but it's going to be that fast."

"Hell, all the folks had in Texas were range cattle and they were more like deer than cattle. No one thought about crossing them."

"You're right. But change is coming."

"I know that, boss. That's why I want alfalfa." He paused and held his hands out to the fire. "How bad are these bandits down there?"

"I don't know, but this new US Marshal wants them mopped up."

Hampt nodded, elbows on knees. "He picked the right man to do it."

Chet wished he felt that certain.

CHAPTER 19

When they woke up in the predawn, Marge stretched and asked, "Where will they live?"

"Who live?" Chet asked, rising to dress in the lamplight.

"Cole and his bride."

"I guess they'll have to rent a place in town. Cole has his savings."

"We better go find them one and a batching outfit."

"I don't know that she married him last night."

"If they took a room at the Brown Hotel, we'll know."

"No, Jenn will know."

"Sure, she lives with her. Hurry and finish dressing. We have lots to do today. You going to ask Simms today about loaning Roamer and not lose your temper?"

"That won't be easy, but, yes, I intend to see him."

"I'll be downstairs in a few minutes. We'll have to take the old buckboard. Cole has ours."

"Bring a warm robe to cover you. It won't be summertime out there."

"Yes, I will."

He looked up at her curt answer. "I only say such things because I worry about you."

She rushed over and kissed his cheek. "I try not to be resentful."

"Other words, you don't take advice easy."

Trying to suppress her amusement, she said, "Oh, I went to finishing school."

"Yeah, Susie warned me."

"I think that was so funny, her saying because of that I wouldn't go camping with you. I'd of done anything to be in your hip pocket. You were hard to convince that you needed me."

"Lucky I saw the light."

Buttoning the front of her dress, she looked up at him and smiled. "I'm the lucky one."

"We both are. I'm going down and see about Monica. Then fix the fireplaces, if she hasn't beat me to it."

He hurried downstairs and saw the fireplaces were filled before he found her cooking breakfast. "Well, we're up."

"I saw the light on up there and knew you'd be scurrying around this morning." Hands covered in flour, she kneaded biscuits on the table. While she cut them with a shot glass, she shook her head at him. "There sure aren't any simple quiet days around here anymore."

"You heard we sent Cole off to get married?"

"There'll be another woman that will miss her man," Monica said, shaking her head.

Hampt was up by then and his threesome came tailing him into the kitchen.

"Did you sleep good, boys and girl?" Chet asked them.

"No," Donna said. "Their feet were cold on me."

Everyone was still laughing when May and Marge arrived to help finish setting the table.

"Monica says we're too busy," he said.

"We all are busier, I think, than we ever were in Texas," May said. "But we have lots more to say grace over out here—and I like it lots better."

"You said it, May. Thanks." Chet hugged her tight.

"And I never would have said a word in Texas, either."

"That's improved, too."

"That day we packed it all up and had the auction, I wanted to cry. I wondered if I'd even fit in this outfit any longer with him and Heck both gone. But it turned out so much better than I ever imagined."

"May, you blossomed in Arizona." Marge smiled at her.

"Look at me. I sure did." She indicated her growing belly and they all laughed about her increasing size.

The team they drove to town wasn't as good as the one Cole had taken. Hampt and his tribe had gone home. The two boys were outriding for him, while he drove the buckboard. What an outfit.

They made it to Jenn's first, and he helped Marge

off and they went inside. Jenn met them talking. "I hope you two got some sleep. I sure didn't. That pesky pair got married about midnight, and by the time we got through celebrating it was three a.m. and I had to open at five."

Marge hugged her. "Did they look happy?"

"Happy as they could be. Yes, I think they were excited and lost at the same time. They're at the Brown and may not come out until he needs to leave with you. He said that you all were leaving again in a few days and he wanted to get married first."

"Can we rent a small house for them and get her set up, so she has a place to live while he's gone?"

"Yes. There's one near me for rent for seven-fifty a month. It needs some paint and a window fixed, but she can stay with Bonnie and me until we get that done."

"Will she like it?" Chet asked.

"She'll be bowled over by it."

"Make the arrangements for it then. I need to go see Simms and act peaceful. I'd like for Roamer to go with us."

"We can handle all that," Marge said, hugging his arm. "You go ahead, but remember your temper."

"As she said, ahead," Jenn said. "Marge and I can handle the rest."

He left and drove to the courthouse. The deputy on the desk looked up in shock. "You got more prisoners?"

"No, I need to talk to Sheriff Simms. Is he in?"

The deputy went to the office door. "Mr. Byrnes is here to see you."

"Show him in," Simms said, and met him with a handshake. "Have a seat."

"I came to see you about a favor. US Marshal Howard Blevins wants me to form a task force and try to stop the Mexican bandits from invading southern Arizona."

"He's the new head man down there, isn't he?"

"Yes. We've never met, but he telegraphed me. I'd like to borrow Deputy Roamer to ride with us, but if he does, when it's over, I want him to have his job back here with you."

"For how long?"

"Six weeks to three months. I don't know for sure, but it could be lengthy."

"I don't see why not."

"Thanks. I'll go talk to him about going along."

"When are you leaving?"

"Within a week."

Simms nodded. "Talk to him. Tell him I'll keep his place open. He may not want to come back after you finish the job."

"I'm sure he will."

"I hope you succeed. There's a vast number of those bandits down there. And I understand they're treacherous."

"I know it won't be any picnic. Thank you."

"Tell the new marshal I'd like to meet him."

"Oh, I'm sure he'll spread out." Obvious the new

Chief Marshal hadn't talked to Simms about the bandit problem.

He left the sheriff's office and went by Frye's livery to see if Roamer was there. He found him and they hunkered down on their heels in the midmorning sun outside the barn, the warming sun shining on them.

"I'm forming a task force for the new US Marshal in Tucson, to try to stop the Mexican raids on the small ranches and outposts on this side of the border. I went on my best behavior and spoke to your boss about borrowing you."

"What did he say?' Roamer twisted his handlebar mustache.

"He said I could have you and he'd keep your job open. Now, we may be gone for months. I don't know how that plays in your life and family?"

"As long as I get paid, my wife and kids will be fine."

"So, you'll go?"

"Hey, I'd rather ride with you than any man living. Who else is going?"

"Cole Emerson, Jesus Martinez, Shawn McElroy, you and I, right now. They say my nephew JD is coming back, and he may join us."

"I know all of them but the McElroy boy." He shifted on his boot heels. "What are your plans?"

"Take four packhorses, and move like lightning to cut them off."

"It might work. We should get lots done anyway."

"If we once get started putting fear in their hearts, they may quit or taper off."

"I like that lightning idea. What else?"

"I can advance you two months' pay right now. And you men will be paid a dollar a day."

"That'll make my wife happy. Send word when you plan to haul out. I'll be packed and ready."

Chet handed him sixty dollars. They stood up and shook hands, then parted.

He went to see Bo next. Busy behind a pile of papers, his land man looked up. "What brings you to town?"

"I'm headed out in the next week to run a task force against the border bandits. I may be gone for a few months. Marge can get hold of me, if you need me. And that about the task force don't need to be told to anyone."

Bo nodded agreement and shuffled some papers around. "There's no news on the Rankin place. It's still in limbo."

"Fine. We can settle on it whenever it happens."

"How are the other ranches doing?"

"Great. When the government finally does pay, it pays well for our delivered cattle. That's what counts."

"Where are your peace keepers today?"

"One got married last night. The other is home, shoeing horses for the trip."

"Keep your fool head down. I need your business."

"How's Jane?"

"A mean witch."

"Liar."

"You defend her. She bites me."

"Tell her I said hello."

When he left Bo, he went by to talk to Ben Ivor at the store. The big man stood up behind his cluttered desk. "Hey, how are you? Can I get you something?"

"No, I just came by to check on you."

"I'm doing fine. That lady is all you said she was, and I'm pleased. She said to tell you hello, if I saw you. She's coming in this afternoon and filing these papers. After she gets through here, I may even have an office system."

"No good or bad news about the machinery?"

"Oh, yes. They said they shipped it, so it should be here on time."

"That's great that the machinery will be here in plenty of time before it's needed."

Before Chet left, he explained to Ben about the task force and his future absence, then he went to the bank to see Tanner.

When he walked in, the banker handed him a telegram. "Good news. They're paying three more months of your paper."

Chet grinned. "We'll be in good shape then."

"I think so. Now, we're breathing anyway."

"No, more than that. We're in fine shape. My man, Sarge, says the agency is pleased with our deliveries. If they keep paying for them, then I'll be fine, too."

When he got back to Jenn's, the bleary-eyed married couple were eating their first meal of the day.

"Your wife and Mom are off renting them a new house," Bonnie said.

"How will I ever repay you?" Valerie asked. She looked awfully dreamy eyed.

"By being happy with him."

"Oh, that won't be hard. Marge and Jenn are busy setting me up in housekeeping. I'll be fine there. Plus, I'll still help Bonnie and her mom in here."

"It's been a long time since I put you on a stage and headed you up here."

"The best day in my life." She beamed at him with teary eyes, then turned and brushed a strand of hair from Cole's eyes. "Thanks for him, too."

Cole sat his coffee cup down. "How're things going?"

"Good. Roamer is going along."

"That's good news."

"Yes, things are coming together."

"I don't see how you hold it all together—it's all so much."

"With lots of help."

Cole leaned over and kissed his bride. She blushed and put her arm on his shoulder. "I better get all the attention I can with him leaving this week, huh?" she asked Chet.

"Aw, he won't forget you."

"I sure hope not. But thanks. You all are being real sweet to us."

"My wife and Jenn I can't control."

They laughed and he ordered lunch from Bonnie.

Clouds were gathering when he and Marge drove home in midafternoon. The day was still a warm one. When they drove in, a jaded ranch horse was hitched at the rack in front of the house. The porch door opened and JD, coffee cup in hand, came out to greet them.

The prodigal was back. Chet felt better, for the moment anyway.

CHAPTER 20

"You're looking good," Chet said, and stuck his hand out to shake his nephew's hand.

"Jesus told me Cole married Valerie last night?"

"We've been tending to them today," he said.

"Wow, she is a neat lady. I wasn't being gossipy. It just surprised me."

"No, they were in serious discussions before, and since we have to leave shortly, he went and married her. Dazed, but they look happy."

"Oh, I hope they are. Tell me about this task force business."

"Let's go inside and drink some of Monica's coffee."

Marge hugged JD. "Good to have you home again."

"Yes, ma'am. It's good to be here. They said down at the lower ranch you're good at forecasting weather. Is it going to snow?"

She held up two fingers. "Those clouds are only harbingers."

JD laughed. "What's that word?"

"Means they are forecasting that the storm is coming."

"I'll use that word. It'll impress everyone at the Palace Saloon."

Chet herded them inside. He turned back and saw Jiminez had already come for the team. Chet told him to put up JD's horse, too, that he was staying. They'd eaten supper when Chet showed him the telegram from Marshal Blevins.

When he finished reading it, he looked up at Chet. "I guess you're going to help him?"

"You want to go along?"

"I think so. I'm not doing anything worthwhile and that might be interesting."

"It could be dangerous as hell."

"I know that from living around you all my life." JD laughed. "Thanks for inviting me along."

"Pick you out a stout horse. The two of you are going to be close companions. Get him shod. Get an extra set of clothes. We may be a while looking for the bandits."

"How long do I have to get ready?"

"Three or four days. Then we leave."

"I'll go in town and see about a few things. Be back here in two days. Jesus can pick me a horse. I'll tell him."

"You can stay for supper, if you like," Marge said.

"Naw, I know him. Once he gets ready to go, he goes. Thanks, Chet. I like the sound of this task force business."

After he left, she asked, "Where's he going?"

"Maybe to get married. I don't know."

Marge stopped and squeezed her chin. "You don't think he's going to see Bonnie, do you?"

"Hell, I have no idea. But it won't be unheard of."

"No, you all rescued her, too."

"He was there, so he knows her and her background."

"Did you think he sounded jarred that Cole had married Valerie?"

Chet threw up his hands at his wife's questions. "I haven't seen him in months. Tonight, he's back and ready to go. That's all I know."

"I'm sorry." She crossed the room and hugged him. "I know he's your Achilles' heel."

He frowned at her. "Whatever is that?"

"Oh, it was one spot that would bring down a great Greek warrior in mythology."

"Remember, I only made six grades in a rural Texas schoolhouse. We hadn't gotten to Greeks by then."

"I don't know if they'd ever gotten there." She kissed him on the cheek and put her arms around him. "Well, you have your task force. Jesus, Cole, Roamer, Shawn, and JD. The lightning outfit."

"Now, if we can get the Mexican bandits to respect us, we'll be back home shortly."

"We'll see about that. Just be careful."

"Yes, ma'am." They went to bed. Another day had closed on his preparations to leave again.

* * *

The next morning, Tom was there early. Chet figured he must have left the lower place at four a.m. He rode up while Chet and Marge were still eating breakfast.

"What's wrong?"

"I wasn't sure when you were leaving and wanted to catch you. Leroy, up on Oak Creek, needs a good team to farm with this coming season. He's doing a lot of work up there. There are some local carpenters need work and can build those cabins you wanted. When the roads clear again, Robert can get lumber up there. They have those plans Marge drew up. You ready to start that?"

"Yes," Chet told him. "I've never seen it, but I understand it's nice. Leroy is a good worker. Let's hold construction to about fifteen thousand dollars."

"I'll watch that close."

"And I agree he will need a team of horses. I saw Frye yesterday, but he never mentioned the California horse trader."

Tom smiled. "It is confusing at times, all we have going on. Robert talked to me. He says if the railroad doesn't come soon they may shut down the mill."

"Well, they will close that mill down if the railroad is all holding them there. Bo said the railroad wanted to sell the entire strip of sections that cross Arizona and they aren't even in New Mexico yet."

"You know Robert's married now. He's concerned about his job."

"If the lumber business goes under, we'll make a place for him and his bride. He's done too good a job as manager up there. You don't have to follow him around to get the job done."

"No, he's great to handle things. He'll be relieved to hear you'll have a place for him."

"Who did he marry?" asked Marge.

"You've seen her at the dances," said Chet. "She wears her blond hair on top of her head. She's the farm girl like Susie kept telling me I needed in Texas."

The three of them laughed.

"I have talked to the young lady and she is very nice," Marge said.

"Nothing is wrong with her. It's just a family joke." Thinking it time to change the subject.

"Tom, JD has agreed to join up and go with us on the border trip."

"That's good. Don't worry about anything here. Everything is running smooth. We can handle it. I got word that the building crew is at Windmilll. Susie is excited."

"If the mill closes, Robert and his wife can stay in the big house. We'll need a family to live there."

"JD and his bride may want to live there," Marge said.

"JD? Married?" asked Tom.

"She thinks it's contagious. Cole married one girl and she thinks JD has gone to marry Bonnie."

"Oh."

Strait-laced Tom was probably taken back by the notion of such a union. But it might not mean a thing to JD. Only time would tell.

After Tom left for home, Chet checked to see how

Jesus was coming along with the shoeing. He found him working on one horse and a ranch *vaquero* working on another. He squatted down on his heels in a sunny spot just outside the alleyway to the barn to watch them work.

"JD said he was going along," Jesus offered between shaping a shoe.

"Yes, he's going, so we now have a team."

"He said he had business in town and asked if we had time to shoe this horse he picked out. So he left him. I told him we'd fit it in."

Chet chuckled. JD'd left, leaving Jesus to do all the work. "So you two got all the hard work."

"We have to do something," the *vaquero* they called Espinoza said, then he laughed and went back to shoeing.

"Where was JD going anyway today? He just got here." Jesus looked over at him.

"Marge says she thinks he is going to town to marry Bonnie."

"Two marriages."

"Hell, I don't know anything, but Cole and Valerie looked happy. We saw them in town."

"Two men from the ranch loaded a wagon with firewood to take to a house they're going to live in, on orders from your wife."

"That's for Cole's house."

"He may never come back and sleep in the bunkhouse again," Jesus said to his shoeing partner.

"Not unless she runs him off."

They all laughed.

* * *

Shawn was back the next day to help Jesus fill the panniers and check the pack equipment. No word from JD until noontime. He and Bonnie drove in using Marge's buckboard. The two were kissy-faced and Bonnie wore a brand-new blue dress.

"This here is Mrs. JD Byrnes," he announced, helping her down.

"Well, lunch is being served," Marge said with an I-told-you-so attitude. She led everyone into the dining room, with Chet bringing up the rear.

"Have you seen Cole and Valerie?" he asked.

"Yes, she's working in my place today at the cafe," Bonnie said. "Cole's stacking wood they brought him on their porch."

Chet thought she looked shiny-faced like a bride, and she had her hand on JD's arm. They did remind him of honeymooners. He hoped to God it worked out for them.

"Bonnie plans to live with her mom until we get back."

"We'll find you a house," Chet assured him.

They ate lunch in quiet conversations. Bonnie acted very demure, but she showed her possession several times by squeezing JD's arm. Maybe it would work—no telling. When they were alone, he'd ask his fortune-telling wife.

"Are we going to leave on Thursday?" JD asked.

"No. On Friday. My wife says it will snow Thursday."

Marge smiled high-headed and passed the bowl of corn. "For those who don't know, I'm not right about the weather all the time."

"Hey, we trust you." JD grinned at her.

"You two going to stay here?" Chet asked.

"No, I want to go see Susie. Bonnie doesn't know her very well and I'd like them to meet."

"Who is going to help Jenn?" Marge asked.

"Oh, she has someone for the rest of the week," Bonnie said. "But she couldn't work today. So Valerie filled in. When the men all leave, she'll have us 'till all of you get back."

So JD was married—good or bad. Time would tell. After the meal, the newlyweds drove on to the Verde Ranch.

When the buckboard made a small dust wake going out, his wife asked, "Will they make it?"

"I have no idea. I can only hope so."

The days flew by. Thursday, they had flakes of snow but nothing big. Word was sent out to all the team members that they were leaving at dawn. Marshal Blevins sent a telegram of thanks and said he'd look for them when they could get there. He asked they meet him at a secret site, so not many would know about them. Otherwise, he was concerned word might travel fast.

They met before dawn and headed south on the Black Canyon Stage Route with five loaded pack-horses in the care of Jesus and Shawn. Each had been chosen for their quickness in leading and ability to move fast when called on. A balky packhorse was a pain that neither Chet nor Jesus wanted to contend with. Heads high, they kept the pace or they were left behind.

The day was long in the saddle with not many words shared. The newlyweds were picked on a little, and they quit the road about sundown. They found a water tank off the road a ways and not near any ranches. After the horses were grained and hobbled and firewood snaked in, the others helped Jesus with the cooking. After reheating the precooked beans and beef he'd brought along, he boiled coffee and they ate well. Everyone knew meals were to be quick so they could move on. As the calendar pushed toward spring, the days grew longer and Chet intended to use all the daylight he could to keep moving.

There hadn't been enough moisture for the Salt River to be high, so he planned to avoid the Hayden's Ferry. His plan was to cross east of the irrigated land and stay in the desert and meet few people. They skirted Superstition Mountain and crossed the Gila the day after that. Their arrival at Jesus's relative's farm above Tucson was quiet.

His family welcomed them and put their horses in the corrals. Jesus's aunt fed them supper and breakfast as well, and when Chet paid her she protested, then gave in. He drew a map for his crew to follow around Tucson. They'd split up to meet at a church called San Xavier that belonged to peaceful Indians.

Chet would ride into Tucson to meet with Marshal
Blevins, then join them on the south side.

They left at dawn, right after breakfast. Jesus's
aunt kissed Chet before they left, saying he was too
generous paying for their food. He put the roan
horse down the main road. By eight that morning he
was inside the county courthouse being welcomed by
Blevins.

A tall thin man with lots of mustache, he ushered
Chet into his office, then sent his assistants to gather
the other people for a meeting.

"I'm so pleased you agreed to do this job. Where
are your men?"

"Going in small parties to San Xavier where we'll
meet tonight. I didn't want any talk about a posse.
We avoided Hayden's Ferry and slept in the desert.
I have five tough men and five packhorses. We're
prepared to take them on."

"That's what I needed to hear. We have telegraph
wires strung to Nogales. I can leave word near the
stations where I think you might be. The one to
Lordsburg also goes to Benson, Tombstone, and
Fort Huachuca. That will give us some contact when
a crime is reported so you might be able to cut
them off.

"They've raided several isolated ranches and small
stores. They steal anything loose and usually rape the
women. But mostly they take the ranch horses. It was
blamed a lot on the Apaches. But they're now in the
Madres or on reservations, so we know it isn't them.
These bandits appear as just drifters or men looking

for work. Then, after the crime, they ride like hell for the border on stolen horses with what else they can steal. I don't know how organized they are, but they must be stopped." He checked his pocket watch.

"I've invited some businessmen and the county sheriff. He knows you well from other cases and spoke highly of your services."

Several men soon arrived—bankers, businessmen, and others—and they shook hands all around. A man named Clinton Sharky spoke for them.

"We know you are a busy man, but we hoped you would take the job. After hearing only a part of all you've done to bring law to the territory, we agreed with Marshal Blevins that you are the one man we need. The sheriffs are supposed to report crimes to you that are committed by border bandits. When and where they happen. Some of them won't and will try to handle it themselves. But we want you to bear down on these raiders and end our problem. If you can convince them they can't come up here and steal us blind and get away with it, we'll pay you two thousand dollars plus your expenses. The government will pay your posse members' fees."

"Thank you. We came as secret as we could. If we can get the reports, we'll cut them off. In time, we'll find as many of the sources they use as we can and eliminate them too. Anyone who shelters or aids a felon will be run off, if not arrested. We find anyone doing something illegal, we will arrest them. I have a handful of damn tough men and we haven't lost anyone so far that we've gone after."

"It won't be easy, Byrnes, and we know this, but you're right about anyone giving them comfort being as guilty as they are. By dealing with them, too, it will help put an end to it."

He was glad he'd made that point clear to the group. The men wound the meeting up by saying if he ever needed a large posse they could send him one in short order.

He thanked them and gathered up his maps, ready to go meet his team.

CHAPTER 21

He left the marshal's office with a dozen maps of southern Arizona, plus numerous reports and descriptions of previous crimes and wanted men. Many of the maps were marked with the reported routes used by the border bandits.

Headed south for the San Xavier church, he felt confident of the support from the head marshal and his group.

He found his outfit camped near the mission where they'd found two fat Indian women to feed them. They feasted on delicious beef, flour tortillas, and roasted vegetables. The women were grateful for the money Chet gave them and told him to come back and eat with them again. Chet promised they would return.

The next day they rode to Tubac. Camped on the thin Santa Cruz River nearby, Chet and Roamer went in to check out the cantina in the small village. The place had a low roof, smelled of unwashed bodies, and had flickering candlelight. The *puta* who worked there was at least seven months pregnant and the bartender was a scruffy old man with a white beard.

"New around here, ain't'cha?" the bartender asked.

"No, we've been coming here for years," Chet said. "What do you serve?"

"I got hot piss for beer and bad whiskey. Which one do you want?"

"How bad is the whiskey?"

In a deep bass voice, he said, "Bad stuff."

"They say lots of Mexican bandits come up here and rob people."

The bartender shook his head. "Or they come from Tucson."

"You saying they don't all come from the damn border?" Chet asked.

"Damn right. They live right up there." He pointed his index finger that direction. "You going to drink or talk?"

"Bring the whiskey. You ever been robbed?"

"Do I look like I have? Hell, no. I shoot them coming in the door and drag them outside for the buzzards."

"Done that lately?"

"Not in six months. My name's Charlie. The whiskey is four bucks. I don't give credit."

Chet slapped the money on the table.

"Bring them a bottle of bourbon and two glasses," Charlie said to the *puta*.

She delivered it, shook her boobs at them, and asked if they needed anything else.

Chet told her no, while Roamer used his jackknife to cut the seal on the bottle. Then he splashed some in the glasses. Over at the bar, three lanky *vaqueros* with big rowel spurs on their boots eyed them suspiciously.

After his first swallow, Roamer coughed. "This damn stuff is worse than he said it was."

Chet took a sip and agreed.

The tallest of the three men at the bar came over and took off his sombrero. "You *hombres* don't live around here?"

"We may," Chet said. "You know any good ranches around here for sale?"

"No real good ones, but some are for sale. Would you want to look at them, if I showed them to you?"

"You sell real estate?" Chet asked, and indicated the chair.

"Thank you. Oh, I do anything to make a living that won't get me in trouble."

"You don't work for a ranch?"

"No, my two brothers and I do day work. I figure if I show you a good ranch, maybe you would make me your *Segundo*."

"You have a glass? We have plenty of whiskey left. Tell your *compadres* to come, too."

He told them in Spanish to bring their glasses over and they quickly complied.

"That is Jose and Bronco, and I am Ortega."

"That's Roamer, and I'm Chet."

Jose let Roamer pour two fingers in his former

beer glass. The other one downed his beer, then held his glass out for two fingers with a polite, "*Gracias.*"

"Where are you from?" Ortega asked.

"Texas," Chet said.

"How big a ranch do you need?"

"What size are they?"

"Most are two sections of deeded land and open range."

"One with good water?"

"There are some fine ones on the Santa Cruz River."

"Where will I find you?" Chet asked.

"Upstream a mile." He tossed his head south. "It has a Two Eight Slash brand. You can't miss it. You need any help, call on us."

The other two said, "*Sí.*"

"Nice meeting you."

"We have to go home now or our women will think we are using Lupe, eh?" Amused, Ortega indicated with a head toss the pregnant woman who worked there.

"They might," Chet said. They all chuckled and the three men left.

"Those three look like the real thing. They might make good help," Roamer said.

"They might find me a good ranch."

Roamer frowned at him. 'What would you do with another one?'

"Put JD to work running it. But, yes, they could be hired to help us if necessary. They were like Raphael's help, good workers, I'd bet on it."

"We're going to headquarter here?"

"First, we need some leads. Then find out how they come and go. Then we'll decide where to set up."

"I see where we've got lots to learn down here, ain't we?"

"Exactly. Cork that bottle and let's get back to camp. We split up tomorrow."

They waved good-bye to Charlie and left. Being the middle of the week, there wouldn't be many more customers coming in. Maybe on the weekend there would be more people around. They'd know more by then, too.

When Chet stopped at the telegraph office, a telegram waited for him and he read it right away.

TWO MEN ROBBED A MAN ON KING'S HIGHWAY TEN
MILES SOUTH OF TUCSON. THEY STOLE A HORSE
WITH A TKY BRAND ON RIGHT SHOULDER. BOTH
ARE MEXICANS.
BLEVINS

Out in the sunlight, he looked at the high rising desert mountains around them. The robbers would probably come that way. "Roamer, you stay around here for a while. I bet they're coming down that road."

Roamer nodded. "Makes sense. I can find that place where we're camping later. Tell them boys not to drink all that whiskey. I put the bottle in your saddlebags."

"Bad as it is, they won't. Be careful. Those two may be tough."

"No problem. Either way, see you later."

Back at camp, he told the crew about the telegram and Roamer looking for the robbers.

Jesus brought him supper and a cup of coffee. "Did Roamer get to eat?"

"I think he may have gone back in the cantina to eat something. If not, he'll be here later."

"I'll save him some food, no problem."

"Tomorrow, I want us to split up. We'll go two by two and see what we can find out about the people, places to hide, and how to get them all the way down this corridor to Nogales. Who would you like to go with?"

"Cole. I think we make a good pair, but you're the boss."

"I think so, too. Send JD with Roamer. Shawn can go with me."

"That would work," Jesus agreed.

Halfway through his meal, he heard several horses coming up the canyon where they were camped. He set down his plate and put his hand on the butt of his six-gun. The entire camp bristled with ready arms.

"Don't shoot, boys. I got the TKY-branded horse and two robbers—both drunker than hooter's goat," Roamer shouted. "I've got them handcuffed, and Charlie helped me tie them in the saddle. I couldn't count the money, but there's plenty."

"Shawn, you and Cole count the money."

"Yes, sir."

"We can do that," Cole said. "Blevins is going to think we're pretty sharp, catching our first ones so soon."

"Just lucky. I thought I'd be up all night waiting." Roamer smiled and shook his head.

"Tomorrow morning," Chet said to Roamer, "you and JD send a wire to Marshal Blevins. Have him meet you at the San Xavier church with his men, so they can take the prisoners on to jail. That way, we can lay low and keep out of the papers, I hope."

JD and Roamer had the prisoners shackled to a tree in no time and made them shut up. Jesus and the others put up the horses. Then Jesus fixed Roamer some food.

When they finally bedded down it was past midnight. The outlaws had eight hundred and forty dollars on them, plus the stolen horse, two others, and saddles. No doubt, they might have lost some of the money, but Chet felt they had most of it, mainly because they had no time to spend it.

He gazed up at the stars. One good deed completed. That was a lucky break; the rest would be much harder.

Jesus made breakfast, with a couple of the other men helping, while the rest saddled horses and pack animals. The once-drunk outlaws were moaning and holding their heads. Must have drunk too much of Charlie's bad whiskey.

After breakfast, the prisoners were loaded and handcuffed to their saddles. Roamer led them on their mounts, and JD led the extra stolen horse. He cautioned them that it might take them a day or longer to meet up with the Marshal, then that long to get back. When they returned, he told them, the others might not be there so check with Charlie for a note telling them where the rest of the team had gone.

Roamer and JD left in a high trot. The others hobbled the packhorses that were left to graze. Chet and Shawn went to the Two 8 Slash ranch. The sign hung over the gate entrance and Shawn bounced off his horse to open it.

The place must have some river water rights for cornstalk stubble showed where it had been harvested the past fall. Several chickens clucked about the place and three *jacal*s served as their homes. Each one had clothes hanging to dry on lines.

A few dogs barked at them and curious milk goats bleated at a safe distance. An attractive woman came to the doorway of the first *jacal* with three small children hanging on her skirt.

"*Buenos dias, señor.*" She smiled big at him.

"Is this where Ortega lives?"

"Yes, him and his brothers."

"Is he off working today?"

"*Si,* what can I do for you?"

"Tell him we camped on the river a short ways past the village. Ask him to come see me tonight. My name is Chet Byrnes. We met last night at the cantina."

"Oh, yes. He says you are looking for a *ranchero.*" She smiled.

"That and other things. No rush. Shawn and I are glad to meet you, *señora*."

"*Gracias, señor.* I will send him there."

"We may not be back until later today."

She shrugged, then smiled like she was pleased. "He can wait." Then she laughed. "He will be there. He liked talking to you, he said."

Two other young women with children stood outside their doors, looking him and his partner over. He waved to them, remounted, and thanked her again before they rode off.

"You said you met their men in the cantina last night where Roamer caught the outlaws?" Shawn slipped off his horse and reopened the gate. When they were through it, he closed it and got back on his horse.

"I think they're brothers or cousins. Real *vaqueros* like the ones on my wife's ranch."

"Will they help us?"

"I hope they will offer us a headquarters and watch our things while we're rangering out here."

"That would be nice."

"If I can, I'll hire the wives to cook for us. We were lucky last night to catch those two. The rest will be harder and take longer, I figure."

"Jesus will like not having to cook, as well."

"I agree. But he beats many cattle drive cooks I've known."

"Sometime, you'll have to tell me about those days. When I was little, Dad made two of them trips to Kansas."

"They made money, but it was tough times."

"How's that?"

"Swollen rivers to cross, stampedes, tornados, storms, and gun-crazy men in the cow towns, plus outlaws to rob you or rustle your cattle. Crossing rivers was a big thing. After my first trip, I swam so much the next summer to get ready for my next drive I thought I was half fish."

"Dad said there was one guy back in Texas got everyone's cattle to take to Kansas. They all knew him, but when he got there he paid off the crew, sold his horses and chuckwagon, and they never heard of him again. Dad lost two hundred head to him."

"There was lots of that went on, herds lost in storms, rustled, ran off bluffs in stampedes and they all died."

As they rode the King's Highway south, heavy traffic on this main road north and south included ox carts that squeaked on wooden axles and carried goods north to Tucson or somewhere else from Mexico. Freighters with twenty-team hitches in a caravan headed both directions. Occasionally, a man or two on a burro rode by, with their women walking behind them with a basket on her head. He tried to imagine Marge doing that and laughed.

"What's so funny?" Shawn asked.

"I thought about my wife doing like that last woman. She'd probably ride the burro and I'd have to carry the basket."

They both laughed and rode on in the warm sun. The roan horse was always a pleasure to ride. Head down and in a swinging walk or trot, he was all business. If you needed speed he had it; if you climbed mountains he was like a cat. He sure beat a head-high crazy horse that wore himself out fighting the bit and the rider.

They stopped for a drink at a roadside well. Several women were in the shallow river across the road, beating clothes on the rocks to wash them. Many were naked to the waist, and the sun glistened on their swinging bare breasts as they worked. It didn't seem to bother them if anyone saw them exposed.

"Great scenery," Shawn said with a grin, and they mounted up to ride on south.

"I guess we all have different ways to live, but these folks seem to make a living down here and don't mind casual."

"A different way, huh?"

"Well, we are seeing lots of it. Men ride, women walk. They wash clothes and don't care. Some even wave at us to be friendly. A different culture is what they have."

"Jesus told me about the rich lady you met in Socorro. He said she was tall and good looking."

"I danced with her and she treated us well. A widow woman who even made Jesus dance with her nieces."

"Was she really rich?"

"Oh, yes, for there."

"If you'd been single, what would you have done?"

"Probably stayed longer."

"That's funny."

"You looking for a rich Spanish woman?"

Shawn reined in his horse "No, just curious. Why are those men in the river with that horse?"

The sorrel horse looked like he might be crippled. "They might be soaking his hooves."

Two men were in the water, with one man who acted in charge. He looked angry at the two working for him. They were all three tough acting and arguing among themselves about what to do with the animal.

"Let's ride on," Chet said, not wanting to make themselves obvious.

"Hey, *gringo*," the burly whiskered one shouted, wading out of the knee-deep river.

Chet reined up and Shawn did, too.

"What do you want?"

"Sell me that roan horse. Mine, you can see, is crippled."

"He's not for sale. Besides, I need him myself."

"How much money you need for him?" He pulled a handful of paper money from his pocket and thrust it forward in a fist. "Tell me. I need him."

"He is not for sale," Chet said in Spanish.

"Gawdamnit. I have the money to buy him. Come back here."

"Go on," he said under his breath to Shawn who moved his mount slightly ahead.

"You want me to shoot you and take the son of a bitch away from you?"

Chet whirled the roan around with his Colt in his hand. "Drop the damn gun or die."

Shock-faced, the man dropped his six-gun, a good thing because Chet was only moments away from shooting him.

"All right. All right. I was only kidding. My horse is lame and I'm supposed to be in Tucson."

Shawn had his rifle on the other men with the loud-mouthed one.

"Wave down a stage. They go there every day. Now, get right back in the middle of the river and stay there till I get out of sight."

"Yes, *señor.*" Walking on pained soles, he soon was back in the water almost to the sorrel.

Chet and Shawn galloped away. Out of sight, they slowed some.

"Who was he?"

Chet shook his head. "I should have found out. But that won't be our last meeting with them, I feel certain."

Shawn glanced back to see if there was anyone following. "He's sure plenty tough."

"He also has a lot of money for a man so poorly dressed."

"Yeah, I noticed."

"Made me think it was less than honestly earned."

Shawn agreed, and they reined their horses down to a walk. Day one was even more exciting than he expected it to be off here in the desert. They'd need to be on the watch for those *hombres*.

They saw lots of country up and down the small river and returned to camp to find Ortega squatted on the ground talking to Jesus and Cole. The lanky *vaquero* rose and laughed. "Sorry I was not home when you called."

"No problem. I wanted to talk to you about our situation. We're a task force sent to clean up the banditry going on here with the culprits running across the border. Now, if we might endanger you or the children and family, please forgive that I asked this from you. We need a place to leave our gear and our packhorses when we don't need them. And a place to camp when we are here."

"Ah, so you are the law?"

"Yes, we are. I can pay you a fair price for rent and you can sell me hay for my horses."

"I would hate to charge you, if you are trying to make it a better place to live."

"No, I want to rent some ground and corral space and also pay you for any services rendered."

"Me and my brothers can always use money. But I would rather be your *amigos*."

"You would be. But some may hate us and take it out on you and your families."

His eyes narrowed when he spoke. "They do and they will die."

"I understand, but make sure your people know the risk. And everyone doesn't need to know what we're doing here until we've completed the job."

"I savvy. Come tomorrow and set up where you want to."

"No, if you aren't there, you tell your wife where you want us to set up."

He grinned big. "I will tell her."

"Just so you know, we've already started our work. Last night, one of my men arrested two outlaws in Tubac. When they got to Charlie's, they were already drunk. They robbed a man and took his horse south of Tucson, and ended up down here. We had word they were coming this way and a description of the horse. Two of my men took them to San Xavier today and the law will pick them up there tomorrow."

"It sounds like you already have a good start on these *banditos*."

"Yes. My nephew, JD, and a man named Roamer took those two to the mission, so that less people know about us. Now, I still want you to show us some good ranches. JD is the one needs the ranch.

"Oh, one more thing. There was a bearded man today with some tough hombres in the river with a sorrel that went cripple, I think. This big bearded guy got out lots of money and went to screaming he wanted to buy my roan. I had to draw my gun and make him go back in the river."

Ortega gave a knowing laugh. "His name is Don McQuire. His father was rich, but he has pissed most of it away. He thinks he owns all this country. He does not mess with me or my brothers. He was testing you."

"I'll remember that. We'll move up to your place tomorrow, if that's all right?"

"Fine. Lots of babies cry around there, but we will watch your belongings. You need some help; we can match guns with that border bunch."

"When we get moved there, you can fill me in on who to watch out for down here."

"For sure. My brothers will be pleased you all are coming, too."

"Here's thirty dollars for the first month's rent."

"Oh, that is too much." Ortega put up a protesting hand.

"You haven't had to put up with us yet."

So the tall *vaquero* rode for home with the money. Jesus and Shawn went to fixing supper, for it had been a long day for all of them.

"That Ortega is a very smart man," said Jesus. "He went to two sessions of school, so he can read and write. Just before you came, I talked to him."

"He's a smart man for doing that. He told us the man who threatened Shawn and I today at the river was a rich man's son who was spending his father's money."

Jesus smiled. "Cole and I saw lots of country, too. Some people we talked to are suspicious and wouldn't tell us much, but when we've been here a while they will open up."

"How many miles away is the young lady you wrote to?"

"Maybe two days' ride."

"After we get going, Cole and JD will want to go back and see their brides. I plan to send them home on the stage for a week. Roamer, too. If things are quiet then, you can go see her."

"I would like to do that."

"We can arrange it."

The three men took turns at guard duty and he told them to wake him if anything was wrong. The nights here were never as cold as up at Preskitt, but they got down into the forties. His blankets kept him warm, but he missed Marge. When they were camped at Ortega's place he'd write her a long letter. This job might consume six months. On the other hand, it might be longer.

How long could he be apart from his wife and ranches? The ranches were in good hands and they could handle them without him, even though overseeing them was his job. But his wife. With a baby coming, she needed him there. Oh, well, nothing to be done about it tonight. He plumped the small feather pillow into a ball and went to sleep on it.

When they moved to the Two 8 Slash, they were the center of attention. They set up the large tarp between two tall cottonwoods. Using poles Ortega found for them, they drove iron rods into them to go into the grommets to support a side wall, then staked them down to make a house to be under. One of the Fernandez brothers hoped it brought them rain and made them all laugh.

After the shelter was up, Ortega brought material and tools to make a long table and benches to sit on. It went up fast. While they unpacked, Maria, his wife, brought them lunch. After the meal, they built a stout rack with poles notched and tied with green rawhide to put the panniers on to keep the ranch dogs out of their things.

Late that afternoon, on horses with salt dried on

their legs and chests, a weary looking JD and Roamer arrived, dismounted, and took off their chaps.

"Nice camp," JD said, looking it over.

"You two all right?" Chet asked.

"Long ride, but three lawmen met us there and took the prisoners. They thought we were lucky getting them two. I told them it wasn't luck; we'd get some more before this was over. I don't believe they thought we could even find any to arrest. Blevins sent you a list of crimes they think Mexican bandits have done recently." He handed Chet the paper.

"All I can say, is those deputies probably only break up domestic fights and arrest drunks," Roamer said with an expression of disgust. "They were neither horsemen, nor real lawmen."

"I savvy that, too. Ortega's family rented us this place for thirty dollars a month. We pay for the hay and they watch our horses and gear. Noontime today, Ortega's wife, Maria, brought us enchiladas and they were good. But I made no deal for them to cook for us. If I can hire them to cook our meals, we'll do that.

"Our first day, we met a tough-talking bearded man who tried to buy my roan. His name is Don McQuire and he has some grubby companions. Ortega says he's spending his father's money."

"We saw nothing but dusty roads and the traffic on it," JD said.

"Now that we're all together, we can make some plans," said Chet. "If nothing comes up in three weeks, we'll take a break and send Roamer, Cole, and

JD home for a week to go mend fences. Jesus wants to ride down into Mexico. Shawn and I will hold the fort down. The Fernandez brothers say they will ride with us if we need them."

"That's great," Cole said.

JD nodded in agreement.

"Tomorrow, we split up again. JD knows Tombstone. You two ride over there and stay in a hotel a couple of nights. Look things over. That space over there is another route south, say from Benson. We need to know the country and the roads the bandits are using to get back home."

After supper, Ortega and his brothers brought their wives and two guitars to the camp. They played music, and everyone danced in the dust with their wives. They were all very proper ladies and everyone had some entertainment. Jose, the youngest of them, was married to Ricky, a tall girl, not out of her teens. No children. Bronco and his wife, Consuela, were looking for number two baby. Maria had three small ones.

"We don't want to take advantage of you," said Ortega, "but our wives would cook your meals for thirty dollars a month and you buy the food. How does that sound?"

"We accept their kind offer. They can buy the food and I will pay them, or give them money to buy it."

"Better if you give them money and they give you the ticket."

Chet agreed.

Maria stepped forward. "Tomorrow, we will start at noon."

"No, it will be tomorrow night before we all get back. If we aren't back, feed the food to your family. They like beef fajitas with onions, sweet and hot peppers, and also your wonderful enchiladas."

"I will be here in the morning to see how your breakfast is done."

"Jesus can show you."

"*Gracias.* If you don't like something we cook, you tell us." The three women standing in the flickering firelight nodded their heads in unison.

Consuela said, "We can always make it better."

That night when Chet lay in his bedroll, he counted his blessings. They had cooks; his men were back and about to go on another scouting party. A good feeling to know things were working out. He wanted to see the Santa Rita Mountain mining area. Maybe hire Ortega to take them there on their first trip. His head on the pillow, he listened to the owls and a nearby coyote howling.

Marge. Things are working out well. I miss you, but we're getting arranged here. Tonight, the Fernandez wives asked to let them cook for us, so I hired them. I'll write you tomorrow. Night, my darling.

The next morning before JD and Roamer left for Tombstone, he told them to just look around and check on telegrams. They promised to do that and headed for Tombstone with bedrolls behind their cantles. Roamer said he didn't like hotel bed bugs.

Maria carried her baby in a sling as she watched Jesus cook breakfast, and they conversed in Spanish like old friends. Afterward, she told Chet she thought she could handle it.

He thanked her, then asked her to buy some canned peaches and tomatoes. "The men love them for a treat. Maybe two cases of each."

Her brown eyes got bigger.

"I can afford them." He wanted to assure a poor rancher's wife it was all right to spend the money on the meals she'd serve them.

"I can do that."

"Good, 'cause we sure appreciate you doing this."

"Oh, *señor*. There is not much way to make money around here. You understand?"

"Yes, I do. But call me Chet, all right?"

"I can do that." Maria smiled at him. "I will tell the others that is your name?"

"Yes."

"You have a wife?"

"Yes, and we'll have a baby in a few months."

"You look happy saying that."

"I am. Very happy."

"I will not make lunch today?"

"Not today, but we'll be back tonight."

"I plan on the fajitas."

"That sounds great. Don't fret. As long as we don't have to cook, we'll like yours."

She giggled as she returned to her *jacal*.

He caught his horse, then he and Shawn went to see about the nearby mines in the mountains. The roads to these places were crudely blasted out notches in the mountainside. So steep, he wondered how they ever hauled in timbers for their operations. They stopped to talk to several dust-clad miners who'd come out for air.

One man spoke about his concern about conveying any gold he found to Tucson.

"Alfred Brannon had a mine up here. Left here with I figure a thousand in gold dust. We never heard of him again. I checked in Tucson and he never made it there. That's my worry."

"You or anyone else has gold to carry out, come see me or my men. We're at the Two Eight Slash ranch, and we'll guard you to get there with it."

"What do you charge?"

"There is no charge." Chet studied the man before telling him, "Keep this information quiet, but we're US Marshal deputies working undercover to stop these Mexican border bandits."

"Well, how about that? I'll only tell people I trust." He shook Chet's hand.

"If you pass on to us any information you receive, or even suspicious people you see, we'd appreciate it. We aim to stop them."

"God be with you, brother. You have a tough job to do."

"We can handle it."

They rode on, meeting several more miners on the way and learning they were all concerned about getting their gold out. He told them to pool their gold for the journey and some of his men would guide them. When he and Shawn headed home, he felt they'd made a good round. Maybe to be more effective, they needed to protect a few such men and stop the robberies.

Maria delivered a telegram that arrived while they were away. It was from JD.

CHET BYRNES

THERE WAS A STAGE ROBBERY HERE. WE HAVE
RIDDEN OUT WITH THE WELLS FARGO AGENT AND
TWO OF THE EARP BROTHERS, PLUS THE INDIAN
SCOUT TO FIND THEM. WILL REPORT MORE LATER.
JD.

"What happened?" Jesus asked.

"JD and Roamer are riding off after stage robbers with a Wells Fargo man, two Earp brothers, and a scout."

"Wow, they already got into it."

"Right off."

"Jesus and I talked to five different ranchers today," Cole said. "Horse stealing is a big problem down here. They can't hardly keep them."

"More Mexican bandits?"

"They say they are."

"We need to keep our eyes open and stop to talk to the suspicious looking ones."

"I bet they take back roads, too, but we are learning them."

"That's why we want to know this country better."
He wondered about the Tombstone stage robbery
chase and his men's part in it. In time, they'd be back
to tell him more.

"Maria is making great food for us tonight," Jesus
confided.

"Beats you having to do it."

"Oh, my, yes."

Supper was a fiesta, and Maria had good red wine
for them to drink with it. All the families joined them
for the meal. Bronco's wife, Consuela, sang Mexican
folk songs in a beautiful voice and played the guitar.

Maria acted a little concerned. "I hope I wasn't
wrong to tell them to come tonight."

"No, we love it. Anytime you're the cook, feed
them."

"I will. It livens up all our lives, huh?"

"Indeed, it really does."

The camp situation had been a good move. He listened to the music and thought about May and her
music. Memories like that made him question why
he was so far away from home. But he'd chosen his
cause—border rangering.

Later, he wrote to Marge and asked Maria to see
that the letter was mailed.

CHAPTER 22

Before the sun came up, a youth rode up asking for Jesus. The boy had ridden the lathered horse a great distance. Jesus hurried over to him.

"What is wrong?"

"They stole six of our horses last night."

"You live where?"

"The Triple X Ranch. My father is Antonio Amadore."

"We met him yesterday. We will saddle up. The nice lady is fixing breakfast, so you must eat with us. Then we can chase down these rustlers."

"My father was very upset. He said you would help us."

"Yes, we will get your horses back. Which way did they go?"

"To the Papago Reservation, like they always do."

"That means west," Jesus told Chet.

"This is Tomas," Cole said. "We met him and his father yesterday, and we already have business, huh?"

Jesus nodded. "They said then that they worried all the time that someone would steal their horses."

They all sat down to eat Maria's breakfast.

When Ortega joined them and learned what happened, he asked, "Any of you ever been on that reservation?"

"No."

"I could go there with you. I have been all over it looking for stray livestock. Ranchers pay by the head to recover their stock that drift over there."

"If she can spare you. Should we take a packhorse along?"

"*Sí.* It is a big place. Not many stores."

Jesus spoke up. "I will set up two panniers to take and that horse can haul our bedrolls as well."

"Do that," Chet said, and turned to Ortega. "We leave shortly."

"I will be ready."

The others nodded their approval. In forty-five minutes, they were ready and left their camp. Tomas road in front with Chet.

"My father really hopes you can find his horses."

"I do, too, Tomas. We'll try."

"This is the only one we have left."

"Well, we better find them then," he said to the boy.

Standing in their stirrups, they trotted their mounts through the rolling desert dotted with thirty-foot tall saguaros. He could smell the flats of pungent creosote brush, then giant patches of pancake cactus spread across the land, with bunch grass all over. The flour-like dust rose from the road and gave him an acrid taste in his mouth. They reached the ranch and Chet spoke briefly to the father while Ortega and Jesus checked the rustlers' tracks and soon had their direction fixed and headed out south. Chet lingered to thank the boy and tell his father they'd try to get the horses back, then left in a short lope to catch up with his posse.

When he joined them, Ortega reined over close. "They think they got all his horses, so they were in no hurry last night. We may catch them."

"I hope so."

They'd reached some hilly country when a few shots rang out. Chet reined up and saw someone blasting away from up on the hillside. Too far away for his .44 pistol to ever be effective. Chet jerked his .44/.40 out. His shots made from the back of the excited roan horse were all around the shooter, sending off dust puffs until finally the outlaw went down holding his leg and screaming.

"Those others are getting away," Ortega told Cole.

"We can handle this one," Chet told him. "Ortega and Cole, you two try to stop them and not get shot. Go after them."

The two rode off in a pounding of hooves. He jammed his rifle in its scabbard and charged up the hillside with Shawn and Jesus. Colt in his fist, he wondered about the man that shot at them. Obviously, his plan was to stall them while the others tried to get away with the horses.

"He was foolish to shoot at us with a pistol," Jesus

shouted as their horses struggled up the steep hillside
with a stretch of girth and leather in the pull. Hooves
clattered on rocks, but they soon gained the crest
and found the downed man and his horse.

"Don't shoot me! I'm bleeding to death."

"They must have found the others. I hear shots,"
he said to his men as they stood over the shooter.

They both lifted their heads and nodded indicating they heard the shots, too.

"Who do you work for?" Chet demanded.

"No one."

"You look like you're going to die. Confess now or
roast in hell."

"My name is Jose. I live in Sonora. My wife is—"
The man keeled over.

"You must have shot him in an artery," Jesus said,
looking puzzled. "He is already dead."

Shawn looked pale. No doubt his first time to
participate in a scene like this.

"He came to do us harm and he died in his boots.
Catch his horse, then tie him across the saddle. I'm
going to see what those boys need.

"Get the gun he dropped, too." He swung on the
roan and took off down the steep slope, dodging
cactus as he rode hard until he hit the flat, then
spurred the horse on.

Ortega was still on his horse, taking shots at the
shooters in the brush. Cole had his rifle out, firing at
them and made a good mark on one of them that
shouted he was hit.

They only made an occasional shot in return.

Then Chet reloaded his rifle and joined Cole on his belly.

"How many are left?"

"I don't know. They won't give up."

Ortega joined them. "Everyone hangs the horse thieves they catch. So they might as well fight to their death."

"If I offer them prison time, would they surrender?"

"No. How is the other one?"

"Dead. I must have hit an artery in his leg."

"Let's all three shoot at once," Ortega suggested.

They did, in a barrage of rifle shots, and then they stopped. In the near silence, only the topknot quail called out with its whet-whew cry.

"Be careful, dying snakes can bite," Chet said as they advanced toward the bandits.

With no further resistance, they moved in but with their guns in hand. They found the three men dead or dying. Beyond help, those dying were soon gone.

With Jesus's and Shawn's help when they arrived, the bodies were soon loaded and all the horses gathered. They rode back to Tomas and his father's ranch with the four dead rustlers and eight horses recovered. He'd file a report for Blevins. The task force was doing its job, but they were far from the end.

Antonio knew none of the dead. He said that he, his son, and his helper would bury them. His wife wanted to feed Chet's bunch, but he told her they needed to get back to their camp at Tubac.

Antonio was in great spirits, poured them all cups of red wine in celebration, and raised his to them.

After they all drank, he said, "I knew they were coming. I was one of the few they had not raided. I will share their horses with a few of my neighbors so they have something to ride, if that is all right?"

"Fine with us," Chet said, and the others agreed. It would damn sure be tough to be afoot out in this part of the desert.

Chet thanked them for their offer to feed them, and for burying the outlaws. His bunch, anxious to get back to camp, headed out.

It was long after dark when they got back. When Maria learned they hadn't eaten, she came down and began fixing supper for them. Some of his worn-out men had to be woken up from a siesta, but her roasted goat, rice, and beans were good and she was cheerful. After the meal, they dropped in their bedrolls. Chet was settled enough by then to sleep, too.

At dawn, they enjoyed the hot oatmeal and coffee Maria had ready for them. Chet was amazed at her resilience and ability to get so much done. Along with breakfast, she brought him another telegram.

A man named Rudy Rayales was found robbed and dead on the road south of Tucson. No other information was available. Not much they could do about that. But he feared there would be more such incidents. So they rested their horses that day, bathed, and shaved. JD and Roamer arrived late in the afternoon from their Tombstone trip and did the same thing. While they were shaving, they told Chet about capturing the stage robbers.

"We tracked them up in the Whetstones. When we rode up, they went to shooting worse I ever saw. Well, that lasted about ten minutes and we had them shot up. I think one was still alive and that breed scout with us went over and finished him off with a bullet to the back of his head. Kinda chilling, huh?" JD asked.

"I guess it's do or die among these border outlaws," Chet said to him.

"Naw, these were white drifters. Probably had cowboy backgrounds. They were losers. When one of the Earps turned one over with his boot, he called him 'Texas trash.'"

"JD's right. They weren't border bandits," Roamer said. "And they weren't going to be taken alive."

"We heard a rumor or two while there," JD said. "If Wells Fargo learns you are planning to hold them up, they'll shoot you first and tell God you died."

Roamer agreed. "That's tough. The Wells Fargo man is sending us checks for a hundred dollars each for helping catch them. Not bad, is it?"

"Not bad at all. After our chase and we returned the man's horses, we got a nice thank-you."

"Well, it was a different situation than I ever ran into," JD said, and shrugged.

So far, they'd scored three hits at the outlaws and it all worked out fine. He had a tough crew and Ortega was all the lawman he thought he would be.

After a good supper that evening, the next telegram came.

CHET BYRNES

RANCHER NEAR PATAGONIA HELD UP AND SHOT.
BANDITS TOOK HORSES. SAM CRANE IS VICTIM. HE
RANCHES NORTH OF THERE. BAR C BRAND. YOU'RE
DOING GREAT WORK.

BLEVINS

When the delivery boy was paid and sent on his way, he turned to Ortega. "You know this Sam Crane near Patagonia?"

"I have met him. He is a tough old man. I bet he fought them."

"He got shot, too. How far is it?"

"A long ride in one day."

"We'll get up early and ride over there. Jesus, get a packhorse ready for a three- or four-day trip."

"Who all is going?" JD asked.

"You and Roamer rest up. The other four of us will go. We'll send word if we need you."

"They're probably across the border by now," Roamer said.

"We'll check that country out. Ortega, you've been to his place?"

"I can find it."

"Okay, plan to take us there."

"Good. I was going to have to build fence for a man. Now my brothers can do that." He laughed.

They rode out at dawn and cut across country to

save time. Ortega's knowledge of the land saved them a lot of time. By late afternoon, with one stop for directions, they were at the Bar C Ranch.

A gray-haired woman met them at the door of her adobe house holding a rifle.

"US Marshals," Chet said, dismounting. "Can we speak to your husband? We understand he was shot by rustlers."

"He's inside in bed. I'll ask him if he wants to talk to you."

She called out in a loud voice. "They say they're marshals. Do you want to talk to them?"

"Where in the hell did they get that many men?"

"Come in. He's crazy. Wants to know where in hell you got all your men."

"Thanks, ma'am." Chet went past her into a room where a pale-faced older man was propped up on pillows in bed with his arm bandaged.

"US Marshal Chet Byrnes, Mr. Crane. We came to hear your story."

"My story? What's yours? I never before saw that many lawmen in one place in this county."

"That's part of the task force out to clean up the border bandit business around here."

"Take a damn sight more men than that, I bet."

"We're working on it one case at a time. We've been here a little over a week and counting arrested and dead ones, I figure we're close to two a day."

"Well, by gawd, there's hundreds of them."

"Tell me about your encounter with them."

"Well, tell him, Sam," his wife insisted, looking bewildered at his reticence.

"They came busting in here about dawn shooting pistols off in the sky and whooping like mad men. Someone was already in my horse pen, running them out.

"I've got a .45 hog leg and I opened the door and shot two of them off their horses. Then they returned fire at me. Creased my right leg, got splinters in my eye when a bullet struck the door facing, and I went down. She had a .22 and shot them up, but they didn't stop. They picked up one of their own and rode off.

"One man they left was dead. They got nine good horses. All had my brand and all were geldings, four to six years old. Prime horses I can sell for up to two hundred dollars. That's a pile of money to me and her."

"Did anyone know the dead man?"

"They said his name was Estevan something. Come from over by Aqua Prieta."

"Nothing else?"

"Naw. If I'd not been shot, I'd a hounded them down myself."

"Good thing you were. They'd a turned around and killed you," she said.

"I get my mail and telegrams at Tubac. My name's Chet Byrnes. You learn anything, write or wire me. I want those bastards as bad as you do."

"I believe you do."

"Don't fight them alone. If you get us any lead, we'll find them."

"When I get stronger, I'll work on that."

"Oh, thanks for coming by. I do believe you will make a difference in these border lawbreakers," she said.

"Thank you, ma'am, for letting me in to talk to him."

"No problem. Sam ain't the rustler chaser he once was, but he won't listen."

"You take care now." Chet tipped his hat and headed for his horse.

Before they were halfway home, it began to rain and some thunder grumbled off in the distance. Ortega knew of a place to camp, so he led them to an abandoned ranch before the sun set.

When putting up the horses, Jesus found a pocket-worn letter on the ground. The rain had dampened it and made the ink run some, but he handed it to Chet.

"May be something worthwhile, someone used this place and lost it down by the corral."

The two-page letter was in Spanish so Chet handed it back to Jesus. "Can you read it?"

"Some," he said and shuffled through the pages. "His name is Alberto—she misses him so—she asks when will he come home to Los Riveria."

"That is south on the Santa Cruz in Sonora," Ortega said.

"I hope you earn much money so we can be married," continued Jesus. "Then she says don't rob any stagecoaches, 'cause they shoot those people. But she hopes he finds many rich men to rob. She asks him to tell her cousin, Rico Chavez, to write his mother who fears for him because a *brujah*—a witch—saw him dead in a dream.

"Then she tells who had a baby and who died in their village. Who messed with another *hombre*'s wife who was with him named Valdez. And she ends up saying for him not to lose his temper with his boss, Leo. Her name is Julie."

"That letter could have been dropped there when they were up here looking to steal Sam's horses."

"Or they could be another gang," Cole said. "We've got some names and a village in Mexico they may have come from. Good find. They sure ain't pastoring no church up here."

They were out of the drizzle, under the nearly dry squaw shade with a fire going to cook supper. Amused, Chet poured some fresh coffee in his tin cup and the aroma went up his nose. Maybe the trip over to see Sam Crane hadn't been a total waste. He wished they'd had fresher tracks to follow, but too many days had gone by before they got there for them to do any good.

CHAPTER 23

They discovered a moonshiner without a federal permit and no tax stamps in a canyon up in the Santa Rita Mining District. An old Arkie named Chester Hammonds ran the still and was mad as a wet hen when Chet told him his operation was illegal and he owed a fifty-dollar fine. He told the man that if he wanted to save the mash in the barrels he'd better get a bucket and feed it to his hogs or they would turn them over and let the mash run out on the grounds. Then his crew went to taking his copper tubing and busting every crock jar that had liquor in it.

They sampled the whiskey and decided it was better than Charlie's brand in the bottle that Chet brought back and what they only used for serious throat ailments.

Hammonds and his skinny wife slopped the mash to the hogs till they couldn't grunt anymore.

"You can't make whiskey less you get a permit and buy tax stamps," Chet told the Hammonds. They

paid him forty dollars of the fine—all the money
they had.

Fines were an issue that deputy marshals handled
in the field, and they collected the money for themselves. It was easier to fine them on the spot than to
arrest them and bring them in for trial and have all
that expense. Like they explained to Chet in Tucson
earlier, most were like this small operation and were
all handled in the same manner.

Glad to be away from the sour mash smell and
stinking hogs, they rode back to camp and bathed.
Laughing about the episode, they all sat down to one
of Maria's great meals.

Jesus told the brothers about the Hammonds'
moonshine operation over the wonderful food and
they laughed about it. Tonight was another fiesta,
music included. Chet was getting more antsy to see
his wife, but he was letting the men go first. JD, Cole,
and Roamer had stage tickets to go through from
Tubac to Preskitt.

Jesus had a packhorse picked out and two panniers, ready to go find his love below the border.
Chet wrote a long letter to Marge telling her he
would be home in two weeks, unless they had more
serious crimes break in the next week. His three men
left on a Saturday morning.

He told Jesus to be gun ready, because he looked
prosperous with a packhorse and his nice new clothes.
Jesus was full of hope and looked forward to solving
the mystery of why she hadn't written him back.

Chet told him, "Remember. Sad things will occur

in all our lives, but you have your faith that you grew up with. God will get you through those times."

"Thank you. I savvy things happen. I will be back in a week. Let no one shoot you. You took a big chance taking me with you the first time. I will never forget that first time. One real scared Mexican boy rode with a big man. I do not feel like that now. *Vaya con Dios, mi amigo.*" Jesus rode off.

Ortega was there and he spoke softly. "He is no longer a boy, either, is he?"

"No, he is my good friend and very capable at his job."

"Oh, I bet you can't wait to go home."

"No, I can't. But I will."

"I know a good ranch closer to the fort. He might sell that place."

"Who owns it?"

"Grover McClelland. But please let me ask him so he will pay me for being a finder, huh?"

"I understand. Let's look at it."

"Sure, soon. What are you doing today?" Ortega asked.

"Noting planned. Only you, me, and Shawn left. What do you have in mind?"

"Go look at some wild horses."

"Mustangs?"

"Not bangtails. There is a wild stallion over west. I want you to see his band. He is a great horse and no one knows where he came from. I would like him and his mares, but I have no place for them. But maybe you could see how good he is."

"Have you ever seen a Barbarossa stallion?" Chet asked him.

"They are all golden horses, aren't they?"

"Yes."

"I saw three of them run at Nogales in the big races over there. Ten years ago and, oh, I wanted one so bad."

"I have one."

"So you are the one who ransomed a girl with a gold horse?"

"That is JD's wife, Bonnie."

"And you sit under this tent and catch two-bit bandits?"

"Someone needs to do it."

Shawn was back from checking the horses.

"Hey, saddle our horses," Chet said. "We're going to look at some wild ones."

"That'll be different."

"We need a change."

"Hey, I love wild horses."

Ortega went for his mount. Laughing, he hugged his wife when he caught her walking down from their *jacal.*

"We won't need lunch," Chet told her. "We're going horse hunting."

She shook her head and sent her hair back so the wind lifted it. "I was there once when we first married. They are beautiful horses and he fears someone will gather them some day before he can."

"We'll go and see what they're like."

"It is a tough trip. But he don't care. Be careful. I will hold supper. You will be back late."

The ride over the western range of mountains was steep and they topped out on the top of a pass where the brisk wind cooled them and their sweaty horses. Acres of brown grass spread out in the distance and two water sources shone in the sun like gems.

"Anyone ranch it?"

"A few do, but it is a tough land."

"How many homesteads are out there?"

"Maybe two dozen."

"In how many miles?"

"A sixty-mile band." Ortega pointed north and then south.

From their perch, the area appeared to Chet like an overlooked empire. He wished he could contact Bo and learn something about the ownership. The south wind was strong and he pulled his hat brim down when they set off going down the steep other side. A place for goats, but he trusted the roan's sure footedness.

New land, new country, and he was impressed. The mild temperature was like south Texas. But rain and water would be the limiting factors. Ortega might be leading them into another great ranch.

They spent the day riding the desert and saw signs, but never found the horse band. To Chet, this was an intriguing land. Some water, but more could be developed. Lots of grass.

"How do you get here?"

"From the south, cross the Papago reservation, or north you can go west on the Yuma road, then turn south and reach it. We are about in the center of the range. I haven't seen anything today but the dwarf antelope that lives here."

"Pronghorn?"

"Yes, about half the size of the other ones."

Hurrying back, they were over the mountain pass before the sun set and rode back to the Two 8 Slash in the twilight. Shawn had been impressed, too.

"Mind if I ask you what you think about that land?" he asked Chet.

"Looks like range country to me. Needs water development—tanks built, springs developed, and maybe windmills, if there is water close by."

Ortega laughed. "I have shared my secret, no?"

"Yes, you did. And it's a good one. We'll go back and look again," Chet promised them.

They all agreed that they'd like to do that.

Maria had some candle lamps on in the tent when they rode up. Shawn and Ortega took the horses to put them up.

She smiled in greeting. "I thought you were lost over there."

"We never saw his horse, but we had a wonderful day. Great country."

She agreed. "Wash up. The food is still hot."

"No messages today?"

"Yes, one." She took it from her apron pocket.

He put the yellow sheet under a candle light to read it.

CHET BYRNES
THE ARIZONA BANK IN BENSON WAS ROBBED TODAY.
THEY STOLE TWO THOUSAND DOLLARS. THREE OR
MORE MEN TOOK PART. TWO TOWNSPEOPLE WERE
SHOT AND A BANK TELLER. A POSSE CHASED THEM,
BUT GAVE UP THIS PM SOMEWHERE BETWEEN
TOMBSTONE AND FT HUACHUCA. NO NAMES BUT
TWO MEXICANS AND ONE WHITE MAN INVOLVED.
IF YOU CAN HELP LOCAL OFFICIALS PLEASE DO SO.
BLEVINS

"What is it, Chet?" Shawn asked.

"They robbed the Benson bank. Three men and rode south. Posse quit their tracks or lost them between Tombstone and the fort."

"What can we do?" asked Ortega.

"In the morning, take some packhorses, cut up through south of the Whetstones and look for them. Being shorthanded, would one of your brothers like to ride with us?"

"I bet he will. Right after supper, I'll go find him."

"No," Maria said. "You men eat. I will ask them to come down here."

The plate of food in his hand, Chet thanked her. The three went to filling their dishes. They soon had their coffee as well and sat down to eat.

The middle brother, Bronco, soon joined them. He was the same lanky cut, twenty-something, image of his brother.

"Maria said you needed more help?"

"We do. Four of my men are on leave. The bank was robbed in Benson. Three men, they say rode south. We're going to try to find out where they went."

"I have no work. Jose can watch the ranch and the women. You plan to leave at sunup?"

"Yes, and thanks."

Bronco smiled. "How did you like Ortega's country?"

"I liked it a lot. I like rangeland. It has some possibilities."

Bronco nodded and went for some coffee.

"He can ride and shoot with me," Ortega said.

"I have no doubts about any of your brothers." Chet smiled, and Ortega nodded in satisfaction.

Chet went to sleep missing his wife, but full of plans to find the bank robbers.

CHAPTER 24

They rode out at daybreak. Bronco rode a head-slinging tough mustang that walked on eggs for half a mile before he calmed down. One of those kind Chet knew about that you'd have to cut his head clear off to kill him.

Ortega convinced him to go farther south than his original plan and swing around through Patagonia to look for sign of them heading south. Someone may have seen them or knew where they went. They reached the area near the fort and shut down to camp for the night. The two brothers knew some people there and wanted to go see them and find out all they could.

"Great idea," Chet said. "We'll be here when you get back."

"They may learn more than we could," Shawn said, unloading the packhorses.

"If there's any information out there, they'll know about it."

They made coffee and ate some dry cheese and

crackers. A coyote howled nearby, bats flew in the night sky, and some desert owls hooted. He sent Shawn off to sleep a few hours before he took over guard duty. Yawning, with a rifle across his lap he dozed lightly while sitting up and woke to the horses nickering to returning horses. The brothers were back.

He walked over to where they were unsaddling.

"Learn anything?"

"One is named Montrose. There is a *gringo* rides with him and a boy. They spent some money at a whorehouse yesterday."

"Where was that?"

"Grainger Springs."

Chet shook his head. "Never been there."

"If that posse had kept on following them, they would have caught them. They said the posse quit way up at Saint David."

"Citizen posses are not too valuable. I'd bet they didn't want to find them. Where did they go next?"

"I imagine Mexico," Ortega said.

Bronco spoke up. "But one of the girls told us they spoke of Tombstone."

"Wouldn't that be dangerous for them?" Chet frowned about that.

"I agree, but they were bold enough to stop at a whorehouse," Ortega said.

"If we only had a horse brand. Descriptions don't do much."

Shawn was up. "You find them?"

"No. Only where they have been."

"I think they may be in Naco," Ortega said. "It is on the border and has plenty of liquor and wild women."

"Let's get some sleep. Can we reach there tomorrow?"

"Oh, *sí*."

Shawn cooked oatmeal with brown sugar and raisins for the crew. He'd watched Jesus do it so much it came out the same. After breakfast, they crossed the desert rangeland and saw many cattle that the brothers said were John Slaughter's. Chet didn't know the man, but evidently the brothers did. They said he originally came from Texas. Coming out on a stagecoach, his wife died and he had two small children to raise by himself.

Chet couldn't help thinking about his own wife and hoped her and the baby were well.

After they arrived in Naco, they stabled the horses on the American side and walked across the international border. The border consisted of just a wide strip of open land that separated the two towns that faced each other. Stations manned by each country's border agents were two shacks ten feet apart, but they mainly handled import and export items.

Oretga led them to a café where he knew the owner and went into the kitchen to talk with him. When he came back to their table, he spoke in a low voice, telling them the men they wanted were in the Red Rose Cantina where they'd been raising hell all day.

"What now?" Shawn asked.

"Who should cover the back door?" Chet asked.

"Bronco or Ortega, they both speak Spanish."

"You go, but don't shoot unless they are shooting, or getting away," Ortega said to his brother.

"I understand."

"Others may flee in the face of gunfire. We want no innocent ones shot."

"I will be careful." Bronco headed for the alley.

"Shawn, you watch who comes out front. Same orders. We'll be in Mexico and we need them back over on the American side and their horses, too."

"Which ones are theirs?"

"I guess they'll have to tell us. Ortega and I are going inside to stand at the bar for a drink and try to locate them."

"Be careful," Shawn said.

Chet agreed, and he and the lanky *vaquero* crossed the open space. Chet felt very conspicuous, but tried to shake his stiffness when Ortega pushed in the creaking batwing doors that needed their hinges oiled.

The smoky room wasn't crowded. Under a wagon wheel light with candles dripping all around it, some men played cards at a large round table. A big man in the back was messing with a *puta*, a lanky black woman. His raucous laughter rang out over some guitar music played by a teenage boy seated on a chair on a small stage.

Ortega ordered them a bottle of mescal and spoke softly in Spanish to the bartender. "Who is that big loud *hombre*?"

"I don't know him. They say his name is Montrose. That kid on the guitar and another named Farley came in here a few hours ago. I guess Montrose has lots of money. He's been spending it like it was water."

"Where is Farley?"

"Playing cards. He's in the dirty white *sombrero*."

Chet paid for the bottle and slipped him a ten-dollar gold piece. The man smiled. "Have fun in Mexico."

"Oh, we will," Ortega promised him.

They poured mescal into their glasses. Chet watched what he could see of the three from the bar mirror. Then the kid got up, put the guitar down and headed for the back door, no doubt to go piss.

"I'll be right back," Ortega said, like a man needing to vent his bladder and headed for the back door.

"Where do you live?" the bartender asked.

"Up by Preskitt."

"You ranch?"

"Yes."

"Is it cold up there?"

"In the winter, it gets that way at times."

"I could not stand to live there if it gets cold. I can't stand it here when it gets cold." He moved on to wait on a customer.

"You make it?" Chet asked Ortega when he returned.

"Yes. The matter is handled."

Montrose was getting louder and the woman squalling and laughing.

Farley stood up and in a loud voice asked Montrose, "Where did the kid go?"

Montrose shook his head. "Why?"

"When he gets back, send him for some food." He belched and rubbed his belly. "Think I'd better take a walk. Be right back." He headed for the back door and Ortega did, too.

When he didn't return after a while, Montrose must have wondered why and he headed for the back door. Chet followed him.

Standing behind the big man who'd stuck his head out the back door to look around, he stuck his Colt's muzzle in his back. "Keep going and be damn quiet about it, or I'll shoot you dead."

"Who in the hell are you?"

"Tell you more later." Then he shoved him on outside.

Bronco stepped up with his gun drawn to cover the doorway.

Chet took Montrose's six-gun out of the holster and stuck it in his waistband. Ortega handcuffed him behind his back. The other two were tied and seated on the ground.

"Which are their horses?" Chet asked under his breath.

"A bay, a dark dun, and a black one," Bronco said. "I'll get Shawn and we'll ride them across the line."

"We'll take them and go down this alley. There's less light shining on the border that way," Chet said.

"See you in Arizona," Bronco said, and hurried to go between the buildings and join Shawn.

"Get on your feet." Chet swept Farley's hat up and slapped it on his head.

"You three bounty hunters?" Montrose growled.

"Yeah," Chet said, and prodded him in the back with his pistol barrel.

"I've got lots of money. I can pay you if you let us go."

"How much?" Chet asked, his foot hitting a bottle in the darkness.

"Thousands of dollars."

"Where is it?"

"At my ranch in Sonora. I swear I'd pay you."

"Why are you robbing banks up here, if you have plenty of money?"

"It's what I like to do."

"Sure. Now, no funny tricks. I can chop your head off and take it in to get my reward."

"Who in the hell are these guys?" the kid whispered.

"Bounty hunters. They play tough. A head, or a body, they don't care," Farley said. "Do as they say."

"All right."

With only the stars for light, they were part way across the open ground that made up the border when Montrose began screaming, "Help! Help! I'm being kidnapped."

Chet busted him on the side of the head and he went face down, silenced. Bronco came riding one of their horses and tossed Chet a lariat. He holstered his gun, nosed the rope around both of Montrose's boots, and shouted, "Go!"

Bronco took a wrap on the saddle horn. Chet beat the horse on the ass with his hat. The horse dug in and the outlaw slid on his back, screaming all the way, and was delivered over into United States territory.

Out of breath and laughing, Chet bent over to get his breath. "That was a great job, boys."

Ortega let out a wild, "Yahoo!"

Chet congratulated them all, then waved his hat at the crowd of border watchers congregated on the boardwalk. "*Muchos gracias hombres.*"

Two guards from the US side ran down with rifles. The man in charge demanded to know what was going on.

"We're US Marshals. And we just extradited three outlaws from Mexico."

He began to laugh and so did the other one. "I've never seen it done like that before."

"Well, it takes all kinds of ways to do this job."

Shawn brought all the horses down to them. They loaded the prisoners, Chet thanked the guards, and they headed back to camp. Chet intended to search them for the money when they got there. He doubted Montrose had any more money in Mexico than he had on this side of the border. Counting their horses, saddles and all, he figured his men would have some good-sized rewards coming.

Like Chet expected, they found the money on the three men. The next morning, he put it all in one bag and they headed for Tombstone and the county jail. He wired the authorities in Benson to meet him there. He also wired Blevins that they had the robbers and most of the loot and where they were headed.

They rode all day, and it was way past sundown when they got to the Cochise County Courthouse. Chet's eyes felt like they were burned-out holes shrunk in his head when he dropped from the saddle. Marshal Blevins was there to shake his hand and introduce him to Sheriff John Behan, a fancy dresser who looked more like a dude than a sheriff.

Two men from the Benson bank were there, the head banker named Cohill, and the other his teller, who took the sack of money they'd retrieved.

When Chet introduced his three men, Blevins blinked.

Standing in the lamplight, Chet laughed. "Four of my men had to go check on their wives. I was short-handed, so enlisted these two to help catch the bank robbers."

"Can I have a story?" a young reporter who'd been hanging around asked.

Blevins stepped in. "The US Marshal's office has a task force working southern Arizona to combat the crime in this district. All I can say is these men work undercover. While doing that, their names and the details must remain undisclosed so as to not inform the criminal element."

"But, Marshal, the town posse gave up and these men found them and brought them in," the reporter complained.

"All you can print is that law officials apprehended the three bank robbers and brought them in."

"That doesn't make much of a story."

"Young man, these men rode miles and worked hard to find these outlaws, and their identity needs to be kept under wraps until their job is done."

"I want that story when you release it, sir."

"You will have it then. Thanks."

Blevins took Chet's arm. "I have a private dining room reserved at Nellie Cashman's restaurant. They're holding it open. Shall we go eat?"

"Sure. We'll put our horses up at the OK Corral Livery and be right up there," Chet told him.

"I want to say, I can't believe what all you've done. It's amazing. Without even a description, and you found them."

"Marshal, we work hard at this. I want these men to have those rewards, and we're also taking their horses, guns, and saddles."

"Sure. The Arizona Bank in Benson offered two hundred apiece on them. I'll get it for them."

"I'll tell them. They'll be very pleased. See you at Nellie's."

When they dismounted at the OK Livery, Ortega asked, "Are we dressed good enough?"

"Good enough for me. Don't worry. There'll be people in there wearing fancy duds like that sheriff back there, and there'll be old prospectors who ain't changed clothes in two years."

Ortega laughed and Bronco joined in. They

strolled up the boardwalk watching all the traffic and commerce going on at night.

"Busy place," Ortega commented.

"Very busy. Twenty-four hours a day. I saw that when we came here to rescue a young woman last fall."

"You get into everything," Bronco said.

"Nearly everything. By the way, Blevins said the reward from the bank will be twice what I told you." Chet led the way across the street and turned south to go to the café.

Shawn whistled through his teeth. "That's a lot of money."

"Yes. It makes the callouses on our butts worth-while."

"*Ah, si,*" Ortega said as they entered the restaurant. When they told the man at the door they were with Marshal Blevins, he showed them to a side room.

When his men stood around looking apprehensive, Chet waved for them to sit down. A waiter poured red wine in their glasses. About that time, Sheriff Behan showed up with Marshal Blevins and Cohill.

Chet only knew what he'd heard about Behan, but felt he was a threat to his organization because of the sheriff's connection with Old Man Clanton. The less the sheriff knew about his outfit the better.

The banker, Cohill, sat beside Chet and appeared friendly. "I understand you have several ranch holdings in the upper part of the state, Chet?"

"Yes, we have land and cattle around Preskitt and

in the Verde Valley. I moved here a couple of years ago and haven't hardly had time to sit down since then."

"How did a man as busy as you find time to do law enforcement?"

"Mr. Cohill, when the law can't do it, someone needs to. Those three robbbers rode right through Behan's backyard. We captured them last night in Naco. Myself, this young cowboy, and those two *vaqueros*. We rode over from Tubac the day before. We found them with only slim descriptions and information we gained from the public."

"I can see why Blevins speaks so highly of you. But tell me, who runs your ranches?"

"A half dozen smart men I hired. I'll put my operation against anyone's. They're well run and making money."

"You have a contract to feed the Navajos?"

"Yes. And we deliver on time and sell them good beef. They were buying cheap beef you couldn't eat whenever they got it there. The deliveries weren't on time and short. We deliver good beef to several points, like the contract calls for."

"Who handles that?"

"A former cavalry sergeant who married my sister. We call him Sarge."

"Who else rides with you, besides these *vaqueros* and the young man?"

"A young man from Mexico who can track a mouse over rocks. A great Texas cowboy, a super deputy sheriff I borrowed, and my nephew who is a good hand."

"Where will you go next?"

"Back to Tubac and wait for a telegram from Blevins."

"I really want to thank you. We've made a first count and they'd spent little of the bank's money. I never expected to see a cent of it again. Blevins says your men will get the reward money."

"They did the work. They took chances. They deserve it."

"I don't disagree, but why pay them all of it?"

"They deserve it."

"All right. Say, I heard today that the big man went to screaming for help when you were bringing him across from Mexico. And that you hit him on the head, then roped his feet together and beat the horse to get him out of there." Cohill was shaking with laugher by the time he finished.

"Well, I wanted him across the line and no problems with the authorities. So we extradited him."

"And you don't take any part of the reward. You are one helluva generous man, my friend."

At that, his men stood up and applauded him, then the rest joined in. Chet stood and made them stop. He said, "The men that ride with me lay their lives on the line every day. I appreciate them and they take care of me, too. Thanks." He sat down.

It's a good night, but I wish Marge was here.

CHAPTER 25

In the morning, they quietly headed for Tubac. Shawn led the packhorses and they rode along with Ortega busy roping odds and ends beside the road.

"You ever roped a mountain lion?" Chet asked. He'd heard men talk about doing it.

Ortega laughed. "One time. And was he pissed off."

"About you roping him?"

"Yes. Oh, he was furious. He got on his hind feet and scratched all the air around him, growling like a rabid dog. Oh, he was so mad. I knew he was going to charge me, and the *hombre* with me was afraid to rope his back legs. If he had, then we could have stretched him out and castrated him."

Shawn was laughing so hard he was crying.

Chet was about to choke on his own amusement. Who but a *vaquero* would think of castrating a mountain lion. Damn, he couldn't even imagine roping a mountain lion.

"So what did you do then?" Chet asked.

"I tossed him the dally and rode like hell to get away."

"He run off with your riata?" Shawn asked.

"*Sí*. He could have had more than that."

The rest of the way back wasn't near as funny. Chet decided if things were fairly calm when the others got back, he'd run home for a week to see his wife and check on the ranches.

His helpers arrived the next day and there were no telegrams. JD and Cole returned looking refreshed, with word that Roamer was on his way, and he arrived soon after. Things remained quiet.

Chet worried because Jesus wasn't back. The fact niggled him half a day before he spoke about it. "Any of you recall where Jesus said he was going to be, or what town down there he went to find her?"

"I think he told me she lived in the Carreeza Valley," Ortega said, looking across the table at his brother Bronco, who nodded.

"*Sí*, he told us one time that she lived there in a small village called St. Maria."

"That is about three days' ride down there. Are you concerned about him not being back?" Ortega asked.

"Yes. Jesus is dependable. Him not being back means something is wrong."

Cole spoke up. "I agree. Jesus is proud to be working with us. He told me he never dreamed he'd have such a job, and he'd never risk losing it for anything. No, he's being detained, or something's wrong."

"Then we better go find him, huh, boss man?" Ortega asked.

"Yes, but I hate to leave here in case hell breaks loose."

"You take Ortega and Bronco. They know the country better than any of us. We get short, or need a guide, Jose can show us the way," Roamer said.

Heads around the table nodded in agreement.

Chet knew he was right. "Maybe nothing is wrong, but we can find out. I'd hate to leave here and not know where he is. Roamer is the boss while I'm gone."

"It has been strange," Cole said. "He wrote her twice lately and she never answered. I figured the way he talked she was waiting for him to send for her. But you never know about women. I was engaged to a girl and went off to Kansas with a herd of cattle. That was in March. I got back the end of September and she was married to a guy I really hated."

"Why? Did she tell you why?"

"Nothing." Cole threw up his open hands. "I guess she just got tired of waiting."

They all shook their heads. Finally, Roamer asked him, "Valerie was still waiting?"

Cole nodded and smiled a slow smile. "Oh, yes, she sure was. Nice lady. I'm proud I found her, or rather that Chet did for me. Boys, I'm a very happy married man."

"That makes two of us," JD said. "I'm like Cole. And we've talked how we both have swell wives almost as great as Chet has."

"Boys, I don't brag much about Marge, but she's a good woman and she'll keep me on track. I never expected to find a wife quite like her, but she's as sincere as any woman I've ever known."

JD spoke up, smiling. "That man didn't always have good luck with women. He had enough bad luck, in fact, to fill a book." He looked at Chet. "Can I tell them?"

"Sure."

"A woman he was seeing was finally going to leave her worthless husband. They murdered her and she wrote the killer's name in her own blood. Bad day. Then a girl he courted in her teens married another man and he was hung for horse stealing. Well, they struck up a romance, but he had to leave Texas and she couldn't leave her elderly parents. So, he hasn't had such a wonderful love life, either. But I can tell you, Marge has been good for him and for all of us."

Everyone nodded somberly.

Chet was amazed. JD hadn't talked that much in years. He'd sounded like a man who halfway understood life. Maybe he was recovering from whatever had eaten him up. Hearing JD made Chet feel good. But his mention of those bad times still made him clutch up some.

"Cole, Jesus isn't here to do it, so will you fix us two packhorses for in the morning?"

"I sure can do that."

Later, Chet went off to sleep in his bedroll. He hoped they found Jesus in one piece. He sure didn't want to have to tell Marge something had happened to the boy. Lord, another distraction to keep him from coming home. But she'd excuse him, since it was about Jesus. At last, he fell asleep.

The morning was chilly. Horses saddled before daylight and packhorses ready. They all wore jumpers against the biting wind. It wasn't below freezing, but the strong breeze was sharp. After breakfast, the three took the King's Highway south for Nogales. Chet would damn sure be glad when spring arrived.

One never knew when it would rain in this country. Midday, it rained hard and thunder rolled across the land. Lucky they had their yellow slickers on. Chet's hat felt like it weighed a ton with rivulets of water coming off the front dip. But despite the soggy weather, everyone smiled and trotted their horse to make time.

They ate a late lunch in a café on the Mexican side that Ortega knew about, and also found them a place to put their horses and to sleep out of the falling moisture. The hip-swaying café owner told them she'd have breakfast ready at five if they wanted it then. It would still be dark, but the road south was easy to maneuver, so Chet agreed. The sooner this was over the sooner he could go home.

The old warehouse was dry at the end where they slept and the next morning a young boy brought them a candle lamp to see to saddle by. Rain still pattered on the roof.

"There will be a lot of flowers in six weeks," Ortega promised him.

"I'll be ready for them." He tipped the youngster who beamed at the coin in his palm.

The food was ready and hot at the café when they rode there. When they finished, he paid her and she told them to come back more often.

That afternoon, the three headed south and reached a ranch that belonged to a friend of the brothers. Benito Orlando was a broad man smiling at the sight of them at his yard gate.

With a big laugh, he shouted to his wife, Nana, to come see who had arrived. The short woman ran out of the house and stood on her toes to hug them. Then she said to Chet, "Come, these are my boys. Anyone who is with them is *mi amigo*."

After they watered the horses and put them into a corral with feed, they headed for the house to eat.

"We will be there tomorrow," Ortega promised Chet with a smile.

Then they would need to find Jesus, the quiet young man who rode with them. All he could do was hope nothing bad had happened to him. He counted on him so much, for his tracking skill, packing, and cooking ability.

Chet followed the others into the nice *casa* where the woman and her help were rushing about to make the food.

Benito heard the story of the task force and what they were doing. He agreed that the bandits needed to be stopped for the safety of people on both sides of the border.

"Where do you live?" he asked Chet.

"Preskitt. My business is ranching."

"How did you get into this law business?"

"I guess because not enough was being done about it."

The man nodded. "I savvy what you mean. How long will you continue?"

"Until someone else can run it."

"I bet they aren't looking." Benito chuckled and Chet had to agree.

"We came down here to look for one of our own who hasn't returned from a week off. He's a very dependable young man. According to my other men, he went to the Carreeza Valley to look for his girlfriend who had not answered his letters asking her to join him in Arizona."

"I wish the best to you on this search, *señor*, and I will pray for your success."

"We sure may need it."

Chet went to sleep troubled about his missing man. They rose early, she fed them, and they rode for the valley. Midday, they were in a narrow irrigated valley with banana trees all over and with many tropical plants he'd never seen before.

The boys stopped and picked some small red bananas growing wild on bushes. They tasted different than any he'd eaten, but he'd seen them in Arizona markets before. They reached the village in midafternoon. A typical small community with a Catholic church and a central well.

They went in a cantina and Ortega asked the bartender about Jesus. The man said he'd never heard of him.

"His name is Jesus Morales," Ortega repeated.

"Not from around here." He hurriedly left to wait on another man down the bar.

Chet shook his head for Ortega to not push it. Something was wrong and he had no idea what it was. But Jesus was either dead or in trouble.

He paid for the beers, but didn't drink his. It tasted too damn bad. Then they rode to the church and dismounted to speak to the priest they found inside.

"Father, a friend of ours came here a week ago to find his bride-to-be and he has not returned. His name is Jesus Morales."

The priest nodded. "He is in critical condition. Come with me."

He took them to a nearby house. On the way, Chet asked what happened to Jesus.

"He was shot."

"Who did it?"

"I was not there. He was brought to me and we have done what we can for him."

Chet looked around. "Is there something evil going on here?"

"Why do you ask that?"

"A bartender would not talk to us about Jesus."

"I am not surprised."

"Then there is some evil power here?"

"My son, this land is no different than the world."

"But where I live, people don't shoot other people."

He led them into a room where the sight of Jesus's pale sleeping face shocked Chet.

"Has a doctor seen him?" Chet spoke in a low voice.

"Oh, yes, and removed the bullet. That was five days ago."

"Why was he shot?"

The priest shook his head.

"Is the young woman he came for available?"

"No."

"Where can we find her?"

The priest crossed himself. "She is dead."

What in hell was going on? He saw the concern on the other two men's faces.

"Who killed her?"

"Six months ago. She took her own life over a situation she was forced into."

"What was that?"

"She was kidnapped and sold into slavery. Taken to Mexico City and she ended her own life. I fear your friend learned of some parties involved in her abduction and was shot when he confronted them."

"Do you know their names?"

"The two men who died were members of the Trucilia family."

"Chet." Jesus was awake, his voice dry and weak.

"Hey, how are you?"

"Better—I think."

"Father has been telling us about how you got shot."

"I am—sorry I could not contact you. I have been—in bed."

"You're in good hands. Sleep and get well."

Jesus nodded, spoke to the brothers, and fell asleep.

In the hall, Chet thanked the priest, his mind on other things.

It would be some time before Jesus could ride out. Maybe they could get a buggy and take him back, at least to their camp. Would the ride kill him? It shouldn't, but he didn't want their efforts to hurt him. Too many unanswered questions.

But they did know something about the problem, and they'd soon know more.

They found a place to board the horses and to sleep. Satisfied they were settled, Chet and the brothers set out to learn all they could about the shooting. Chet found a street vendor lady who fixed them supper on her small grill. Soon, they dug into the large tortilla wraps.

Ortega asked her small questions, one at a time, so as not to alarm her. She knew about the shooting. Two men escaped, she said.

Then she gave them two names. "They are mean

men and many fear them. Alfredo and Domingo Noreaga."

"What happened to Truc—"

"He shot them. Then these other *hombres* came and shot him."

"Who are they?"

She shrugged. "Cousins. Bad men, too."

"Where can we find them?" Ortega asked.

"They have a place up the valley."

"What does it look like?"

"A *ranchero*, huh?" She shrugged her thin shoulders.

"I guess we can find it."

She agreed with a nod. That was the end of her answering any more questions.

They walked along the quiet dark street. Chet wished he'd gone back to check on Jesus, but he'd do that in the morning.

At the livery barn he told the brothers, "By now, they know we're here. From here on, be careful every minute."

"And they know why we came," Ortega said with a nod.

"We need to keep up a guard tonight."

"You take the first. Wake Bronco when it's his turn. I'll take the last one."

"That sounds fair, but wake me if either of you see anything suspicious."

Both agreed, so he sat his shift, then woke Bronco for his turn to listen to the night sounds.

An edge of discomfort went along with him to his bedroll. Not over the brothers, they were tough and would fight tooth and nail for him. It was the situation. An enemy he could not measure, nor did he know them on sight or their strength. And any unknown weakness they had that he could use to take them down. Sleep buried his concerns.

"We have company, *señor*," Ortega whispered in his ear.

Colt in his fist, he nodded. "How many?"

"Five or six. They rode up and tied their horses a block away about a half hour ago. Then they went and drank some whiskey with some *putas*. I heard them say there are only three to kill. I cut their cinches and came back here. That three means us. And at dawn."

Bronco joined them and squatted down. "What do we do?"

"Stealth. We need to get one or two of them before the sun comes up."

"Bronco and I will handle it." Ortega nodded and his brother stood to join him.

Chet told them, "Be back here before dawn."

They nodded, then were gone in the night. He checked all the rifles to be sure their chambers were full. His cartridge pistol was loaded. He moved some empty crates to make barricades. Later, he put the stuffed bedrolls out in front so they looked like someone was sleeping in them.

The night was quiet, except for crickets and sleeping horses grunting. He shifted the Colt from his fist to the other hand and dried his palm on his pants several times. At last he heard his men coming back.

When they rejoined him, there was a crease of pink on the horizon. Guns at hand, and behind the crates, they faced the two open doors backlit by the budding dawn.

Ortega said, "There are only three left. The ones in back won't help them."

"Thanks. We needed that advantage. Get down. They'll think we're sleeping in our bedrolls."

CHAPTER 26

"There they are!" Gunshots rocked the building and when the gunsmoke cleared, three silhouettes stood in the smoky doorway. The three bedrolls smoldered from the bullets in them. Their laughter rang out in the empty warehouse.

"We got them three *bastardos*," a loud voice declared as they holstered their guns.

"Not yet," Chet said in Spanish.

Three rifles shattered the silence. The three gunmen crumpled to the dust.

"We will go get the others," Ortega said, and he and his brother went out the back door. Chet stood over the men still in the throes of death and kicked their guns aside.

Curious townspeople had begun to dare look from across the street. Women caught up their children and dragged them back to the safety of the onlookers. Then a few brave men ventured halfway across the street.

"Are they dead?" one man asked.

Chet was aware of every man in the crowd. He didn't feel a threat from any of them. "If they aren't dead, they're dying."

"Those are bad men," an older woman said, tossing her head toward them.

"No, ma'am. They're only dead men now."

Ortega and Bronco came around the corner with five horses and two dead bodies on them. They dumped the bodies beside the others.

"We need their guns?" Bronco asked.

"Round them up. We need a wagon and a team."

A man stepped forward, sombrero in hand. "I have a wagon and team, *señor.*"

"I need you to take my wounded man back to Arizona. I'll pay you fifty dollars."

"I will take him for you."

"Find two thick mattresses for him to lie on. I'll pay you for them. Meet me at the doctor's in thirty minutes. Now, where is the undertaker?"

Another man stepped forward. "I am, *señor.* What can I do for you?"

"I want them buried." He indicated the men on the ground.

"Oh, *señor,* I will need coffins and services. Let me see, that would be—"

"Hey, I said buried. Ten bucks apiece and cover them up."

"That is very unusual, *señor.*"

"Not for trash. I can get several people to dig a grave for all five and bury them for that. Take it or leave it."

"I will bury them."

"Good.

"Okay. Come load them up and you get the money."

"*Sí.*"

Ortega returned to say the packhorses were loaded and ready to go, and the man with the wagon and team were there.

"Good. Take him to the doctor's office and get Jesus comfortable in the wagon. Make sure he has two mattresses. I'll be there after this man loads these bodies."

"We can handle loading Jesus."

The undertaker returned and loaded the bodies into a hearse. Chet paid the man, then swung on the roan horse. He scattered a handful of pennies in the street for the children. They rushed screaming to find them and he rode off.

Jesus looked stronger lying under covers in the morning coolness. Chet rode up to pay the nurse for her care. The woman took his twenty and thanked him. "He is a kind man," she added. "I will pray for him."

"Thank you," he said, and rode after the wagon.

With few problems, they reached Nogales in three days, and a doctor there examined Jesus. He told Chet, "He is recovering and healing, but his body needs time. He must have lost a lot of blood. I think if he takes things easy, in a few weeks he'll be his old self."

They loaded him back in the wagon and went on to Tubac. When they arrived at the Ortega ranch, everyone was excited.

Chet paid the Mexican wagon driver and thanked him. "You can stay and rest a day before you go home, if you like."

"They say they will have a fiesta tonight?" he asked.

"I bet they'll have one for him. You're welcome to stay for it."

"*Gracias, señor.*"

As soon as they were settled, Chet went over the mail. In his absence, things had been quiet. He read his wife's letter carefully. The bank had received more government money for the cattle. Things were smooth with Sarge, Tom, and Hampt. Everything was all right with Reg and Lucie. She missed him.

After a visit with his men, he left Roamer in charge and planned to catch the stage in Tubac that night. JD rode with him to town to bring his horse back to camp, leaving the party makers celebrating Jesus's return. At last, it was his turn to go home, carrying letters for their wives from JD and Cole.

"You still think a ranch west of here could work?" JD asked.

"You interested?"

"Yes."

"Could your wife stand the isolation out there?" Chet asked him.

"I think so. If I can afford to send her home every few months."

"Think on it then. Bo can put us one together, I'm certain. Be lots of work."

"I like the warmer climate. This desert is different, but there's grass over there and it needs more water development. If you decide to do it, I'd like a shot at the job."

"I'll consider it and talk to Bo some when I'm at home. This task force business suiting you now?"

"Yes, it is. I think people really appreciate what we're doing."

"You've sure done your share to make it work."

"Thanks. You have a safe trip."

JD went back to the ranch and Chet waited in the stage office. Fresh horses were soon hitched for the trip to Tucson. They'd make one more horses change and he'd be in Tucson after daylight. From there, he'd take the stage north to Hayden's Ferry, then the Black Canyon Stage from that point on home. He'd damn sure be tired of rocking stages by then.

The trip was uneventful, with mostly drummers and one stuffy army officer going to the fort. Usually, there was at least one woman, but none rode this time. When they started up the steep grades north of Hayden's Ferry, he knew the temperature would drop sharply, so he had on his jumper and a blanket to wrap up in.

They arrived in Preskitt in the dark and Jiminez met him. They loaded his gear into the buckboard and the young man drove him home under the stars. On the way, the stable hand told him things were going smooth at the upper place.

When they reached the ranch, the lights were on in the house and several rigs parked around in the yard. Marge came out on the porch in a coat that didn't hide her growing pregnancy. They held one another for a long while and kissed.

"How is Jesus?"

"He'll be fine. He's getting his strength back. The doctor in Nogales said he must have lost a lot of blood. But he'll be fine."

"You didn't bring him home?"

"Not to ride on those swinging coaches. My back feels broken now."

"Come in. Everyone is here. I'm sorry you don't feel good."

"I feel good enough to see you and the rest of our family."

"Good." She kissed him on the cheek and they went inside. It was damn sure wintertime up here—still cold.

Everyone was there—the expecting wives, Susie and May, and their men. Millie and Tom. Hugs and kisses from all, and he even kissed Monica who beamed at him.

His butt braced against the wall, he looked over all of them in the living room. "I can say it's sure good to be home. We still have more work to do down there, but we're making progress. I was gone a week to get Jesus and no telegrams reporting crimes came in.

"Jesus is doing fine, but it's a sad story. The girl waiting for him was kidnapped and sold. The priest said she couldn't stand what had happened to her and committed suicide. Jesus was evening the score for her and was shot in the back. Those men who did that to him no longer live in this world."

There was a room full of nods of approval. "He'll be back to duty in a few weeks. JD is more himself than I can recall. He's anxious to have a ranch to run down in southern Arizona. Warmer down there."

They all got a chuckle out of that.

"Chet," Tom said. "I hate to tell you, but Hoot passed away this week. I know how he helped you get that ranch and what he did for the rest of us when you went to gather up this crew. We laid him in the ground two days ago."

"Thanks. He was a great help to me and my start in the territory, and a good friend. I thought a lot of him. I know you must have given him a good send-off." He looked down at his dusty boots and the room went quiet.

After a moment, he cleared his throat and turned to Sarge. "Are the cattle sales still going well?"

Conversations in the room started back up as Sarge answered him. "All our plans have worked well this winter. They have even been shocked that we delivered them on time."

"We have a steady stream of cattle coming to us from the local ranchers," Tom said.

Hampt spoke up. "I'm ready to plant when we get a weather break and it warms up."

"I guess Reg and Lucie are all right?"

Marge nodded. "Their letters are cheerful."

Susie agreed. "Our house is coming up, Sarge tells me."

"I guess all I have to do is wait for the babies to get here. Raphael all right?"

"Oh, yes. He wanted to come tonight, but something came up."

"I'll see him tomorrow or whenever. If you have a problem, you'd better tell me or it won't get fixed."

Millie stood up. "I want to tell you how much I appreciate my house. Thank you, Chet Byrnes, we all love you."

Susie came by and he kissed her forehead. "I look around and see four of us expecting. Must be the water out here."

He hugged her close. "Ain't we lucky?"

"Yes, we are, brother. You be careful down there."

"I will. Love you."

He spoke to Tom and Millie next. "Sorry I missed Hoot's funeral."

"He was fine, just slipped away peacefully in his rocker."

"How is Robert?"

"The mill is still running near full capacity, and he's married, you know?"

"Yes, I remember, the tall blond girl."

"By the way," Tom said, "I bought those horses for the haying. We need to ship Reg the machinery and horses when spring comes. Sarge and Hampt have theirs and their horses. I can hire enough boys for those jobs next summer. I rented more alfalfa ground down in the valley. We'll need it."

"Good. I count on all of you to keep these places going. Keep water development on your mind.

People that succeed in this business solve those problems."

They ate Monica's cake and goodies and then turned in.

In his own bed with his wife at last, he drew her close. "I was sure anxious to be back here with you."

"Well, don't hold anything back; you won't hurt me or him."

He chuckled. "I won't then."

CHAPTER 27

Marge said she'd stay home while he went to town and did his business. The cold snap had a good hold, and he rode horseback on one of her father's saddles. The big bay horse Jiminez called Baldy, because he had a white face, walked on eggs out to the crossbar. After that, he settled down and Chet short-loped him into town. The trip to town didn't even wind the big horse, and he stopped at Jenn's Café. He was mobbed by the two wives, and after kisses to his cheek, he handed out their much sought-after letters.

"How's Mexico?" Jenn asked.

"Dusty and poor."

"Like always."

"Like always." He told her Jesus's story and about the task force.

"Sounds like you have it held down."

"Only for a short while until some new warlord rises up and raids across the border again."

"No one used to stop them. Oh, Hoot passed away

last week. I knew he was bad off, but your people made him feel at home."

"We did the old man right. I hate I wasn't back, but I'm certain he's forgiven me."

"Oh, yes, I'm sure. What next?" she asked.

"We go back, for a while anyway."

"I really believe those two girls are happy in their new lives. I hope so. I made some bad mistakes in my life at that age, but—aw, hell, I hope they make as good a deal as you have out of it."

"Me, too."

When he arrived at the bank, Tanner was happy. They had a nice visit over the growing ranch bank account. Ben at the mercantile smiled when he checked with him. He asked Chet to have a seat and closed the office door.

"Kathrin and I are going to have a baby. My divorce will be final any day and we'll be married. I never thought I'd have an heir. I'm lots older than you. But I'm about to bust my buttons, and that's because you saw something in her and gave her a chance."

"I'm happy for both of you. You deserve happiness." He reached out and shook his hand. "Ben, we're getting ready for hay. I guess all is well here?"

"Tom ordered more harness and it should be here soon. When will we ever get a railroad out this way?"

"It will be years away."

"I suppose you're right. How is your outfit down south doing?"

"Fine. We're arresting a lot of thieves and murderers."

He rode by Bo's and his office was closed. That struck him as funny and then he saw the note.

Closed for family emergency.

He remounted and rode to the doctor's office. He found Bo pacing the outer room.

"What's the matter?"

"Jane. She's losing the baby and I may even lose her. What will I do?"

"Stay sober."

"I'll do that. There's the doctor coming out." He turned and almost cried. "Oh, God, Chet, she's dying."

"You can go in and see her," the doc said, and shook his head sadly. "We've done all we can, but I fear you will lose her."

"Thanks. Come on, Chet. I know she'll want to see you."

Jane was always small, but she looked like a pale child under the white covers. Her voice was soft and rusty sounding. "Chet, you find him another. He don't need another bottle, but he'll need a woman to remind him of that. God, I love you both so much."

"I'll do that, Jane. Trust me." He squeezed her cold small hand.

"Good, then I won't worry anymore."

Bo fought to keep back tears. But the power of God was sweeping her away and Chet knew it would be swift.

Bo fell on his knees, mumbling prayers to save her.

But that last ounce of life dripped out of her. Jane died.

He and Marge attended the services at the Methodist cemetery. Bo asked Chet to say a few words, and when the time came he stepped forward to speak. His words rolled out into the wintry weather on steamy breath.

"God brought Jane to us. She was an orphan who'd made her way here from back east. She married Bo and they had a good life, both finding strength in each other. His business expanded and she was the force that pushed him ahead. They were expecting their first child, but God needed both the child and her in heaven. But our father will give him the strength he gained from their union to continue his life as a sober citizen. Amen."

"Amen."

Bo touched his arm. "I will do that."

Marge was overcome and told him so walking to the buckboard. "You find words that impress me a lot. Maybe that's why I married you. Where does all that come from?"

"Ah, I just try to let it come from my heart."

"And you do." He helped her into the buckboard, then wrapped her in a blanket. "Let's go home."

"Yes. Let's do that." He climbed on the seat and clucked to the ready horses. They went home, smartly trotting the team in the unwarming bright sun. Harness jingled and hooves padded the hard surface. And he had his wife with him.

"Two months?"

"Yes, they should be here then."

"They?"

"I think at times they may be twins. Don't count on it." She shrugged under the blanket. "I've never been this far along before. It isn't a lot of fun, but I look forward to having him or her here."

"Well, you aren't the only one who's never been this far before."

They both laughed and he drove up to the house.

They took a nap after lunch—an excuse to cuddle and make love. But who cared? He had lots of questions to be answered, and the unexpected death of Jane was another thing to think on. What would Bo do? Go crazy? Probably.

His days at home passed swiftly. Soon it was time to go back to the task force, so he kissed his wife goodbye. Jiminez drove him to the stage stop and he climbed aboard the southbound coach after sundown. Days were getting longer and he knew spring had probably sprung down south. Everyone had promised him flowers there after the winter rains.

When they reached the New River Station, the sun came up and showed him the fragile looking paintbrush flowers and a hundred more varieties in fairy-like circles that carpeted the desert floor. He recalled Texas springs, when the blue bonnets and the other wild flowers did that. How he'd loped through miles of it then. Maybe after the loss of two close friends, this was a good omen.

He hired a buckboard to take him to the ranch

from town. Maria met him, surprised he was back so soon.

"Jose is here. The rest left this morning. There was a robbery of a shipment of silver and gold east of the Chiricahuas. Marshal Blevins said they needed lots of help over there. They said for you to wait here for their return."

"I'll go see if I can help them."

"They said to make you stay here."

"Oh, they worry too much about me."

"Then Jose must ride with you."

"Maria, you will need someone here."

"If anyone wants to die, we can shoot them. You either take Jose or you don't go."

"All right, we'll need a packhorse and tell him we leave in two hours."

She half laughed. "Good, he has time for his wife."

"Will she need more time?"

"Maybe. Ricky is strange. I said too much. He will be ready." She blushed, shook her head, and hurried off to get things done, holding the hem of her dress up as she ran for the *jacal*.

He laughed to himself after she left. Jose's wife must be different. Maria seldom complained about anything.

The two rode out in a long trot leading the pack-horse. They had maybe a two day ride or longer to find his task force. No easy job. Jose never complained, so Chet guessed he'd settled with his wife. They camped that evening on Sonotia Creek near

Patagonia. Jose was an efficient camp helper, and they soon had supper cooking.

"Was Jesus feeling strong enough to go with them?"

"He really did feel good and wanted to go. Ortega said he could rest in camp if he got tired."

"Good, he's tough enough."

"He told us more about the girl he lost. A shame."

"He never spoke about her to me."

"She must have been lovely."

"Well, I have buried so many people lately, I hope that's over for a while."

Jose nodded. "That is not fun."

The next day, riding east over the open range country, he decided to take the pass over Muleshoe Mountain to reach the San Bernardino Valley where the robbery occurred. They pushed hard and stopped at a widow's place for the night, deep in the narrow canyon below Muleshoe Mountain pass.

She fed them and Chet went to sleep in his bedroll. He suspected the woman had other plans for his helper. He had no interest in her himself and soon found sleep.

Jose woke him before daylight. Squatted beside him, already in his boots and spurs, he spoke softly. "The border bandits have put out a reward for your death."

"Which ones?" He sat up in the cool premorning air.

"She does not know, but the way she explained it, they are offering five hundred dollars for the *gringo* that leads the task force. That is you."

"We've really made some enemies, haven't we?"

He agreed with a smile. "But I do not think I can protect you good enough. I do not have Ortega's skills at this business. We need to go back today. This country I do not know, and it sounds like they have many out looking for you. If not, she would not know that much about it."

"You don't trust her?"

"No. She is too easy to seduce. You know what I mean. She would tell someone you were here if they honeyed up to her. I know she must be lonesome, but she is too lonesome, huh?"

"All right, let's ride over the pass and down the valley."

Jose pinned him with a serious expression. "When we come back, we will not stop here?"

"That's fine. But if I can help the men, I'd like to lend them a hand."

"I have the horse packed."

"You didn't sleep, huh?"

"No. Her word concerned me much about your safety. The last thing Maria told me was you are very important and I should let nothing happen to you."

"Thanks for the concern. We'll be fine."

"I really hope you are right."

They saddled and rode off before a light showed in her *jacal*.

The steep canyon slopes bristled with junipers, and in the dim dawn light they looked to Chet like stations for ambushers. The hard climb shed stones under their horses' hooves until they reached the top and a cool wind swept across their faces and their sweaty hard-breathing horses. He looked back. The deep canyon looked less dangerous with them on top. The road went steeply off the pass into the valley below.

He could hardly imagine a heavy-loaded wagon going off this pitch. Obviously, though, they had, for some wrecked wagons' shattered remains could be seen off the edge of the road. His roan horse's stiff-legged descent agreed with his calculations. They reached the small village at the base and found a street vendor who made them some breakfast. She was toothless and smiled a lot while she squatted down cooking.

"You go far today?" she asked.

"Clear to hell," Jose told her.

Chet almost laughed. She was getting no information from him. Probably just as well. If they had killers out looking for him, any information would be valuable to a poor villager.

"What is your name?" she asked Jose.

"Ramon Garcia."

"What is his name?"

"John Smith."

He paid her and they went for their horses. Chet said, "Let's go, Ramon."

"*Ah, sí, Señor* Smith," he said, and never cracked a smile.

Her food was not wonderful, but they ate the stuffed tortilla in the cool shadows of the canyon.

They rode on down the canyon where it opened

up on the east side of the mountain into the desert flat. When they reached the next small village, Jose went into the cantina and asked about their men passing through.

When he came out, he told Chet they were there two days before. The bartender thought they went to Lordsburg, fifty or sixty miles north.

"Where would you think they'd go down there?" Chet asked, not satisfied they'd gone to Lordsburg.

"San Bernardino is the town on the border. I think they would go there. It has border entry. The pack train must have been going there to bring the ore in or out."

"I'm for going there." They set out across the flat desert. A land with less cactus and more grass marked with some mesquite, they reached the village in late afternoon.

Jose recognized a horse that belonged to his brothers at a hitch rack and reined up. "Get off your horse, *señor*. Someone might shoot at you. I will find him."

Chet stepped down, though he saw no danger from the dust-floured residents of old men and women and some half-naked children. A bleak-looking place. Farther down the street were some adobe warehouses marked with an export-import sign.

In a short time, Ortega came out with Jose and smiled. He had several purchases in a sack.

"Good evening, *señor*."

"Great to see you. Where are the others?"

"At the Peralta family ranch, about ten miles east. It is a good place to camp and I know the ranch foreman."

"Any luck on finding out about the robbery?" Chet asked.

"I can tell you on the way, but everyone is fine. I don't like this place. Jose said they have a price of five hundred dollars on your head. In this piss-poor place, that is a fortune, and we need to move on."

"Fine. Let's go." Chet saw no threat, but the brothers knew the border better than he did. They rode a long way but saw ranch lights at last. They rode by the main adobe buildings and corrals.

Ortega spoke to a rifle-armed guard. "These are my kinfolks," he told the man, and they went on to a small spring-fed lake under some cottonwoods.

Chet's pleased crew got up from around the campfire to shake his hand.

"Good to have you back," Roamer said. "There must be thirty dead mules about ten miles or so north of here. Unburied corpses laying around. The canyon is run over in buzzards and anything that eats the dead. None of us can figure out what really happened, except the pack train ran into a large band of heavily armed gunmen and were shot to pieces. Every pannier is gone. Most of the packsaddles are gone, and the bodies were stripped of clothing and any identity. Must have happened some time back. Ortega talked to some people who said it was a major operation, and they felt the men rode for Old Man Clanton. But there's no way to prove it, so we have little to go on."

"How's everything at home?" Cole asked.

"No problems I could learn about."

"That's good. All of us over here, and we're not learning a thing."

Chet agreed. They might just as well go home. He bet Sheriff Behan never sent anyone over to even look at the site. Win some and lose some.

"Jose, tell them what she told you over in Muleshoe Canyon last night."

Jose told them about their overnight stop and what the widow told him about the warlords in Mexico putting a price of five hundred dollars on Chet for his death.

"We had not heard that over here," Ortega said. "But chances are they'd never pay it."

"And if I was dead, who would complain?" Chet teased.

"Your wife would," Cole said. "We ain't letting them do that."

"Hell, no," JD said. "Who are these guys offering this reward? I'd like to go find them and end their misery for them."

"They will show up," Ortega told him.

"Let's go home tomorrow. You've run out of leads. Even if Clanton did it, we can't touch him in Mexico without an army."

They all nodded in agreement.

Chet laid in his bedroll a long time before he went to sleep. He never took defeat well, but this horrendous crime would have to go unanswered. A well-planned robbery. No witnesses. Someone must have seen those outlaws ride in and ride out, but no one was talking.

CHAPTER 28

The trip back to headquarters took two long days of hard riding. But when he dropped heavy from the saddle in the starlight and heard the brothers' women's voices welcoming their husbands home, he felt good.

"*Señor* Chet, are you hungry?" Maria asked, sounding concerned.

"No. I'll be fine. Too tired to eat anyway."

"Ortega said you rode a long ways."

"Miles and miles."

Jesus took his horse and led him off with his own.

"Thanks, see you in the morning," he said to his now solemn man.

"There were no telegrams," said Maria.

"That's good news."

"Good night." Then she rushed off to her *jacal.* Her husband was home.

He wished he was—but sleep came easy. Waking up was hard. He dressed and went to the tent where Maria was busy feeding the crew pancakes and oat-

meal. About half of the crew were up. He didn't
blame the others for sleeping in. Hey, they had no
work pressing them.

She poured him some coffee. "Pancakes or oatmeal, or both?"

"Pancakes will be fine. Send someone to town
today and buy some good beef and some onions and
sweet peppers, and some red wine, huh?"

Her sweet face perked up. "We will have a *fandango* tonight?"

"Yes, we need one."

"I am glad you are back. We need to liven up,
don't we?"

"You know how. If you need more money, let me
know."

"I can use my bill and you can pay it later."

"You have a deal."

When it warmed up, he took a bath and shaved.
Poor folks in Preskitt were shivering and he was lying
in a hammock perfectly warm. The men busied
themselves with resetting shoes on the horses and
repairing tack.

Jesus came over with a crate to sit on. Chet swung
his legs over the side of the hammock. It looked to
him like his man wanted to talk and he was ready. He
couldn't suppress a large yawn.

"Hard ride back here yesterday," Jesus said.

"Yeah, but I'm glad we're here."

"Oh, yes. I came to talk to you. My life, you know,
has changed. I had such plans, but they were all
around her coming to be with me. My life is like a

derailed engine I saw one time, that banditos had blown from a train. It simply laid there. A little steam escaped from it and some smoke from the furnace— but it just laid there and no one could put it back on those tracks."

Chet began telling him. "A woman I once loved would not leave her husband who abused her. One day, I went to her ranch and found her murdered by my enemies. It was a bloody crime and she wrote the killer's name on the sheet with her own blood. In that same room, she had left a letter to tell her husband she was leaving him."

"Oh, I heard you tell this story. She was leaving him for you, huh?"

"Yes, but I never let the husband read the note."

"I see what all you must have gone through. Yes, like my story, that is a sad one. How did you forget it?"

"Got busy fighting a range war that was piled on me."

"I see. You say life goes on."

"It does, Jesus. There are other good women in this world."

"I will look."

"Pray, too. It helps. Things won't be quiet for long. We'll get busy again. You won't have time to worry about much else."

Looking brighter, his man thanked him and went on. He hoped he'd done him some good.

Maria came back from town in the buckboard before time for the lunch that Ricky was preparing.

She unloaded her supplies and said she had a letter for him and went to find it.

The letter was from Bo, and brought memories of Bo's recent losses before he even opened it.

Dear Chet,

I learned about a man who has several sections of land in that region you were interested in. There are few improvements. He ran some Mexican cattle down there and let them fatten. So there are some pens—or were—and a few rough headquarters. His name is Hans Krueger and he lives in Los Angeles, California. I suspect he ranches over there.

I have included a map of his holdings and land relative to where you are. The Rankin deal has been postponed again by the courts. Do you want the store in Camp Verde? It is for sale.

"NO!"

I am sober and regret it every day. I did get drunk once and hated it. I know now why you don't drink. But my life is not the same without her.

Bo

"What have you got?" JD asked, dropping by and taking a seat on the bench.

"A map to a ranch we may go look at."

"Where is it?"

Chet pointed at the map. "This is Tubac. The land

is west over those small mountains and lays up and down the basin on the other side."

"What's wrong with it?"

"Water for cattle, for one. No ranch improvements, but there might be corrals and some *jacals* left."

"You went over there, didn't you?"

"Yes. Lots of grass, but it's the lack of water that hangs it up."

"When can we go back and look some more?"

"Any time. Crime has slowed up a lot. I know we don't have all of them rounded up and it's only a lull, but I think a few of us can go look it over."

"I'm ready." JD looked pleased.

"I'll talk to Ortega. He knows that country."

"When you get ready, let me know."

"I will."

He caught Ortega later and told him he wanted to take another look at the land to the west.

"Fine, who goes?"

"You, Jesus to cook, and JD who wants to run it, if I think it will work. I have a map of the pattern of the sections the man in California owns. They say he brought cattle from Mexico and fattened them out there. Must not have worked too well."

"I never knew when he did that. There are remains of corrals, but I never talked to any *vaqueros* who worked there then."

"My land man had that story. But the remains of corrals say it probably happened."

"Oh, yes, and these horses are not scrubby mustangs. I would say some good stallions escaped, and those horses over there have more Barb blood."

"That makes sense."

"When do we go?" Ortega beamed.

"Day after tomorrow, if we have no problems."

"I will be ready."

No telegram came and Chet left the camp in Roamer's hands who Bronco was teaching to braid a riata cut from a whole steer hide. Chet and the others left before dawn with two packhorses. Their horses, fresh from their rest, struck out on the move.

Chet was behind Ortega's horse when he reined up. He followed the man's pointing finger. A large mountain lion loped along the ridgeline. Too far away to shoot. Chet nodded. "That was a big old tom."

"Yes, he could kill a horse."

"Or me," JD shouted at them.

Chet agreed and they moved on.

On the pass, they rested their horses and then settled into the steep decline. On the less steep trail, JD rode up beside Chet.

"You say the route in here from Tucson is flatter?"

"Yes, for all purposes, it's flat and you can see for miles up and down this land."

"Good. These damn mountains would be tough to get in or out of here."

"The way down to Mexico is also an open door for rustlers."

"That makes it interesting, don't it?"

"Could be a tough place to ranch."

"No tougher than the Verde place was when you bought it."

"It is still a challenge to make a profit. But we'll have steers to sell this fall."

"Where could we sell these cattle?" JD asked.

Chet shook his head. JD understood some of the problems they'd face building a ranch out here. He'd not seen a dry cow pie near any waterholes, and that meant there was no maverick population like they found on Reg's operation. But they hadn't seen the entire ranch on that first trip.

Ortega swung them south to a small natural lake fed by a spring where they'd leave their packhorse and gear and set up camp. Jesus remained to set up things for cooking. They rode on, eating some burritos Maria sent with them.

When Ortega found some fresh horse apples, Chet was pleased. In a short while he had his glasses out scoping the herd they'd found. A large blue roan stallion was the monarch of the herd of brood mares with many great looking colts. He passed the glasses around.

Ortega nodded. "They are good horses."

"How many bands are here?"

"I don't know, but I have seen this stallion, and there are others."

"It would be interesting to cut off the colts," JD said.

Ortega agreed. "But there must be a bachelor herd of males he has cut away from these mares."

"Right. Have you seen them?" JD asked.

"Only their heels."

"Interesting, huh, Chet?"

"Yes. That's why we came to appraise this place."

"You have any ideas?" JD asked.

"Water worries me."

"The stud uses the lake. Where is there more?"

"Maybe south," Ortega said, and they rode in that direction.

After a few hours in the saddle, Chet saw through his glasses palm trees in the heat waves. Palms had been planted by the Spaniards centuries ago. They showed up in many places in the southwest desert around water sources. That meant water, so they headed that way.

Obvious, too, was the smell of smoke on the wind. When they arrived at the source, they found people who were probably squatters on the property. Dust-floured and hard looking, some pregnant, the women came out of their canvas hovels with small children around their tattered skirts.

Ortega rode in and told them hello. They nodded, but their faces were solemn.

"Where are your men?"

The women's turned-up palms were his answer.

"Are all of you dumb?" he asked in Spanish.

Chet noticed they'd grown some corn and crops in the past summer season.

"Ask if they have food," Chet told him.

He did and one woman said, "*Poco.*"

Chet gripped his saddle horn and nodded. "I heard her. They don't have much."

Ortega rode back to them. "What can we do?"

"We'll send some food back to them tomorrow."

He swung his horse around and told them they would send them some food. The women nodded at his words and crossed themselves.

They rode on and an hour later they shot two buck deer. They loaded them on their horses and rode back. The women came out looking shocked and his men hung the carcasses up on some cross arms for the women to butcher.

"Can you dress them?" Ortega asked them.

"*Oh, si, gracias, gracias.* God bless you all."

Chet nodded and they headed back for camp. The range had lots of forage, but water was the weakest part. Windmills were expensive to drill and set up. Plus this much land would require hundreds of them. And he'd bet all of this land didn't yield well water. He had lots to think about. How many other squatters were out there, besides those desperate women and children?

"Where were their men?"

"I have no idea. They must be off working in the valley up by Hayden's Ferry."

"Could they have starved before they got back to them?"

Ortega nodded grimly.

Chet shook his head. The notion made him sick, thinking of those small children starving. It reminded him of the Indians they'd helped at Camp Verde when the Indian agent was starving them. And of the breeds on the Verde they fed until Marge's church took over.

During the ride back to camp, the women's situation rode hard on his thoughts. He couldn't settle all the problems in this world, but he didn't have to stand by and let such things continue, not if he could help it.

Back in camp, Jesus was glad to see them and had plenty of food cooked and a Dutch oven cobbler. He got the acclaim of all the crew when they finished eating.

Chet told him about the squatters, and he agreed to take them half a sack of beans and as much flour as he wouldn't need before they returned to camp. Ortega drew him a map on an envelope.

"I'll get them the food tomorrow."

"They appreciated the two deer we gave them, so they'll like what you have to give them, too."

"I'll find out where their men are, too. Maybe a poke in the ass would help them, huh?"

Chet laughed. "It wouldn't hurt them none."

It had been a long day. Lots of country, but not much water. That was why that German never used it but once. Chet didn't want a one-time experience. He'd had enough of them in his life.

His mind was on his wife, full of a baby or two. Life would be back to normal by summer again. Maybe they could even use the Oak Creek place. He hoped Leroy and Betty Lou worked it out up there. And Reg, he'd go see him on the next trip home. Not that

he thought he and Lucie couldn't run the ranch—
simply be nice to see them again. He fell asleep wondering about the cattle drive to Gallup.

The next day, they rode three abreast up the
valley. Jesus was going to take the supplies to the
women, and they were going to look over the north
section of range.

By midafternoon they approached some buildings
and corral. Smoke came from a rusty stovepipe—
probably a cooking fire. There had been cattle signs
for over two hours, but they didn't see any.

"Is that on your map?" Ortega asked. "I have never
been up here. I didn't know these were here."

There was an X on the map about where they
were, but it was unexplained. A stock dog barked and
a man armed with a rifle stepped out to squint at
them.

"We may have trouble. Be careful," he warned.

"Who the hell are you?" the rifleman asked.

"I could ask you the same."

"This is Buster Weeks's ranch. I'm the foreman,
Larry Masters. What'cha want anyway?"

"He owns this ranch?"

"You hard of hearing? I said this was the Buster
Weeks's ranch."

"I talked to Hans Krueger of Los Angeles, California. He says he owns this ranch."

"Well, he fed you a line of bullshit. Buster Weeks
owns it lock, stock, and barrel."

"How many acres?"

"Hell, a section, I guess. I've been down here two

years looking over his cattle. Ain't no Hans Krueger
ever been around."

"How many cows does Buster own?"

"You the damn tax collector? Count them your-
selves."

"Mr. Masters, you don't understand. I'm a US Marshal and I'm asking you how many cows he has out
here."

"About two-fifty."

"Thanks. How long will it take for you to round
them up and get your ass off this ranch?"

"You crazy? Marshal or not, I'm not leaving here
till Buster Weeks tells me to."

"Does he live in Tucson?"

"Yeah, why?"

"Because I'm going up there and tell him what to
do, so you'll have to do it."

"You don't know Buster Weeks. He'll blow your
damn head off. He owns this place."

"He may own a place close by, but this is not his
ranch headquarters."

"We'll see about that."

"Where in Tucson does he live?"

"Got a ranch up north at Oracle Junction. He'll
damn sure straighten your wagon, mister, about who
owns this land."

"I doubt that."

They turned their horses to leave. The place was
respectable enough and if it supported two hundred
fifty cows, they could sure start there. There was a
small lake lined by gnarled tall cottonwoods. So the

supply of water had been there to keep them alive, and a good spring piped through a number of large round rock and mortar tanks.

Out of hearing, JD rode in beside him. "You really think this is on Krueger's property?"

"Yes, and that makes sense. Weeks, I bet, figured out he was gone from the territory and moved in to use it."

"You know him?"

"No, but I will in the next by and by."

"What next?"

"I'm going to hire a lawyer in Tucson that specializes in land cases and start there. I'll have Bo get an option to buy the land from Krueger, contingent on removal of all squatters, and for him to give me permission to move against them. That might shake him, if he fears lots of lawsuits will lower the value of this place."

JD laughed. "That dumb cowboy back there didn't know who he was dealing with, did he?"

Chet shook his head. "How many *vaqueros* can we get to gather Weeks's cattle and drive them to Tucson?"

"A hundred enough?"

Chet shook his head. "Oh, that's way too many."

Ortega mimicked him. "Oh, they are cheap workers."

"He might sell them to you cheap?" JD threw in.

"He might just do that," Chet agreed.

"I've heard about Weeks from somewhere," Cole said. "I wish to hell I could recall where it was at."

"I thought the same, but I couldn't name the place."

"I bet it was in Texas. I'm sure he was in some big deal back there before we left."

Chet tried to put Weeks name with different things to try to recall any past association. Weeks Cattle Company? Weeks Freighting? Weeks Commission Company? None fit, but he knew that name from somewhere in the past. He'd get to meet him, since he'd thrown the gauntlet down with his ranch foreman.

"Reckon he has any *vaqueros* working for him?"

"Oh, I am certain he does. I do not know them."

"Ortega, if you rode up here tomorrow and stayed out of sight, could you talk to some of them away from the house?"

"No problem. If they ride out, huh?"

"I think they do. What does he pay them?"

"Twenty a month, maybe." Ortega shrugged.

"You can pay them a few dollars for them to tell you how the ranch operates."

"How many you want?"

"Two or three. But tell them not to worry, when we get the ranch they'll have work."

"I can try."

"They can use a few spare *pesos*?"

"Ah, *sí*. That will work."

"You're thinking now, Chet." JD chuckled. "Boys, he covers every bet he makes. I'll bet we'll own the Rancho Diablo in no time at all."

"We calling it that?" Chet asked.

"Damn right. And I hope the Fernandez brothers will all come work for us."

"Oh, I imagine we will," said Ortega. "Maybe only two of us. One can run our place at Tubac, no?"

"I'd say so. How many cows do you have now?" Chet asked.

"Two dozen."

"I'll make you a loan to get your count to a hundred. Then you will have some income for the one that runs it."

"That would be generous of you. What will you do next?"

"Ride to Tubac tomorrow to get hold of Bo. Go to Tucson and hire that lawyer and find out about this Buster Weeks."

"How are we splitting up?" JD asked.

"Jesus can cook and ride with you two. Cole can go with me, so my wife doesn't bitch, and you three can make contact with those *vaqueros*. Then you three come back to Ortega's ranch. We may be back from Tucson by then and have the whole thing rolling."

"I believe we'll have another big Byrnes ranch operation here," JD announced.

"You good at laying adobe bricks?" Chet asked him. "Why?"

"Your wife is not going to want to live in a hovel out in nowhere."

JD nodded slow like. "I guess I can sure learn how."

They laughed at his reluctant reply.

"Hell, I called it Rancho Diablo. It may be that for me, huh? But if I have to, I'd learn how to lay adobes."

"If you need a builder, I can get him and an army from Mexico to build it," Ortega promised.

"Saved by the man," JD shouted, and stood up in his stirrups. "Thanks, partner."

"No problem. I want some of those unseen bachelor horses to break," Ortega said.

"When they are ours, you can pick them."

"Good enough." The older brother's smile filled his face.

They made camp and Jesus reported the women were in disbelief that Chet would do all that for them besides the two deer, and thanked him.

"You missed it," JD said. "We're in the process of buying the whole damn place. And we have squatters on some real good headquarters, running their boss's cattle."

"Who's that?"

"Buster Weeks."

Jesus shook his head.

"We don't know him, either."

But we will run him off. Chet knew he faced a large fight, but it could be won. And he had a few good hands in the fight—Bo for one. And he had the money to move it. A tough lawyer came next.

CHAPTER 29

Marge asked their lawyer in Preskitt to recommend one in Tucson, then sent Chet a telegram with the name of Russell Craft. And that's why Chet found himself in the law offices of Jensen, Craft, and Rosewood.

The office walls were lined in walnut paneling and the man behind the desk was in his forties. Despite the warm temperature, he wore an expensive suit, with a tie and starched white shirt.

"What can I do for you today, Mr. Byrnes?"

"Do you represent, or does your firm represent, Buster Weeks?"

"No, but I know the man. Why?"

"I'm in the process of buying some property that he's squatting on."

"And you want him removed?"

"Him and three hundred cows, plus calves, yearling horses, and people."

Craft leaned back in his expensive rollback leather chair and tented his fingers. "Have you ever met Buster Weeks, sir?"

"No, and I don't care if I ever meet him."

"They say he has a violent temper."

"I'm not here looking for advice on my personal safety. I'm here to talk to you about what I can do to evict him."

"Do you own the property involved?"

"I will have an option from the seller on it shortly and the right to evict any squatter."

"May I ask where this land is?"

"Southern Pima County."

"You are certain this man is squatting on this land?"

"No doubt."

"How much land is involved?"

"Close to forty-eight thousand acres."

Craft frowned. "My God, man, that is an empire."

"Eight sections, you figure it."

"And the current owner?"

"A man named Krueger."

"I have some roll-down maps. Let's look at it on one of them." Craft went over and pulled down the map. He soon located the land. "Here is the property. Where is Weeks squatted?"

"See that X? Right there is where he's headquartering his operation." Chet used his finger to show the spot.

"You have not spoken to Weeks?"

"I spoke to his foreman down there, Larry Masters.

He told me to go to hell. He said Weeks owned the place."

"It is obvious the X was there to mark the headquarters of that plot of land."

"There isn't any doubt."

"Would you like to speak to Mr. Weeks about amicably talking this over in my office?"

"We can start there. I should have a telegram within the next two days giving me authority."

"I will invite him here, say Friday at two p.m. Where do you live, Mr. Byrnes?"

"Right now down at Tubac. But my ranches are at Presksitt."

"Oh, isn't that inconvenient?"

"If he can't make it, wire me at Tubac."

"Very well. This may all be settled out of court."

"I'm not a betting man, but I'd bet you ten he won't agree to leave."

Craft laughed. "You may know more than I do about this man."

"No, I haven't met him, either, but I got the impression from his man that was not his way."

"Let's say it is all a mistake and he thought he really did own it?"

"Let's say how he saw it was deserted and moved in figuring the owner would not be back and he could use it for free."

"How long has he been there?"

"Three years, I suspect, from what his man said to me."

"Where up north is your ranch?"

"Preskitt Valley, Hackberry, Camp Verde, and up on the rim east of there."

Craft paused and nodded. "You are not an ordinary cowboy then."

"I'm down here with a secret task force to halt the crimes committed south of here near the border. I work for US Marshal Blevins."

"The new man?"

"He's pretty serious about putting a stop to it."

"He obviously has a man who knows how to find them."

"Thanks."

"No, thank you. We will see what Weeks wants to do next."

"Wire me."

Chet left the office. Cole was squatted on his boot heels in the shade, with both horses switching flies. He got to his feet. "How did that go?"

"He's inviting Weeks to a meeting here at two p.m. on Friday."

"He thinks that he'll move?"

"I doubt it, but we can learn what he thinks, if he shows."

They rode south and didn't arrive in camp until late that night.

When he woke the next morning, Roamer had a short telegram for him.

CHET
THERE IS A DEATH THREAT ON YOUR LIFE.
ONE OF MY DEPUTIES HEARD ABOUT IT ON
THE BORDER. HE COULD NOT FIND A SOURCE,

BUT WANTED ME TO PASS THAT ON TO YOU.
BE CAREFUL.
BLEVINS

"The word is out on you." Roamer shook his head.

"Talk's cheap." Then he explained what the lawyer said and where they would start on the eviction notice.

Roamer, JD, and Ortega planned to make a round down to a suspected outlaw hideout in the Huachuca Mountains and struck out the next day with a packhorse. That left Shawn, Cole, and Jesus to guard him so he could attend the meeting in Tucson on Friday.

After they left, a telegram from Bo arrived.

CHET
WE HAVE AN OPTION FOR FORTY THOUSAND
DOLLARS, IF AND WHEN THE SQUATTERS ARE
DRIVEN OFF THE LAND. YOU HAVE FULL
AUTHORITY TO DISPOSE OF THEM. I DON'T
KNOW, BUT THAT IS DIRT CHEAP LAND. BO

Chet sent one back to him.

BO
SEND RUSSELL CRAFT THAT INFORMATION AT
JENSEN CRAFT AND ROSEWOOD ATTORNEYS IN
TUCSON A.T. PRICE IS RIGHT IF WE CAN WRESTLE
THE LAND AWAY FROM WEEKS. YOU DID GOOD.
CHET.

"That's a helluva price," Cole said when he showed him the message.

"That's a helluva dry place, too."

"What did JD call it? Rancho Diablo?" Jesus asked.

"Right. He called it that himself."

"You can make it work. I truly believe you can."

"Good."

They went back to Tucson on Thursday and Chet learned that Weeks and his lawyer were coming to the meeting.

"His attorney has some land claim he's bringing that shows Weeks owns those ranch quarters."

"I doubt the owner of the land would have bought it and made that setup without a survey."

"Whatever, we'll need to have it surveyed." Craft drummed his fingers on the desk.

"We can do that, but if he's wrong, I want to charge him pasture fees. That way, if he's bluffing, he might not be so insistent on staying."

"Oh, he's blustery. I imagine we'll have a confrontation in my office. But we must be lawful, unless his threat is real."

"I totally understand. I will be here at two p.m. tomorrow."

"Yes, and we shall see. This lawyer, Townsend, talks a lot, too."

"I'll remember that."

Chet and his men went back out to Jesus's aunt's place and spent the night. He'd brought a lot of food from the open market, and they held a big *fiesta* with some of the neighbors. His aunt was very excited and thanked him for the treat.

Midday on Friday, they were back at the lawyer's office. A big red-faced man in a brown suit, and wearing a new Boss of the Plains silk-wrapped-brim hat, was introduced to him as Buster Weeks. They didn't shake hands.

"Byrnes, next time, come see me. Don't threaten my foreman."

"Next time, don't squat on a ranch I'm buying."

"You may be a big man in the north. You ain't shit down here."

"Gentlemen," interjected Mr. Craft, "we are here for a discussion, not a fight."

"I think Mr. Weeks had an appointment here," Jarman Townsend, his lawyer, said.

"Everyone sit down," Craft said. "Now, Jarman present your claim for the land."

The gray-haired man who looked a little red-eyed from a bout with a whiskey bottle the night before cleared his throat and handed Craft a paper. "Here's the property you are talking about."

Craft went to his wall map and read the description. "This calls for sixty acres."

"That's where the gawdamn ranch is located. North of that Krueger property," Weeks said.

"A surveyor can settle this," Craft said.

"We don't need a gawdamn surveyor. They can't find their ass in this country. Some greasers built those damn buildings on the place I bought from

Santos. That bunch Krueger sent didn't know where they were at setting it up years ago."

"Survey it then," Chet said, already weary of this mouthy sumbitch.

"Do you know what those bastards will charge you to do that?"

"I don't care. They will find you are way south of his northern line and you can pay for the survey and also three years' pasturage."

"Hell, I ain't agreeing to that."

"You know you're wrong, so go on. We will have it surveyed. Then we'll meet you in court."

"You'll find I'm right. I intend to fight you. I own those ranch headquarters."

"Gentlemen, let's sit down again," Craft said. "Jarman, does your client intend to refuse negotiations at this time?"

"Yes, we believe that the ranch headquarters are not located on Krueger's land."

"Then we will survey and see you in court."

Chet knew that would take time—as much as six months' litigation, but in the end they would win this case. Still, it involved a lot of money, but he had the place bought at the right price to afford some litigation.

"Good day, gentlemen," Craft said, and Townsend and Weeks left. The latter looked like a snarling dog going out the door, but Chet had no fear of him. He still couldn't place if he'd really met him before; some thread of the man niggled him, but no memory came forth.

After talking with Craft about their plans, he and his men headed back to Tupac.

"How long will the survey take?" Cole asked.

"Oh, two months. I bet nothing is ever in a hurry down here."

"Will we be there when they do the survey?"

"We may. Craft has a copy of the original plat, which included the points of reference the surveyors made when they surveyed it for Krueger in 1867. Craft felt they were valid. He wasn't sure how Weeks had been able to buy sixty acres in such obscure country. Our attorney also mentioned that might be a doubtful deed. He plans to investigate it closer."

"What do you think?" Cole asked.

"I was thinking Weeks may have a partner who figured all this out and he's only the front man."

"Oh, who would that be?"

Chet turned up his palms. "I guess that is for us to find out."

They got back to camp late that night. JD was still up and eager to hear the results of the meeting.

Busy stripping out the wet latigo leather on his cinch, Chet considered the meeting he'd had several hours earlier. "Weeks is a windy Texan with lots of bluff. He wants to fight us in court."

"So how long will that take?"

"I figure six months at least, but we're in for the whole thing."

"Nothing is easy."

"Nothing. You ready for the wait?" Chet asked.

"Hell, yes."

"Good. It may shred all our patience. Tomorrow, I'll send Bo a telegram and tell him our results."

"I bet he's anxious, too. Oh, you got a telegram today." JD scrambled to go get it.

"From who?"

"Your banker. He's collected four more months' cattle deliveries."

"That's great news." Whew, that really was good news. The total operation was moving forward.

"I thought so, too."

Jesus took Chet's horse to put him up.

Chet ate some fruit—red bananas and citrus—then went off to find some sleep in his bedroll. Made him more homesick than ever, but he slept hard.

A man came in the morning to tell them about a bloody ranch raid made by bandits and offered to take them there. Dallas Gabbert rode a rough-looking bay gelding. He hadn't shaved in some time and his clothes were threadbare, but he sounded real and concerned. Chet, Roamer, and Cole rode with him to the site.

"Did anyone contact the sheriff?" Chet asked him while on the way.

Gabbert shook his head. "I don't know. I heard about you and your men and figured you could do more than he could."

"I don't compete with sheriffs."

"Hell, I been hearing all kinds of reports how you been getting them bandits."

"We have gotten some."

"Well, by God, they killed Nellie Justice, her boy, and the hired man. She never hurt no one."

When they got there late in the afternoon, the scene was grim. Gabbert had drug their bodies inside the *jacal* to save them from buzzards. He'd even covered her naked corpse with a blanket. The bloody sight of her body that Chet saw under the candle lamp was ugly. A small woman in her thirties who looked tough. The boy of ten had his throat cut, and the Mexican man was shot in the back of the head, execution style.

If only he'd brought Jesus to track.

"Three horses rode out," Cole said. "One had a Chet-broken-shoe."

Chet chuckled. "I was thinking we needed Jesus."

Cole shrugged and smiled. "I knew we had to find their tracks."

"Good job. I think we need to contact the sheriff in Nogales for Santa Cruz County. I met him once. I think his name is Garcia."

Gabbert nodded.

"Roamer, you ride in there and find him or his man and have them bring the coroner out here. I'll make a map of the crime scene and send that with you for him."

"We'll leave you some signs," Chet said to Roamer. "We've got some jerky and should find food along the way. You do the same."

"You going to try to track them?" Roamer asked.

"If they left a track."

"I'll find you."

"Fine." Chet wasn't certain how Gabbert and the sheriff got along. Why did he ride clear to their camp to report a crime that happened in the jurisdiction of a sheriff? That was why he chose Roamer to go see the chief law official.

Roamer left for Nogales. In the late afternoon, Chet, Cole, and Gabbert headed east. He had concerns that the outlaws wouldn't go far, but Gabbert had a notion they were going to a hideout in Nogales.

"There's a ranch over there where lots of them bandits hide out. It's easy for them to slip off into Mexico from there."

Chet yawned. "Thanks, you can guide us. We'll chance catching them."

The darkness of night finally made their traveling dangerous. They slept a few hours in their bedrolls, ate some more jerky, and washed it down with canteen water. In the predawn, Chet decided he needed to find out more about their guide. Several things about the man and his part in the raid vexed him.

"Gabbert, why don't you level with me? I think you know who murdered those folks."

"I never lied to you."

"No, but I don't have all the story."

Cole listened close as they stood by their horses under the stars.

"I never killed her."

"I didn't say you did. Tell me the entire story."

"Me and that damn sheriff had our outs."

"Outs? What's that mean?"

"I traded for a horse someone had stole. He came

to arrest me for stealing it. I got in a fight and was arrested. I never stole nothing. I was having an affair with her. He knew that. I figured that was why he'd accuse me of the crime." The man was crying by then.

"Gabbert, tell me about these men that we're headed for."

"Aw, they raped her about six months ago. I ain't no hand with a gun. She begged me not to go over there and kill them. She wouldn't tell the sheriff, either."

"They raped her?"

"They were drunk and rode over there and raped her the first time. I just hoped they didn't do it again. I was drunk that night and didn't go see her. Yesterday, I rode out there and found them dead. I figured the sheriff would arrest me for doing it."

Gabbert was still crying. "I don't know why she put up with me. But she was a good woman."

"Who are these men we're going after?"

"Joe Guzman. Theo somebody, and Anthony Diaz."

"What do they do?"

"Small crimes."

"She have any money?"

"Not much."

"Guzman the leader?"

"Yeah, he's in his thirties. Them other two are maybe twenty."

"Women and kids there?"

Gabbert nodded and wiped his nose on a dirty sleeve.

"What now, Chet?" Cole asked.

"How far away are they?" Chet asked the weeping man.

"Two miles."

"I know you're sad and I believe your story, Gabbert, but we'll need evidence that they were there."

"I saw they took both her dresses."

"Huh?" Chet asked, ready to mount up.

"They took both her dresses. She only had two. One was her working dress, the other her good one. She didn't have no dress on when I found her. Both were gone."

"We'll find them, and we'll have a good case."

By the time the sun started to rise, they rode up to the place with their guns drawn. Gabbert, of course, didn't want a gun.

"Guzman, come out empty handed. The law's here," Chet yelled.

A woman screamed and Cole jerked his horse's head around and fired a shot in the ground to stop a half-naked man attempting to run away. "Get the hell back here."

The younger man stopped and raised his hands. "Don't shoot. Don't shoot."

Another young one wearing only his pants came around with his hands in the air.

"Watch them." Chet decided Guzman must have run out the back and he charged his roan horse around the *jacal*. He spotted the near naked man headed for the chaparral riding bareback. He fired a warning shot in the air and the man stopped his horse.

"Get your hands high. Now, dismount, and don't move or you're dead."

Chet stepped down and took handcuffs from the saddlebags. The man's hands shackled behind his back, he headed him back and led his horse.

Cole had the other two seated on the ground. Gabbert held a Mexican woman in her teens who kicked and thrashed around.

"This is Nellie's dress she has on and the other one is inside."

"Good. Where is the money?" He punched Guzman in the back.

"She didn't have any money."

"No, you found some money. That's why you killed her."

"How do you know that?" Guzman acted insulted.

"Hell, you raped that woman before and didn't kill them. It was over money, wasn't it?"

"It was all his idea," one of the younger men said.

"Shut up."

"I want the money," Chet insisted.

"I don't have any money."

"I want an answer, and my time is short."

"How did you find us?"

"Gabbert showed us the way."

"That old drunk. I should have killed him, too."

"Now show me the money."

Chet shoved Guzman ahead of him into the house where the outlaw nodded at a large jar. When Chet looked inside, he saw a sack. He lifted the heavy sack onto the table and opened the drawstring. It was full of coins and bills and a letter inside that he took out and opened.

To Who Reads This: If I die this money goes to my friend Dallas Gabbert to raise my son Abraham.

Nellie Justice

"What does it say?" Cole asked.

"Gabbert is out of debt. She left all this money to him to raise her boy. Make that woman get out of that dress. It's evidence."

"We may have to take it off her." Cole looked at him with a frown.

"We can do that. Let me talk to her."

Chet turned to Gabbert. "Close up that bag and letter and take good care of it."

"Yes, sir. This is some mess."

Chet nodded curtly and went outside. He told the woman in Spanish to take off the dress or they'd take it off.

She acted indignant, but she stomped inside, undressed, and flung the dress at him. "There, you *bastardo*!"

He swept it up, ignored her nakedness, and went outside. Laughing to himself, he gathered that dress and the other one Gabbert found. The man was seated on the ground, crying again.

"Quit feeling sorry for yourself. Did she own that place where she lived?"

"Yeah, she owned it. Why?"

"Well, I bet the judge will give that to you, too. She left a will of sorts for you to take care of her son."

"He was killed."

"You still look like her heir. I'll help you settle it. It was something she wanted."

"Damn those bastards. What are we going to do with them?"

"Take them to jail and see they hang."

"Good."

"You need to sober up and stop feeling sorry for yourself."

"I will try."

"I don't mean try. I mean do it. She must have seen something in you. Why don't you try to live up to it?"

"All right. I will."

Cole put a noose around each of the men's necks and made a chain of them. "We're going to Nogales. We have Gabbert's money and the two dresses they stole after they killed her. Let's move, and if they don't trot, drag them."

Midmorning, they met Roamer and a deputy sheriff coming to find them.

The deputy looked over the prisoners. "You got any proof against them?"

"Yes, Nellie Justice's two dresses, and the money they stole."

"How can you prove it's hers?"

"It has her will in the same bag as the money."

"Roamer says you're US Marshals."

"We are. You can wire Marshal Blevins and find out who we are."

"I'm sure my boss has. Messing up a murder scene is a crime."

"I doubt a jury would find it so. To leave bodies out for buzzards is not the right thing."

"How come did you get notified and we didn't?"

"Lack of faith." Chet shrugged.

"Huh?"

"The man felt you were prejudiced and he wanted it solved."

"You don't have any authority in our local law."

"Hey, I'm not going to stay here and argue with you. Any citizen can arrest any criminal and bring him to justice."

"You ain't anyone as important as you think you are."

"Listen, we solved a heinous crime. We have the killers and the evidence. Since you're such a legal expert, I'll talk to the judge and prosecutor."

The deputy sulled up. They rode on. Roamer was chuckling when they went on—the prisoners grumbling about the pace.

Roamer gave Chet a head toss. "I'm glad he took you on. I've listened to his bitching since I notified them of the crime."

"I plan to hire a lawyer to represent Gabbert when we get there. This all is crazy. But I agree he'd never of stood a chance if he hadn't called on us."

Roamer agreed.

"You should have been there. The woman was wearing one of her dresses and wouldn't take it off. I told her to take it off or we would."

"She took it off?" Roamer chuckled.

"Yep." Chet nodded. "And she threw it at me."

"No rocks in it?"

"No, but if she'd had some she'd have thrown them, too."

"We're going to Nogales then?"

"Yes, we need to set up some help for Gabbert. I'll hire him a lawyer and we'll get a bank to count the money and hold it. Plus have her will straightened out."

"What next?"

"I don't know. Just part of our project down here, is all I can think of."

"What about the big ranch?"

"Oh, that will take some time. Then it'll end up in court."

"You figure they have a claim?"

"I don't think Krueger made any deal that large that would hold up. And my lawyer wonders how Weeks got sixty acres out there in the middle of nowhere. That's all being investigated."

Roamer shook his head in disbelief. "You do things I'd never even try, but you make money and help lots of folks. Sharing that Navajo cattle deal is really great for our neighbors."

"You think JD can run this place?" Chet asked, knowing he and JD had been doing things together.

"I think he'd do a good job. He talks a lot like he's anxious to settle down with his wife."

"I think he's made a turn anyway."

When they reached King's Road, the prisoners were exhausted. Chet hired a rancher with a large wagon and a big team to haul the prisoners. By evening, the murderers were in the Nogales County jail and Chet met with the prosecuting attorney and sheriff. After a fiery meeting with the sheriff, they agreed the money and the will needed to be put in the bank while her estate was probated by an attorney the prosecutor recommended as honest.

The sheriff was still trying to protest the action of the task force in the case, until the prosecutor finally told him to shut up, and that ended his mouthing off. The official complimented Chet on his efforts. It was late when the three had supper and bedded down in the livery.

Gabbert met them for breakfast in a café and told them the attorney, Jim Elmore, was handling his case. He acted and looked sober. When the meal was over, Chet took him aside.

"I'll pay that lawyer's fee and help you, if you stay sober. You want to drink, you tell me and I'll quit."

"I'm going to try hard. I appreciate your helping me, and she would too for seeing what she wanted is done."

"No, no try. Don't drink."

"Yes."

They left Nogales and were all day getting back. Jesus came out to greet them.

"Anything wrong?" Chet asked, dismounting.

"No. No telegrams, no letters. I went to town and got some more frijoles, corn meal, and flour for those squatters. I figured they'd about ran out, huh?"

"Good idea. Where's JD?"

"Since we had no problems, he and Ortega went to shoot a desert bighorn ram."

"That might be fun."

Jesus agreed, but didn't act interested.

"While you're down there with the squatters, find out where their husbands might be. They need to come and get them. They have no way to raise enough food out there and they face starvation."

"I will see what I can find out."

"Someone needs to ride with you over there."

"I will get Cole, but you must keep Roamer here to look after you."

"Yes, Mother. You two be careful. I have some bad feelings about Weeks. I don't trust him."

Jesus smiled. "I am only doing what she told me to do."

"I know. I'll keep Roamer close by."

"Good."

Chet wrote Marge telling her about Gabbert and the murders, and some about the land case with Weeks. Then he told her how he missed her, but he'd come home in a few weeks to see her.

CHAPTER 30

When JD and Ortega returned from their hunt, they had a fat mountain sheep. The head was a handsome trophy and Chet congratulated them for their success. He figured that head would one day hang on the wall at the new ranch's main house.

Maria planned a *fandango* with Chet. Though Chet appreciated her concern for everyone on the team and for providing their meals, he also found her to be very intelligent. It didn't take a lot of schooling to be people-smart like Maria. Some folks learned it—others never did understand a thing about how it worked.

As the days lengthened, many things pressed on his mind. Things were slow for the task force, so he turned his attention to the squatters. Jesus returned from feeding them with no answer as to where their husbands had gone off to. They didn't know what happened to them. All they knew was they were supposed to come back for them some day.

"I think any hope of them coming back for those women is like smoke. It's gone on the wind," Chet said.

Jesus frowned in concern and agreed.

"How many are there?"

"Three older women, two younger ones, seven kids."

"In the end, we may need to load them into a wagon and take them to Nogales or Tucson. We could find them a couple of *jacals* and maybe they'd eventually find new husbands."

"Maybe." Jesus made a face.

Chet chuckled. "You think they're too ugly to appeal to anyone?"

Jesus nodded. "They are not pretty."

"I don't need to feed them forever, so we need a solution. Plus they might die out there. Did they walk to get where they are?"

"Many of those poor people coming up here for work walk."

"Why didn't they take the King's Road?"

"Maybe they got lost?"

Chet shook his head wearily. "They really are lost."

Was it deliberate? Did their husbands dump them there? He thrust it all out of his mind and concentrated on getting ready for the *fandango*. Maybe the celebration would take his mind off the squatters as well as the lack of work for the task force.

Everyone was in a festive mood that night. The music was good and the barbequed sheep proved delicious. His crew danced with the brothers' wives and laughed a lot. Chet turned in early, with plans to write Marge another letter in the morning.

Come morning, he was up early and drinking Maria's fresh coffee.

"When you finish your work here, we will miss all of you," she said.

"Yes, we've made some great friendships among your family. We'll stay in touch."

"I am grateful for your offer to buy us cows for our ranch. We will pay you back, and, in time, we too will have a real ranch." She brought the first Dutch oven full of biscuits over and offered them to him.

"No problem."

"Tell me about your wife. She must be a great lady."

"Marge has been very good for me. She's more than I ever expected to have in a wife. We're very close. She's a great horsewoman and rides jumpers. But having lost two babies, she hasn't ridden since she learned she is to have this one. We hope that makes the difference. She misses her riding a lot, but is dedicated to having this one."

"I will burn a candle for her," Maria said. "I am so glad you found us. We have worked hard, but with a herd of cows of our own the ranch will now grow. You are a good encourager, too."

"You've made this place home for me and my men and I thank you."

She blushed, nodded, and excused herself.

While their law enforcement efforts waned, it gave him time to reflect. Working out the details for buying a huge dry ranch taxed his brain. And he needed to gather more information about the squatters, those abandoned women. Then there was Weeks's ranch operation and how to handle it. Oh, well, since he took over the family operation as a teenager, he always had his head crowded with problems.

Maybe he'd take a nap in the hammock and let the problems rest. *Marge, I miss you.*

CHAPTER 31

Everyone was in camp to enjoy the big meal Maria cooked for their supper. It was drawing toward evening, with the warm day coming to a close. After the recent rains, the surrounding desert looked like a vast flower garden with the wild flowers that carpeted it.

Earlier, they received a telegram from Blevins about a ranch raid near Benson. The message had come late in the day and Chet assigned Roamer and JD to handle it. They'd ride out the next day to check on the situation.

Cole and Shawn were going to look in on some problems they'd heard about down at Patagonia. That left him and Jesus to take the next call. Jesus had recovered completely from his wound, but Chet felt he still needed to take it easy.

After their meal, their hosts played some music and they savored an evening of gentle breezes before splitting up and going to bed. Chet found his bedroll and was snug in it knowing the temperatures would drop overnight. Sleep soon sailed him away.

Come morning, two sets of his men had already left to handle their assignments. Chet settled down to catch up on his expense log. Keeping track of expenses wasn't a job he enjoyed, but recording their expenses was important if he was to recover his costs as agreed to by Marshal Blevins.

When a rider came into camp looking saddle weary, Chet glanced up. Unshaven, the man rode a roman-nosed gray horse as gaunt as he looked. He dropped out of the saddle, hitched up his size-too-big dirty black wool pants, and asked Jesus where his boss was.

Chet rose from the long table under the tarp and closed his account book. "Good day, sir." He extended his hand.

The man didn't offer to meet his handshake, and Chet looked harder at him. "What can I do for you?"

"I can show you where the men are that killed old man Sam Crane down by Patagonia."

"Oh?" Chet hadn't heard that Sam died from the wounds he received during the attack on his ranch six weeks before. "Who did it?"

"What'cha gonna pay me?"

"For information that pans out, twenty bucks." Something wasn't right about this man. Was he a snitch, or was he up to something else? "How much do you know about them?"

"I can lead you right to them. There's three of 'em."

"Well, where are they?"

"If I'm going to take you there, I need fifty."

"That's a little steep."

"You want them or not?"

"All right, how far away are they?"

"Oh, a day's ride. But I want the gawdamn money before we go one step."

"I never caught your name?"

The man's steel-blue eyes narrowed. "I never told you my gawdamn name. Besides, you don't need my name."

"Mine's Chet Byrnes. I'm a US Deputy Marshal and I'm in charge here."

"Well, ain't that totty? I'm Jack Smith and I ain't got time to screw around with you. You want his killers or not?"

Chet studied the man. He wore a sweat-blackened holster and his gun butt had scuffed wood handles. A half-dozen corroded .45 bullets were stuck in the belt. It must have been cartridge modified. The hammer and body parts showed they'd been worn a lot. He didn't consider Smith, or whoever he was, as a *pistolero*, but no doubt he could use it. So why was he wanting to show his hand for a reward on men as tough as those killers?

"You're certain they killed Crane?"

"Why in the hell—" He snatched off the once light-colored hat with the indented crown and slammed it on the table. "Listen, you either want them or not." He used his fingers to comb back his wavy gray-streaked hair. "What do you think I'm here for anyway?"

"I'm not too sure. That's why I'm asking you." Chet stood his ground. From the corner of his eye he saw Jesus, who'd moved closer and wasn't missing anything the man said or did.

Smith slammed the weather-battered hat with the uneven brim back on his head, jerked the clasp on the rawhide strings, and set it tight under his chin. Then he turned hard on his run-over boots with his pants tucked inside. His Mexican spur rowels rang. Under his breath, he said, "Fuck you, I'll go elsewhere and find me someone who'll pay me."

"Smith, I'm not through talking to you. Turn around." Chet expected the man would try to spin around and draw on him. The web of his own hand rode on the cool steel of his gun butt.

"Don't touch that gun." Jesus's words sounded colder than ice. His .45 ready in his fist, he cocked it.

The man's hands at once spread out from his body, and he stood frozen. Thwarted from drawing, his fingers opened and closed. "I never came here to fight with you."

"You've got a damn unfriendly way of talking to me, mister. Jesus, take his gun."

"There ain't any need in that." An impatient expression crossed his face.

Jesus stepped in and disarmed the man, tossing the gun onto the long table. By then, both Ortega and Jose came on the run from their *jacals*. Ortega carried a rifle, his brother a pistol.

Chet held up his hand to stop them from shooting. "Now tell us who you really are."

"My name's Frank Kinkaid."

"Where do you live?"

"Tombstone—anywhere I can live." He shrugged his narrow shoulders.

"You didn't ride clear over here from Tombstone for a fifty-buck reward to tell me where three killers are." Chet folded his arms across his chest, and he and his three men listened close for the man's answer.

"All right. They paid me a hundred to get you to ride over there so they could ambush you."

"Who are they?"

Kinkaid began to shift his eyes from man to man, to take in the effect of his words. "I only know one of them is called Arthur Hatfield."

Chet asked Ortega, "You know anyone by that name?"

Ortega shook his head. "Where does he live?" he asked Kinkaid.

"I don't know. They have a place down on Patagonia Creek."

Chet interrupted to fill in the brothers. "He came here wanting me to pay him fifty dollars to say where Sam Crane's killers are."

"Sam's dead?" Ortega frowned.

Kinkaid said, "They buried him last week at the Burro Creek School cemetery."

The men shook their heads almost in unison. No one had heard of his death.

Chet hoped Sam's widow was doing all right. He turned back to the drifter. "Describe Hatfield."

"Maybe fifty, big mustache, wears a black hat, kind of a dresser—lacy shirts and a suit coat. Carries a short-barreled sheriff model Colt in a shoulder holster. He gambles a lot in Tombstone and lives with a whore south of there on a small ranch. He speaks Spanish real good, and his men are all Mexicans."

"Why does he want me dead? He breaks the law?"

Kinkaid nodded. "His men shot up Crane and took those good horses he had."

"Where did they go to?"

"They say Old Man Clanton's." Kinkaid shook his head. "Hatfield knew I was broke. Two days ago, outside the Birdcage, he pulled me off the sidewalk out in the dark and tells me, 'Here's a whorehouse token for Louisa.' Then he held the brass coin up in the starlight to show me what it was. Then he tells me to go use her and meet him at midnight over at Blackman's stables and he'd have a job for me.

"I asked him what kind of job, that I wasn't no killer or bank robber. He told me to never mind, just meet me and he'd pay me well."

When he paused, Chet said, "Go on."

Kinkaid shrugged, wet his lips, and glanced around at the others. "I bedded her. God, I'd marry her if I could afford her. Then I went and waited at the stable for him. He was so damn late getting there to meet me, I fell asleep in that sweet-smelling alfalfa hay. But I was dead broke . . ."

"Keep talking."

"I ain't broke no law. What're you going to do to me?"

"Never mind that. Tell us the rest of your story."

"He showed up. Said he wanted me to tell you I knew where Sam Crane's killers were hiding and lead you to his place. His men would ambush you and your men. I took his money and rode over here. Hell, he might of killed me if I'd said no after he gave me that token for her and the hundred dollars. He said just lead you over there. His men would be laying in wait to shoot you."

"Why?"

"He said 'cause you had the entire bunch of border bandits scared to come over here anymore. He couldn't make any money, because he couldn't get them to come over and rob anyone for him. I'm not lying." He acted more nervous every minute.

"Boys, I guess we're doing a helluva job to have them try this."

His men laughed and relaxed somewhat.

"Kin I go now?"

"No. You're going to take us to that place on the creek. You have to earn that money he paid you."

"Oh, shit. They'll kill me, so I won't talk. I mean, I don't want to die. He's got some mean sons-a-bitches down there."

"Name them."

"Butcher Crab, One Eye Elms, and I don't know the Mexicans' names."

"You heard of them?" Chet asked the brothers.

"Crab broke out of prison below the border. Elms is a slick knife man," Ortega said. "I thought they were down in Mexico."

"I guess he hired them recently. He really talked like if he could get rid of you, he'd have no more trouble making raids again."

"You've seen them at Tombstone?" Chet asked.

"Oh, yeah. That place is so busy, no one bothers to arrest anyone unless they break the law in town. Then you get your head busted in."

"After we raid this ranch on the creek, then you can show us this place Hatfield has, right?"

"I can draw you a map."

"You ain't listening to me," Chet said, glaring at him.

"Yeah. Yeah. I can do that."

"Tell me about the bloody raid over in Skeleton Canyon where the silver pack train was robbed."

"I wasn't there. I mean, I wasn't nowhere near that."

"You've heard stories. I want to know all about it."

"They said the word came down the coins had been stamped at Silver City and the pack train loaded with them was coming back. It was in a telegram in code sent to Tombstone. A rider took the message to Old Man Clanton's ranch and give it to him. I don't know if that old sumbitch can even read. But he called in all his cattle rustlers and the rest of his men to lay that trap. I heard his men scouted that train—knew their every move—from Lordsburg clear on down to the morning they hit them. They brought their own pack train and hit them at dawn."

"I thought Clanton had so much business selling

beef to the Army and the Indians he didn't need money?"

Kinkaid sent a hard look at him. "Yeah, he does. But he won't ever get enough. He hordes it."

"What are we going to do with him?" Jesus asked, indicating Kinkaid.

"Handcuff him, so he don't leave. Tomorrow, Cole and Shawn will be back to go with us. We'll start at the creek place and take it. Then, the next day, we'll arrest his boss, Hatfield."

"He ain't no boss of mine."

Chet looked directly at him. "I want to be sure you go with us to get them," he said right in Kinkaid's face, who stumbled backing up from him.

"Put a handcuff on him and put him on a chain."

"I ain't going to—"

"Damn right. You ain't doing one thing to warn them, either," Chet said.

"Maria is bringing lunch. Have a seat, *hombre*," Ortega told their prisoner.

He obeyed, but looked dumbfounded at his new situation.

Chet's mind raced. They had to surprise the outlaws when they struck them. This could prove to be as serious a situation as any his posse had handled so far. In past situations, the wanted criminals were on the run. These killers were dug in, to ambush him and his men at any cost.

"I'd like you to go along," he said to Ortega. "Those other two will be ready to ride in the morning."

"*Si*. I would love to get my hands on that bunch, too."

Chet clapped him on the shoulder. "We'll get them."

This could be the big break in the border criminal activity—which meant they might all be able to go home soon. That notion pleased him mightily.

CHAPTER 32

Five of them, plus the antsy snitch Kinkaid, rode out early the next morning to find Hatfield's place on Patagonia Creek. Not knowing how long they'd be gone, they took a packhorse along. Chet's plan was to scout the place first from the backside and locate the outlaws. The willows in the bottom were head high to a man on horseback, so he knew not to ride into the ranch from that direction. He suspected they'd post a shooter there to ambush them.

They made camp north of the ranch and Ortega, Cole, and Jesus took off on foot to check out the ranch. They left Shawn with Chet and Kinkaid in the camp. In a few hours, they were back.

Under the stars, with no fire so as not to be noticed, Chet squatted on his heels with his men in a circle. They talked in low voices.

Cole began with a report of what they'd found. "There are four men at the ranch. That big guy named Butcher Crab, a skinny gray-headed guy that Ortega says is Elms, and two *pistoleros* we couldn't put handles on, but they're tough enough looking. They carry rifles all the time and are serious killers, we have no doubt."

"They act like they're nervous about something. One of them came back while we were down there, probably from being posted to ambush whoever came through the willows," Ortega added.

"Good. I have a stick of blasting powder. We can cut it in two, then load and deliver to wake them up," Chet offered.

"Load it," Cole said.

The rest nodded their agreement.

"Should we drop in before sunup?"

"Yes. They all sleep under a squaw shade in hammocks. I doubt they have any guards posted. A couple of sticks of blasting powder should wake them up disorganized as all get-out," Cole said.

"What about Kinkaid?" Jesus asked.

"Chain him to a tree," Chet said, and his man moved to do that.

They made a small shielded fire to see how to cut the stick in two parts, load and fuse them. Then they moved on foot to take their places around the camp, moving slowly so as not to be heard, in case someone was awake.

They surrounded the outlaws' shade. Chet and Shawn on the west side, Jesus and Cole on the east side, and Ortega on the south end where their horses were corralled. Shawn and Jesus were to light the fuses and deliver them with a toss. Everyone would be ready for an explosion of the outlaws when they went off.

Dawn finally peeked its peach-pink light over the eastern mountains. Fuses were lit and the sticks tossed in under the shade. The explosions were near simultaneous and even lifted the shade's thatched roof some in a cloud of dust.

Blinded and staggering, they came out empty-handed and shocked to meet the posse's guns. Hand-cuffed, the four were seated on the ground in their underwear under Chet's sight while his men saddled horses for all of them. They grumbled and cussed.

"Where will we take them?" Cole asked.

"Tombstone jail. But if he's home, I want Hatfield next. Word gets out that we have his men, he may run for it."

With the outlaws' horses ready, Shawn and Cole ran to get their own mounts and collect Kinkaid. In a short while, the caravan was on the road. Chet intended to avoid riding by Patagonia so no one could be forewarned. They pushed hard and by midafternoon were south of Tombstone and, according to Kinkaid, close to Hatfield's ranch.

The place sat isolated in a broad grassy valley between the Huachuca Mountains and the hills that shielded it from Tombstone. They stopped to rest in a dry wash and dismounted their prisoners. After they relieved themselves, they sat in the sand draw eating jerky washed down with canteen water.

Chet and Ortega went to scope out the ranch house surroundings. The woman Kinkaid spoke about came out to draw water from the well. There was no sign of Hatfield, but if he was there, he might be sleeping. According to Kinkaid, he gambled a lot in town at night.

"What should we do, boss?" Ortega asked when they slipped back from their high point.

"If he's here, take him."

"Ride straight in?"

"We can do that," Chet said. "Let's talk to the crew."

Back in the draw, every one of his men gathered to hear their results.

"She's here, but he may be sleeping. No telling. Why don't three of us ride up there and arrest him?" Chet asked. "If he's here."

"You stay here," Cole said. "No sense in you being on the point here."

Jesus agreed. "Cole is right. We are here to protect you."

"Listen, guys, this is my job. You can protect me, but I'm the lead man in this outfit. I won't ask you to do what I won't."

"I think, this time, we should ride down there," Jesus argued.

Chet waved them aside. "I'm going. Cole, you and Jesus ride with me. Ortega, I want you to come in from behind, in case he tries to escape. We'll give you half an hour to get in place. Shawn can watch the prisoners."

Ortega saluted him and left on the run, rifle in hand. While they waited, the prisoners grumbled.

Chet drank from his canteen. The sun was heating up and the breeze was out of Mexico, not over twenty miles south of them.

At last, they mounted their horses and left Shawn in charge. The bunch grass was thick and brown, waving in the wind. Quail ran about whet wooing out of sight. A few longhorn cows raised their heads to study the threat of the riders, then went back to grazing.

No sign of anyone at or around the adobe *jacal*. Then a woman screamed. A man cussed and the door filled with a man in a black suit drawing his gun from a shoulder holster.

Chet drew his own, stood in the stirrups, and aimed at the smoking gun in the doorway. Something struck him like a sledgehammer blow, and he felt the blast of the bullet in his chest. The six-gun slipped from his hand. He saw the shocked face of Jesus as he holstered his own gun and grabbed for Chet's horse's bridle.

"Kill that son-of-a-bitch," Jesus swore at Cole, who rode past while he tried to steady Chet in the saddle so he didn't fall off his horse.

It was all a bad dream. Chet hurt deep, and the whole world felt like it was at arm's length. Jesus was on the ground, struggling to ease him out of the saddle and get him down.

"What in the hell will I tell Marge?" Jesus asked, scrambling to lay Chet on his back.

More shots, heard only dimly, and Jesus said, "They've got Hatfield. He won't shoot anyone else.

Hang on, Chet. We're going to hitch his wagon and get you to the doctor in . . . Mother of God, please be with him. Oh, I pray so hard for him. He is my father . . . please, save him, dear Mother."

"How bad?" Cole asked.

"He is still alive. Get the wagon. He needs a doctor. There are many in Tombstone."

Cole shouted, "You've got to live, Chet—" He rushed off shouting at Ortega. "Get the wagon hitched. He's still alive."

Chet's world went black. Next he knew was when he came around for a short while when he was being transported in a wild ride. Jesus was trying to keep him steady on a mattress while they raced for Tombstone.

"They are bringing the prisoners," Jesus assured him as he drifted in and out of consciousness.

Then he smelled chloroform and found himself lying between stiff fresh sheets. Someone was talking about telegraphing Marge. Upset, he tried to protest. In her condition, she didn't need to come. But he had no voice, and then he was sent deep under a dark wave that offered to take him away from the pain.

No. He had to swim out of this. He gritted his teeth, but away he went off into oblivion.

CHAPTER 33

The *Tombstone Epitaph* came out with newsboys hawking the latest news: "U.S. Marshal Shot in Arrest Incident!"

According to U. S. Marshal Blevins, his chief deputy, Chet Byrnes, was shot last Wednesday while arresting Arthur Hatfield at his ranch south of Tombstone. Byrnes has been in charge of the federal force trying to stop the activity on the border where the outlaws cross over to strike at isolated ranches and businesses. Byrnes, working with several men, had rounded up an outlaw gang hiding in the Patagonia area and was going to arrest and charge Hatfield as their leader.

When they approached his ranch house, Arthur Hatfield reportedly shot Marshal Byrnes. His men brought Marshal Byrnes to Tombstone and Doctor John Engles stated that his patient was on a life and death watch after being treated for a serious gunshot wound.

Marshal Byrnes' wife, Margaret Byrnes, is reported to be on her way to his bedside, coming from the Byrnes ranch near Prescott. The marshal is a large rancher there who has been volunteering his time to help clean up the crime in southern Arizona. We are paying close attention to this lawman's struggle to live.

All the men arrested by his posse have been transported to Tucson and face charges in federal court on various crimes, ranging from the murder of an area rancher to planning to kill a federal officer. The list of those men include Arthur Hatfield, Butcher Crab, One Eye Elms, Manuel . . .

A Special Note to My Fans

Dear Readers,

Thanks to all of you for your support and fan mail. Without you, I'd be a crotchety old man wondering what to do next. I'm grateful for the sales of this series, and hope this one entertains you like those in the past.

This is the fifth book in the Chet Byrnes series. If you're new to these books, they're written so each book stands alone, but they also reflect back on Chet Brynes's life that is over his shoulder. So you might want to go back and read the books leading up to this one. (Listed on the front.)

This book makes one hundred and thirty western novels I've written over the last twenty-five years. I've been fortunate to win some awards: two Spurs, a couple of Spur Finalists, the coveted Cowboy Hall of Fame Wrangler Award, and the Will Rogers Award for the first book in this series, *Texas Blood Feud*. But as proud as I am of those, your e-mails are equally rewarding.

I try to make these novels accurate to the times, but the needs of fiction sometimes take a few shortcuts. For instance, I learned from a great writer and historian friend, Johnny Boggs, that in 1872 New Mexico had no state prison system. The Yuma prison system in Arizona wasn't built then, either, and convicts served terms in county jails in both territories.

My term as President of Western Writers of America runs through 2014. It's a great organization for anyone who writes western history, fiction, songs, or poems. Their website is www.westernwritersofamerica.net.

I'm working full time on writing more for you about the Chet Byrnes family and their lives. I know you have many questions about his future, but that will have to wait until book 6. I hope you're going back and reading the past adventures of this once-Texas-based ranch family and how Chet had to move them to Arizona Territory to escape a family feud.

Outlaws moved west to escape the forces of the law. At our nation's birth, they fled over the mountains to the West from the East Coast to escape justice. In the open country of the West, they spread out to bring grief to the God-fearing settlers brave enough to settle among the war-like Indians and that element of the population gone bad. Settlers brought their Bibles and good manners to this region, and their firearms to preserve it.

From the star of the Texas Rangers, sheriffs, and town marshals, to the US Marshals, the men wearing the badges brought the wild ones to the bar of justice, but the job was long and hard. And the list of prisoners who escaped state prisons and were never found again tells you how tough it was for the law to apprehend them.

The switch to cartridge shells for Colt arms came around 1872. Compared to the cap and ball models, they were much more dependable, but all cartridges sold were not that perfect and could misfire. The gun could be reloaded quite a lot easier, but they cost much more to shoot. However, they didn't cross fire and explode in the shooter's hand like the old models did.

I'll keep spinning yarns, so check my website— dustyrichards.com—for my new releases. I also have an author's page on Amazon.com, and I answer e-mail at dustyrichards@cox.org.

> Sincerely yours—and happy trails,
> Dusty Richards
> November 2013